"Earth is real," Dumarest insisted. "A world, old and scarred by ancient wars. The stars are few and there is a great, single moon which hangs like a pale sun in the night sky."

"It's a legend," she said. "I have heard of them. Worlds which never existed, like Jackpot and Bonanza, El Dorado and Camelot."

"There is only one Earth and I was born on its surface. One day I shall find it."

The saga of Earl Dumarest, born on Earth, taken far across the galaxy, and left to find his way back has become one of the classic series of modern science fiction. With a growing readership, the demand for these exciting novels of one man's determined heroism in a quest for the world mankind had forgotten has grown to a high intensity. DAW Books now brings back to print two such novels, long unavailable, but always in high demand.

MAYENNE

and

JONDELLE

by
E. C. TUBB

DAW Books, Inc.
Donald A. Wollheim, Publisher

1633 Broadway, New York, N.Y. 10019
DEC 1 5 1982

FIRST PRINTING (DOUBLE EDITION), APRIL 1981

1 2 3 4 5 6 7 8 9

DAW TRADEMARK REGISTERED
U.S. PAT. OFF. MARCA
REGISTRADA. HECHO EN U.S.A.

PRINTED IN U.S.A.

MAYENNE

To
Hilda Elizabeth Mitchell

Chapter
❖ ONE ❖

Dumarest heard the sound as he left his cabin, a thin, penetrating wail, almost a scream, then he relaxed as he remembered the Ghenka who had joined the ship at Frell. She was in the salon, entertaining the company with her undulating song, accompanying herself with the crystalline tintinnabulation of tiny bells. She wore the full Ghenka costume, her body covered, her face a mask of paint, the curlicues of gold and silver, ruby and jet set with artfully placed gems which caught and reflected the light in splinters of darting brilliance so that her features seemed to be alive with jeweled and crawling insects.

She was, he assumed, no longer young. No Ghenka in her prime would be found on a vessel plying this far from the center of the galaxy; rich worlds and wealthy patrons were too far apart. Someone on the decline, he guessed, unable or unwilling to meet rising competition, going to where she would be both novel and entrancing. Not that it mattered. Whatever her age there was no denying the trained magic of her voice.

He leaned back against the wall and allowed the hypnotic cadences to wash over his conscious mind, dulling reality and triggering sequences of unrelated imagery. A wide ocean beneath an emerald sky. A slender girl seated on a rock, her hair a ripple of purest silver as it streamed in the wind, the lines of her body the epitome of grace. A fire and a ring of intent faces, leaping flames and the distant keening of mourning women. Ice glittering as it fell in splintered shards, ringing in crystal destruction. Goblets shattering and spilling blood-red wine, the chime of chan-

5

deliers, the hiss of meeting blades, harsh, feral, the turgid
chill of riding Low.

"Fascinating." The low voice at his side broke his reverie. Chom Roma held unsuspected depths of artistic ap-
preciation. The plump hand he raised to stroke his jowl,
matted with hair and gaudy with rings, trembled a little.
"Fascinating," he repeated. "And dangerous. Such a song
can lead a man into memories he would prefer to forget.
For a moment there I was young again, a slim boy flushed
with the triumph of his first sale. And there was a girl
with lambent eyes and skin the hue of a pearl." He fell
silent, brooding, then shook his head. "No, Earl, such
dreams are not for men like us."

Dumarest made no comment; softly as the entrepreneur
had spoken his voice had been a jarring irritation. There
would be time for talk later, but now the spell was too
strong and, he agreed, too dangerous. A man should not
become enamored of mental imagery. The past was dead,
to resurrect it, even by song-induced stimulation, was unwise.

Ignoring the Ghenka he concentrated instead on the
salon and the company it contained. Both were familiar
from countless repetitions; a low room fitted with tables
and chairs, dispensers against a wall, the floor scarred with
usage and time. The assembly a collection of men and
women with money enough to afford a High passage, their
metabolism slowed by the magic of quick-time so that an
hour became a minute, months shortened into days. Yet
even so the journey was tedious; in this part of the galaxy
worlds were none too close, and entertainment, because of
that, the more highly appreciated.

The song ended and he heard a ragged sigh as the bells
fell silent, the company blinking a little, silent as they re-
gretted lost imagery, then breaking the tension with a
storm of applause. A shower of coins fell at the Ghenka's
feet and she stooped, gathering them up, bowing as she
left the salon. Dumarest caught her eyes as she passed
close to where he stood, deep pits of smoldering jet
flecked with scarlet. Her perfume was sharp, almost acrid,
and yet not unpleasant.

Quietly he said, "Thank you, my lady, for the display of

your skill. A truly remarkable performance. The company is honored."

"You are most gracious, my lord." Even when speaking her voice held a wailing lilt. "I have other songs if you would care to hear them. If you would prefer a private session it could be arranged."

"I will consider it." Dumarest added more coins to the heap clutched in her hand. "In the meantime again receive my thanks."

It was dismissal, but she did not leave. "You go to Selegal, my lord?"

"Yes."

"I also. It may be that we shall meet again. If so it would be my pleasure."

"And mine," said Dumarest.

Still she lingered. "You will pardon me if I cause offense, my lord, but, as you probably know, I travel alone. To one in my profession such a thing is not wise. Also, on Selegal, I will be unfamiliar with the local ways. I am not suited to the arrangement of business ventures. Perhaps, if you would consider it, something could be arranged."

Dumarest caught the note of appeal, the desperate need that broke through the stilted formality which was a part of her professional training. A woman alone, most likely afraid, doing her best to survive in a region foreign to her experience. Yet he had no intention of getting involved.

Before he could refuse she said, "You will consider it, my lord? At least your advice would be of value. Perhaps we could meet later—in my cabin?"

"Perhaps," said Dumarest.

Chom Roma drew in his breath as the woman moved on to her quarters. "A conquest, Earl. The woman finds you pleasing and a man could do worse than take her under his protection. Had she made me such an offer I would not have hesitated." Envy thickened his voice a little. "But then I am not tall and strong and with a face that commands respect. I am only old Chom who buys and sells and makes a profit where he can. A stranger to courts and the places where the rich and high-born gather. A woman can tell these things."

"Some women do not regard that as important."

"True, but the Ghenka is not one of them." Chom

glanced down the corridor to the closing door of her cabin. "She lives for her art and herself like all her kind. Could you imagine such a woman living in a hut? Tilling fields or working in a factory? She needs someone to stand between her and the harshness of life. A strong protector and someone to take care of unpleasant details. I wonder what happened to her manager. Perhaps he tried to sell her and she had other ideas. A knife in the dark, a drop of poison, who can tell? These things happen." He shrugged, thick shoulders heaving beneath the ornamented fabric of his blouse. "Well, Earl, such is life. What now? Shall we try our luck?"

Dumarest glanced to where the gambler sat at his table ringed by a handful of players. Harg Branst was a thin man with prominent ears, his features vulpine and touched by advancing years. A true professional, he wore no rings and his nails were neatly trimmed. He rode on a profit-sharing basis, as much a part of the ship's furnishings as the steward and cabins. He looked up from his cards, met Dumarest's eyes, and made a slight gesture of invitation for him to join the game.

Chom spoke in a whisper. "Have you noticed his good fortune? Never does he seem to lose. Now, to me, that is against all the laws of chance."

"So?"

"Perhaps something could be arranged between us? I have a little skill, and you are no stranger to the gaming table. It would be a kindness to teach him a lesson."

Dumarest said, dryly, "At a profit, naturally."

"All men must pay to learn," said Chom blandly. "Some do it with their lives. We need not be so harsh. It will be enough, I think, to trim his wings a little. Working together it could easily be done—a matter of distraction at a critical moment. You understand?"

The palming of cards, the switch, the squeeze when, convinced that he could not lose, the gambler would allow greed to dull his caution. It could be done, granted the basic skill, but unless the man was a fool the odds were against it. And no man who earned his living at the tables could be that much of a fool.

"The cost of the journey," urged Chom. "A High passage safe in our pockets when we land. Insurance in case of need. You agree?" He scowled at the lack of response. "A golden opportunity, Earl. Almost a gift. I cannot understand why you refuse. We—" He broke off as if knowing it was useless to argue. "Well, what else to kill the time? Daroca has some wine. Come, let us test his generosity."

Dumarest frowned, the man was beginning to annoy him. A shipboard acquaintance, met when he had joined the ship at Zelleth, the entrepreneur was becoming a nuisance. Deliberately he looked away, studying the others in the salon. Two dour men, brothers, Sac and Tek Qualish, consultant engineers now intent on their cards. Mari Analoch, hard, old, with eyes like those of a bird of prey, a procuress seeking to open a new establishment. A squat amazon, Hera Phollen with her charge the Lady Lolis Egas, young, spoiled, eager for excitement and adulation. Vekta Gorlyk, who played like a machine. Ilgazt Bitola, who played like a fool. The man who waited with his wine.

"Earl?" Chom was insistent.

"No."

"You have something better to do? More study, perhaps?" Chom smiled as Dumarest turned to stare into his eyes. "The steward was careless and failed to close the door of your cabin. I saw the papers you had been working on. Such dedication! But I am not after charity, Earl. Daroca wants to meet you and I think it would profit you to meet him." He paused and added, softly: "It is possible that he might be able to tell you something of Earth."

Eisach Daroca was a slight man, tall, dressed in somber fabrics of expensive weave, the starkness relieved only by the jeweled chain hanging around his neck, the wide bracelets on his wrists. He wore a single ring on the third finger of his left hand, a seal intricately engraved and mounted on a thick band. His face was smooth, soft, the skin like crepe around the eyes. His hair was clubbed and thickly touched with silver. A dilettante, Dumarest had decided. A man with wealth enough to follow his whims, perhaps jaded, perhaps a genuine seeker after knowledge. An eternal student. Such men were to be found in unexpected places.

He rose as they approached, smiling, extending his hand. "My dear Chom, I'm so glad that you managed to persuade your friend to join us. You will join me in wine, Earl? I may call you that? Please be seated."

The wine was an emerald perfume, delicate to the nose, tart and refreshing to the tongue. Daroca served it in goblets of iron-glass, thin as a membrane, decorated with abstract designs, expensive and virtually indestructible. A part of his baggage, Dumarest knew, as was the wine, the choice foods he ate. Not for him the usual basic, the spigot-served fluid laced with vitamins, sharp with citrus, sickly with glucose, which formed the normal diet of those traveling High. Everything about the man spoke of wealth and culture, but what was he doing on a vessel like this? Bluntly he asked the question.

"A man must travel as he can," said Daroca. "And it amuses me to venture down the byways of space. To visit the lesser worlds untouched by the larger ships. And yet I do not believe there is virtue to be gained by suffering hardship. There is no intrinsic merit in pain and, surely, discomfort is a minor agony to be avo'ded whenever possible. You agree?"

"At least it is an interesting philosophy."

"I like my comforts," said Chom. He lowered his empty glass. "The trouble is in being able to afford them. More often than not it isn't easy."

Daroca refilled his glass. "And you, Earl? Do you also enjoy comfort?"

"He's had too much of the rough not to enjoy the smooth," said Chom before Dumarest could answer. "I can tell these things. There is a look about a man who has lived hard, a set of the lips, the jaw, an expression in the eyes. The way he walks and stands, little things, but betraying. As there is with a woman," he continued, musingly. "You can tell the one who is willing and the one who is not. The one who is seeking and the one who has found." He took a mouthful of wine. "What did you think of the Ghenka?"

"She has skill." Daroca glanced at Dumarest. "More wine?"

"Later, perhaps."

"Is the vintage not to your liking?"

"It is too good to be hurried."

"As is interesting conversation. I contend that intelligent discourse is the hallmark of civilized man. As yet I have found no evidence to shake my conviction, but plenty to uphold it. You are satisfied with the wine, Chom?"

The plump man dabbed at his lips, his second glass almost empty. If he caught the irony he gave no sign of it. Instead he said, "She is more than skilled. The Ghenka, I mean. She is a true artist. Did you know that it takes twenty years to train such a one? The voice has to reach full maturity and they begin learning as soon as they can talk. Twenty years," he brooded. "A lifetime. But with such a woman what more could a man want?"

"A place of his own, perhaps," said Daroca softly. "A home. Children to bear his name and continue his line. Some men are not so easily satisfied, as I am sure Earl would agree. The mood of a moment does not last. It holds within itself the seeds of its own destruction. Passion is a flame which devours what it feeds on. The satisfaction of conquest, of possession, fades to be replaced by new aims. The happy man is the one who finds contentment with what he has."

Dumarest made no comment, sitting back in his chair, watching, savoring the wine. He was curious as to why Daroca should have wanted his company. Boredom, perhaps, but that was too facile an answer. The salon held others to whom he could have given his wine. An audience, then, someone to listen while he spoke? But why the crude and grossly coarse entrepreneur? Why himself?

Caution pricked its warning and yet the man seemed harmless enough, even though it was obvious he had arranged the meeting. And even if he weren't harmless there might be information to be gained. It was barely possible that he knew something of Earth and, if he did, the time would be well spent.

Dumarest looked down at his hand. The knuckles were white from the pressure with which he gripped the goblet. Deliberately he relaxed. Haste now would gain nothing, and hope was not to be encouraged. Also, Chom could have lied.

Quietly he said, "I understand that you have traveled much and far. May I ask why?"

"Why I travel?" Daroca shrugged, a gesture of pure elegance when compared to Chom's heaving shoulders. "As I told you, it amuses me to visit other worlds, to study other cultures. The galaxy is incredibly vast when considered in terms of habitable planets, and there are intriguing backwaters, lost worlds, almost, rarely visited and of an engrossing nature to one like myself who is a student of mankind. May I return the question? You also travel. Your reason?"

"I have a restless nature," said Dumarest. "And I like variety."

"A kindred spirit," said Daroca. "Shall we drink to our mutual interest?"

He was casual as he lifted his goblet, but his eyes were shrewd. A dilettante, perhaps, but Dumarest recognized that he was no fool. Only such would have taken him for a man of cultured leisure, even if Chom had not spoken as he had. Travel took money and a High passage was not cheap. Those who couldn't afford it rode Low, sealed in the caskets usually reserved for livestock, doped, frozen, ninety percent dead, gambling their lives against the fifteen percent death rate for the privilege of traveling cheap.

To such travel was a mania or a grim necessity.

"He's looking for something," said Chom as Daroca lowered his glass. "A planet named Earth."

"Earth?"

"That's right." The entrepreneur reached, uninvited, for the wine. "A crazy name for a world. You might as well call it dirt, or ground, or soil. Earth!" He drank greedily, and dabbed at his lips. "A dream. How can there be such a place? It doesn't make sense."

"A mythical planet?" Daroca shrugged. "There are many such. Worlds of supposed fantastic wealth, once found and then, for some reason, lost or forgotten. Once I went in quest of such a place. Need I say that it was a futile search?"

"It has another name," said Dumarest softly. "Terra. Perhaps you have heard of it?"

For a moment time seemed to congeal, to halt as he waited, his outward calm belying his inner tension. Perhaps, this time, he would receive a positive answer. Perhaps this wanderer would know the way to the planet he sought. Then, as Daroca slowly shook his head, the moment passed.

"You have never heard of it?"

"I am sorry, my friend, but I have never been to the world you mention."

"It doesn't exist, that's why." Chom was emphatic. "Why do we sit here talking about such things? There is wine to be drunk and beauty to admire. A pity we could not combine the two. Come, Earl, stop looking so bleak. At least you have the consolation of wine and there is always the Ghenka. A pleasant combination, yes?"

"For some," admitted Daroca. "For others, perhaps not. Such men are not so easily pleased. But I offer a toast. To success in all we attempt." He paused and added softly: "To Earth!"

"To a dream," scoffed Chom. He emptied his glass in a single gulp.

Chapter
◆ TWO ◆

The Lady Lolis Egas was bored. She lifted an arm and watched as the sheer fabric of her gown slid, slowly at first, then with an acceleration so fast it was impossible to follow, down the smooth length of her arm. It was a trick induced by the drug in her blood; the use of quick-time held peculiar dangers and played visual distortions. The sleeve had moved at a normal rate, only to her and those with her had it seemed to travel so fast.

As the cards which left the dealer's hands, the container which one of the players knocked from its place, the coins which the old harridan insisted on throwing instead of, as was normal, sliding them across the surface of the table.

The lifted arm, now bare to the shoulder, was flawless. She turned it, allowing the light to catch the gems on wrist and fingers, the great sapphire of her betrothal ring shimmering with ice-cold fire. It was a good ring and there would be more like it, clothes too, rare perfumes, expensive foods. Alora Motril of the House of Ayette would make a good husband.

But the nuptials were yet to come and, now, she was bored.

"Perhaps you should rest, my lady." Hera Phollen recognized the signs, and made the suggestion more from hope than any conviction that she would be obeyed. Her charge would be no trouble once asleep. "We have far to go and you will want to look your best when we arrive."

"Am I so ugly?"

"You are beautiful, my lady."

Hera's voice was deep, her hair short and her face seamed, but she was not a man and Lolis had little desire

14

for the adulation of women. She lowered her arm and turned, studying those in the salon. Vekta Gorlyk? Perhaps, but there was something cold about him, something remote; he would offer little sport. Polite, yes, and with time it would be possible to arouse his passion, but he lacked the ability of quick interplay, and while it would be amusing to shatter his reserve, it would take a patience she didn't possess. Ilgazt Bitola? He was young with a foppish manner of dress and his face held a certain weakness which she had long since learned to recognize. He would be willing to amuse her and yet the conquest would be too easy. Who then?

Her eyes drifted toward the table at which the three men sat. She dismissed Daroca at once, he was too world-wise, too cynical and, perhaps, too cautious to respond to her bait. The entrepreneur was too gross. Dumarest?

Softly she said, "Tell me, Hera, could you defeat that man?"

"In combat, my lady?"

"Naturally, what else?"

"Perhaps, my lady. It is something I would prefer not to put to the test."

"Afraid, Hera?"

The gibe was too obvious and the girl too transparent to arouse anger. Quietly she said, "My lady, I am to deliver you safe and unsullied to your husband to be. If it becomes necessary I will kill to achieve that aim. And there is no man alive of whom I am afraid."

Lolis could believe it. The amazon was trained and incredibly strong, a fitting guard for such as herself. A man she could have seduced, but not Hera, and the woman was dedicated to her profession. Yet it was amusing to tease her.

She rose and stretched, accentuating the curves of her body. At the gaming table Ilgazt Bitola watched and called an invitation.

"Are you going to join us, my lady?"

"Gambling bores me," she said. "And I am already bored."

"So?" He was eager to please. "Perhaps that could be

cured? An examination of the vessel, for example. Just you and I. Alone."

"I have already seen the ship."

"But not all of it, my lady," he insisted. "There is an unusual beast in the hold and one well worth your attention. I am sure the handler will not object." He let a stream of coins fall ringingly from his hand. "I have the means to persuade him if you agree."

She shrugged and turned away so as to face the three men sitting over their wine. Smiling, she approached them. Daroca courteously rose.

"My lady?"

"May I join you?"

"Certainly. A moment and I will summon the steward to bring more glasses."

"That will not be necessary." She stooped over the table, ignoring Chom's lascivious eyes, the inhaled breath of Hera's disapproval, and lifted Dumarest's goblet. She drank and replaced it, the mark of her lips clear against the crystal. "Thank you."

It was a simple approach, and, from experience, predictable. He would now lift the glass and drink and make some remark as to how sweet her lips had made the wine. Casual banter without real meaning, but which could lead to other things. She would sit beside him and they would talk, and, later perhaps, she would no longer be bored.

The prospect excited her, his masculinity triggering her overdeveloped sexual characteristics so that she felt the biological reaction begin to take command. Watching, Hera felt a quick disgust. Couldn't the stupid young fool recognize the difference between men? Did she think that Dumarest would react as, say, the entrepreneur would in similar circumstances? Across the girl's shoulder she met his eyes, and relaxed as she saw the quiet amusement. There was no danger here.

Chom said, "Sit, my lady. Your presence sweetens the wine and, should you care to drink from my glass, my happiness would be complete."

She looked at Dumarest. "And yours?"

"Happiness is not such a simple thing nor is it so easily obtained. If you would care to finish the wine, my lady?"

He rose and offered her his chair. "I have drunk enough. You will excuse me?"

It was rejection and she felt a surge of anger so intense as to make her feel physically ill. Hera's smile made things no better, but the time for revenge was not yet. Later she would think of a way, but, for now, it was important to salvage her pride.

"I had no intention of staying," she said coldly. "You presume to think otherwise. I will see you later, Daroca, when you have more congenial company. In the meantime I have other things to do." To Bitola she called, "You were going to show me something in the hold. How long must I wait?"

Harg Branst riffled the cards, cut and dealt sliding each across the table. He said, "You have made an enemy, Earl. If I were you I should be careful. That guard of hers is an ugly customer."

Mari Analoch scowled at her hand, rings flashing on her wrinkled fingers. "She's a stupid, oversexed bitch, and that kind are always trouble. I should know. In my business they are more bother than worth. The men like them, sure, but they love to set one against the other and they can change at the drop of a coin. Do you call these cards?"

"I'll change hands if you want," said Chom. "They can't be worse than mine."

The dour brothers said nothing, playing with a grim determination. Vekta Gorlyk carefully stacked his hand. Dumarest watched the neat precision of his movements, the immobility of his face, the eyes which alone seemed alive. Odd eyes, veiled, secretive.

Daroca moved coins to the center of the table. "I'll bet five."

"Earl?"

"And five more."

"She's going to Ayette," said Mari. "Getting married, so I hear. The poor fool doesn't know what he's letting himself in for. He'll pay for every ounce of pleasure he gets and he'll be wearing horns before a month is past. I'd bet on it."

"Bet on your hand," suggested Harg. "And you're

wrong. She's marrying high and there'll be enough guards around to keep her pure. Even so, Earl, I wouldn't visit that world if I were you. Chom?"

"I'll stay."

"Mari?"

"This hand is like the girl, pretty to look at but useless for anything else." She threw the cards aside. "With your luck, Harg, we should be partners. How about that? I've a nice little place lined up on Selegal, and if you've got some cash you could do a lot worse. With me running the girls and you the tables we should do well. Interested?"

"I might be," said Harg. He leaned back, knowing there was no need for high concentration, that the game had lost its sharp edge and that the players were sitting more for social reasons than anything else. And the prospect was attractive. He was getting tired of the limited life of endless journeyings broken only by brief halts at various planets. And, always, was the possibility that his luck might run out, his skill become blunted. The woman offered security. "I might be interested," he said again. "Let me think about it."

"How about you, Earl?" Mari was shrewd, her eyes calculating as she glanced at where he sat. "My experience, Harg's luck and you to give protection. We split the profits three ways and it won't cost you much to buy in. In my business you need a strong man around to keep order and take care of the parasites."

"Try the amazon," suggested Earl. "She might be interested."

"And you're not?"

"No."

"He spends his life throwing away opportunities," said Chom. "The Ghenka, the girl and now you. Some men have too much luck." He frowned at his cards. "I'll take two."

"Wait your turn," said Harg. "Earl raised and now it's up to Daroca."

"Take it easy," Chom pleaded as Daroca fingered his coins. "Think of the poor."

Mari snorted. "Let the monks do that. That's one good thing about this journey. No monks. I was on a ship once carrying two of them. The Universal Brotherhood might

do a lot of good work, but there are times when they
don't belong. You know, they made me feel guilty. Not
that they said anything, but they're so damned self-sacrific-
ing. How can men bear to live like that? Poverty is something I run away from, but they go out of their way to
find it."

"They do good work," said Dumarest. He looked at
Vekta Gorlyk. "Don't you agree?"

"Yes," he said. "I agree."

His voice was flat, like his face, devoid of expression, a
dull monotone which gave no added emphasis to his words.

Dumarest said, watching, "You don't find many in this
part of the galaxy. Not like you do in the Center. But
there seem to be plenty of cybers about, and that's odd
when you think about it. If the Cyclan is established out
here, then why not the Church? You have an opinion?"

"I haven't thought about it. I don't travel much. I
wouldn't have noticed."

"Cybers go where the money is," said Chom. "Money
and influence. Those who aren't welcome in high places
wouldn't see them. What's your trade, Gorlyk?"

"I am a dealer in rare and precious books."

"Books!" Chom raised his eyes and shrugged. "And who
buys those? Museums and libraries and eccentrics. You
could trade for a lifetime and never see a cyber. Now if
you were like Earl here, a man who gets around and
moves high, then you would. Well, let's get on with the
game. Daroca?"

"I'll stay."

Dumarest sat back as the play went its course. Chom
spoke too much of things he could only assume and he
wondered at the entrepreneur's reason. Envy, perhaps? It
was logical, yet somehow it didn't seem to be the answer.
A man in his profession would have early learned the
value of silence. It almost seemed that he was advertising,
warning, even, but why and to whom?

He looked again at Gorlyk, studying, judging. The man
had certain disquieting characteristics. His emotionless impassivity, the dull monotone of his voice, his precision
even. A cyber could feel no emotion; an operation performed at puberty divorced the brain from all physical
sensation so that he was a stranger to hate and fear, pain

and envy. Food was a tasteless fuel, the rarest wine less commendable than plain water. They were living machines who could never experience love and whose only pleasure lay in mental achievement. The knowledge that the predictions they made extrapolated from available data were correct.

Dumarest felt an awareness of danger. If Gorlyk was a cyber in disguise, divorced from his scarlet robe, his shaven skull covered with a wig or natural hair, then the Cyclan knew exactly where he was and where he was going. And that was the one thing he had done his best to avoid.

Daroca looked up from his cards as footsteps sounded down the passage outside. He frowned as others followed, their vibration loud in the silence of the salon. "Something odd," he said. "Trouble, perhaps?"

"That bitch has seduced the crew and they're after her." Mari was contemptuous. "Forget it. Deal, Harg."

"Something's wrong," said Chom. His voice reflected his fear. "The engines, perhaps?"

"If they go you'd never know it," said Mari. "You'd be dead." She cocked her head, listening, then rested her ear against the table. "There's a lot of noise somewhere," she reported. "I can pick it up loud and clear. Sounds like a fight of some kind."

Dumarest followed her example. Transmitted by the metal structure he could hear thuds and what seemed to be shouting. As he rose the door of the salon burst open and a uniformed man came inside.

Officer Karn did his best to be casual. "Harg," he said. "You're wanted in the hold. Quickly."

The gambler made no move to obey. "That isn't my department."

"Captain Seleem gave the order. If you want to ride on this ship again you'd better do as he says." His calm broke a little. "Damn you, don't argue with me. You're wanted in the hold. Now move!"

Reluctantly Harg threw down his cards and headed toward the door. As he opened it the distant sounds became louder. Dumarest caught the officer by the arm as he was about to leave.

"What's wrong?"

"Nothing that need concern you. If you will all stay in the salon you'll be quite safe. Unless—" He broke off, studying Dumarest, his height, the sheer gray of his tunic and pants, the high boots and the hilt of the knife riding just below his right knee. "I can't demand this," he said. "But we're short of men. If you could help?"

"What needs to be done?"

Outside, walking down the passage, the officer explained. "Some fool bribed the handler and got into the hold. We're carrying a beast for the zoo on Selegal. Because of its peculiar metabolism it couldn't be frozen, so we held it in a cage. Somehow it broke free. Now we're trying to get it back."

Dumarest listened to the noise. "An animal?"

"You haven't seen it yet," said Karn grimly. "Wait until you do."

Seleem stood outside the closed door of the hold, Harg and the steward beside him together with two other officers. They carried ropes and nets and the steward held a hypogun. The captain nodded to Dumarest as Karn explained why he had brought him along.

"Thank you for offering to help. We need all we can get. You know what happened?"

"I can guess. Bitola and the girl?"

"Her guard too. The girl managed to get out, not the others. She was hysterical and I've got her safe in her cabin, asleep." He glanced at the instrument in the steward's hand. "Have you trapped game before? Good. You probably know more about it than any of us. Can you give us some advice?"

"Keep clear," said Dumarest. "Move fast, don't hesitate and don't fumble. How big is this thing?" He frowned at the reply. "That big? And fast? There are enough of us for three teams. I'll go with Harg, Karn with the steward, the two officers together. Approach it from three directions. It can only move in one direction at a time and, when it does, the other two teams move in with the nets. Muffle it, rope it, hold it fast. And hold it," he emphasized. "Weaken and it will break free."

"Three teams," said Seleem. "Six men. What do I do?"

"You've got a ship to run. If we don't make it you'll

have to laser it down." Dumarest glanced at the steward.
"Let's get on with it."

The hiss of the hypogun as it blasted drugs into his
bloodstream was followed by an immediate reaction.
Dumarest drew a deep breath as the neutralized quick-
time ceased to affect his metabolism. The lights bright-
ened, the noises from beyond the door slowed so that he
could determine the sound of metallic crashing, the shatter of crystal, a solid, repetitive thudding. Gently he took
the instrument from the steward's hand, careful least he
should bruise flesh or break bones. Like the others the
man stood as if made of stone. He shook himself as
Dumarest fired at his neck, the others treated before he
could completely recover. They tensed, nets and ropes in
hand, ready as Seleem opened the door.

Inside lay chaos.

The caskets had been smashed, the wiring, the lights
and metal plating. Blood spattered the gleaming fragments
and a shapeless something lay before a twelve-foot cube
of thick bars. The handler, Dumarest guessed, or the
guard or even Bitola, but he wasted no time making certain. The broken lights had robbed the place of illumination, only a single tube casting a glow over the cage, the
rest in crawling shadow.

From behind came Harg's strained whisper. "Earl?"

"Wait."

To walk into danger was worse than stupid. Before he
entered the hold Dumarest wanted to locate the beast. He
stared into the shadows, wondering where it could be. The
thing had sensed their approach, or it had caught the light
streaming through the open door, and it had stilled all
movement.

"Get something heavy," he ordered. "Throw it past me
into the hold. Hurry."

He heard Seleem grunt and then something flew past his
head to crash against the floor. In the shadows something
moved, a bulky shape, scaled, legged, gem-like eyes in a
circle around a pointed head.

Dumarest lunged into the compartment, Harg following,
the others spreading to face the beast. As it sprang into
the light from the open door it stood fully revealed.

It was taller than a man, the head elongated into a savage beak and mounted on a prehensile neck. The body was like a pear, rounded at the base and ringed with clawed legs. At the height of a man's waist smooth tentacles hooked, the ends split into finger-like appendages, circling the body. The eyes were set in circles of bone and stared in all directions.

"God!" Harg sounded as if he were going to be ill. "What kind of thing is that?"

An offshoot of evolution, the result of wild mutation, that or perhaps it was perfectly fitted to its natural environment, Dumarest neither knew nor cared. He cried a warning as light glinted on the shifting scales, the words drowned in the sudden scrape of claws on the metal floor, and one of the officers screamed as the pointed beak ripped out his life.

"In! In, damn you!" Dumarest lunged forward, the net streaming from his hands. It settled on the lifting head, was ripped to shreds by the hooked tentacles. Before other nets could join the first the thing was free and rushing again to the attack.

This time the steward died.

"Get together," shouted Dumarest to Karn and the remaining officer. "Spread the net between you. Harg, grab hold." He flung the end of a rope toward the gambler. "Now run past it. Move!"

He raced toward the door, Harg running twenty feet to one side, the rope stretched between them, the beast in the middle. The rope hit, held, and, still running, the two men passed in a circle about the beast, trapping it in another loop of rope.

"Hold it!" Dumarest ordered as the beast lunged against the restraint. "The net, quick now!"

He hauled as the beast moved toward Harg, white-faced, sweating with terror. His boots slipped on the blood staining the floor and the gambler yelled as a tentacle tore at his sleeve, ripping the fabric from his arm and raking an ugly gash down his bicep. Dumarest ran to one side, rested his boot against the edge of one of the shattered caskets, and heaved.

Harg released the rope.

The thing came like a thunderbolt, a waft of sickening odor and a blur of lashing tentacles. Dumarest staggering

back, off balance with the sudden release of tension, felt
the hooks tear at his chest, the clawed feet at his stomach
and legs. He dropped the rope and flung himself aside as
the vicious beak dented the metal where he had stood.
Blows stung his back as he rolled, regaining his feet just in
time to avoid the thrusting head.

Automatically his hand fell to the top of his boot, and
lifted the knife, its razor edge catching the single remaining light.

Seleem, from where he stood in the open door, yelled,
"Don't kill it!"

Dumarest ignored the command. He was fighting for his
life, blocking the lash of tentacles with his left arm, the
knife in his right slashing, cutting, lopping the ripping
hooks, stabbing at the circle of eyes. Green ichor spattered
his face, his head, stinging as it touched the naked flesh. He
backed away, wary for his eyes, chest heaving, body in a
fighter's crouch.

"Don't kill it!" shouted Seleem again. "Karn, Grog, get
it!"

They ran forward with their net as the beast lunged
toward the open door. It had been attracted by the captain's shouts, the blaze of light and, perhaps, the possibility
of escape. Karn fell aside, one hand to his face as his
companion doubled, screaming, hands clutching his ripped
stomach.

Too late Seleem tried to close the door. The beast hit
the closing panel, threw it back against the captain, slamming him against the wall. Dumarest followed it into the
engine room, saw it lope toward the massive bulk of the
generators. The pointed head darted forward, the beak
slamming against the metal cover. It boomed, dented, but
held. Again the head slammed forward. A third time.

"The engine!" Seleem staggered from where he had
been crushed. "Stop it!"

Dumarest lifted his knife. His arm swept back, forward,
the blade a glittering icicle as it left his hand. It struck the
beast just below the circle of eyes and buried itself to the
hilt. The thing reared, pointed head lifting, and from the
open beak came a deep, gurgling ululation.

Then the head slammed down again, the beak ripping
through the plating, burying itself in the mass of delicate

machinery beneath. Fire blossomed around it, a gush of released energy, searing, incinerating, filling the compartment with the stench of roasting flesh. It spread, melting the casing, the carefully constructed parts inside.

"God!" whispered Seleem. "The engine!"

It had died, as the beast had died, as they would all die unless it could be repaired.

Chapter

◆ THREE ◆

Karn had entered the engine room, the gambler at his side. They watched as Dumarest walked to the dead creature and tugged his knife free. The blade was warm to the touch and stained with the acid ichor. He wiped it on his tunic and replaced it in his boot.

"Help me get this thing clear of the generator," he said. "Make sure the power is disconnected."

Together they lugged it from the ruined machine and dropped it against a wall. It was heavy for its bulk and death had coated it with a nauseous slime.

"It's dead," said Seleem. He seemed to be numbed by the loss. "I was to be paid on delivery and there's a penalty clause. I'll be ruined."

Shock and injury had disturbed the balance of his mind and he sought refuge in comparative trivia.

"I told you not to kill it," he said accusingly. "I warned you that it was something special. How am I going to meet the penalty? A lifetime in space," he mourned. "Twenty years as a captain. Five as an owner. Now I'm finished. You shouldn't have killed it."

"I didn't," said Dumarest.

"You could have," said Karn. The blood on his face gave him a peculiar, lopsided appearance. "I've never seen anyone move so fast. For a moment there I thought it had you, the time when Harg let go of the rope, but you managed to move out of its way. And when you fought it!" He shook his head, doubting what he had seen.

Harg said, "Earl, about that rope. I couldn't help it. The pain got me and I couldn't hold it with one hand. I'm

26

sorry, but I just couldn't hold it. You've got to believe that."

"He believes it," said Karn. "If he didn't you'd be dead by now." He kicked at the dead beast. "Damned thing. Three good men gone and all because some stupid bitch had to be clever. She must have opened the cage for some reason and look what happened."

"No," said Dumarest. "She didn't open the cage."

"Her friend, then. It's the same thing."

It wasn't that either, as Dumarest had known from the first. He glanced at Seleem, still trembling, then at the ruined generator. It presented no great urgency; if it could be repaired a few hours wouldn't matter, if not, then time was of no importance.

"Let's go back to the hold," he said. "There's something I want to see."

The shambles seemed worse than before now that the need for violent action was past. Dumarest stood looking, checking, verifying his suspicions. The dead officers and the steward lay where they had fallen. The handler was a shapeless huddle before the cage, recognizable only by his tattered uniform. Bitola was close to the door, the amazon sprawled even nearer and a little to one side. Her face was badly ripped and the beak had smashed her chest, but her expression was recognizable. Determination. She must have thrust her charge through the panel, slammed it, and turned to face the beast. Or perhaps the girl had been given time to escape and had closed the door herself. Now it didn't matter.

But she and the others had been on quick-time and it would have been impossible for her ever to have moved fast enough had she been near the cage when the creature broke free. They must have been leaving, actually at the open door, when it had attacked.

To Seleem he said, "What did they tell you about the beast? The shippers, I mean. Did they warn you it was intelligent?"

"No." The captain looked at his trembling hands. "They said it was just an animal. Something for the zoo. It couldn't be frozen or given quick-time. They supplied it in the cage and all I had to do was to feed and water it at regular intervals."

Karn said, "What are you getting at, Earl?"

"The shippers lied. That thing was more dangerous than they told you. Or perhaps it underwent a metamorphosis of some kind. What kind of lock was fitted to the cage?"

"It was simple enough. A pressure plate which had to be pushed and then slid to one side and then down. An animal couldn't figure it out unless—" He paused and then added, slowly, "I see what you mean. The damned thing must have let itself out and it couldn't have done that unless it had intelligence of some kind. But what was the point? I mean, if it was intelligent, surely it would have known there was no possibility of escape."

How to tell the workings of an alien mind? And yet some things were common to all life forms. Dumarest looked at the smashed caskets, the broken lights, the dark corners in which things could safely lurk.

He said, "The beast could have been a gravid female. It may not have wanted to escape as we use the term, but to settle its young."

"Hell," said Karn. "That means we have to search every inch of the hold. Now?"

"You saw the big one. We don't know how fast they grow."

"Now," decided the officer. He frowned, thinking, his hand touching the dried blood on his cheek. "I'll fix some lights and get some help. This is an emergency and the passengers will have to cooperate. Captain?"

Seleem winced as he drew in his breath. He seemed to have recovered his full awareness, probably helped by the knowledge that, as the shippers had failed to give due warning as to the intelligence of the beast, he was no longer responsible and no longer liable to the penalty he had agreed to pay for failed delivery.

"Do as you think best, Karn. My chest hurts, my head. I took a beating when that thing slammed me against the wall. And we've lost too many men. There's only you and myself left now." He looked at Dumarest. "How about you? Have you worked on ships before?"

"Yes."

"I'm needed at the controls. We both can navigate and Karn knows something about engineering, but we need someone to take care of the passengers. As from now you're my third officer with pay starting from the time we left Frell. Your passage money will be returned. Agreed?"

"Agreed."

"I'll need you all to sign a deposition as to what happened, but we can do that later." Seleem took a careful breath. "Now I'd better get back to the control room. Karn, keep me informed."

"He's hurt," said Dumarest as the captain moved slowly away. "He could have cracked ribs and maybe some brain damage. Have you a medic on board?"

Karn looked at the crumpled body of the steward. "We did, not now. Suggestions?"

"Mari Analoch might know something about medicine; get her to look at the captain. The Qualish brothers are engineers; they can start work on the generator. Gorlyk and Harg can help me to search the hold while you check for life-support damage. Right?"

"Right," said Karn. "You know, Earl, you're going to make a damn fine officer."

Mari Analoch said, "You're a fool, Earl. I heard all about it when I fixed up Karn and the gambler. Why the hell didn't you run when you had the chance? Fighting that thing the way you did. It could have ripped your face and taken out your eyes. I don't like to see a good man wasted."

She sat on the bed in his cabin, a tray of medicants at her side, a sheet wrapped around the expensive fabric of her gown. Her hair was slightly disarranged and her cosmetics, untended, betrayed the age she fought hard to conceal. A hard woman, ruthless and practical, but she had volunteered to help.

"You shouldn't listen to gossip," said Dumarest. "And I had no choice. Had I tried to run it would have got me."

"So you say. Now get those clothes off and let me inspect the damage."

"Seleem?"

"He's all right. A couple of cracked ribs and slight concussion. I put him under slow-time and he'll be fine in an hour."

She watched as he stripped, the protective mesh buried in the plastic of his clothing glinting as it caught the light through the scarred material. It had saved him from the ripping hooks and claws, but though it had withstood penetration it had done little to nullify the whip-like impact of the blows. The hard, white surface of his skin was striped and marred with purple bruises, his left forearm a mass of welts.

And, clear against the skin, sharp against the bruises, were the thin cicatrices of old wounds.

"Lie down," she ordered. "On your face." Lotions stung his back and brought a soothing numbness. "You're a fighter," she said, and he could feel the tip of her finger as it traced the pattern of his scars. "Ten-inch blades and the winner take all. Right?"

She grunted as he didn't answer, moving down his body, the swab in her hand moving over his hips, his legs.

"Turn over. Are you ashamed of it?"

The light was behind her, limning her hair with a halo of brilliance, casting her face in shadow and softening her features so that, for a moment, he could see something of what she had once been. Young and soft with a determined line to the jaw and lips which could smile, but rarely with her eyes.

"No," she said. "You're not ashamed. You're like me, doing what has to be done and making the best of it. A girl can't fight in a ring, but she can get by in other ways. A man now, that's different. The ring takes care of the weaklings." The swab moved over his chest and down to his stomach. "The ring," she said. "I've watched a thousand fights, but I could never understand why they do it. For money, yes, that I can appreciate, but why else? Do you get a kick out of it? Is it fun to kill a man? Some say it is. I don't think you're one of them."

The swab moved lower, passed over his loins, moved without lingering to the tops of his thighs. He relaxed, thinking, remembering. The blood-hunger of the crowd, the eager anticipation of blood and pain, the shouts and yells and the stench of sweat and fear. The grim knowledge that it was either win or die or, if not that, to be slashed and cut for a savage holiday. And, always, the conviction that luck could not last forever, that a single slip, a mistake, a patch of blood beneath a foot, the sun reflecting from a polished surface, anything, could tilt the balance and defeat all skill.

"Earl?"

He realized that she waited for an answer.

"Do you, Earl? Fight because you like it?"

"I fight only when I must." He was curt, not wanting to discuss it. "Have you finished?"

She was in no hurry, admiring the shape of him, the firmness, the touch of his skin as she let her fingers trail over the edge of the swab. Any woman could be happy with a man like this, and she wondered why he traveled alone. Not for the want of opportunity, of that she was convinced. Old and cynical as she was, yet even she could feel herself respond to his nearness. Had she been thirty years younger, twenty even—but it was useless to dream. The curse of her sex, she thought wryly. The biological need, not for passion, but to be with a man she could respect. The type of man she had never found—or had found too late.

"Mari?"

She had lingered too long, perhaps betrayed herself, and that was something she had never done before. Not even as a young girl, when she had first learned that what is said and what is meant are not always the same thing. She turned and dropped the swab into her tray.

"No damage," she said. "You'll be as good as new soon. Did you finish clearing the hold?"

Harg would have told her of the fifteen eggs they had destroyed, each as large as a doubled fist, each pulsing with life, but he told her again, not wanting to be hurtful.

"Seleem was a fool to have carried the thing," she said. "A bigger fool not to have sealed it in something solid. And insane not to have lasered it down at the beginning." She paused, then said quietly, "Just how bad are things, Earl? I would appreciate the truth."

"The hold is wrecked, Mari, but it can be repaired. I've got Chom and Gorlyk working on the caskets and Harg is rewiring the refrigeration units. Karn is confident that he can repair the generator. It's only a matter of time."

"And in the meantime we drift," she said shrewdly. "The field is down. Earl, why waste time repairing the caskets?"

"We have time. And it gives us something to do."

"To stop us thinking?"

She was too shrewd. The Erhaft field no longer protected or moved the vessel, and they were vulnerable to the hazards of space. Debris could impact the hull, a wandering meteor, even, rare, but always possible; a dozen things to threaten their lives.

"Suppose we can't repair the engine," she said thoughtfully. "What then? Do we drift until we die of old age? Or—" She broke off, frowning. The chance of rescue between the stars was so remote as to be inconceivable, but closer to a planet? "The caskets! Earl, do you think we'll have to ride Low?"

He smiled and shook his head. "You've too vivid an imagination, Mari. Anyway, would it be so bad?"

"I've done it before, when I had to, but twice was enough. And this would be different. We'd never know if we would be found. Damn it, Earl! I asked you not to lie to me!"

"I haven't lied." He reared up from the bed, his hands hard as they caught her arms, his face close to her own. "Listen, we hope to repair the generator. I'm sure we can do it, but only a fool takes no precautions. It may take longer than we know. All right; at the worst it may be impossible. But we still have a chance. In the caskets we can wait as the ship drifts to some habitable world when we can be rescued. That is why I am repairing the equipment in the hold. Now you know, but if you open that great mouth of yours and talk about it I'll close it for good. Get it?"

It was a language she understood.

Alone, Dumarest leaned back on the cot, closing his eyes and trying for sleep. He was overtense, the muscles jerking beneath his skin, his adrenalin-flushed blood denying relaxation. From somewhere came a thin, high keening, the Ghenka, he guessed, at practice or mourning the dead. Soon they would have to be evicted, the crewmen certainly, and he doubted if Lolis would want to have the body of her guard preserved for planetary burial. Bitola would go with the rest. A short, empty life quickly ended.

Well, perhaps he had been lucky. For him, at least, death had come quickly.

He turned, one hand by accident touching the metal bulkhead. The alloy was dead, lacking the faint vibration of the field, and he turned again, finally opening his eyes and looking at the ceiling. It was smooth, the paint fresh and bright. Seleem kept a good ship.

The keening rose, broke, then commenced again on a different key, a different song. It seemed louder than before and his mind began to fill with images, a woman with hair of spun silver and limbs of elfin grace. Another, this time with hair like flame and eyes of emerald. Kalin, who had given him so much. Whom he could never forget.

The song guided his thoughts in a chain of associated ideas. Kalin, and the secret she had given him; the Cyclan members who wanted to regain what had been stolen from their secret laboratory. The sequence in which the fifteen molecular units needed to be arranged to form the affinity-twin. Fifteen units, the last reversed to determine dominant or submissive characteristics. A combination which could be found by trial and error—given time. Too much time for the impatience of the Cyclan dedicated as it was to total domination of the galaxy. The possible number of arrangements ran into the millions; if it were possible to assemble and test one each second it would take four thousand years to try them all.

But, once found, it would give power incredible in its scope.

The artificial symbiote, injected into the bloodstream, would nestle in the base of the cortex and take control of the entire nervous and sensory system. The brain containing the dominant half would take over the body of the host. The brain of a cyber would reside in each and every person of influence and power. They would be puppets sitting on thrones and moving to the dictates of their masters. The Cyclan had once owned the secret, but now Dumarest had it, and the Cyclan would move worlds in order to recover it.

He had been forced to fight and run to keep it from their hands too often.

And, always, there was the danger that the Cybers' predictive skill had set a trap into which he would enter.

Gorlyk, perhaps?

He rose with sudden determination. If the man was working for the Cyclan there could be evidence in his cabin. He was working in the hold and it would be a simple matter to make a check.

Once dressed, Dumarest left the room and headed down the passage toward Gorlyk's cabin. The door was locked, but he had the steward's master key. Inside it was dark, the air heavy with a musty odor. Light blazed as he turned the switch and looked at the neatly-made bed, the cabinet, the piled suitcases, the small things a man carries to give him comfort and the illusion of home. A block of clear plastic held a single bloom of yellow laced with green, the styles a flaming scarlet against stamens of dusty black. A box of carved wood chimed when he opened the lid, a simple tune reminiscent of meadows and lakes. A string of well-thumbed beads, a tiny plaque bearing an abstract design, a bowl intricately decorated with women and beasts.

Souvenirs, perhaps. Little things collected during travel, or they could hold a greater significance to their rightful owner. A cyber would never have tolerated such emotional unessentials, but a cyber in disguise could have deliberately assembled them as a part of his deception.

Dumarest examined the cabinet. It held nothing but clothes, a single change of apparel together with a scarf of fringed and embroidered silk. The cases were heavy and locked with simple combination devices. He stooped, resting his ear against the mechanism, his fingers gentle as they turned the dial. A minute click, another, two more and the lid rose at his touch. Inside rested a heap of shabby books.

He lifted one, riffling the pages, smelling the odor of must rising from the volume. The paper was yellow and had obviously been treated with some form of plastic in ancient times, but the coating had worn thin and the revealed paper showed signs of decay. He had no idea as to the volume's value or worth. The title was in faded gold, tarnished, indecipherable. He looked again at the interior. The print was archaic and hard to read. He scanned half a page before deciding that it was some form of fictional romance. More deception? Or was Gorlyk exactly what he claimed to be?

He checked the rest of the contents, finding nothing except more books, replacing them as he had found them and closing the lid before spinning the dial. He looked under the mattress, ran the tips of his fingers along the frame of the cot, and searched the artifacts for signs of hidden compartments. A second case revealed no more than the first. The third held thin manuals dealing with mental disciplines, a large case of assorted drugs and several packets of dried vegetation. One of them seemed to be fungus of some kind, another a type of grass. Hallucinogens, perhaps? The basis of a health diet?

Dumarest replaced them and noticed a fold of paper protruding from one of the manuals. It was covered with a mass of neatly-written figures all in groups of seven. He turned it over and looked at the hatefully familiar tracing of the Cyclan seal.

Chapter
◆ FOUR ◆

Captain Seleem raised his cup of basic, drank and said thoughtfully, "Vekta Gorlyk? No, I have no personal knowledge of the man."

"Has he traveled with you before?"

"I think so. A few times, at least, but I cannot be certain as to the dates." Seleem drank again, emptying the cup. His eyes were bright and clear, but his face bore the marks of deprivation. Slow-time had speeded his metabolism so that he had lived days in an hour. Unconscious, he had starved. Had the treatment lasted longer he would have died. "You have a reason for your interest?"

Dumarest handed him another cup. "I was curious. He seems a strange person and I wondered if you knew anything about him. Where did he join the ship?"

"Phengala."

It was the world from which the ship had come to Grill, where Dumarest had joined it. It had gone then to Frell and had been scheduled to stop at Selegal and finally to arrive at Ayette. Then the ship would retrace its journey, serving a handful of worlds on a fairly regular schedule. There would be other ships each doing much the same. Did each carry a minion of the Cyclan?

Seleem moved cautiously in his chair. His brain was clear, but his chest still ached and when he breathed deeply he knew pain. Ribs took more than days to heal; he should take more slow-time and get himself fit as soon as possible. But first he had to restore his wasted tissues.

Dutifully he drank more basic.

"I've arranged a rota for the passengers," said Dumarest. "The men are doing what they can. Mari has taken

36

over the steward's duties, and the Lady Lolis is still asleep. I've kept her under quick-time," he added. "The rest are normal."

"The Ghenka?"

"In her cabin. There is little she can do, but I will get her to relieve Mari when it becomes necessary."

Seleem nodded, appreciating the crisp report which gave information without a mass of trivial detail. But he had to be certain of one thing.

"Are you sure no trace of the beast remains? No undiscovered offspring?"

"We checked thoroughly. Nothing remains."

Seleem sat back in his chair and stared at the screens, the assembled instruments which ringed the control cabin. Normally those instruments would be busy, questing with their sensors, guiding the vessel through the immensity of space. They were still functioning as their power did not depend on the drive-generator, but now they were quiescent. Without the Erhaft field the ship was practically immobile.

Bleakly he stared at the stars revealed in the screens. They showed no sign of movement, appearing as static brilliant dots scattered thinly over the darkness, a smear of distant galaxies like a coil of gleaming smoke. A touch and the Center came into view, a host of suns each ringed by many worlds, curtains and sheets of light, great clouds of luminous gas, the whole interlaced with busy commerce. But here, where the stars were few and distances immense, ships were not plentiful.

"How long?" asked Dumarest.

"Until we reach Selegal?"

"There or somewhere else."

"Too long." Seleem was grim. "We have no velocity to speak of now that the Erhaft field is down. We are drifting at a fraction of the speed of light and the galactic drift makes a mockery of our original course. We shall arrive somewhere, given luck and sufficient time, but it could take centuries."

"Or never," said Dumarest.

"That is correct," said the captain. "There is no point in lying to you. Unless we are attracted by the gravitational field of some star we could drift for an eternity."

It was as he had known. Dumarest looked away from the captain where he sat in his big chair, his face drawn in the soft illumination from the screens. Seleem looked older than he should, too old for his deprivation, his face sagging with the inner knowledge of certain extinction should the generator fail to be repaired. A red light shone on one of the panels like a watchful eye. The possibility of rescue was astronomically remote, but hope was eternal. When the field had collapsed the automatic beacon had begun to emit its call for aid.

The response was nothing but a thin wash of static, the sounds of dying atoms carried on the radiation of space. It was an empty sound, eerie, somehow frightening. The universe was too vast, too impersonal, and men were too small and insignificant in comparison.

Randomly, Seleem touched a control, and abruptly the sound changed. The thin, empty wash of spacial background noise became filled with a wailing lilt, crying, appealing, the sound of a soul in torment and carrying within itself the epitome of abject loneliness.

"What's that?" Seleem's eyes darted about the control room. "Dumarest?"

"Listen."

It came again, sobbing, a somber dirge of perfect harmony, rising to fall into pulsing tones, lifting again to a crescendo.

"Something outside!" The captain reached for his instruments. His hand trembled as he made adjustments. "Loud and strong and very close," he muttered. "But from where?"

He glared at the screens, but they showed nothing new. He adjusted them so as to scan the area all around the vessel. Nothing.

"A malfunction, perhaps?" Seleem made rapid checks. "No. Everything is in order. Someone is broadcasting on a general band. Ultra-radio at high emission from a source very close." He cut the volume and the wailing lilt faded to a mournful echo. "What can it be?"

"It's the Ghenka," said Dumarest, listening. "It can't be anything else."

He heard the song as he approached her cabin and wondered at the anguish it contained. He knocked and she fell silent as she opened the door and stepped back so as to allow him to enter her room. She had discarded her costume, the gems and paint, and now wore a simple dress of some clinging fabric. It rose high about her throat, full-sleeved, tight at the waist and falling to just below her knees. One side was slit almost to the hip to allow ease of movement. It flamed with a brilliant scarlet and, for a moment, he paused, half expecting to see a cowl, a shaven skull, the great seal he had reason to hate.

Then she switched on a brighter light and the illusion passed and he could see her as she really was.

A woman, no longer young, but not as old as he had suspected. Certainly not old enough to have run from competition, the wealthy worlds and rich patrons on which she depended. Her face was smoothly contoured, the mouth wide and generous, and what he could see of her throat was slender and unlined. Her hair was a rich bronze, closely-cut and fringed above the eyes. Her lips were full and soft, the lower almost pouting.

She inclined her head and said, "My lord, this is an honor."

"You know my name," he said. "Call me Earl. We have no need of formality."

"As you wish, Earl. My name is Mayenne."

"And you were singing. Why?"

"It is my trade. A skill must be practiced if it is not to weaken." She hesitated, then added, "And it gives me comfort. I am much alone."

Too much alone, he thought with sudden understanding. A toy to amuse the rich, an artist trapped by her training and achievement. Ghenkas were always remote and, on the ship, she had been mostly ignored.

Dumarest examined the cabin. The bed was unmarked, but the cabinet and small table were not as tidy as they could have been. A clutter of cosmetics, sprays, the gems she wore, all lying in a muddled heap. On the floor, fitted into a compact case, stood the familiar shape of an ultra-radio transceiver. Casually he picked it up.

"An unusual thing for a Ghenka to be carrying, Mayenne," he said. "A recorder I could understand, but why a radio?"

"It was a gift and it gives me comfort. With it I can listen to messages and music from many worlds. Surely there is no harm in a person owning a radio?"

"No harm," he admitted. "But to use it when there is no one to listen? You know our situation, girl. What did you hope to achieve?"

"Nothing."

"You sang into it just to amuse yourself?"

"Not to amuse. I was lonely and afraid and space is so empty. I hoped to pick up a message or some sign that we might be rescued. There was nothing but the sound of emptiness. It sounded so alone that I sang to comfort it. To comfort myself. Can you understand?"

Dumarest remembered the bleakness of the static he had heard in the control room, the eerie feeling it had created. It would not be hard for a person trained as the Ghenka had been in tonal efficiency to imagine the sound held words, almost recognizable, almost human. It was perfectly understandable that she could have sung back to it as a man might talk to a tree or to something which could not possibly answer. Loneliness took many strange paths.

He set down the radio and sat on the cot. "There is no need for you to be afraid. In a little while we will have repaired the generator and be on our way. On Selegal you'll make friends and no longer be alone."

"You are trying to be kind, Earl, but it will not be like that. It never is." She sat beside him, so close that he could feel the warmth of her body, the pressure of her thigh. "People do not accept me readily. Women hate me because of the influence they think I have over their men. Men desire me, not as a woman to be loved, but as a prize to be displayed. The rich are condescending and the poor are envious. Those who employ me try to cheat. Do you wonder why I need protection?"

"Guards can be hired and managers employed."

"You, Earl?"

He sensed the invitation, the unspoken offer of more than money if he agreed. The pressure of the thigh increased and the lips were close to his own.

Flatly he said, "No. I have other things to do. Perhaps Chom could help?"

"That man?" Her tone held a sneer. "He is an animal and a thief. Did you know that he tried to break into the dead man's cabin? I heard a sound and looked into the passage and he was trying to open the door."

"Bitola's cabin?"

"Yes. A short while ago. What else could he have been doing but seeking to rob the dead?"

It was possible and most likely true. The entrepreneur would not let such an opportunity pass, but Dumarest wasn't shocked and he doubted if the woman was either. They had both lived and learned the hard way. The dead had no use for their possessions, but the things they left could mean comfort to the living.

But, if she had seen Chom she could have seen his own search of Gorlyk's cabin. He thought about it, then decided against. Her door opened in the wrong direction; he would have seen the panel move. Yet was she all she appeared to be?

Would a Ghenka normally be carrying a high-powered ultra-radio of expensive make? A gift, she had said, but from whom? And why?

"You are troubled, Earl," she whispered. "Let me sing to you. Not all my songs are sad. I can create joy and passion and even forgetfulness. Listen!"

She began to hum, the soft tone rising, breaking into a ripple of cadences, words beginning to emerge, honeyed as they spoke of love and the satiation of desire. She caught his frown and, without breaking the song, immediately altered the pitch and rhythm, the words still soft and honeyed but now whispering of other things. Of home and a fire and the laughter of children. Of winds across an empty space and the triumph of growth. Another slight adjustment and he felt himself begin to sink into a reverie shot with mental images of an endless quest, of endless stars, of hardship and fulfillment to be achieved. And, always, beneath the words, the song, was the recognition of aching loneliness and the promise that it would be eased.

Unsteadily he said, "Enough, Mayenne."

Her hand touched his cheek, soft, gentle, the fingers trailing in a lingering caress.

"Earl, my darling. So long have I sought you. So much have I needed you. Do not leave me now."

He sank beneath the weight of her body and felt her warmth, her sudden hunger and consuming need. The scent of her perfume was a cloud accentuating his induced desire and his hands rose and touched the line of her back and shoulders, the helmet of her hair.

"Mayenne!"

The light died as she touched a switch and then there was only darkness, the lilting, singing whisper of her voice, the soft, demanding pressure of her silken flesh.

The bodies were gone, the mess, the smashed lights and crystal of the caskets. Even the floor had been cleaned of blood and ichor so that the hold seemed as if it had never witnessed pain and death and violent struggle. Dumarest raised a lid of one of the cabinets, sheet metal instead of the normal transparency, and felt the gush of frigid air rise from the interior. He closed the lid and switched on the mechanism, watching the temperature gauge as it fell. Satisfied, he moved to the others, testing each in turn. Again he moved down the line, this time checking to make sure the warming eddy currents were working at optimum efficiency. Finally he accepted the fact that the caskets, at least, were fully operational.

The generator was something else.

He paused in the engine room and glanced at the dismantled parts lying in neat array on the bench. Karn looked up from a sheaf of blueprints and nodded a welcome.

"Earl, satisfied with the hold?"

"It's as good as it will ever be."

"I wish I could say the same about this damned engine." The officer sounded as tired as he looked. Lines were graven on his normally smooth face and his eyes were sore, bloodshot.

Dumarest said, "Why don't you get some sleep?"

"Later."

"There's nothing that can't wait a while. Anyway, the Qualish brothers can handle things while you rest."

"They get on my nerves," said Karn. "They might be good engineers, but when it comes to repairing a machine all they can think of is replacements. Hell, to listen to them you'd think we had a factory just around the corner. They can't seem to get it into their thick heads that we have to make do with what we have."

"You're tired," said Dumarest.

"Sure I'm tired, but what has that got to do with it?" Karn shrugged as he met Dumarest's eyes. "So I'm being unfair," he admitted. "They aren't ship engineers and they can't help the way they think. And, from their point of view, they are right. The parts do need replacing. In fact we need a whole new generator and we'll get one as soon as we can—if we can."

Dumarest caught the note in the officer's voice.

"If?"

"It's bad, Earl. You're an officer now, so I'll give it to you straight. I think the Qualish brothers may have guessed, but they haven't said anything. If we get that generator going it will be a miracle."

"As bad as that?"

"I think so. Do you know anything about an Erhaft generator? They're factory-assembled and turned and they aren't meant to be torn apart. The worst that usually happens to them is that they get out of phase, but always there's a warning. Sometimes a ship is lucky to make a landing, but that's because some greedy captain pushes it hard and takes one chance too many. But that's about all."

Dumarest said, "Not quite. Sometimes an engine will fail."

"That's true," said Karn grimly. "But when it does no one knows anything about it. The ship just vanishes. Sometimes the collapsing field volatizes the structure; if it doesn't the ship just drifts until the end of time. We didn't volatize. One day, maybe, we'll form the part of another legend, a ghost ship which carries a crew of skeletons on a trip from nowhere to the same place. Something for people to talk about when they've nothing better to do. Hell, man, you've heard a dozen similar yarns in your time."

"Often," said Dumarest. "But we're not going to become one."

Karn made a sound deep in his throat. Fatigue and

despondency had colored his mood. He gestured to the dismantled generator.

"Look at it," he said flatly. "When that damned beast hit it was like shooting a bullet into a chronometer. The impact damage was bad enough, but when the energy went it really messed things up. We've stripped the whole thing and checked each part against the specifications. Most can be used, a few can be salvaged, but some will have to be replaced. Our spares are limited and will have to be adapted. The wiring is no problem and we can do something about the wave-guides, but the crystals are something else. From what I can see we are going to need three of them. They have to be the exact size, shape and structure. Tell me how to get them and I'll tell you when we can reach Selegal."

"Grow them?" suggested Dumarest. "Possible?"

"It's how they are made," admitted Karn. "But that would take equipment and measuring devices we haven't got. Try again."

"Is it possible to adapt or improvise?" Dumarest frowned, thinking, conscious of his lack of specialized knowledge. "An ultra-radio contains the same type of crystal, doesn't it? Would it be possible to assemble them in some way so as to regenerate the Erhaft field?"

He shrugged as he saw Karn's expression.

"I'm not an engineer and I'm shooting in the dark. I don't know what to suggest; all I am certain about is that, if you admit defeat, none of us has a chance. Now why don't you get some sleep? A tired mind is useless when it comes to solving a tough problem. You could make a mistake, overlook something, do irreparable damage." His tone hardened a little. "You put me in charge of the passengers, but you're as human as they are. Are you going to walk to your cabin or do I have to carry you?"

"Insubordination, Earl?"

"No, Karn, good sense and you know it. Now tell me what has to be done and then get some rest."

Karn sighed, admitting defeat. "All right, Earl, I'll do as you say. But if you can't find me those crystals there is only one thing to be done." He paused, then added softly, "You can pray. I can't think of anything else."

Chapter

◆ FIVE ◆

Lolis smiled and looked at the men gathered around the table in the salon, Harg, Chom, the silent Gorlyk. She breathed deeply, inflating her chest, conscious of their eyes. Chom purred as he gestured to a place at his side.

"Be seated, my lady."

Like the others he looked tired, worried, his eyes sunken in the puffiness of his cheeks. Against them Lolis was newly-risen, the effects of quick-time barely worn off, her eyes fresh and body relaxed from sleep and rest.

She said, "Where is Dumarest?"

"At his duties." Harg riffled his cards for want of something better to do.

"Do we need him, my lady?" Again Chom gestured his invitation. "I would offer you wine but things are not as they should be. Daroca has become morose and our new steward, or should I say stewardess, is careful of the supplies. But we have cards and conversation and they are enough to while away the tedious hours. Come, sit beside me and I will tell you of an adventure I had on a planet circling a triple sun. The girls held the power on that world and followed a strange courtship. I was younger then, and handsome in my fashion. I also owned jewels of rare value. Had I not been careless I might have ruled there yet."

He paused, waiting for her invitation to continue, but she had no time for boring reminiscences.

Harg said, "Your guard is dead, did you know?"

"And Bitola also." She was casual. "Yes, the old hag told me."

"And four other men," continued the gambler. "The

45

ship damaged and others hurt. Was it worth it to see the beast?"

He was being unfair but her casualness annoyed him. That and her arrogance. The incident was an unpleasant memory, for her to be swiftly forgotten; her only regret was at the loss of a servant and amusing companion. The cards made an angry rasp in his hands. Perhaps, if he could persuade her to play, some of the gems of which she was so enamored would fall his way.

The prospect entranced him: to be rich, with money enough to take up Mari's proposal, a half-share in a profitable enterprise. He could forget the acid taste of fear in his mouth. He had been on spaceships too long not to have recognized the danger of their position. The rest might believe that all would be well, but he had seen the captain and could read Karn's expression. A little more luck, he prayed. One last safe planetfall, a little money to see him through and he would be content.

He looked up as Mari entered the salon. She was bedraggled, her hands showing marks of labor, and she stood glaring at the girl.

"So you've finally decided to join us," she snapped. "Didn't I tell you to start work in the kitchen?"

Lolis shrugged. "I am not a servant."

"And you think I am?" Mari fumed her temper. "Listen, girl; this is one time you have to earn your keep. Things need to be done. The men want a soft bed when they have finished their labors and they can't be expected to prepare their own food and take care of their cabins. So get to it."

"I am not a servant," repeated Lolis stubbornly. "And how long does it take to prepare basic? How long to make a bed?"

"Try it and find out."

"Not long," said the girl. "I have been trained in order to maintain a palace. In my father's house the servants were never idle. You are quite capable of doing what needs to be done. And," she added with a sneer, "you should be used to making beds."

"Bitch!"

"Hag!"

"By God," said Mari, shaking with rage. "If I had you

in one of my houses I'd take the skin from your back. I'd teach you manners, you chit. I'd have you crawl and beg forgiveness. I'd break your spirit."

"Mari!" Harg was concerned. Selegal was far from Ayette, but assassins could be hired and the girl was of the type to bear a grudge. "She is tired," he said to Lolis. "She doesn't mean what she says. You must forgive her, forgive us all. This has been a time of great strain."

"She is old," whispered Chom. "And jealous. You understand?"

It pleased her to be gracious. Smiling, Lolis said, "You have good friends, old woman. On Ayette I would have my husband teach you a lesson you would never forget. Now bring me food, quickly."

"When it is time."

"I said immediately."

She had gone too far. Lolis knew it as Mari advanced toward her, hands lifted, fingers hooked to rip at mouth and eyes. Her face had hardened into an animal-mask of sheer, vicious ferocity and the girl looked at death and worse than death, the ruining of the beauty of which she was so proud.

"No!" she said, backing away. "Touch me and I'll tell Dumarest."

"You think he'd care?"

"He loves me!"

The effrontery of it stopped Mari as nothing else could, turning her sudden anger into ribald amusement.

"You? A man like that in love with you? Girl, you dream."

"I saw him," said Lolis. "He looked into my cabin and I could read his eyes. Had I been fully awake he would not have left me."

She meant it, decided Mari. A twist of the imagination, a wish-image born of half sleep and boredom and perhaps a little more. He had rejected her, and such an unpleasant memory could not be tolerated. And so she had built a fantasy which fear and terror had brought into the open. That and perhaps something more. She wanted Dumarest to be in love with her so that, perhaps, she could take revenge for the imagined slight.

A child, Mari thought, *and I was going to treat her as I would a woman.* But even children had to learn.

Aloud she said, "Girl, you forget something. Days have passed while you were dreaming under quick-time. Earl is with the Ghenka."

"He wouldn't."

"Why not? Because you are a woman and you are here and, to you, no other woman could beat you at your own game? Earl is a man, child; what would he want with a stupid girl? The Ghenka wanted him and I think she is in love with him. He could be in love with her. Why not? They make a good pair."

There was a note of wistfulness in her voice, caught by Harg if no one else; then he saw the look in Chom's eyes and knew he wasn't alone. But the entrepreneur was subtle. Instead of the anticipated jest, cruel because of its truth, he said, "Mari, you are overtired. . . . My lady, the journey is not yet over and who can tell what tomorrow may bring? As every gambler knows, the one who wins today can lose all in a matter of hours. And," he added meaningfully, "few men enjoy the fruit which falls too easily into the hand."

The message was plain enough for even Lolis to understand. She was young, nubile, fresh, rich and lovely. Earl had taken what was at hand. Now, when he had a choice, he would be hers for the asking. And why not? With Hera safely out of the way, who was to bear tales? The entrepreneur could be bought, Harg threatened, Mari accused of spite and Gorlyk . . .?

Deliberately she sat beside him and rested her hand on his arm.

"We have been strangers for too long," she murmured. "Tell me about yourself."

In the control room Seleem was dying. He sat slumped in his chair, face waxen, breathing shallowly, the air rasping in his chest and throat. Sweat dewed his features and Mayenne wiped it away with a scrap of scented fabric. He smiled his thanks weakly.

Dumarest stared bleakly at him, knowing there was nothing he could do. The internal injuries he had suffered had been more serious than they had imagined. Splintered ribs, perhaps, lacerating the lungs. Or a ruptured spleen—he had no way of telling. Slow-time had cleared his mind, but it would take more than rest to mend his body.

"You must eat," said Mayenne to the captain. "Please try to take something. Daroca has some food of his own which could tempt your appetite."

"Later."

Helplessly, she looked at Dumarest. The subdued light caught the bronze of her hair, filling it with little splinters of brilliance so that she seemed to be wearing a helmet of burnished metal. She had changed her dress, sensing, with her womanly intuition, that scarlet disturbed him. Now she wore a gown which matched the color of her hair. It too caught the light, the glow and the starshine from the screens, adding to the illusion that she was a warrior dressed in glinting mail.

Dumarest said, "Captain, we need you and your skill. You must take food."

"The philosophy of a traveler," Seleem said softly. "Eat while you are able because you can never be sure when the opportunity will arise again." He coughed with a liquid gurgling and blood showed at his lips. "Later."

"Earl," whispered Mayenne. "Is there nothing we can do?"

A doctor could have operated, repaired the broken body and used the magic of slow-time to accelerate healing, keeping the captain unconscious and artificially fed. But Dumarest lacked the necessary skill and the ship was not equipped for such treatment. The only thing he could do, the normal practice in such cases, was to freeze the captain in one of the caskets until they could reach proper facilities.

But Seleem was needed at the controls. And the captain refused to abandon his command. He said weakly, "Report on the condition of the generator."

"Karn has reassembled what he could. Now he and the Qualish brothers are trying to find some way to replace the ruined crystals."

"Karn is a good man," said Seleem. "Not as good an engineer as Grog, but he will do his best."

"I know that," said Dumarest.

"A good man," repeated Seleem.

He fell silent, brooding, regretting past mistakes. He should have killed the beast instead of trying to recapture it. He should not have used so many of his crew. He should have run from the door or closed it earlier. He had been greedy and now he was dying and the ship was dying with him. They would all die.

Dumarest said, "Mayenne?"

"Yes, Earl?" She followed him as he moved toward the door of the control room. "Is there something you want me to do?"

"Stay with him." He glanced to where the captain sat facing his instruments, the screens. "Get him to eat. Keep him alive and, more important, keep him from dying before his time. We need his skills. If Karn ever gets that generator working he will have to stay by it. Seleem is the only navigator we have."

"I understand."

"Daroca has done his best, but Seleem seems easier with you. Perhaps you could sing to him." He paused and added, "Happy songs. He must be kept cheerful."

"All my songs are happy ones now, my darling." Her arms lifted, closed around his neck and pulled his face closer to her own. Her lips were soft and gentle, then firmed with rising passion. "I love you, Earl. I love you. My life is yours. Remember that."

Her life, her love—for what little time remained.

Dumarest closed the door behind him, his face bleak as he heard the wash of static from the radio, the empty, eerie sound. And then came the notes of her song, soft, warmly human, a mother crooning to her child, a woman to her lover. Comfort for the dying captain, his tormented mind eased with induced imagery.

He heard voices from the salon and glanced inside, seeing the gambler dealing cards to Chom, Lolis sitting close beside Gorlyk. Mari entered, bearing cups of basic. She saw him and called for him to enter.

"Food, Earl. Shall I take some to the captain?"

"Yes, Mayenne too. Has Daroca eaten? The others?"

"Daroca's in his cabin; he didn't want anything. I've attended to the Qualish brothers and the officer. Double rations; they need the energy." She handed him a steaming cup. "And so do you. Sleep too; you've been working too hard, Earl. Now sit and get that down."

Her voice was falsely harsh to cover her concern. He smiled and took the cup and sat close to the girl. Lolis glanced at him, then returned her attention to Gorlyk. Let him be envious, a little jealous, perhaps. Later she would make him her own.

"And you mean you can do that?" she said to Gorlyk with feigned interest. "Really train your mind so as to improve its efficiency?"

"Certainly. It is a matter of conscious discipline. For thousands of years men have known that, by mental exercise, they could control their metabolistic behavior. For example, I could thrust a steel rod into my flesh and I would not bleed, feel pain, nor would the injury leave any trace or scar. When I was very young I saw a troupe of entertainers at a fair. They walked on broken glass, pierced their flesh with needles, held their hands in fire. The sight intrigued me and I determined to learn their secrets."

"Fakirs," said Chom. "A trick of the mind."

"Mental conditioning," insisted Gorlyk. His voice had warmed from its normal dull monotone; now it held a trace of warmth and pride. "Rigorous discipline exercised over many years. The brain is everything, all else of minor importance. Emotion is wasted energy. To feel hatred or anger is a weakness. Such things are the result of glandular secretions and, by mental control, can be prevented."

Slyly Lolis said, "And love?"

"An emotion detrimental to mental well-being."

Chom laughed and said, "It is fortunate for you that your mother did not subscribe to your teachings. Right, Earl?"

Dumarest made no comment.

"Love is everything," said Lolis. "I can't imagine what life would be like without it. To train yourself to be an unfeeling machine." She gave an exaggerated little shiver. "Horrible!"

"But efficient," said Gorlyk. "Love is not essential to the perpetuation of the race. Parthogenesis or artificial insemination could take care of later generations and such births could be strictly controlled on the basis of mental attainment. Think of what such a system would mean. The race would constantly grow in mental prowess; only those showing the highest ability would continue their line. The rest would be eliminated from the genetic pool. It would mean the millennium."

"Or sheer, unadulterated hell," said Harg. "Surely life is a matter of variety? Your plan would make all men the same."

"No," said Gorlyk. He paused, searching for an example. "Take this ship. Men designed it, built it, sent it traveling between the stars. Now it is obvious that there must be an optimum design for a vessel based on its function and purpose. Over the course of time ships have become more or less standardized. Trial and error have resulted in a pattern which we all know. Not perfection, but a greater efficiency when compared to earlier models. If we do it with ships, then why not with men?"

"And women?" Lolis glanced at Dumarest. He was drinking his basic, apparently uninterested in the conversation. "Would you like all women to be the same, Earl?"

"In many ways they are," said Chom before Dumarest could answer. "In the dark, at least."

She ignored the crudity. "Earl?"

To Gorlyk he said, "Have you heard of the Cyclan?"

For a moment the man hesitated, a shadow in his eyes; then he said, "I am not sure of what you mean."

"The Cyclan is an organization like those you speak of. It is dedicated to the mind. Emotion plays no part in its dealings. I find it strange you have not heard of it."

"A dealer in books," scoffed Chom. "Where would he have met a cyber?"

A hundred places, perhaps, Dumarest thought. The goods he dealt in were rare and costly and those who would buy them would have money and influence. And he carried a tracing of their seal.

Dumarest said, "Gorlyk, have you ever met a cyber?"

Again he paused slightly before answering, as if he were considering his reply—or tailoring it to suit the occasion.

"Yes," said Gorlyk. "Once. I was most impressed."

Impressed enough to have fashioned his life on what he had seen? To have copied the seal which the cyber would have worn emblazoned on the breast of his scarlet robe?

It was possible and a cautious man would not have

given an outright lie to a simple question. But Dumarest did not press the point. There would be time for that later.

However, unless Karn could repair the generator, there would be no need.

Daroca called softly from just within the open door of his cabin. "Earl! A moment?"

He seemed no different than he had before. The somber clothing was neat and clean; his face was unmarked by worry or doubt. He stepped back as Dumarest entered the cabin, and gestured to a chair.

"Some wine?"

"No, thank you."

"This is a special vintage," urged Daroca. "Something which I would venture to guess you have never tasted before." He produced a bottle fashioned of ebon glass, the darkness flecked with crystalline shimmers. Into a pair of the iron-glass goblets he poured what seemed to be a flood of bubbles suspended in an amber fluid. "A novelty," he said, handing Dumarest one of the glasses. "A secret of the vintners of Hammashend. I think it will amuse you."

Dumarest looked into his goblet. The bubbles were of various colors, floating, lambent spheres, touching, parting, never breaking their individual boundaries. He sipped and felt a cool tartness. Again, and this time he felt a globule break against his tongue. Immediately his mouth was filled with the taste of honey.

"A host of different flavors, each trapped in its own liqueur," said Daroca. "No two drinks are the same. It adds a new dimension to a social grace." He paused and added, "And such things should be enjoyed before it is too late."

"You know?"

"Our position? Certainly. I would be a fool if I did not."

"The others?"

"The girl has no mind for anything but herself. Harg, like all gamblers, is a philosopher. Chom?" Daroca shrugged. "An animal who will fight to the last in order to survive. Gorlyk has his mental discipline." He smiled with quiet humor. "It will be interesting to see him put it to the test."

"And yourself?"

"I am not afraid to die. No," Daroca corrected, "that is not wholly true. I am afraid of the lost opportunities death will bring. The places I shall not see, the things I shall not do. Stupid, perhaps, but to me death has always represented unfinished business. I am a methodical man, Earl. More wine?"

"No."

"Later, perhaps." Daroca leaned back in his chair. "Of us all I would guess that our situation bears hardest on you. You are a man of action, used to making his own way and, in a sense, controlling his own destiny. Now there is nothing you can do but wait. How long, Earl?"

Dumarest shrugged. "Karn is doing his best."

"Which we both know isn't going to be good enough." Daroca sipped at his wine, looking surprised at the flavor he had discovered. "Roses," he mused. "Or, no, the essence of shleng. Interesting."

"You aren't going to die," said Dumarest. "The caskets are repaired and are waiting. When it is time they will be filled."

"So I have heard. No, not from Mari, but I guessed she knows. The brothers were talking, and I have my own intelligence. Why else should you have them made ready? However, Earl, what else is that but anticipating the inevitable?"

"You will be alive," said Dumarest harshly. "You will have a chance. We all will."

"A fighter," mused Daroca. "You never give up."

"No," said Dumarest. "I never give up." He rose from his chair. "Was that all you wanted to talk about?"

"Wait. You haven't finished your wine."

Dumarest looked down at the goblet. He didn't want the wine, novel though it was. He didn't want to sit and talk about what he already knew too well. Daroca was probably bored, but there were others with whom he could converse. And the cabin, with its soft furnishings, seemed to stifle, pressing close with its metal and plastic.

"Wait," said Daroca again. "Please sit and finish your

wine. And let us talk a little. About Earth," he added softly. "Terra."

"You said that you'd never heard of the place."

"I said that I'd never been to that world," corrected Daroca as Dumarest resumed his chair. "That is true; I never have. Does it really exist?"

"I was born there." Dumarest sipped at his wine and his mouth filled with a sharp astringency reminiscent of dust. "An old world, scarred by ancient wars, on which life is not easy. There is a moon, huge and silver in the sky. The stars are few, and ships rare. I left as a mere boy, stowing away, and I had more luck than I deserved. The captain was old and kind. He could have evicted me; instead he allowed me to work my passage. Later, he died."

He sipped again, remembering the endless journeyings, the strange worlds as he moved deeper and deeper into the Center of the galaxy. Always traveling, until he moved in regions where even the very name of Earth was unknown.

"You came from that world," said Daroca musingly. "Can't you get back? Haven't you the coordinates?"

"No."

"But surely they can be found? There must be records."

"No," said Dumarest again. "I told you, Earth is a world which has been forgotten. The very name causes amusement. No one seems to know where it is."

"A mythical planet," said Daroca. "Or one which is assumed to be a mythical planet. I went on a quest for such a world once. Eden. A planet of supposed beauty and eternal life. I actually found it, or a world bearing that name. Needless to say, it was not what legend implied. A harsh world with a peculiar race of introverted people with ludicrous claims. They insisted that all mankind had originated on their planet, that it was the source of every race on every world in the galaxy. An obvious impossibility. But Earth?" He shook his head.

"And Terra?"

"They are the same, you say? If so, perhaps I can help you. I have heard the name before. There is a cult which holds that, like the Eden I told you about, all life originated on one planet. They call it Terra."

"The Original People," said Dumarest.

"You know of them?" Daroca sounded disappointed. "I'm sorry, Earl. I thought I could be of help. It seems that you already know all I can tell you."

"Perhaps not. Do you know how to contact the cult? Where they are to be found?"

"No."

It was the answer he had expected, but Dumarest was not disappointed. Earth was close, of that he was certain. Clues won over the years had guided him to this sector of the galaxy, and it could only be a matter of time before he would know exactly where it was to be found. Clues won on Toy, on Shrine, on Technos and Dradea. The threads winding close with, perhaps, the final answer to be found on Selegal.

"You are fortunate, Earl," said Daroca softly. "I envy you."

"Why?"

"You, at least, have a reason for living. A goal at which you can aim. I—" He broke off, shrugging. "Well, never mind. But to drift is not always a pleasant thing. Shall we finish the wine?"

Chapter

◆ SIX ◆

Dumarest woke to a pressure on his shoulder and the sound of an urgent voice.

"Earl, darling! Wake up! Wake up, Earl!"

It was Mayenne. She lifted her hand as she saw his opened eyes and stood quietly beside the bed as he sat upright. He felt weak, disorientated, his head spinning with vaguely remembered dreams. Daroca had kept him talking, and he had lingered, sensing the other man's need of companionship. Had some of the globules contained hallucinogens? Damn the man and his exotic wine!

Mayenne said, "Please, Earl. Hurry."

"A moment." He rose and rinsed his head, the cold water helping to wash the cobwebs from his brain. While dressing, he said, "Seleem?"

"He isn't dead, Earl, but something has happened to him. I went to the salon to prepare him some food, and when I returned he said that he'd heard voices."

"Voices? Another vessel?"

"I don't know."

"Did you hear them?"

"No. Earl, he looks so strange. He kept asking me if I could hear anything and I couldn't. So I came for you."

Seleem turned as they entered the control room. The lights were out, the chamber lit only by the telltales and the starglow from the screens. He was upright in his chair, eyes bright, shoulders squared as if his body had summoned up a reserve of energy.

"Dumarest," he said. "Check the screens. Negative?"

"Negative."

"Yet there has to be something out there. I heard it. Listen."

He touched a control and the thin wash of static poured into the room.

"Negative," said Dumarest. "Captain, maybe you'd better let me give you something."

"I'm not mad," snapped Seleem. "And I'm not suffering from delusions. I tell you I heard something."

"Voices, Captain? A response to our beacon?"

"No, not voices. It was more like a song. A sound like the girl makes. You remember? We heard it once together."

When she had sung into her radio and broadcast her voice to the stars. Dumarest met her eyes.

"No, Earl. I wasn't responsible. I swear it."

"But you were singing to the captain."

"Yes, but I'd left to get him food. There it is." She pointed to an untouched cup of basic standing on the chair-table. "I didn't sing and I didn't broadcast. You have my word for that."

A delusion then, the crying need for Seleem to save both himself and his command, causing him to fit imagined words to the empty static. Dumarest drew a deep breath, knowing that he had been a fool to hope.

"I heard it," insisted the captain. "It came loud and clear. I couldn't have been mistaken."

Dumarest said, "Mayenne, do you remember the song you sang before you went to get the food?"

"Yes, Earl."

"Sing it again."

"Now?"

"At once, Mayenne. Please."

He watched as the notes soared around him, filling the cabin, merging with the background wash of static. Seleem gave no response, sitting as before, and the telltales remained quiescent. A forlorn hope, but it had to be tried. At times ultra-radio had freakish ways, and, if nothing else, it would prove by negative response the captain's delusion.

Seleem stirred as Mayenne fell silent.

"It was something like that," he said. "Not exactly the same, but something—"

The radio burst into life.

It was a reflection, thought Dumarest wildly. A return

of what had been emitted, bounced back from some scrap of cosmic debris. Crystals, perhaps, vibrating in sympathy and rebroadcasting what they had received. And then he noticed the subtle differences. The song was not exactly the same: not even a mirror-image. It was as if someone had heard a shout and answered it with a blast of similar sound.

"There!" Seleem was trembling. "I told you I heard something! I told you!"

"Sing again," Dumarest ordered. "Use sequential notes in varying series and pause between each group."

"Earl?"

"Do it!" Urgency sharpened his voice, making it hard. "Aim for a response. If it is identical, it could be a reflection. If not, it could be the result of intelligence. Hurry."

He timed the song, the answer, checking and testing as Seleem adjusted his controls.

"Too low," he said after a prolonged space of silence. "Higher? Sing higher!"

The girl had a tonal range more than twice that in normal use. Her voice was a trained instrument capable of delicate variation and pure harmony. A Ghenka could smash glass and curdle milk, kill bacteria even, with the power of her voice. Dumarest felt the ache in his ears as her tones soared, saw the captain's eyes become suffused with blood and felt the thin vibration of the control panel on which his fingers rested.

"Enough!"

Tensely he waited for the response. When it came, there could no longer be any doubt. It was not a reflection.

Dumarest spoke into the radio. "This is a ship in distress. Do you understand? We are damaged and without motive power. We need assistance badly."

Nothing. The screens remained empty, the radio silent. Seleem stirred fretfully in his chair.

"Try again," he urged. "Dumarest, there's a ship out there somewhere. We've got to remain in contact. Try again."

"We don't know that it is a ship," said Dumarest. "All we can be sure of is that something, somewhere, is emitting a signal." He boosted the radio to the limit of its power. "Listen," he said harshly. "You out there, *listen.*

This is a ship in distress. We have suffered damage and
are drifting. Unless we get help, we'll all die. Locate our
position and come to our aid. *Quickly.* We have no time
to waste."

Again no response.

"I don't understand this," muttered Seleem. "It answered the girl, why not you?"

Pitch, frequency, perhaps even the casual dictates of cu-
riosity, how could they tell? Dumarest caught Mayenne by
the arms.

"Sing to it. Attract it. Bring it to us, somehow. I don't
know how," he said as he saw the question in her eyes.
"But it answers you, and that is enough. Call to it, girl.
Bring it close."

"But, Earl—" Her hand rose and touched her throat.
"For how long must I sing?"

Even a trained voice had its limitations. Dumarest
checked the panels, found the recorder and switched it on.

"As long as you can," he said flatly. "And then we'll use
the tape. Now, Mayenne."

Karn entered the control room as she began. He stood,
listening, as she sang for her life, the lives of them all. Her
voice rose in a plaintive wail, shrilling, sobbing with a terrible yearning, calling, pleading in the universal language
of despair.

As she paused he said, "Captain, I—"

Seleem cut him short. "Be quiet. We are in contact with
something. Listen."

The song rose again, a little different than before, but
still tearing at the nerves with the same impact. Karn felt
a bleak helplessness, a fury at unresolved suffering and
pain, a burning determination to help and aid whenever
the opportunity arose.

The answer came in a roar of sound.

It blasted from the radio, lilting, wailing, seeming to
hold a question. Dazed, Dumarest flung his hands to his
ears. Karn caught Mayenne's look of anguish and heard
Seleem's cry of pain. Then the sound changed. Now it no
longer posed a question, but held decision.

The ship moved!

On the screens the stars shifted, flickered and were replaced by others, sparse and dull against the sky. A hand-

ful of somber points were backed by unending darkness, broken only by the smears of distant galaxies.

A world hung before them.

Seleem cried out and flung his hands at the useless controls. Dumarest caught a glimpse of harsh roughness, of rounded nubs which could once have been mountains, and then they were closer, hurtling toward a deep valley barely visible in the weak light of the stars.

"Earl!"

He heard the cry and felt Mayenne grip his arm. He caught her to him, cradling her tight, giving her the useless protection of his flesh as his skin crawled to anticipated destruction.

"Earl," she whispered. "Kiss me good-bye."

He felt the touch of her lips, the softness of her hair against his cheek, the warm pressure of her body as, helplessly, he waited.

And then, incredibly, the ship came harmlessly to rest.

"God!" Karn was sweating; his hands shook as he dabbed at his face and the trickle of blood from his bitten lips. "Landings like that I can do without. Are you all right? Earl? Mayenne?"

"Yes," she said. Like the officer, she was dazed. With her emotions set on approaching death she was slow to recognize the abrupt transition. Her eyes widened as they stared past Dumarest to the big chair. "The captain!"

Seleem was dead. He lay sprawled on the padding, blood edging his mouth, his eyes filled with the terror he had known at the last. Shock had sapped the remaining strength from his weakened body. Karn gently closed the staring eyes.

"A good man," he said bleakly. "And a damned fine captain. I know just how he must have felt. A dead ship and a certain crash. All he'd ever worked for on the edge of destruction and not a damned thing he could do about it. A hell of a way to end a life."

Dumarest said, "You're in command now."

"In command of what? A useless vessel stranded on an unknown world? You know why I came to the control room? It was to tell the captain that we didn't have a hope in hell of ever being able to repair the generator. I've tried everything I know and it isn't enough."

"It's still your command. And you have decisions to make, responsibilities. There are the passengers; have you forgotten?"

"No," said Karn. "I haven't forgotten. But how am I going to explain? One minute we were in space, the next . . .?" He shrugged. "What happened, Earl?"

"You saw it. You should know."

"Instantaneous transmission. I saw it but I still don't believe it. It goes against all the accepted laws of nature. The energy requirement alone would have been fantastic." Karn looked at the screens, at the rough terrain outside. To either side the cliffs framed a solitary star. "Something moved us," he said wonderingly. "Shifted us from where we were to where we are now. And where is that? Somewhere remote, that's obvious. We must be at the edge of the galaxy. But why?"

Mayenne said, "I called for help. Something answered."

"You call this help? The ship stranded and the captain dead?"

"That was an accident," said Dumarest. "He was ill, dying, and the strain was too great."

"So they couldn't help that, but why bring us here at all?"

Karn moved to the radio and boosted the gain. To the silence he said, "This is the commander of the vessel which has just landed. We are in distress and require immediate aid. Reply if you receive me."

He snarled at the lack of a response.

"Listen," he stormed. "You brought us here and you killed a man in doing it. Now talk to me, damn you. Talk!"

A rush of noise and then a single word came.

"Wait!"

Mayenne caught Dumarest's arm. "Earl! They answered! They can understand!"

"Then why don't they talk?" Karn adjusted the radio. "What are we supposed to wait for?"

"Wait," said the radio again. Then, in a disjointed rush, the voice said: " . . . Need to correlate data . . . communication . . . stimulation of reserve . . . unrelated form of reference . . . micro-currents of various transmitters oc-

cluded by engrossing irrelevancies . . . time . . . inconsistent
with . . . manjhala hish . . . secal. . . ."

"Crazy," said Karn. "What's the matter with that opera-
tor? He doesn't make sense."

"He sounds so cold," said Mayenne in a whisper, as if
afraid of being overheard. "Like Gorlyk does at times.
Flat, dull, like a machine."

The radio emitted a series of clicks, a high-pitched whistle and then a dull, rumbling grating sound which fell to a
sonorous booming.

"Damn you," said Karn. "You're getting on my nerves."
He glanced at Mayenne. "Perhaps she should sing to it
again."

"Use the tape," said Dumarest. "We recorded her last
songs."

It was worth a try and they had nothing to lose. As
Karn engaged the spool, he studied the screens. The edge
of the cliffs seemed a little different from what they had
been before, the bleak stone hazed with a mist of light. He
blinked, wondering if his eyes were at fault, but the soft
glow remained.

Karn rested his hand on the control. "Here goes.
Maybe, this time, we'll be sent back home. Right on the
field at Selegal would suit me fine." He froze as the radio
broke into new life.

". . . compounded error . . . communication by means of
vibrating membranes . . . no . . . vibration conducted
through gaseous medium . . . no . . . unessential . . . signal
medium restricted to limited range of cycles . . . correlate
with electromagnetic emissions . . . malfunction. . . ."

The cold voice held a frightening detachment. Dumarest
thought of a tiny insect lying on a path, a hand sweeping
it up and carrying it to a laboratory, there to mount it, examine it, perhaps dissect it. Would the creature comprehend the forces which had moved it? The musing of the
technician probing into its life?

"Earl," whispered Mayenne. "I'm afraid."

Had she grasped the analogy too?

Before he could ask, sound thundered around them: a
blast of noise so intense that it created physical pain. It
was as if the very walls of the vessel quivered to invisible

energies, vibrating in the aural spectrum, but so strongly that they could only cringe and wait for it to end.

"Stimulus inappropriate," said the radio. "Adjust."

Again the ship quivered with sound.

And the planet spoke.

It needed no mouth; mouths are only a means of vibrating gases. It needed no radio; it could control the passage of electrons, the emission of energies, as a part of its integral existence. All that was required was a diaphragm which could be vibrated within a range discernible to the ear. And the ear itself contained such a diaphragm.

To such a being it was a small thing to correlate words, to assign meanings, to construct the terminology and extrapolate from proven data. A man could do it, given time.

They could understand that. The sense of purpose and the taint of frustration was understandable too. Beyond understanding was the element of time.

It was old.

It had gained awareness and, inevitably, it had acquired an emotion. Just when it had made that acquisition had engrossed it for an eon during which suns had faded into embers and the area of space in which it drifted had become desolate and cold. The need for survival had driven it to regions where suns were hot and space full of needed radiation. But those suns in turn had died and again it had moved.

On such a scale time ceased to have meaning. The repetitive pageant had unfolded itself so often they were like the pages of a book; suns flaring to die, their planets disintegrating into dust; its own bulk maintained by manipulations of which it was a master.

It had crossed intergalactic space, a planet-sized intelligence which had been attracted by a song.

And it was bored.

Karn entered the salon and joined the others where they sat at the table, all congregating as if for mutual comfort and protection. There was no need for explanations; all had received the message. He nodded to Dumarest as he took a cup of basic from the tray which Mari had provided.

"I've taken care of the captain. Sealed him in one of the caskets for later burial. He'd want to be evicted into space, not planted in that thing out there."

"A worm," said Harg. "It made me feel about an inch high."

"But it can help us," said Lolis to Dumarest. "It can do anything. Surely you can make it repair the ship and send us on our way?"

"We can't make it do anything," he said flatly. "We can only ask."

"But you will do that?"

It was Karn's responsibility, not his, but he didn't bother to argue with her. Later they would ask. Later they would do what had to be done. But it would be at Tormyle's convenience, not theirs. Tormyle, the name the world had given itself.

Daroca touched Mayenne on the arm. "Perhaps if you sang to it again?" he suggested. "Bribed it, perhaps?"

Chom thoughtfully rubbed at his chin.

"You know, Earl, there are opportunities here. The thing must hold secrets of tremendous value. The way it shifted us, for example. If we could obtain such knowledge we could demand our own price."

He was serious, Dumarest decided. The man's natural defenses had narrowed his horizons to regions he could comprehend. To him the giant intelligence on which they rested was nothing more than a potential source of wealth. And he was right. The human mind could only grasp so much at a time. An enemy was no more to be feared because it was large. A virus could kill as surely as a planetary brain.

"I must talk to it," said Gorlyk. "I think you should elect me as your spokesman. I am the only one here with the training to deal with it. A machine must appreciate logical thought and I have devoted my life to perfecting mental discipline."

Karn said, "Why do you call it a machine?"

"Could it be anything else? No organic life could have lived for so long. Nor could it have grown so huge."

"It is bored," said Daroca. "Could a machine feel emotion?"

"A brain, to remain active, must be constantly supplied

with fresh stimuli," said Gorlyk. "To me it is self-evident that Tormyle cannot be the product of natural life. Therefore it must be a fabrication. Perhaps a self-perpetuating device of some kind."

"Not so fast." Sac Qualish stared down at his hands. They were rough, scarred with recent labor. "That thing comes from a long way away. We have no idea as to what life-forms are to be found in other galaxies. All we know is that it's bored and it wants us to provide intellectual stimulation. Can you do that?"

"Certainly."

"I couldn't." Sac glanced at his brother. "Could you, Tek?"

"No. I've been thinking about it and I know just how Harg feels. Like a child faced with a genius. A bug on a carpet waiting to be crushed."

Karn said, "It didn't say anything about intellectual stimulation. It just said that it was bored and hoped to relieve itself. That we would relieve it. Nothing was said as to how."

"What else could it be other than by mental stimulation?" Gorlyk looked around the table. "Do you agree I should be our spokesman?"

Chom said, musingly, "Not so fast, my friend. There could be certain advantages in being spokesman, but it would take a man used to devious ways to make the best of them. And not for himself alone, but for all. I am such a one. In my profession it is essential to have a ready tongue and nimble wit—two things you lack."

"Tormyle would not appreciate dealing with a liar and a thief," said Gorlyk coldly.

"You dare to call me that!"

"Your actions prove it. Shall I elucidate?"

"Shut up," said Harg.

"Our lives may depend on the correct choice. I insist on being the one."

"Be what you like," said Mari quickly. Nerves were taut and, like the gambler, she knew too well how soon a quarrel could become more vicious than words. "Just get us out of here and I'll give you a permanent free pass to any house I own. That's a promise."

"Don't be so free with what isn't yours to give," snapped

Chom. "I do not like to place my life in such hands. Earl?"

"Leave me out of it," said Dumarest.

"You then, Karn. You are the captain now. It is for you to make the decision."

"Toss for it," said the officer bitterly. "Or play cards. At least it will keep you from each other's throats."

"I'm willing," said Harg.

"I'm not." Daroca was firm. "Gorlyk is right when he says that our spokesman, should we need one, must be the best man available. Our lives could depend on the way he handles the situation. With respect to all present I submit that it should be either our captain or Dumarest. Karn will be needed to take care of the ship. Earl?"

"A good choice," said Mari. "You agree, Harg?"

The gambler nodded. Gorlyk said, "Why must the choice lie between them?"

"They are both officers," said Daroca mildly. "The only ones we have now. It could be that Tormyle will only have respect for established authority. I don't know, but officer or not, Dumarest is my choice."

Lolis said, "And mine. Earl, darling, you will agree?"

"I will think about it."

"And other things, darling?"

The invitation was plain, and he caught Mari's scowl, the sudden hardening of Mayenne's lips. But he was in no mood for the casual interplay of personal relationships. The girl was a fool and promised to be a nuisance.

Flatly he said, "My lady, you waste your time."

"Why, Earl? You go with the Ghenka; why not me? Am I so ugly?"

They were all under strain. A sharp retort would have been easy but unnecessarily cruel. Deliberately he softened his tone.

"You are very beautiful, my lady, as you well know. But you have much to learn." To Karn he said, "Captain, I think we should resume our watch."

The view had altered. There was a softness about the valley which had not been there before. Above, the single star winked and seemed to waver as they watched.

"Air," said Karn wonderingly. "But the planet is airless." He checked an instrument. "Three pounds pressure and rising. Earl?"

"It is making a place for us," said Dumarest. "An environment in which we can survive outside the ship. It has probably sealed the valley with force screens of some kind." He remembered the haze he had noticed earlier. "It could be manufactured from the stone, water perhaps, even food."

"Like God," said Karn wonderingly. "Creating a world to order."

Chapter

◆ SEVEN ◆

It was a paradise.

Dumarest stood just outside the open port of the vessel and breathed air which was rich and warm and filled with delicate perfumes. The valley was thick with exotic plants, bushes and flowering trees covering the barren harshness he remembered. Above the space between the cliffs was a shimmer of light as warm and as bright as any sunshine.

"It's beautiful," whispered Mayenne. "The kind of place I have always dreamed of. If I could live here, with you, Earl, I would want nothing else."

"It built well," admitted Karn.

Well and fast, using information taken from their own minds, Dumarest thought. He watched the others drift to either side, their voices clear on the scented air.

"A langish," said Daroca wonderingly. "I haven't seen one since I was a boy. They grow only in the foothills of the Jade Mountains on Klark."

Mari laughed as a fungus popped and released a cloud of spores to hang shimmering in the air.

Sac Qualish pulled golden ovoids from a tree.

"Taste this fruit, Tek. It's really something." He snorted as his brother hesitated. "Hell, if Tormyle wanted to kill us it wouldn't have to poison the fruit. Go ahead, there's nothing to worry about."

Karn said, "We should stop them, Earl."

"We can't, and Sac is right. I don't think we have anything to fear from the fruit and vegetation." Dumarest watched as Mayenne plucked a flower and held it to her nose. Pollen rose and she sneezed.

69

Lolis danced on a patch of lawn, blossoms wreathing her hair.

"This is wonderful," she called. "When I am married I will have a place built exactly like this. A love bower. Earl, come and join me. Let us explore."

She frowned as he made no move to obey.

"No? You then, Gorlyk."

"Wait!" Karn was unsure of himself, out of his depth and not knowing just what to do. "I think we should stay together. It wanted us outside; well, we are here, but maybe we should stay close to the ship."

"You worry too much," she called. "There's nothing to be afraid of."

Dumarest wished he could be as certain. He reached for a leaf and let it lie in his hand, not plucking it, holding it on its stem. Was it real or an illusion? The valley appeared to be a haven, but it could contain nothing except air. The rest might exist only in their minds.

He heard laughter. Lolis was dancing again, Gorlyk looking foolish in a lopsided garland of flowers which she had thrown over his head. The Qualish brothers stood beside the tree, their faces smeared with juice from its fruits. Mayenne was lost in a dream as she wandered, gathering flowers. Even Karn seemed to have relaxed.

He opened his blouse and bared his chest to the warmth of the sky.

"Paradise, Earl. The thing which people have looked for since the dawn of time. We could have found it."

"At a price."

"We can pay it. There are ten of us and between us we should be able to provide Tormyle with what it wants. And it can't be really bad, Earl. Would it have provided this garden if it was?"

A beautiful garden—if there was no serpent.

Dumarest felt the leaf quiver in his hand, vibrating, forming words.

As every leaf vibrated, so did the very molecules of the scented air.

"I am Tormyle."

It was a statement of fact as cold as ice and carrying the bleak detachment of a machine. Startled, they waited.

"You are sentient forms of life each containing an electromagnetic unit of intriguing complexity. Why do you not use it to communicate?"

"It's talking about our brains," said Karn wildly. "How can we answer that?"

Gorlyk took a step forward as if to attract attention.

To the air he said, "We are aware of our physical limitations. We are in the process of evolution and will, in time, be able to achieve mental communication. Now we use machines to obtain the same ends."

"Understood."

A silence and then Dumarest tensed as he felt the impact of invisible energies. A soft pressure enfolded his body, questing, probing before it vanished as suddenly as it had come. From their expressions he knew the others had suffered a similar experience.

"Soft," droned the air. "And different. You are of two kinds. Why is that?"

"For reproductive purposes," said Gorlyk quickly. He was determined to be the spokesman. "We represent both sexes. Male and female. The female bears the young." He added. "I am a male."

"Understood."

It was toying with them, Dumarest thought. Asking what it must already know. If it could have searched their minds in order to discover the things needed to fashion a suitable environment, then surely it must have gleaned other knowledge. And yet it was in the nature of a machine to verify all data. If it was a machine.

He said, "Will you repair our vessel?"

"Don't talk to it," said Gorlyk. "I am the spokesman. We agreed."

"Shut your mouth!" Chom snapped. "We aren't here to play games."

Dumarest ignored them both. He said flatly, "I asked you a question. Will you answer?"

The leaves rustled. "Dissension. A conflict of electromagnetic units. But there is more. I find it engrossing."

"Don't listen to him," said Gorlyk. "Tormyle, I am the one to whom you should speak."

"A metabolic alteration for no observable cause," said the air. "Increase in temperature and muscular tension. Some aberration of the cranial unit. Explain."

Anger, thought Dumarest. Gorlyk's training had let him down. He must be feeling rage at the interruption and overriding of his assumed authority. A cyber could never lose his temper. One minor problem, at least, had been solved.

Aloud he said, "He is feeling a strong emotion."

"Explain."

"He wants to hurt me. To destroy my function."

"Explain what you mean by emotion."

"A strong feeling caused by internal or external stimuli."

"Feeling?"

"Joy, hate, anger, love, fear, hope." Dumarest added: "I can't explain them. They have to be experienced. To the majority of our kind they make life what it is."

"Stimuli?"

"Opposition, possession, loss, achievement, failure, success." Dumarest paused. How to explain abstracts to something so alien? "I can't make it clearer than I have. You either know what I'm talking about or you don't. Obviously you don't."

The air stirred and Tormyle said, "Insufficient data to resolve unfamiliar concepts. Detailed examination essential before further progress."

Gorlyk vanished.

He went without trace, one second standing with his face turned toward the brightness of the sky, the next completely gone with not even a clap of air rushing to fill the vacuum he must have left.

Lolis screamed. "I felt it. Like a great hand snatching him away. I was standing right beside him and I felt it!"

"He must be somewhere." Karn ran to where he had been standing. The grass was unmarked. "Search," he ordered. "Spread out and look everywhere."

"No," said Dumarest. "It will be a waste of time. We all know what happened."

"Tormyle," said Daroca. "Do you think it is responsible?"

"You heard it. What else?"

"A specimen, snatched away for detailed examination." Mari dabbed at the sweat which had appeared on her face. "The poor devil. I never did like him, but at least he was human. Not like this." She stared uneasily at the vegetation shrouding the walls of the valley, its floor. "Perhaps we should get back into the ship."

It would make no difference and they found it impossible. The port had been closed and sealed. Like it or not they had to stay in the open; they clustered close at the base of the ramp.

Mayenne said, "Earl, what will happen to him?"

"Gorlyk? He will be studied."

"But how?"

"I don't know."

"Killed?"

Dumarest impatiently shook his head. Gorlyk was gone and it required little imagination to guess what would happen to him. Taken apart cell by cell, perhaps, tested and probed to destruction, torn apart in search of an elusive thing called emotion. Or perhaps Tormyle had more efficient means. Perhaps the planetary intelligence could test without destruction.

"It's watching us," Chom said broodingly. "I can feel it. Like spiders crawling on my skin."

"It's busy," Mari said shortly. "It's got no time for us at the moment."

"A brain like that could have time for a thousand things at once. Do you think it's as restricted as ourselves? And have you never done two things at the same time?"

"Yes," she admitted. "Often."

"And you have only a small brain," said Chom. "Think of what Tormyle can do. It's incredible."

He shivered a little and hunched himself small as if to escape the notice of a watching eye. It was a feeling they all shared. The primitive defense to cringe, to hide, to wait until danger had passed. But in this place there could be no hiding.

Dumarest said, "We had better eat. Let's gather fruits and see what else is available."

"You want us to go in there?" Mari jerked her head toward the undergrowth. "After what has happened?"

"You didn't want to search," reminded Karn. "You said it would be a waste of time."

"It would, and I'm not talking about making a search.

But we just can't sit here. Tormyle will do as it wants and there's nothing we can do about it."

"A philosopher," Chom sneered. "Well, Earl, this is something you can't tackle with that knife of yours. I suggest we find some way of buying our way out of here. Has anyone any ideas?"

Their voices blurred as Dumarest left the company. With Mayenne at his side, he headed into the underbrush. The bushes pressed close, but they were soft and devoid of spine or thorn. Water gushed from one side and they found a narrow brook flanked by mossy banks. Clusters of some grape-like fruit hung thickly from low branches and Dumarest gathered them, sitting, eating with quiet deliberation.

Mayenne said, "We aren't going to be able to leave here, are we?"

"We don't know that."

"I feel it." She sat close beside him, the bronze of her hair pressed against his cheek. "So much to happen so fast," she murmured. "A few days ago and my life seemed arranged. Nothing but work and travel and a slow fading as my skill died. Do you know what happens to old Ghenkas? They move lower and lower down the social scale. A few open schools of elocution. Some manage to find themselves a husband, but men are few who would be willing to tie their lives to entertainers of such reputation. Most kill themselves. Did you know that, Earl?"

Eating, he shook his head.

"You find that strange? But then you wouldn't know what it means to watch a part of yourself die. The voice loses flexibility, cracks, holds broken tones. To a Ghenka that is death. It is better to leave with a little pride. Each of us carries a gem which, when sucked, will yield poison. There is no pain."

"You have no way of knowing that," he said quietly. "But you are not going to die."

"By the gem, no. I had thought about it, but then I met you and—" She broke off, drawing a deep breath. "I love you, Earl. My life began when I met you. Still I cannot believe that you love me in return."

"Why do you find that strange?"

"I am a Ghenka."

"You are a woman who can sing like an angel," he corrected. "And you have given me happiness."

"As others have done?"

She reached up and touched him as he made no answer, letting her fingers trail across his cheek, the hard line of his jaw.

"As others have done," she said, and this time it wasn't a question. "But they lost and I have won—for now."

The brook made a little rippling sound and he wondered where the water came from and where it went. From the wall of the cliff, he assumed, manufactured from the rock itself, vanishing beyond the protecting force fields which must seal the valley. He finished the last of the fruit and washed his hands, ducking his head deep into the stream. The water was cold, filled with tiny bubbles, tasting of iron.

"Earl!" She lay on the bank, arms lifted, eyes expressive. "Earl!"

"You should eat something."

"I am hungry," she admitted. "But not for food. Must I starve?"

He held her close and felt the tiny tremors which ran beneath her skin. A creature afraid and needing reassurance. She saw the bleakness of his face.

"Is something wrong?"

"No."

"Do you feel that we are being watched?" Her laugh was a low caress. "My darling, does it matter if we are?"

He was not thinking of that. Tormyle had taken Gorlyk as a specimen to be examined, but Gorlyk was a male. To be thorough, a female would have to be examined also. Mari, Lolis or Mayenne. Which would be chosen?

She cried out from the pressure of his arms.

The sky never changed. Always it seemed as if it were noon, and Dumarest could only guess how long they had been away. Mayenne walked beside him, eating fruits he had gathered, golden juice on her lips and cheeks.

"You're a strange man, Earl. Here we are with all this trouble and yet you insist that I eat."

"An empty stomach doesn't help clear thinking," he said absently.

"But to worry about details when we've such a big problem. Aren't you concerned about the future?"

The future was to come; the present was at hand. Life was the extension of a moment and he had learned the lesson too well for it ever to be forgotten.

The group at the base of the ship seemed the same as before. Dumarest could see Chom's squat bulk, the more graceful shape of Daroca, Karn's open blouse, the two Qualish brothers, Mari.

"Earl!" Mayenne caught his arm. "Lolis isn't with them."

Lolis, young and fair and full of grace. Nubile and eager for love, a little foolish perhaps, more than a little selfish. Why had she been chosen?

"She went shortly after you'd left," said Karn dully. "Vanished just like Gorlyk. One second she was sitting there, making a garland out of some flowers, and then she was gone. Damn the thing!" he exploded. "Does it intend to kill us all?"

"It's playing with us," said Harg. "Like a cat with a mouse." His hands trembled as he dealt out cards. "One after the other. First Gorlyk, then Lolis; who next? Mari, perhaps? Chom? Me?" He grunted as he turned over the jester. "The fool," he said. "We're all fools. Why didn't we stay safely at home?"

"I've checked the ship," said Karn to Dumarest. "I tried to get inside. There are lasers there, weapons we could use if we had to. But it's still sealed tight."

"Weapons won't help us." Chom had overheard. "We need to use more subtle ways. The thing must be intrigued, bribed, seduced into letting us go free. A bargain must be made."

"We've been over this," said Karn. "We have nothing to offer."

"I disagree." Daroca brushed a fleck of pollen from his sleeve. "We know the thing is bored. We know that it needs something to hold its interest. A problem, perhaps. A paradox of some kind. There is one about a barber; do you know it?"

"There is a village in which all men are shaved by the barber," said Harg. "No man shaves himself. Question, who shaves the barber? Incidentally, every man in the village is clean-shaven."

"Stupidity!" snorted Mari. "Do you think Tormyle would be interested in a riddle like that?"

"He might be," said Daroca. "There is no answer, you understand. If all men are clean-shaven, and no man shaves himself, and all are shaved by the barber, then the barber cannot be shaved. But he is clean-shaven. Can you grasp the paradox?"

Mari said, "If our lives depend on a thing like that, then we had best end them now. Earl, can't you think of something?"

"Daroca could have a point," he said. "It's worth considering. It would do no harm to give it something to think about. Who knows? We may be lucky."

A voice said, "What is luck?"

It came from the base of the vessel and they turned, staring. Mari gave a choking noise and Chom sucked in his breath.

"God!" said Karn. "What is that?"

"I am Tormyle." The thing lurched forward. "What is luck?"

It was grotesque, a child's fantasy of an ogre, something which should have been a man but wasn't. It was tall and broad and the face held certain disturbing familiarities. Gorlyk, distorted, could have looked like that. Gorlyk, swollen, stretched, partly melted and then frozen into a parody of a human shape.

Again it said, "I am Tormyle. What is luck?"

Harg licked dry lips. "The combination of fortuitous circumstances. Why—"

"Why do I appear before you in this guise?" The voice was not as cold as before. It almost held interest. "To be viable in any frame of reference communication must be of an equal nature. It occurred to me that perhaps my previous method may have disturbed you. I learned much from the original specimen."

Dumarest said, "And the second one? The girl?"

"She is of a more complex character. My investigation is proceeding."

"You've killed them," said Mari bitterly. "You've torn them apart."

"Destruction was essential for the complete reduction to elemental parts. But it is of no importance. The sample was small and can be replaced by your normal reproductive methods. Tell me about luck." It nodded as Harg explained. "I understand. The selection of variable choices so as to arrive at a desired result. To you it is important?"

"Yes," said the gambler.

A hand lifted, pointed. "You?"

"We had bad luck," said Mari. "That's why we're here."

"So the acquisition of luck is a prime directive?"

"Yes," said Harg.

"No," said Mayenne.

"Explain."

"A person has a certain thing which is of major importance in his life," she said. "Harg is a gambler and so he wants good luck. To me that isn't so important."

"What is?"

"Love."

"Love?" Tormyle sounded puzzled. "The word is familiar. The second specimen was obsessed with the concept. Love is what you did beside the stream?"

"That is part of it, yes."

"There is more? Yes. An intangible. An emotion. Data is accumulating. A correct decision to attempt communication by this method. More prime directives." The hand lifted. "You?"

Karn said, "I want command. Responsibility."

"You?"

Chom said, "To live in comfort."

"You?"

Dumarest said, "To survive."

"The basic prime function of any sentient being." Tormyle sounded approving. "A policy is being formulated to achieve the desired result. Later you will be notified. There will be darkness. You will rest."

It vanished.

The sky went dark.

They slept.

Chapter

◆ EIGHT ◆

Chom rose, muttering, his face creased as he stretched. "I ache," he complained. "At least Tormyle could have given us softer beds."

Dumarest glanced at the sky. It was bright again, shimmering. He felt stiff and unrested. They had lain where the thing had left them, falling into immediate unconsciousness when the sky had darkened. A forced period of sleep which had contained little of value.

Around him the others had risen. Daroca dusted down his clothing, the great ring on his finger flashing with reflected light.

"What have we learned?" he demanded. "It came to us and spoke; have we learned anything new?"

"A policy is being formulated," said Harg. "Something to achieve the desired result. What result?"

"The alleviation of its boredom," said Chom. He winced as he rubbed his back. "And we have nothing to offer it. Nothing."

Karn came from the vessel where he had been testing the port. "Still sealed. Earl, what should we do?"

He was the captain and should have made the decisions, but he was used to space and the obedience of machines. In this environment he was at a loss.

"We must get organized," said Dumarest. "We need food, shelter, beds, weapons."

"Weapons?"

It would give them something to do and, armed, they would feel less helpless.

"We don't know what Tormyle intends," explained Dumarest. "It is only good sense that we should prepare for anything we can imagine. We need beds so that we can rest in comfort. Food to maintain our strength. Shelter in case the environment is changed. But most important of all is that we remain active."

"Why?" demanded Chom. "We are helpless. Must we run like a rat in a wheel for the sake of movement?"

Daroca said, thoughtfully, "The analogy is a good one. When I was a boy I kept some insects in a jar. They were clever things and they amused me with their constructions. At times I used to tear down what they had built in order to watch them build again. After a time they ceased to spin their fabrications, and so, bored, I destroyed them. Earl is right."

"We are not insects."

"We are men," said Dumarest harshly. "No matter what Tormyle thinks of us, we are men. The moment we forget that we deserve to die."

"The man of action," said Chom. "But there is more to life than physical endeavor. There is the logic of the mind."

"Logic?" Daroca shrugged. "All men must die, and so it would be logical to anticipate the inevitable. Do you suggest we all terminate our existence?"

The entrepreneur scowled.

"You twist my words," he complained. "If we could think of something to intrigue Tormyle we could be gone in an hour. I still say we should concentrate on that."

Karn made his decision. "We'll do as Earl says."

There were difficulties. The gathering of ferns for the beds was simple, but they had to make baskets in which to hold the fruit, and Karn frowned as Dumarest mentioned water.

"We'll need pots. There could be clay in the soil, perhaps, but how can we harden it?"

"With fire." Dumarest sighed as he recognized the other's limitations. "Daroca has traveled and must have experience of nonmechanical cultures. And the Qualish brothers should know something of primitive engineering skills. A fire can be made with a bow to generate friction. Baskets can be woven from leaves; some of these plants could contain gummy saps which would make them water-tight. There are big leaves which could be sewn with a needle of wood and thread of fiber."

"And the material for spears? We need long branches. You have a knife, Earl. Will you gather them?"

A clump of slender boles reared to one side, slim, topped with feathery tufts, each twice the height of a man. Dumarest cut one down close to the ground and examined it. The material was hollow, like a tube, but one end could be sliced at an angle so as to make a point. He chopped it to an eight-foot length, poised it and threw it toward Karn. It stuck, quivering, in the soil.

"Will they do, Earl?"

"Try it."

The Qualish brothers came toward them as Karn threw the crude weapon.

Sac lifted it and flexed it in his hands. "Highly elastic," he commented as it snapped back into its former shape. "We could make bows out of this. All we need are some feathers for the arrows."

"Leaves would do," said his brother. He took the shaft and flexed it in turn. "Anything will serve for use as a flight. Our problem is in finding something suitable to use as a string." He plucked at his clothing. "Maybe we could tease out a few threads and wind them together. It's worth a try."

"Cut some more, Earl," said Karn. It had been a comfort to hold the spear. "As many as are suitable."

Dumarest returned to the clump. The knife in his hand flashed as it sheared through the slender boles, the feathery tips rustling as they fell. He reached for one to slice off the end and froze.

Tormyle stood before them.

It had changed. Now it no longer looked grotesque, but massively human. The rounded skull rose seven feet above the splayed feet. The neck was thick, running into sloping shoulders, the arms and chest corded with muscle. The face was a graven image and slanted eyes glowed from beneath prominent brows.

It said, "The original specimen considered this to be an optimum form. You agree? No. Some have reservations. I find it intriguing that there is no accepted norm for the shape of individuals of your species. However, it will serve for the matter at hand. I intend to test your prime directive. Certain limitations have been imposed for the purpose of this experiment."

"I don't understand," said Karn. "What do you mean?"

"The prime directive of any sentient life-form is to survive." A thick arm lifted and pointed at Dumarest. "You stated that on the previous occasion. Correct?"

"Yes," said Dumarest.

"You have repeated that conviction since wakening. In you it is very strong. In others not so strong. I am intrigued by the differential. Explain."

"All men want to live. Some are more eager for life than others."

"A variation of intensity. I understand. The strongest, then, should be tested. Failure will result in complete termination."

"My God!" whispered Karn. "Earl, it intends to fight you."

Dumarest backed as it advanced, knife poised in his hand, sword-fashion, edge upward so as to slash. To thrust would be useless; the corded muscle would be tough and even if penetrated would trap the blade. And he had no certainty that the thing held familiar organs. It was shaped like a man and there should be a heart, lungs and a brain. But how could he kill a planetary intelligence?

Tormyle said, "This body is fashioned after your own. The destruction of certain areas will cause it to cease functioning. Remember that you are representative of your species. Begin."

Dumarest threw himself to one side as it ran toward him. The knife blurred, hit and dragged as he drew it back in a vicious slash. Red fluid like blood gushed from Tormyle's side. A man would have clapped a hand to the wound, hesitated and perhaps withdrawn so as to resume the attack with more caution. Tormyle did not react like a man. Before Dumarest could recover his stance the thing was on him.

A blow jarred the side of his head and he tasted blood as he went down. A foot slammed into his ribs, lifted and stamped down at his face. It missed as he rolled and sprang to his feet. Again the knife lashed at the corded muscle and a long cut opened across the belly. Intestines should have bulged, bursting free to hang in red and blue ribbons; instead the wound gaped like a cut made in clay.

Tormyle moved back.

"We recommence," it said. "You have unnatural advantage. For the purpose of this test we must be even. The implement in your hand must be discarded."

Dumarest snarled and threw the knife.

It halted an inch before one of the deep-set eyes, hovered a moment, then spun through the air to land with a thud an inch from Karn's foot. Before it had landed, Dumarest had attacked. He ran forward, dropping, his right boot swinging in a vicious arc to the thing's left knee. It hit with the dull snap of bone. As a hand snatched at him he had rolled clear. Immediately he sprang to one side and kicked again, this time at the other knee. Crippled, the thing fell.

"Interesting application of mechanical principles," it said. "However, compensations can be made."

On its knees it shambled forward, hands outstretched.

Dumarest hesitated, glancing at the knife. If he ran for it, Tormyle would recommence the contest and he would have neither the blade nor the advantage he had won. An advantage gained only because the thing was unused to physical combat and lacked the hard-won experience Dumarest possessed.

But it could learn. Already it was moving faster, the big hands reaching out to rip and tear. To stop it bare-handed might be impossible, but it had to be tried.

Dumarest ran forward, jumped and landed just behind the broad back. He lifted his hand, stiffened the edge and swung it like an ax at the base of the neck. Again, a third time, then Tormyle had turned and the big hands gripped his thigh.

Dumarest stabbed it in the eyes.

"Ocular vision now destroyed," said Tormyle. "Severe damage to upper region of torso and lower region of guidance mechanism." It gurgled as Dumarest chopped it in the throat and then, quickly, slammed the edges of his palms at the biceps and nerves which would control the hands if the thing had been a man.

The grip of the fingers slackened. Dumarest pulled free, lifted his doubled fists and brought them crashing down on the thing's temple. Bone yielded beneath the sledgehammer impact. Again and the weakened skull showed a noticeable impression.

"Extensive damage to frontal lobes of directive unit," said Tormyle. "Had this fabrication been a sentient organism it would now be incapable of function. The test is over."

It vanished.

Between the mossy banks the stream made a liquid susurration, the surface flecked and dancing with light from the glowing sky above. Dumarest stripped and dived, hitting the water with a shower of spray, arching his back and arms so as to glide just beneath the surface. The water was as cold as before, numbing with its impact and he rose, gasping, ducking to scoop up a handful of fine grit from the bed. Standing in the water he rubbed the grime and stains from his hands. More grit and he cleaned his clothing; then he spread out his tunic and pants to dry. His thigh showed ugly bruises where Tormyle had gripped the flesh and his hands were sore and swollen. Lying on the bank, he let them trail in the water, the cold numbing and reducing the tenderness.

It was warm and the sultry air held the scent of growing things. Against the cliff the bulk of the ship reared, tall, incongruous in the valley paradise, and thinly he could hear the sound of voices. One of the Qualish brothers calling to the other, and the answer, Mari's higher voice, all muffled by the screen of vegetation. He turned at the sound of movement, a lilting thread of song.

"Mayenne?"

The song died and was replaced by a soft laugh. The rustle of disturbed leaves came closer.

"Is that you, Mayenne?"

He frowned as there was no answer and rose, stepping to where his knife stood half buried in the soil. Before he could reach it, she stepped from the undergrowth and stood smiling before him.

"Lolis! But—"

"Are you disappointed, Earl? Did you expect Mayenne?" She smiled and came closer. "What can she give you that I cannot? Earl, my darling, must you be so blind?"

She looked as he remembered, tall and young and very beautiful. She wore a thin gown of some diaphanous material which clung to the curves of her body. It parted as she sat to reveal the long lines of her thighs, the upper swell of her breasts. One hand patted the ground at her side.

"Come, Earl, sit and talk to me. Why do you look so surprised?"

He said harshly, "I thought you were dead. We all thought that."

"Dead, Earl?" Her laughter was as sweet as the tinkle of the water. "Do I look as if I am dead? I am here before you. Let us make love."

He ignored the invitation, sitting close beside her, his eyes probing her own. There was something beneath the surface, a touch of hardness he had never noticed before, an assurance she had previously lacked.

Quietly he said, "What is your name, my lady?"

"Lolis Egas. I was to have been married to Alora Motril of the House of Ayette."

"Was to have been?"

"I think that I have changed my mind. He no longer appeals to me. Come, Earl, let us make love."

"On the journey here, in the ship, there was a man who took you to see a beast. His name?"

"Really, Earl, does that matter?"

"His name?"

She did not hesitate. "Bitola."

"And your guard? You remember her name also?"

"Certainly. Hera Phollen. What is the matter, Earl? Why do you ask so many questions? Don't you trust me?"

For answer he reached out and took her wrist between his fingers. The flesh was smooth, warm and silken to his touch. He gripped and watched as the indentations he had made filled to leave small pink patches against the whiteness of her skin.

Flatly he said, "Lolis is dead. Both specimens were tested to destruction. Why did you select this shape, Tormyle?"

"You guessed," she said. "How?"

"Lolis was young and beautiful, but she would never have acted as calmly as you have done. You may have stored every fact you discovered in her mind, but her emotional interplay eluded you. What do you intend?"

"At the moment, nothing."

"And later?"

"That I have yet to decide." She leaned back on the mossy bank, turning so as to face him, smiling as if she were exactly what she appeared to be. "I like this form so much better than the other, don't you, Earl? And it allows for free communication. I decided that it would be best to appear in a shape familiar to you all. The other tended to create disturbing aberrations. A facet of the thing you call emotion. What would you call it? Fear. What is fear?"

"The anticipation of personal hurt or destruction."

"But you were not afraid when we fought, Earl. Why was that? Can't you experience the emotion?"

"Yes," said Dumarest bleakly. "I know what it is to be afraid. But fear has no place in combat. A man afraid is a man as good as dead. He slows, hesitates, misses his chances. When you are fighting for your life you have room for only one thought. To survive. Nothing else matters."

"Not even love?"

"Lolis would have put that first," he admitted. "But the girl was a romantic who had yet to learn the essentials of living."

"You miss her, Earl?"

"No."

"Could you have loved her?"

"How can I answer that?" He was impatient. "You have no idea as to the meaning of the word. What is love? Who can answer? Love takes many forms. To some it is a weakness, to others a source of strength. A man can love many things, his wealth, his life, his home, his children, his wife, his mother, his sisters and brothers, but each love is different from the rest." He added, "And some men never love at all."

"Are you one of them, Earl?"

"No."

"You have loved," she said softly. "And a man like you would love deep and well. You could tell me about it and teach me what it is. The girl thought she knew what love was, but now I see that it was a love of self. A facet of the prime directive of survival. For you love has a different meaning. I must discover what it is."

He said, "You could call it the converse of being cruel."

"Cruel?"

"You are being cruel in keeping us here. Why don't you repair the ship and let us go?"

"Later, perhaps."

"Can you do it? Repair the ship, I mean?"

"That?" Her laugh was pure merriment. "That has already been done. A simple matter of selected forces and synthesis of the missing parts. Your vessel is very elementary, Earl. I could build you a better one."

"That won't be necessary. Now, if you will unseal the ship, we'll be on our way."

He was being optimistic and he knew it, but it was worth a try. He was not disappointed when the girl shook her head.

"No, Earl, not yet. There are still things I have yet to learn. About luck, for example. The selection of fortuitous circumstances." She paused as if listening. "At this moment Harg is selecting a fruit from a tree. It is one of a cluster, and half of them are filled with a substance destructive to his metabolism. If his luck is good he will choose one which is harmless. Correct?"

Dumarest looked at his hands; they were clenched, the knuckles white. For a moment he was tempted to grab the girl by the throat and strangle her to death. But it would only be a temporary thing, and Harg could still select wrongly.

She said again, "Correct?"

"Yes."

"And if he picks one which is lethal, his luck would have been bad. Is that so?"

"Yes," said Dumarest again.

"He has chosen," she said after a moment. "And his luck was good. Now what made him pick that fruit and not one of the others? How often could he do it? What factor determined his selection?"

"An intriguing question," said Dumarest. "And one which has engrossed some of our finest thinkers for millennia. As yet they have found no answer. Perhaps you could."

"I will consider it."

"And, in the meantime, will you see that the fruits and everything else are harmless? If not, you will lose your specimens."

She smiled, teeth white against the redness of her lips, her throat. "You are concerned. Do you love them all so much?"

"That has nothing to do with it."

"What then?"

"I'm a specimen too," reminded Dumarest. "And my luck needn't be as good as Harg's."

"But concern is a part of love?"

"Yes."

"And what else? Sacrifice?" She rose before he could answer and waited until he stood before her. "A most intriguing concept and one which I must fully investigate. I will devise a plan. In the meantime there will be no further random experiments. The fruits and all else in the valley will be harmless as before."

"And the ship? When can we leave?"

For a moment she looked a young and lovely girl pondering on which dress to wear for a special occasion, and then he saw her eyes, the cold detachment, and remembered who and what she was. Remembered too that she could destroy them all at a whim.

"When I have discovered what love is," she said. "Not before."

Chapter
◆ **NINE** ◆

Chom lifted the bow, drew back the string and let fly. He swore as the arrow thudded into the dirt a good ten feet to one side of the tree they were using as a target.

Daroca said, "You plucked. Don't jerk the string back as you release. Just straighten the fingers when you're ready. See?" He demonstrated, the arrow hitting the bole. "Try again."

"What's the use?" Chom scowled as he rubbed his left arm. "I can't hit anything and the damn string's flaying my arm. I'll stick to a club."

"It's a matter of practice," insisted Daroca. "You have to keep trying. Wrap something around your arm to give protection. Pull the notched arrow back to the point of the chin and use the barb as a foresight. Look at what you are aiming at and release without plucking."

"I'll still stick to a club," said Chom firmly. "You learned how to use a bow when you were a boy; I didn't. I had no time for games. Anyway, what good is a thing like that against Tormyle?"

Harg said, "We won't be fighting Tormyle; not exactly. We could be up against something like Earl fought. Man-shapes or animal-forms of some kind. All we know is that we are to be tested in some way and have to be ready to meet anything that comes."

Chom made no further objection. Instead, he squatted and recommenced work on his club. A large stone had been wedged in the split end of a thick branch and lashed tight with strips of material pilfered from his blouse. Now he tied more strips so as to make a loop which could be slipped over the wrist.

To one side Dumarest was making knives.

He sat before a heap of the thin boles he had cut and sliced them at an angle. The edges of the hollow stems made sharp edges and a wicked point. He left the round handles untouched.

Mayenne said, "Will they be any good, Earl?"

"These?" He lifted one of the crude knives. "They can cut and thrust and will kill as surely as a blade of tempered steel. All we need to do is to wrap some thread around the hilts so as to stop the hand slipping along the edges."

She hadn't meant that and he knew it, but had deliberately misunderstood. As he reached for another foot of stem, she caught his hand.

"You were a long time at the river, Earl. I tried to join you, but there was a barrier of some kind which prevented me. What did it look like?"

"Tormyle? I told you. Like Lolis."

"She was very beautiful."

"So?"

"And you were bathing and naked and—" She broke off. "I'm sorry, Earl. I guess I'm just jealous. But when I think of you and her in the same place where we found happiness, well . . . forgive me?"

"For being in love?"

"For being a stupid fool. What does one woman more or less matter? And she isn't a woman, not really. Did you?"

"No."

"Would you have?"

He was coldly deliberate. "If it would have bought our freedom, yes. But it wouldn't and I didn't."

"I'm glad, Earl."

He smiled and stroked the edge of his knife down the length of wood. It was not as sharp as normal and he reached for a stone to whet the blade. Over the thin rasping Mayenne said, "When, Earl? Did it say?"

"No."

"Nor what we could expect?"

"I told you what she said. When she knows what love is, then she will let us go. Not before."

"She?"

"It, then. Tormyle. What difference does it make?" Cautiously he tested the whetted edge. "Try handling one of these knives. Get used to the feel and heft. Practice sticking one into the ground. When you do hold your thumb over the end and aim for a point about three inches below the surface." He frowned as she made no move to obey. "Do it, girl. Your life could depend on it."

Mari called out as Mayenne picked up one of the wooden slivers.

"Teach your woman to use a knife and you buy trouble, Earl. Haven't you learned anything in life?"

"To dodge," he said, matching her humor. "To fight when I can't and run when I can. Have you made that sling yet?"

"All finished." She held up a thonged pouch. "Can you really use one of these?"

For answer he slipped the knife into his boot, rose and took the sling from her hand. A pebble the size of an egg rested in the dirt. He picked it up, fitted it into the pouch and, holding both thongs, swung the sling about his head.

"That tree," he said. "The cluster of fruit."

The sling spun faster, whirring through the air, the stone hurtling as he released one of the thongs. Juice and pulp spattered the bole where the fruit had hung, the sound of the stone a soggy thud.

"I used to hunt with one when a boy," he said. "Game was small, scarce and agile. A sling was all I could afford."

"Not even a bow and arrows?"

"They were Daroca's idea. The Qualish brothers made them."

"And you don't think they'll be of much use?"

"Daroca can use one, but that's all. It takes a lot of practice to hit what you aim at with a bow. A crossbow would be different, but we can't make them with what's at hand."

Not if they were to have any stopping power, he thought. For that they needed a strong prod, heavy bolts and cord they didn't possess. And a heavy crossbow was troublesome to load. At close quarters a spear was as good. Closer and a club was better.

Karn came from the base of the ship, the Qualish

brothers at his side. The officer looked tired and haggard, his eyes revealing his frustration. Logic told him it would do little good to gain entry into the vessel, but to him it was home and he wanted to be in the familiar surroundings of his command.

"Nothing," he said to Dumarest's unspoken question. "We tried to force an entry through the emergency hatch. The whole ship's sealed solid. Are you sure it has been repaired?"

"So I was told."

"It could be a lie." Karn scrubbed at his chin. "But what would be the point in that? If only I could make certain."

"We'll try again," said Sac Qualish. "Later."

His brother said, "Should we build more weapons, Earl? We could make a catapult of some kind. Or construct an earthwork of sorts. A ditch and sharpened stakes in a ring around the ship."

"No," said Dumarest.

"You don't think it'll be necessary?"

"There's no point in tiring ourselves out making something we may not need. I don't know when this test is going to begin, but we want to be fresh to meet it. You'd better get some food and rest now. You too, Karn. There's not much more we can do but wait."

Wait and hope and practice and try to find the answer to a question. What was love?

And how to explain it to an alien intelligence who had no conception of the meaning of the word?

They had built a fire, a small thing of weak flames and a thread of coiling smoke which rose like a feather in the still air. Mari threw on a handful of dried leaves and set others to bake, coughing a little as the fumes caught her throat. Chom held a fruit speared on a thin wand and roasted it. He lifted the dripping mess, tasted it and spat his disgust.

"Fruit," he said. "Well, I suppose we could make wine if we had to, but I would give it all for a bite of decent meat."

Karn muttered in his sleep. "Seleem," he murmured. "Yes, sir. Full cargo on Ayette. Three riding Low."

Mayenne began to sing.

It began as a low dirge, tremulous, haunting, a bleak call for help from the midst of snowy wastes and endless deserts, the empty expanse of enormous seas and the barren vault of the skies. It rose a little, a thread of pure sound in which lurked words like ghosts, fragments of half heard, half understood communication, touching buried memories so that the past lived again. Gath and the endless winds, the fretted mountains, the medley of voices, the composite of all the sounds that had ever been or could ever be made. A voice whispering.

"I love you, Earl. I love you!"

Another.

"A thousand years of subjective sleep. A milliard of dreams."

A third.

"There will always be a welcome for you on Toy ... on Jest ... on Hive ... on Technos ... on Dradea."

More.

"No, Earl! No! ... ten High passages ... the Ram, the Bull, the Heavenly Twins ... five hundred, ten-inch knives, to the death ... I love you, Earl. I love you!"

And another, utterly cold, speaking across the galaxy with frigid determination.

"Find him at all costs. Failure will not be tolerated. The man Dumarest has the secret the Cyclan must repossess. Find him!"

A bell chiming.

"Charity, brother. Remember the credo of the Church. There, but for the grace of God, go I. Charity ... charity ... charity."

The song wavered a little, soared almost to a scream, then plunged into a throbbing undertone reminiscent of drums.

Daroca sighed. "Artistry," he murmured. "Never have I heard a Ghenka sing so well."

"If I can remain alive," said Chom with feeling, "and if I can gather the needed wealth, I shall buy a Ghenka for my private pleasure."

"A recording would be cheaper," said Harg.

"True, but would it be the same? I think not. No true artist sings exactly the same twice; each performance is unique to itself. And the mood is important—how could any recording guess my thoughts, the way I feel, the adaptions essential to the creation of the moment? No, my friend, I have made my decision." He speared another fruit and held it over the flames. "Perhaps this one," he murmured. "At least it may not dissolve into a pulp."

Mari said, "Earl, look at the ship. Something is happening."

A light glowed around the supports, a will-o'-the-wisp luminescence bright even against the glare of the sky. It gathered itself into a ball and drifted toward them. It touched the ground a few feet away. Touched—and changed.

An insect, thought Dumarest wildly. Standing upright, winged, haloed with light, the face a mask of perfection.

"An angel," whispered Mari. "Dear God, an angel!"

A figment of some old religion caught and fashioned from the aroused images of her mind. A fragment of legend brought to solidity by the magic of Tormyle. For a moment it stood resplendent and then it was gone and in its place stood a familiar shape.

"Lolis!" Chom's fruit fell unheeded into the fire. "My lady!" He rose, bowing, his hands outspread. "I know, of course, that you are not the person we knew by that name. But it will serve. A lovely name for a lovely woman. My lady, I understand that you wish to know the meaning of love. I can teach you. In my travels I have come against it in many forms and have mastered them all. My heart is yours to command."

She said, "The shape I wore before did not please you. It should have. Why didn't it?"

"I am a simple man, my lady, and used to simple ways. Not for me the esoterics of mysterious cults. I buy and I sell and do what I can to please. Love, to me, is the desire to serve. To serve, to teach, to guide. To give pleasure and, if in return I gain a little joy, it is the joy of giving. If I could talk to you, my lady, alone, I am sure that we could find matters of mutual interest."

Mari said, "I don't trust that man. He's trying to make a private deal. Doesn't the fool realize that he's not talking to a normal woman?"

She had spoken softly but her voice had carried. Daroca

glanced at Dumarest, then at Karn. The officer cleared his throat.

"As acting captain I represent these people. Any arrangements should be made through me."

"Captain?"

"I am in command of the vessel." Karn was bleary-eyed, freshly woken and unrested by his tormented sleep. He made a vague gesture toward the ship. "Tell me the price for letting us go."

The girl smiled, young and lovely and as fresh as a spring morning. She moved a little closer to where the fire plumed its thread of smoke. To one side Mayenne slammed her wooden knife viciously into the ground.

"We know the price," she snapped. "The thing wants the answer to a question. It wants to know what love is. Love!" she repeated bitterly. "How can you teach a planet what that is? How can you love a world?"

"It's possible," said Daroca softly. "If the world is home."

Earth, perhaps; but it wasn't the same and Dumarest knew it. Daroca was playing with words and this was no time for semantic games. It was no accident, he thought, that Tormyle had chosen to appear in a female guise. It could have copied Gorlyk's form as easily as that of Lolis. Why had it chosen to appear as a woman? He glanced to where Mayenne stabbed at the ground in symbolic murder. Had she reason for her jealousy?

Aloud he said, "We are not in the mood for games. You have made a decision; tell us what it is."

"Impatient, Earl?"

"We spoke once of cruelty. To keep people in suspense is not kind when their lives depend on your decision."

"And love is the converse of cruelty. I remember. And you, Earl, could never love a person who is cruel." She glanced at Chom. "Could you?"

"Love, my lady, knows no limitations. I could love you even while dying in your embrace."

She raised her arms and reached toward him and he moved toward her as if without a will of his own. His boots trod in the fire and scattered the ashes so that he became wreathed in smoke. In the smoke they embraced, his thick arms clasping the slender figure, her own arms around his plump torso, the hands pressing against his back.

"Love me," she said, and squeezed.

Chom made a sound like an animal in pain. His muscles bulged, the flesh of his cheeks mottling with a purple effusion of blood, his eyes starting from their sockets. Desperately he fought against the constriction and then, abruptly, relaxed, his face strained as he stared at the girl holding him close.

"Not the same," she said. "Not the same at all."

"My lady!" he wheezed. "My lady, please!"

She released him and he staggered back, tearing at the collar of his blouse.

"The problem is one of definition," she said. "To be genuine love must be strong, this much I have gathered. But love seems to hold many forms, and which is the right one? To discover this I have devised an experiment. It should be conclusive."

"Wait," said Harg. He stepped forward, a small man, aged, yet holding a strange dignity. "Listen to me, Lolis ... Tormyle, whoever you are. I don't understand all this talk of love. Maybe I've been unlucky in my time, but no woman has ever wanted me for her own and I've never felt strongly about anything. Certainly not strongly enough to fight and die for it. And I guess that is what you intend. So let's cut out all this nonsense and decide things one way or the other. A turn of a card. High card, you win and do with us as you please. Low card, and we win and you let us go. Quick, simple and decisive. You agree?"

"A gamble," she mused. "A test of the thing called luck. Do you all wish to participate?"

"Yes," said Dumarest quickly. "We do."

He caught Chom's arm as the man opened his mouth to protest and caught Daroca's look of sudden understanding. It was a wager they couldn't lose. Harg had framed the terms well; already they were in Tormyle's power to do with as it wished.

"Harg is in love with the laws of chance," she said. "For him joy lies in winning, and the touch of cards and dice are equal to a caress. Luck is his mistress and good fortune his deity. A strange thing," she mused, "that a sentient being could hold such high regard for something so intangible. But the concept is intriguing. Yet the wager is wrong. He stands to lose nothing."

Dumarest said, "You heard the terms. Do you agree?"

"To the gamble, yes. But not on those terms. Each must risk his own fortune. Harg will be first. If he wins, I will set him down on a safe place. If he loses, then I will take his life."

"A safe place," said Harg. "What do you mean?"

"A world on which you could survive. One of your habitated planets." She paused. "Ayette? Yes, the world you know as Ayette."

"You can do that?"

It was possible. To an entity which had snatched the ship across light-years in a second anything was possible. Harg had asked only for reassurance. When it came he produced his cards.

"Wait," said Dumarest sharply. "It's your life, man. Remember that."

"My life," said Harg. "Such as it is."

"Don't be a fool," said Mari harshly. "Go to the table expecting to lose and you'll be ruined for sure. As a gambler you know that. Stay with us and you've got a chance. Lose and you've got none at all." Her lips tightened as he riffled the deck. "Remember our agreement? Shares in a new house? Don't do it, Harg."

He ignored her, riffling the deck. He held them out on the flat of his palm.

"Choose."

"You first."

He cut quickly, trusting his life to the luck he had wooed over too many years. The cards made a slight rasping sound and he held his choice low, not looking at it, eyes instead on the young girl as she reached for the pack.

"A lady!" Sweat burst out on his forehead, clung like dew to his upper lip. His laugh was bitter as he turned up his own selection. "A jester! Well, I was always a fool. What now, Tormyle?"

He died.

He did it slowly, horribly, his flesh melting and seeming to run like wax in a flame. His limbs arched, became grotesque and his body puffed so that, as he fell, he looked like some monstrous spider. And, as he fell, he screamed.

Dumarest moved. He was a blur as he reached and snatched a spear, lifted it, thrust it with the full power of arms and shoulders into the shrieking mass. The sharpened point sliced deep, penetrated the heart and brought instant oblivion.

As Harg slumped into a lifeless heap he jerked free the spear and threw it at the smiling face of the girl.

The point, ugly with blood, dissolved into splinters, the shaft lifting to fall to one side.

Quietly she said, "That is twice you have used weapons against me, Earl. Will you never learn?"

"You bitch!" shouted Mari. "You dirty, sadistic bitch! Did you have to do that?"

"He wagered and he lost." And then, to Dumarest: "You killed him. For love?"

"For mercy—something you could never understand."

"Because he was in pain? Yet had you left him alone he would not have terminated his existence. I was altering his structure, adapting it to a new form. An experiment to discover how malleable your species is. Now, perhaps, I shall have to use another." Her arm lifted, pointed at Tek Qualish. "You."

He vanished.

To Mayenne. "You."

She followed.

To Mari and Karn. "You also."

They went and she followed.

Daroca had rebuilt the fire, gaining some small comfort from the flame, huddling close to it as his forebears had done in ancient times when the red glow had spelled safety and the communion of kind. Facing him, Sac Qualish sat with his head in his hands mourning his brother.

"A bad business," said Chom. He glanced uneasily over his shoulder to where Dumarest was busy selecting spears. Harg had gone, not even a patch of blood marring the ground where he had fallen. "A warning, perhaps? Harg tried to be clever, but he forgot that he was not dealing with a young and ignorant girl. How can any man hope to best the might of a planetary brain?"

"He tried," said Dumarest curtly.

"He tried and failed and died with your spear in his

heart. You were too quick, Earl. You should have waited. If the girl spoke the truth he could be alive now. Changed, but alive."

"As what?" Dumarest dropped two of the spears and hefted two others. "A thing to crawl in the dirt? A crippled freak?"

"He had a clean death," said Daroca. "No man could ask for more. If the same thing happens to me I hope that Earl will be as merciful." He shivered and held his hands close to the flame. "Is it my imagination or is it getting cold?"

Dumarest glanced up at the sky. It seemed lower than before and the upper regions of the ship shone with a sparkling frost. Around them the leaves seemed wilted, hanging limply from their stems. He walked toward the ship and felt the bite of numbing cold. Returning, he headed down the valley and felt the familiar heat. Back at the fire he said, "It's localized and spreading."

Chom was shrewd. "To keep us away from the vessel? But what's the point? It's sealed and we can't get in anyway."

"We'll find out," said Daroca. "When it's ready to let us know." He threw more leaves on the fire, added slivers of wood and leaned back from the rising smoke. "I've been thinking. We know that Tormyle is bored. We also know that it wants to discover the meaning of the emotion we know as love. But it is alien and that could well be impossible. What happens if it fails?"

"We die," said Chom bleakly.

"Perhaps not, at least, not in the way you mean. Time cannot mean the same to Tormyle as it does to us. I think that, while we continue to amuse it, we will continue to survive."

"Amuse?"

"Intrigue, then. Interest would be a better word. What do you think, Earl?"

"I think we should get armed," said Dumarest. "And be ready to move."

"To where?" Sac Qualish lifted his head. His face was strained, bitter, his eyes red. "To run in a circle until that thing takes us like it did my brother? To take us and tear us apart like it did Gorlyk and Lolis? To change us like it did Harg? Do you remember what he looked like? When I think of Tek like that it makes me want to vomit."

"Shut up," said Chom, and added, more gently: "Tek wasn't the only one. He took the Ghenka too, remember."

"And Mari and Karn," mused Daroca. "Now why should it have made that selection?"

"Does it matter?"

"It could," insisted Daroca. "The girl was, is, in love with Earl. Tek and his brother are very close, and brotherly love can be very strong. Karn? Well, he is in love with his ship."

"And Mari?" Chom blew out his cheeks and shook his head. "Once I thought that she might have a fancy for Harg, but he is dead now. You perhaps? Are you in love with her?"

"No, but her profession is to deal in love, or what too many people call it. It is her business and her thoughts must be conditioned to regard her houses as palaces of joy, mansions of endearment, abodes of love. We know the difference; but would Tormyle?"

"A professional dealer in the emotion it seeks to understand," said the entrepreneur slowly. "If our situation wasn't so perilous I would find the concept amusing."

But there was nothing amusing in the growing cold, the sealed ship, the too recent memory of the way Harg had died. And still less in the voice which whispered from the wilting leaves, the very air itself.

"The experiment begins. Those who were taken will be found at the end of the valley. Your actions will determine their continued existence. Go now."

"Tek alive!" Sac sprang to his feet, his eyes glowing. "Did you hear that? They're still alive!"

Alive and waiting to be rescued, the bait in an alien trap to determine an emotion impossible for their captor to comprehend.

Chapter
◆ TEN ◆

The valley had changed. The cold welling from the region of the ship had blighted the vegetation and turned the stream to ice, but it was more than that. Now every leaf held a hint of menace as if things watched from behind its cover and thin threads glistened with silver between the trees.

A maze, thought Dumarest, through which they were being guided, spurred by the advancing cold and urged by the bait lying ahead. Mayenne and the others. Thought of the Ghenka lengthened his stride. She would be waiting, hoping. He could not fail her.

Yet, even so, he was cautious.

"Wait," he snapped as Sac Qualish plunged ahead. "Take it easy. We don't know what may be waiting for us."

"My brother is waiting, that's all I care about."

"Can you help him if you're dead?" Dumarest halted and glanced around. The trees soared high, their feathered tops hiding the sky and casting patches of thick gloom. The ground felt soggy and he trod carefully down a narrow path. They had left the cold behind and, here, it was still warm.

Chom sucked in his breath as something moved to one side.

"What was that?"

A thing, a shape, something fashioned at Tormyle's whim. It appeared again, low, crouching, eyes like gems in an armored carapace. A watchdog, perhaps, to keep them on their way, or perhaps something to be feared more than that.

101

Dumarest said, "Daroca, your bow."

"You want me to kill it, Earl?"

"If you can." He watched as the other man took aim, drawing back the arrow, holding, then releasing the string with a vicious hum. The arrow whispered between the trees and hit with a hollow thud.

It was like bursting a balloon. There was an empty plop and a scatter of segments. Chom sighed his relief.

"If that's all we have to face we haven't much to worry about." He lifted his club and swung it against a tree. The stone made a dent in the soft bole. In his other hand he carried a spear and two of the wooden knives were thrust in a band tied around his waist. "We could stand off an army of the things."

"Perhaps," admitted Dumarest. "But not if we get separated. And there could be something else. Keep close and cover each other. You to one side, Chom; you the other, Sac; Daroca, take the rear." He paused and added, "And keep an arrow on the string, just in case."

He moved ahead, spear extended in both hands, ready to thrust or block. It was a clumsy thing compared to the quick mobility of the knife he was used to, but it had the advantage of length. Like the others, he carried wooden knives. Sac had a club. Daroca had his bow. Like savages, they plunged into the deepening gloom.

"What now?" Sac fumed his impatience as Dumarest halted again. "Damn it, Earl, we'll get nowhere like this. Why don't we just push on and find the others?"

"Through that?" Dumarest pointed with his spear. Ahead the path was crossed with silver threads.

"If we have to, yes." Sac pushed ahead. His spear touched one of the strands. The ground opened beneath it.

He yelled once as he fell and then Dumarest caught him by the arm, dropping the spear and flinging himself to the edge of the opening. Below gaped emptiness, a hollow void smoothed as if by machines. Sac hung, suspended, his spear falling like a splinter to vanish in darkness. His face, strained, turned upward to look at Dumarest.

"Earl! For God's sake!"

He was heavy and the ground at the edge of the hole loose. Dumarest gritted his teeth and concentrated on clamping his fingers about the arm, feeling the weight of the body tear at his muscles as the dirt below him fell into the hole. Then Chom had gripped his ankles, hauling back with all his weight. Sac rose, caught at Dumarest and heaved. One foot lifted to rest on the edge of the hole and, with a rush, he was safe, sweating as he rolled on the dirt.

"Trip wires," said Chom. "I don't understand this. If Tormyle wants us to reach the end of the valley, why does it make it so hard?"

"Perhaps it wants us to give up," suggested Daroca. "But then why the cold? We have no choice but to move. Rats in a maze," Daroca said thoughtfully. "I saw an experiment like that once. Food was placed at one end and the rats at the other. They wanted the food, but they had to move through the passages to get it. And there were dangers, things which drove them to frustrated madness, other things which killed. The idea was to find the most clever rat or the one with the greatest compulsion."

"We aren't rats," said Sac. He stood, trembling, looking at the hole. "You saved my life, Earl. I was falling, as good as dead, and you saved me. From now on you give the orders and I'll obey."

Dumarest looked at the silver wires, the shadowed path. To one side came the hint of movement; who could tell what lurked above?

He said, "We go back."

"To the ship?" Sac hesitated; he had made a promise which already he found hard to keep. "But what about the others? My brother?"

"We'll skirt the valley and keep the cliffs to one side. That way we'll only have to watch our flank."

"If we can get to the cliffs," said Daroca quietly. He lifted his bow and pointed with the arrow. More shapes had appeared, clustering, moving as if to a plan. They were difficult to spot and details were vague in the gloom, but they looked different from the one he had shot.

Chom drew in his breath.

"They're cutting us off," he said grimly. "Earl?"

"We charge. Together now and stop for nothing. Keep an eye open for wires and miss the trees. There is a clearing back a little way. Make for it and, if we have to, we'll make a stand. Now!"

He led the way, running, spear at the ready and eyes darting from side to side. A glint of silver showed ahead and he veered, the others following in his path. Another and he sprang aside, a third and he regained the trail he had left. Before him something rose from the ground, mandibles snapping, rearing half the height of a man. The spear caught it in the thorax, spilled a flood of ichor and ripped free as Dumarest jumped. His boot hit the flat head and the rounded back; then he was running to turn and stab fiercely at a worm-like thing which hissed and coiled and then vanished.

"Earl!" Chom came running, with Sac and Daroca following. "Behind you!"

He spun, dropping to one knee, the spear point sloping before him. A beast, striped and fanged, was in the air. The point sheared into chest and lungs, the slender shaft snapping beneath the weight. Dumarest dropped it, whipped out a wooden knife and plunged it into an eye.

"Quick!"

He was running again while behind him came the thrum of a bowstring, the soggy impact of Chom's club. Sac cried out, swearing, and pounded after the rest. Ahead lay the clearing, a patch of open ground coated with soft grass and edged by slender shafts. Dumarest raced toward them, the knife lifting from his boot, slashing, turning the hollow stems into fresh spears.

Panting, he looked around.

Nothing.

No nightmare beasts or shapes from delirium. No silver threads. No attack. Only himself and the others, gasping, hands strained as they gripped their weapons. And, as he watched, their breaths plumed in streams of vapor from the sudden cold.

"Madness," said Daroca. He stumbled and dragged himself upright with a visible effort. His face was lined, haggard, suddenly aged. Gone was the smooth dilettante who had ridden the ships down the odd byways of space for the sake of novelty. Now he, like them all, was a man struggling to survive.

"Madness," he said again. "What kind of test is this? What has it to do with the determination of love?"

Dumarest said nothing, plunging ahead, the soaring cliffs to his left, the massed vegetation to his right. As he had guessed the going was easier, a wide patch of debris lying between the cliff wall and the undergrowth, and though it was strewn with boulders they were making good time. Since they had left the clearing, they had seen no silver threads, no lurking shapes.

Only the numbing cold had followed them, forcing them to keep moving.

"We could make a fire," said Chom. "Sit and rest and maybe sleep a little. Food too; there must be fruit on some of those trees."

"We'd freeze," said Sac.

"Maybe not. If we showed determination, what would be the point in killing us?"

"We keep going," said Sac doggedly. "My brother is waiting."

"Then let him wait!" Chom slammed his club at a boulder, chips flying from beneath the impact. "What is your brother to me? If he's dead, there's no hurry; if he's alive, he can be patient. If we sit and refuse to move, she may come to us again. Words could accomplish more than this journey."

Dumarest said, "Remember Harg? What happened to him?"

"He gambled and lost."

"Do you want to take the same chance?"

The entrepreneur scowled. "No, but need it come to that? We have played her game long enough. If she wants love, there are four of us here to give it to her. No woman respects a man who acts like a mouse."

"She isn't a woman," said Dumarest. "Why don't you remember that?"

Dumarest realized it was easier for them to think of Tormyle in familiar terms: somehow a woman was less frightening than a totally alien being. But she was no more a woman than the shapes which had attacked them, the planet on which they trod. She, it, was all of them and more.

Daroça stumbled again, dropping his spear in order to catch a boulder and save himself. He clung to the stone, panting, sweat dewing his face despite the chill. Old, soft, he could no longer stand the pace.

"Leave me," he gasped. "I'll come after you as soon as I can."

Chom beat his hands together; his skin was mottled with the cold.

"He'll die," he said dispassionately. "If you are merciful, Earl, you will give him a fast end."

"Kill him?" Sac looked from one to the other. "You must be joking. You just can't kill a man like that."

"No?" Chom shrugged. "You have a weak stomach, my friend, and a selfish mind. The product of a soft world with neat laws and easy comforts. But I have lived on harsh planets and so has Earl. On such worlds a man must rely on his friends. What would you do with him? Carry him? We have far to go and are weak. Leave him? He will sit and freeze and shiver, then finally sink into a coma and die a miserable death. A thrust of a spear, a pressure on the carotids and it is over. Quick, clean, merciful."

"Barbaric!"

Sac was wrong, but Dumarest didn't argue. The man was a product of his culture and not to blame for the unconscious sadism which would condemn a man to lingering agony in the mistaken belief that he was being kind. But Chom was wrong also; the mercy of death was not a thing to be casually given to save inconvenience. Daroca was exhausted, ready to give up, but all men held within themselves unsuspected reserves of energy.

He said, "Daroca, listen to me."

"Leave me, Earl. Let me rest."

"If you stay here you'll die," said Dumarest harshly. "Is that what you want, to commit suicide? Now stand up, man. Up!" He gripped the blouse and pulled Daroca upright, away from the support of the boulder. Deliberately he sent the flat of his hand across the sunken cheek. Again, a third time, the blows measured to sting. He saw the shock in the sunken eyes, the dawning of anger. Rage was an anodyne to apathy and apathy could kill.

"Earl! Damn you!"

"You hate me," said Dumarest. "Good. And you hate this valley and Tormyle and what it is doing to us. You hate it so much that you aren't going to let it win. You're going to reach the end of the valley with the rest of us. All you have to do is to keep putting one foot before the other. A child could do it."

Daroca touched his cheek, the red marks left by Dumarest's fingers.

"No, Earl. I haven't the strength."

"I saw a woman once on Jachlet. She crawled ten miles with two broken legs. Haven't you the guts of that woman?" His hand lifted again, poised to strike. "Now move, damn you! Move!"

Sac took the lead, Daroca stumbling after him, leaning on his spear, the bow slung over his shoulder. Chom stayed close and Dumarest took the rear. Before them the cliff wall curved to the right, blending with the vegetation ahead. Above, the shimmering sky threw an even brightness. There was no sound, only the rasp of their boots, the sound of their breathing, the gasps of the exhausted man.

It was like a nightmare in which there was continuous movement but no progress. A false world of unreality in which anything could happen, the cliffs, the sky itself the product of a whim. The boulders grew larger, cracks appeared in the surface, and once the air became filled with drifting motes of sparkling dust.

Chom wiped at his sleeve and ran the tip of his tongue over his lips.

"Sweet," he said. "Like sugar."

Dumarest cautiously tasted it, gathered a small heap in the palm of his hand. It had a strong flavor and a texture like that of nuts. Food, perhaps, a gift from Tormyle? A reward for good behavior?

"Leave it," he said. "Don't eat it."

Chom frowned, "Poison?"

"No, but we have no water and it will aggravate our thirst."

They pressed on. The sparkling motes vanished as the valley stretched before them. Ahead thrust a jutting wall of rock, a barrier over which they had to climb. A crevasse had opened to their right which was impossible to cross.

"We could go back," said Chom. "Take a detour through the undergrowth."

Dumarest looked back the way they had come. The crevasse curved so as to enclose them in a narrow segment and, as he watched, it widened, moving close.

"We climb," he said. "We have no choice."

At first glance the wall was sheer, but then he saw minor imperfections, cracks, fretted and splintered stone, a ladder which an agile man could climb. Sac went ahead, Chom following, crawling up the face of the wall like an ungainly spider, thick shoulders heaving as he lifted his bulk.

Daroca said, "I can't make it, Earl. I haven't the strength."

"You'll make it."

"How? Can you give me skills I don't possess? I have no head for heights and I couldn't support my weight. You have no choice but to leave me."

Dumarest studied him. He was drawn, pale, haggard with fatigue. A man at the limit of his reserve. But he was slim, light and could be carried for a short distance. Carefully he studied the face of the wall. The others had reached halfway to the summit, scrabbling as they sought for holds. As he watched, Chom slipped, hung suspended by one arm and then, with a burst of energy, swung himself to safety.

But there was another route, one which offered more promise: a slanting crack running high across the wall, a ledge, a series of fretted places.

Daroca said, "You'd best hurry, Earl. The crevasse is very close."

It was feet away, moving as he watched, widening, the bottom invisible.

Dumarest threw aside his spear.

"Climb onto my back," he ordered. "Put your arms around my neck. Hold tight, but don't throttle me. Close your eyes if you have to, but relax. Don't fight against me."

"No, Earl. You can't do it."

"Move, damn you!"

The stone was granulated, sparkling with buried minerals, little gleams appearing to vanish inches before his eyes. Steadily he moved upward, balancing the weight on his back which threatened to tear him loose, muscles cracking as he gripped and hauled. He reached the slanting crack and moved along it, boots wedged tight to support his weight. In his ear the sound of Daroca's breath was a rasping susurration and he could feel the heat of the man, his sweat, his barely controlled fear.

"Relax," he said harshly.

"Earl!"

"I've climbed mountains before carrying a pack as heavy as you. We'll make it."

He reached the end of the slanting crack, groped upward for a fresh hold and felt rock crumble beneath his fingers. For a moment he swayed, fighting for balance; then his searching hand found a nub of stone, a rounded boss which he gripped as his boot rasped at the wall. It found a hold and he heaved upward, his other hand lifting.

"To the left," whispered Daroca. "A foot to the left and three inches upward."

Dumarest grunted. "Too far. Look for another higher but closer."

"Up," said Daroca. "More. To your right. There!"

It helped. Face close to the stone, Dumarest inched upward, guided by the whispering voice, using discarded handholds as resting places for his boots. He felt his muscles begin to weaken, the sting of sweat in his eyes and the taste of blood in his mouth as he clung desperately to the rock. The weight dragging at his back seemed to have increased and he knew that if he didn't make the summit soon he wouldn't make it at all.

Grimly he resisted the thought, concentrating on each movement as it came, not thinking of the inevitable result should he slip or lose his precarious balance. From somewhere above came the sound of voices and they spurred him on. If he could hear them they must be close.

"Earl!" Daroca's voice was a strained whisper. "I'm slipping. I can't hold on!"

"Lock your hands." He felt the sudden shift of balance, the backward tug. "Damn you! Do as I say!"

He choked as the locked fingers pressed against his throat, then tensed the muscles of his neck as he sucked in air. Another foot of upward progress, two more, and he paused, fighting the blackness which edged his vision.

Daroca's foot found a resting place and he heaved, easing the pressure of his hands.

"Earl, I—"

"Shut up. Look for holds. Tell me where they are."

Dumarest listened, memorizing, then inflated his lungs. With a smooth surge of energy he recommenced to climb, hands following a preconceived pattern, calling on the last of his strength. A yard, three, and then he felt hands grip his arms, pulling, dragging him and his burden to safety over the edge.

He rolled, feeling Daroca fall away, rising on all fours, head low as he sucked air into his tortured lungs. His arms were quivering, the muscles of back and shoulders, his calves and thighs. Above the surge of blood in his ears he heard Sac's voice, high, brittle with surprise.

"The valley! It's changed!"

Chapter
◆ ELEVEN ◆

There had been stone and a gentle slope leading from the edge of the cliff to a cluster of vegetation, trees thick with bushes filling the area to either side while, beyond, a curtain of mist had reared. The slope remained, some of the trees and a scatter of bushes, but where they had been thick now they were sparse, gathered in small copses interspersed with an emerald green sward. Where mist had curtained the end of the valley a thing of dreams now stood.

It rose in a mass of soaring towers, delicate spires and graceful cupolas, crenellated walls bright with streaming banners. A fortress such as had never existed in reality—the needs which had made such a thing imperative based in an age when its construction would have been impossible.

Dumarest examined it, eyes narrowed, catching the glint of metal against the somber stone. Helmets, perhaps, or the heads of spears, the glints vanished as soon as they were seen, flashing like will-o'-the-wisps, tiny flickers which teased the eyes.

Beside him Chom released his breath in a gusting sigh.

"Magic," he said. "Or madness. What game is the creature playing now?"

"A castle." Daroca rubbed at his red-rimmed eyes. "And are those soldiers on the walls?"

"It wasn't there before." Sac seemed dazed by what he had seen. "And then, as you came over the edge, Earl, it suddenly appeared. The mist seemed to solidify, the trees to blur and then—" His arm rose, making a helpless gesture.

"A castle," Daroca said again. "The concept of chivalry

111

and of romantic love. Has Tormyle locked the others
within those walls? Are we supposed to rescue them? And,
if so, how can the four of us storm that citadel?"

"We'll storm it," said Sac. "If we have to. My brother's
in there. Right, Earl?"

"Four men," said Chom. "No weapons to speak of. You
must be mad."

"Earl?"

"Shut up," said Dumarest. It was no time to quarrel.
"We'll do what has to be done, but first let us find out
what it is. Are you fit to move, Daroca?"

"With care, yes."

Dumarest nodded and led the way down the slope
toward the enigmatic building. The ground was soft
beneath his boots, the trees and bushes bright with clustered blooms, great floral stars of red and purple, globes
of violet and azure, trailing fronds of scarlet and lambent
green. An illustration from a child's storybook, he thought.
Something stolen from a vagrant memory. Mari's perhaps,
or even Karn's. Men who spent their lives in space had peculiar ideas as to recreation.

The slope flattened and then began to rise toward the
castle. Details still remained vague; the walls were clear
enough, the turrets and banners, but the hints of metallic
gleaming defied true description. They could belong to the
accouterments of men or things fashioned in the likeness
of men. Or they could be the offshoot of opposed energies.

Chom came grumbling from where he had examined a
clump of bushes. "No fruits. Nothing to eat or to assuage
our thirst." He grimaced at the glowing sky. "And it seems
to be getting warmer."

The heat increased as they progressed until the sweat
was running down their faces. Dumarest eased his collar
and tried not to think of rippling streams, the chill impact
of crushed ice against his teeth. At his side Daroca stumbled and halted, panting.

"A moment," he pleaded. "If we could sit for a while
and rest I'll be fit again. An hour, surely, can make little
difference."

Sac forged ahead. "My brother is waiting. We have no
time to rest."

His brother, Mayenne, the others. Yet exhausted men

would be of little use in what could be waiting ahead. Dumarest slowed, then headed toward a clump of trees. Shade, at least, was there to be enjoyed.

From the castle came the sound of a trumpet, hard, imperious.

It came again, a compelling note which seemed to hang in the crystalline air, urgent, summoning. A third time and Daroca sucked in his breath.

"The drawbridge," he whispered. "Look!"

It was a slab of wood, thirty feet high, ten broad. As they watched, it lowered, moving quickly, silent until it reached the ground, where it came to rest with a dull thud. Beyond it gaped an opening, dark, fretted at its upper edge with the teeth of a portcullis. Again the trumpet sounded and something came from the darkness toward them.

Like the castle, it was a thing of dreams: a tall figure mounted on a horse, both mount and rider plated with gleaming metal which shone like gold in the light from the sky. A lance rested in one gauntleted hand, the tip rising in salute as the thing came to a halt facing the little group. From within the closed helmet boomed a hollow voice.

"Welcome."

A herald, thought Dumarest. A part of the furnishings of this present fantasy, as was the castle, the drawbridge, the portcullis. Tormyle at play—but there was nothing childish in the stakes of the game it had engineered.

He said, "We have come for our friends."

"Those you seek are within the walls," said the hollow voice. "If you can enter, you may take them."

"If?"

"There are formalities. Customs to be observed. A ritual to be followed."

Chom snarled his anger. "More tests? Will the thing ever be satisfied? What more does it want us to do?"

"My brother!" Sac fought against Dumarest's restraining hand. "Let me go, Earl! Tek is waiting!"

He would have to wait a while longer. The game Tormyle had devised had to be conducted on the rules it had determined.

To the herald Dumarest said, "I don't understand what you mean. Explain."

"The explanation is obvious."

"Not to me."

"Earl!" Sac tore himself free and raced toward the lowered drawbridge. He reached it, put one foot on the planking and then spun as something buzzed from the darkness and enfolded him with gauzy wings. Still spinning, he fell as the shimmering creature vanished back into the darkness.

Ignoring him, Dumarest said, again, "Explain."

"That should not be necessary," boomed the herald. "You have a saying which provides all answers. Love will find a way. Therefore—find it!"

There was no food, no water, little shade and the temperature was rising all the time. From beneath the scant protection of the trees Dumarest stared thoughtfully at the castle. The herald had gone and the drawbridge had risen; all he could see were walls of stone, the towers, banners and the enigmatic glints of metal. A puzzle. A box containing the hostages. A stronghold which, somehow, he must find a way to enter.

He heard the rustle of movement and turned to find Daroca at his side.

"A peculiar construction, Earl." He nodded toward the castle. "I have been examining it too. Those towers seem to serve no useful purpose. See? They do not widen into overhangs so as to protect the base of the walls and they are too high to serve as viable platforms for archers. And who in their right senses would build a castle overlooked by the cliffs at the rear? The drawbridge, too; there is no moat or trench and so no need of such a bridge." He tilted his head, squinting. "My eyes are not as strong as they could be. Are those men on the walls?"

"An illusion," said Dumarest. "I've been watching them. A man would turn his head, alter his pace a little, be curious if nothing else. They aren't men." He added, with sudden impatience, "But we know that."

"True," admitted Daroca. "We are the only men on this world—us and those within the walls. But old habits die hard. We see a fragment of something familiar and fill in details from our own knowledge of what should be. A cas-

tle should contain armored men—therefore we see them.
And yet the herald seemed real enough."

Real as the trees were real, the grass beneath their feet,
as real as anything on this peculiar world. Dumarest turned
and looked to where Sac Qualish was lying. The buzzing thing had rendered him unconscious; now Chom was
cooling his forehead with a mass of leaves.

"He's coming round," he said as Dumarest stepped
toward him. "He's stirred a couple of times and once he
gave a groan." He lifted the leaves and used them as a fan
to cool his own face. "What was it, Earl? The thing which
attacked him? It looked like a giant butterfly to me."

"I thought it was a web," said Daroca. "Something like
the mesh-symbiotes of Chemelophen. Not that it matters.
The castle is obviously protected against direct attack."

Chom wiped his face and licked at his fingers, scowling
at the taste of salt.

"First the cold," he grumbled. "That was to get us moving toward this end of the valley. Now the heat—how
long can we last before taking some sort of action?"

"Not long," said Daroca. "But what kind of action can
we take? Aside from illustrations I've never even seen a
castle, much less learned how to take one. Earl?"

Sac groaned before Dumarest could answer. He stirred
and sat upright, one hand to his head, his face creased
with pain.

"What happened?" He frowned as they told him. "I
remember something which buzzed, a sting as if I'd
touched a live wire, and then nothing. You should have all
followed me," he accused. "Together we might have been
able to get inside the castle. Instead you were content to
argue with that creature of Tormyle."

Chom said, "You talk like a fool. What did you gain by
your action? What would any of us have gained? This is a
time for thought, not stupid heroics." He threw aside the
wad of leaves. "The herald spoke of customs, a ritual
which should be followed. Have any of you any idea of
what it meant?"

"It also said that love would find a way," reminded
Dumarest.

The entrepreneur shrugged. "Maybe, but I am not in
love."

"Not even with your own life?"

"That, perhaps." He rose, eyes shrewd in the rounded planes of his face. "A spur to the intelligence, you think? Find the answer or die in this heat? Daroca, you are a man of intelligence and one who claims to have studied many strange cultures. Can't you solve this riddle?"

As the man hesitated Dumarest said, "You spoke of chivalry and the concept of romantic love. Just what did you mean?"

"A legend, fable rather, but one based on fact. At least I think so. There was a time in some remote past, probably on a primitive world, when men built strongholds and wore armor and fought with simple weapons. They had a code of behavior which we know as chivalry. Kindness to the weak, help for the afflicted, adherence to a given word—a society which probably never existed but which the romantic wish to believe actually had. The legend probably arose from when men fought to exist on newly-settled worlds and had to band together against a common enemy. Something of the sort is to be found on Kremar and Skarl."

Dumarest was patient. "I know that. An aristocracy given to symbols and ritual. And the rest?"

"Romantic love?" Daroca shrugged. "An ideal based on a concept of purity. A man could love a woman for everything but the reason normal men love women. A distortion which placed high value on fetish instead of natural, sexual desire. A form of insanity, of course, but not without appeal to those who yearn for a reality which could never exist."

Chom made a sound of disgust. "Madness. And where could a thing like Tormyle gain such ideas? From Mari?"

"From Tek." Sac Qualish rose painfully to his feet. "As young men we were interested in old legends and codes of behavior. At one time we thought of writing a book based on stories which are enjoyed by children and which seem to be found on most worlds. Tales of great heroes and mighty deeds."

"And women who are more—or less—than human." Chom laughed. "You should have got married, Sac. A woman in the home would have cured such dreaming. But how does it help us to know all this? Will it help us scale those walls?" His broad hand gestured toward the crenellations, the glints of metal and streaming banners. "Destroy the things which are no doubt waiting for us?"

"You asked a question." The engineer was sullen. "I answered."

"With nonsense," snapped Chom. "With words when we need lasers and explosives."

"With ideas," corrected Dumarest. "With the answer we need."

Daroca looked his surprise. "Earl?"

"Tormyle is logical; we know that. Therefore this fantasy must contain elements of logic based on the things we see: a castle, banners, a herald wearing full armor. Tek's fantasy brought to life. Romantic love and what it means."

"I see." Daroca drew a deep breath. "You know," he said, "I think you've known all along what has to be done. The only thing which can be done. You knew, Earl. Admit it."

"Admit what?" Chom glared his bewilderment. "What are you talking about?"

"The way into the castle. The only way. Sac?"

The engineer was thoughtful. "A challenge. If all this is based on Tek's imaginings, then the castle will hold a champion. We must challenge him—it—and thus gain victory. But how can we do that?" He looked at what they carried, the crude weapons of wood and stone, remembering the armored creature on the horse, the thing which had buzzed and stolen his senses.

Dumarest said, "Chom, give me your club."

There was no sound as he walked toward the drawbridge. The soft ground muffled his boots so that he seemed to be walking on velvet. The heat now had grown so that the air quivered; breathing was a thing of conscious effort. Already they were suffering from the effects of dehydration; soon they would be too weak to do anything but lie and wait for death.

From above sang the single note of a trumpet.

Dumarest ignored it, concentrating on the planks of the drawbridge. As he got closer he could see anomalies—the planks were too exposed to fire, a thing never permitted in a real stronghold, and the ground lifted as it reached the walls instead of falling into a trench or moat. The walls, too, were seamless, the rough surface artificially streaked with what would have been mortared blocks. A facade, he thought, covering what? The rugged walls of the cliff perhaps. A cavern. A pit leading to the heart of this strange world. Anything which Tormyle desired. He could only trust in the logic of the machine and the determination of the thing to learn what it could never know.

The drawbridge was very close. He stepped to one side, cautious in case it should suddenly be lowered to crush him like an insect beneath the heel of a boot. Again the trumpet sounded and, as the clear note died, he sent the massive head of the club thundering against the wood. Twice more he beat the panel, hard, measured strokes, the stone gouging into the planks.

Something fell from above.

It buzzed, shimmering, twisting like a near-invisible skein of thread, bright colors shot with ebon, silver merging with scarlet. It shrilled and darted toward him, wide wings spread so as to engulf him, the buzzing higher and taut with menace.

Dumarest sprang backward, the club lifted, falling, lifting again to hammer once more at the wings, the shimmer, the tiny body he could see at the center of the mobile web.

As it squashed the buzzing died. For a moment the webs were still, multicolored lace spread on the sward and then, in a moment, both crushed body and wings had vanished.

From beneath the shelter of the trees he heard Chom's bellow of warning.

"Earl! The bridge! It's coming down!"

He sprang backward as the great slab of wood swept down from where it rested against the walls, reaching safety as the end jarred against the ground. Logic, he thought grimly. A double-edged weapon. Though there was no moat one was implied and, by beating against the structure, he had, in a sense, attacked the castle by frontal assault. The attack had been answered by the buzzing thing falling from above.

Three feet from the end of the drawbridge he stared at the dark opening, the fretted portcullis, the flanking walls of stone. A glimmer showed in the depths, the sound of hooves and the herald, magnificent in golden metal, advanced with lance at rest, the point aimed at his breast.

Dumarest said, "I challenge you!"

"Challenge?"

"You spoke of formalities, customs, a ritual to be observed. Send out your champion and let us fight. If I win, then the prisoners you hold are mine. The laws of chivalry demand that this be so."

The booming voice said, "You would fight me?"

"Yes."

"For love?"

"For life."

"The prime directive," mused the creature in the golden armor. "But why you, Earl? Why must it always be you? Have the others no desire to continue their existence? Or is your love for the woman so strong that it has overridden all caution and logical consideration? You will fight, you say. And the others?"

Dumarest said harshly, "Let us keep to the point. This is your game, Tormyle, your rules. Will you keep to them or not?"

For a long moment there was silence as if the thing were checking possibilities, weighing consequences, gauging the logic of the situation. And then, "I accept. In one hour we will fight."

Chapter
◆ TWELVE ◆

It was a long hour. The heat did not increase, for which Dumarest was thankful, but still the air remained oppressive, the sweat streaming from his body robbing him of precious salt. Sac, recovered, stared gloomily at the castle, his eyes narrowed as he tried to determine the nature of the enigmatic glints on the crenellated walls. Daroca too was wrapped in introspection, musing, his ringed hand lifting often to touch his cheeks, the lobe of his right ear. Only Chom was practical.

"That thing is armored, Earl. Wooden spears will be useless against the metal. Before you can use a club you'll have to get close, which means dodging the lance and whatever else it may be carrying. The bow?" He shrugged, thick shoulders heaving beneath his blouse. "How will you handle it, Earl?"

Sac said abruptly, "There! On that tower! Look!"

Dumarest followed his pointing hand and saw nothing but vagrant glimmers.

"He's gone. But I'm sure I saw him. Tek was standing watching. The others too."

Were they images created by imagination and the need to be reassured? Chom echoed his impatience.

"Dreaming won't help us. You're an engineer; can't you think of some way to help Earl defeat that creature?"

"No."

"Think, damn you! His life depends on it. All our lives. If you hope to save that brother of yours, quit staring and use your brain."

"I'm not a fighting man," said Sac dully. "I don't know anything about weapons. But what about the mount it

120

rides? Metal is heavy and if he could be thrown, it might help."

If it could be thrown. If the champion would be the herald. If it were a normal man with human limitations. Dumarest fought the inclination to regard it as anything more. If the champion was invulnerable, then he could not hope to win. But in that case there would be no point to the conflict. The rules of the game, he thought. The insane fantasy constructed by the world-intelligence must offer the hope of success or the entire experiment would be useless.

His knife whispered from his boot.

"Give me your blouse," he said to the engineer. "Daroca, search around and find me some stones. All you can get, any size, bring them to me here."

"Earl?"

"Do it!"

The knife sliced through the fabric of the blouse, cutting it into narrow strips which Dumarest plaited together to form three long cords which he joined together at one end. The stones Daroca had found were too small. His blouse yielded more material which Dumarest fashioned into pouches. He filled them with stones and lashed them to the free ends of the three cords. Rising, he spun the device over his head, faster, faster, releasing it to fly, spinning over the clearing to hit and wrap around the bole of a tree.

"Neat," said Chom as he unwrapped it. "Where did you learn to make a thing like that?"

"On Marakelle. They hunt small animals which are very fast." Dumarest jerked at the cords, tightening them and checking the pouches which held the stones. "A trained man can bring down a running beast at a hundred yards." He sorted other stones for use in the sling. Both weapons would serve to attack at a distance, but for close-quarter work he had nothing except the knife and the club. Neither were much use against an armored man.

"We could help," said Daroca abruptly. "If we all attack at the same time, it would make things easier. We could distract its attention if nothing else."

"No," said Sac.

"Why not? Are you afraid?"

"The challenge was for single combat. If Earl should be killed, then our turn will come." Again the engineer stared at the walls of the castle. "If Tormyle allows it. If it doesn't kill us all or let us die for want of food and water."

Chom said, "Stop talking about food and water. Earl will do his best; if he can't win, then we are as good as dead." His big hand ripped a mass of leaves from a tree. Wadding them, he thrust them into his mouth, chewed, then spat in disgust. "Nothing. Even the taste is vile. All you can do now, Earl, is to rest."

Rest and wait as he had done so often before during the moments before combat. To force himself to relax, to ease the tension which could weaken if maintained too long, the keen edge of concentration blunted by overstimulus. Dumarest lay in a patch of shade, eyes closed, apparently asleep but, as Chom knew, far from that. A man summoning his energies for violent action, a killing machine ready to explode.

From the castle came the sound of the trumpet.

"Now," whispered Daroca. He drew in his breath with a sharp hiss as the clear note sounded again. The drawbridge lowered and the champion rode from the darkness into the light of the glowing sky.

It was not the herald. It was not a thing of golden grace but big and broad, wearing black metal spined and curved in baroque monstrosity. The animal it rode was not a horse but a scaled thing with six legs and a long, prehensile tail. Jaws gaped, showing rows of savage teeth and fire spurting from the cavernous throat. A giant lizard or a dragon from fable, a part of the fantasy which Tormyle had constructed.

Chom sucked in his breath. "Earl! How the hell can you ever beat that?"

Dumarest watched as it came over the planking. The rider, cased all in black metal, carried a long lance, a mace, a sword and shield. A pennant fluttered from the lance, forked and bearing a device of red and yellow on a field of green. The thing itself, if constrained to human limitations, was no real danger. The armor would slow it down, the weapons it carried of use only at close quarters. The dragon was another matter.

It was green flecked with red, the scales limned with scarlet, the eyes, hooded by bony protuberances, gleaming like jewels. It was fast and quick and agile. The tail could swing like a club, the teeth rip like a hundred knives, the spurting flames burn and incinerate. Helpless before it he would be easy prey for the rider with his long lance.

Daroca said, "It's giving you no chance, Earl. None at all."

"We can't let him face it alone." Sac was trembling. "If we're going to die we may as well all go together."

Dumarest ignored the comments and checked his weapons, inflating his lungs. As the dragon and its rider reached the end of the drawbridge he stepped from beneath the shelter of the trees. He was ready as it came toward him over the soft ground.

The eyes were the only vulnerable point and, protected as they were, it wouldn't be easy to hit them. He stood, the loaded sling in his hands, judging time and distance. As the beast came closer he began to rotate the sling. It hummed through the air, making a thin, vicious sound. The dragon heard it and paused, head lifting, jaws gaping and bright with fire. The rider touched it with hooked spurs and the beast lowered its head, claws ripping at the dirt as it loped forward.

Dumarest waited, tense, concentrating on the glowing jewel of an eye, ignoring the gleaming tip of the lance, the teeth, the spurts of flame. The thongs of the sling were taut against his hand. One final turn and he released the stone, running as it left the pouch. He heard it hit, the soggy impact it made and then the dragon roared, head rearing, turning, blood streaming from the ruined eye.

Before the rider could regain control, Dumarest had raced forward, knocking the tip of the lance to one side, gripping it in both hands, and continued to run alongside the stricken dragon. Leverage did the rest. It was impossible for the rider to maintain its grip on the weapon without turning in the saddle and it could turn only so far. Dumarest tore it free, jumped over the lashing tail and ran another hundred yards before turning, lance in hand.

From the air Lolis whispered, "Well done, Earl. So very well done."

So far, perhaps, but the danger still remained. He had lost his sling, the thongs and pouch trampled and burned and the lance was poor exchange. He poised it as the dragon advanced, grounding the butt and aiming the point at the pulsing throat. An unthinking beast would have charged against it, but the dragon was more than that. Half blinded, fuming with rage, it had instilled cunning and the rider on its back recognized the danger. Dumarest felt a gush of fire and saw the wood of the shaft begin to smoke, the metal point glow with sudden heat. He ran as the tail lashed like a whip toward him. Turning, he threw the lance with all the power of his back and shoulders. It slammed into the side of the beast's neck and blood spurted from a gaping wound. Before it could recover he was spinning the bolas, the weights stretching the cords as he hurled it at the jaws. It hit, spun tight, cutting short the plumes of fire.

Then Dumarest was running forward again, reaching for the lance which had been shaken from the creature's neck, gripping it as the tail slammed against his side with numbing force. He rolled, fighting for air, seeing the clawed feet rise above him as the beast reared ready to rip out his intestines. A second and he would be dead—but a second was long enough. He crouched, lance upraised, the point burying itself into the scaled hide as the dragon crashed down, the metal shearing through flesh to impale the heart beneath.

Again the air whispered a compliment.

"So fast, Earl, so very fast. But you have not won yet."

The rider still remained. It had been thrown clear of the dying beast and now stood, grim in black plating, shield and sword ready for action. Against it Dumarest had nothing but his knife.

He circled warily, watching as the thing turned to face him. It was like a machine, a robot without discernible weakness, armed and armored against any attack. Dumarest lunged, the knife held like a sword, the point glittering as it swept toward the visor. The shield lifted, the sword hissed as it cut the air, the tip ripping the plastic of his blouse as Dumarest sprang back just in time.

Fast then, but careless, the creature should have used the point to thrust, not the edge to slash.

Again Dumarest lunged, leaping sideways as he feinted with the knife, forcing the thing to turn to guard its rear. He edged toward it, feinting, ducking, darting like a wasp at the armored shape, using his speed to avoid the sword, the slamming blows of the shield.

Then Dumarest sensed the dead creature at his side and turned, springing over it, stooping to tug at the lance. It was buried too deep. He released it as the sword whined down, the edge aimed at his head. He caught the blow on his knife, feeling the jar as he turned the blade. He snatched with his left hand at the mailed arm and threw himself backward as he gripped the limb.

Caught off balance, the armored figure toppled over the body of the dead beast. Before it could recover, Dumarest was on it, the knife in his hand stabbing at the visor, grating as it slipped through the eye-slits. Beneath him the figure heaved once and then was still.

Chom's voice roared in triumph:

"You have beaten it, Earl! You have won! The champion is dead and the prize is ours!"

But nothing was dead. Dumarest dragged free his knife and looked at the unstained blade. He jerked open the visor and saw nothing but emptiness within the helmet. A hollow man who had fought and would have killed, but could lose nothing in return.

Then the armor was gone, the dragon, the castle itself with the high walls and crenellations, the banners and soaring towers. The fantasy was over. Where it had stood was nothing but the merging cliffs of the valley.

And Mayenne.

She stood in a transparent cage, looking very small and helpless, her hair a glowing helmet of purest copper in the light from the shimmering sky. Beside her stood Karn, his eyes sunken, anxious. In an identical cage, yards distant, stood Mari and Tek Qualish.

Both cages were suspended on chains fastened to the ends of slender rods protruding from the cliff wall. Between them ran a narrow causeway at the far end of which was set a tall lever. To either side gaped an abyss.

Dumarest walked to the edge and looked down. The bottom was invisible. He looked to either side; there was no way to reach the cages aside from the causeway. The ground too had changed, the soft emerald of the sward replaced by a stony barrenness, the sparse trees once again the thick mass of vegetation they had previously known.

Chom came panting toward him, Sac and Daroca close behind.

"What new deviltry is this?" The entrepreneur scowled at the cages, the people within. "You won the bout, Earl. The prize should be ours now. Have we yet another test to pass?"

"Ingenious, isn't it?" Karn's voice came clearly from the confines of his cage. "A novelty devised by Tormyle. It told us all about it. You can save half of us—but only at the expense of the rest."

Dumarest stepped onto the causeway and examined the lever.

"Don't touch that!" said Karn sharply. "Not yet anyway."

"You'd better explain."

"Yes," said Karn. "We were meant to do just that." His arm made a vague gesture. "We're suspended, as you see. That lever will swing one cage to safety, depending on which way it is thrown. To the left, us; to the right, the others. The cage chosen will drop to the causeway and open. The other will fall into the abyss. I don't have to tell you what will happen to the occupants if it does."

"Mayenne?"

"It is as he says, Earl. We two against the others. You have to decide." She paused and added, "There is a time limit. Ten thousand heartbeats. At the end of that time both cages will fall."

Over two hours, more than enough time for thought. Beside Dumarest, Sac Qualish whimpered like a dog.

"I don't believe it! Tek, she's lying, isn't she? She has to be lying."

His brother was calm. "No."

"Mari?"

"She's telling the truth as it was given to us."

Dumarest said, "Is there any way you can get out of those cages? Is there anything we can do to get you out?"

"No." Karn was positive. "I've been over every inch of it."

"Tek?"

"We're in sealed boxes. As far as I can make out both cages are solid." His calmness was unnerving, the resignation of a man who had accepted the inevitable. "As Mayenne said, it's for you to decide."

A decision no man should ever have to make, Dumarest thought. As Sac edged toward the lever Dumarest said, "We must think about this. Discuss it. I suggest we all sit in the shade."

"No," said the engineer. "I'll stay here."

"You'll do as Earl says." Chom closed his big hand over the other's arm. "We'll gain nothing standing in this heat. Come now. You too, Daroca. We'll go back to where we watched the fight."

Back beneath the trees Daroca slumped against a bole, Chom squatting like a toad at his side. The entrepreneur frowned at the suspended cages.

"It must have got that idea from Mari. Some houses of pleasure specialize in displaying their wares in such a fashion. The rest? Well, Karn would know about opposed balances, Tek also."

"And cruelty?" Daroca forced himself to sit upright with an obvious effort. The man was dying, thought Dumarest dispassionately. They would all die unless the temperature fell and food and water was provided. "This shows a refinement usually only to be found in highly sophisticated cultures. An application of mental torment. Who is to decide and how? No matter who is chosen, the winner will also lose. It will not be pleasant to carry the memory of those he has doomed to extinction."

"Nobody is dead yet," said Dumarest. "And perhaps nobody will die. You're an engineer, Sac. Is there any way we can lock the mechanisms?"

"Without being able to study it, how can I tell?"

"You could try. Even I know that a stone in the right place could wreck any machine ever built. No," he said sharply as Sac made a move toward the causeway. "I don't want you to touch anything. Not yet."

"Don't you trust me?"

Dumarest made no answer and looked instead at the

cages, the abyss and the causeway. With fire they could burn down trees and set the boles so as to prevent the cages from falling. With rope they could lash them fast in some way. But they had no rope and no time to make it and they would never be able to fell trees in time.

"A problem," said Chom musingly. "And one of which I am glad to have no part. You, Earl, are concerned with the Ghenka. You, Sac, with your brother. Only one can be saved. Perhaps you had better draw lots to decide which."

"No," said Sac.

"Fight then? You would be foolish to do that. Earl would surely win."

Dumarest said flatly, "There will be none of that. We didn't fight our way here to kill each other at Tormyle's whim. I have another suggestion."

Daroca stirred. "Which is?"

"We do nothing."

"And let them all die?" Sac stared disbelievingly. "No. I can't agree to that. Damn it, Earl; you forget that Tek is my brother!"

"And you forget that if it hadn't been for Earl you would be dead," snapped Chom.

"I've not forgotten. But I'm alive and so is Tek. I want to keep him that way."

Daroca said quietly, "I suggest we lower our voices. It can't be pleasant for those in the cages to hear our discussion. Now, Earl, what did you mean when you suggested that we do nothing?"

"What else can we do? Fight? Kill half in order to save the others? We've jumped to Tormyle's tune long enough. Each test we've faced has been followed by another. Now I say it's time to call a halt. We sit and do nothing. If it wants to kill us all, there is nothing we can do to stop it. But I'm damned if I'm going to cater any longer to its sadistic pleasure."

"A bluff," said Chom shrewdly. "Is that what you think, Earl?"

"I don't know. I hope so."

"You hope?" Sac stared at his clenched hands. "Is that all?"

"You know the alternative."

"Tek alive and the others dead. Yes, I know it, but Tek will be alive. Alive, do you hear? Alive!"

"Be silent!" snapped Daroca. "Remember they can hear you!"

"I don't care if they can!" The man was almost hysterical. With an effort he forced himself to speak more quietly. "Listen, Earl. I owe you my life and I won't forget it. Anything I can give you is yours for the asking. But not this. Damn it, man; you can always get another woman. I can never get another brother."

"Logic," said Chom blandly. "And I am sure that we all appreciate it. So let us be logical. I was wrong when I said that I had no interest in this problem. I had forgotten the captain and, as we are being logical, he must be considered. Of what use to save the others if we have no one who is capable of handling the ship? Of them all Karn is the most important and the fact that the Ghenka is with him is a happy accident for Earl. Save one and you save both, and the captain must be saved if we are ever to leave this insane world. My regrets, Sac, but it seems your brother must be sacrificed for the common good."

"No one will be sacrificed," said Dumarest sharply.

Chom shrugged. "No? You are one man, Earl, among four. I vote for the captain. Daroca?"

"I say we wait and do nothing."

"Two to wait, one to save the captain. It seems, Sac, that you are in a minority." Chom added softly, "Unless, of course, you decide to side with me."

Dumarest said, "There will be no decisions. If any of you choose to commit murder then you will be the first to die. Now sit down, Sac, and relax. There is nothing to do but wait."

"We can talk." The engineer moved toward the stony ground. "There are things I'd like to say to my brother—and have you nothing to say to Mayenne?"

He spun as Dumarest glanced toward her, swinging the club he had snatched up to smash at the unprotected skull. Dumarest caught the movement and threw himself aside in time to avoid the full impact of the blow. Instead of crushing bone and brain it glanced off the side of his head, sending him to his knees, half stunned, blinded with pain.

He heard Daroca cry out, Chom's voice exploding in a

curse and the rasp of boots against rubble. He staggered to his feet, right hand lifting with the knife. Then he dropped it as he realized the impossibility of the throw. Already Sac was at the causeway and racing toward the lever at the far end. Quickly he scooped up a stone and threw it with the full strength of his arm. It hit the running man between the shoulders, sending him sprawling, his outstretched hands touching the lever. He rose as Dumarest reached for another stone. As he poised it to throw he heard the deep thrum of a string, the vicious hiss of an arrow.

Sac cried out, lifting his hands to the shaft buried in his throat, twisting, falling, the weight of his body hitting the lever.

It was thrown toward the left.

Chapter

◆ THIRTEEN ◆

Chom laughed and tore at the smoking meat, filling his mouth so that juices ran down his chin. He chewed and swallowed and reached for wine, filling a goblet full of lambent gold.

"Come, my friends," he said. "Let us celebrate. Tormyle has been most kind."

Food for the rats, thought Dumarest bleakly, comforts as a reward for successful endeavor. A house had appeared from nowhere, a table loaded with meats and fruits, wine and a dozen varieties of pastry. The entrepreneur was enjoying himself.

"Come," he said again. "Earl, Mayenne, all of you. Eat, drink and be glad that you are alive. A song later, maybe, after other matters have been taken care of." His leer left nothing to the imagination. "I'll be content with simpler pleasures. Synthetic as it may be, this meat is the finest I've ever tasted. The wine also."

Daroca nibbled fastidiously. Karn chewed with a vague abstraction as if his thoughts were elsewhere. Mayenne sipped at some wine.

"Earl?"

She wanted to talk, to relive the episode, to feel again, perhaps, the relief she had known when her cage had swung to safety. Dumarest preferred to leave things where they belonged among the dead memories of the past.

"Eat," he said. "You must be starving."

She frowned. "Why do you say that? We ate only a short while ago. At the ship, remember?"

Time, he thought. Moments for her had been hours for

131

them. Had she been kept in some form of stasis? It didn't matter. Not now.

"Earl," she said. "I must know. I heard you talking while I was in the cage. Would you really have sat and waited and done nothing?"

The truth would have hurt. He said, "Does it matter?"

"No," she admitted. "Not now. But I wonder what would have happened if Sac hadn't forced a decision. Would we all have died? Would Tormyle have repented?"

He moved, restless in his chair, conscious of the futility of the discussion. Conscious too of other things. Chom was celebrating, using their assumed victory as an excuse to eat and guzzle wine, but they had really won nothing but a respite.

"Poor Sac," said Mayenne after a moment. "And his brother. Mari too. They didn't deserve to die as they did. Killed for nothing at all."

Dumarest said, "Don't think about it."

"I won't," she promised. "But you saved my life, Earl. I shall never forget that."

"Thank Daroca, not me. He fired the arrow which killed Sac."

"Daroca?" Leaning forward, she touched his hand. "I must thank you," she said. "For what you did. It was a wonderful shot. Bad for Mari and Tek, but good for me and Karn. Earl too," she added. "I will never give him cause to regret your skill with a bow."

He reached for wine, sipped and said, "I wish I could take the credit, Mayenne, but I didn't use the bow. I lacked the strength to pull the string. It was Chom who shot the arrow."

Chom? Dumarest looked at where he sat, a man who had denied all skill with a bow. A lucky shot, perhaps? It was a facile answer, but not good enough. Until now he had assumed Daroca had killed Sac but, if so, why had he denied it?

Karn sighed and said to no one in particular, "How can I explain? When we get back to Ayette, what can I tell them? All those passengers dead, the captain, the ship delayed."

Chom blinked his amazement. "That worries you?"

"They will want to know." Karn was insistent, clinging, Dumarest realized, to familiar routine, familiar problems.

"Tell them the truth," said Chom.

"You think they will believe it?"

"They will have no choice. You have witnesses and can pass any test they may devise for the determination of truth. But why go to Ayette at all? The galaxy is wide, my friend, and now you have a ship of your own. With some adjustment I'm sure that none of us will complain if you chose to open a fresh trading route. Partners, maybe?" Chom smiled at the thought. "A regular income, comfort assured for old age, a nice home on some nice world. What do you say, Earl?"

"Karn has his duty."

"And duty is sacred?" The entrepreneur shrugged and reached for more wine. "We have only one life, my friend. We owe it to ourselves to spend it as best we may. Karn would be a fool to waste his opportunities. You agree, Daroca?"

"It is a philosophy I have heard before."

"So short of words?" Chom lowered his goblet and thrust aside his plate. "What's the matter with you all? We have come through great dangers and have won the test and all you can do is to sit and brood. Tormyle has proved to be generous." His hand waved at the house in which they sat. "Soon we shall be on our way with a ship and a galaxy to rove in. There are worlds I know on which we could do well. Contract labor for the mining planets, for example. Peasants who would sign away their lives for cheap passage. Cargoes which the squeamish hesitate to touch. All ours for the taking. And, friends, ours by right. We are the victors and to us go the spoils." He beamed and Dumarest realized that he was more than a little drunk. "How about it, Daroca?"

"Do as you please—once I have landed on a civilized world."

"You then, Earl. Of us all you have the greatest right. You are truly the victor."

"Of what?" said Dumarest harshly. "Of meat and wine and a place to sleep? Or are you thinking of the dead?"

"They are gone," said Chom. "We are alive. Come, Earl, let us drink to that at least."

"Go to hell," said Dumarest, and rose from the table.

Mayenne followed him outside to where the shimmering sky threw its monotonous light. The abyss had closed; the mechanisms of the test had vanished. Now there was nothing but the merging cliffs and the stony ground at their feet. The temperature had fallen so now it was like a pleasant summer's afternoon on a gentle world.

He turned. The house was low, rambling, a place of colonnades and pointed windows, fretted woodwork and peaked roofs. Over it hung trees bearing scented blossoms and flowers glowed in profusion on all sides.

"It's beautiful," whispered Mayenne. "Earl, darling, if we could only have a house like this for our own, how happy I would be. There would be room for guests and parlors in which we could entertain. And other rooms where children would be safe. Our children, Earl. I am not too old to give you sons."

And daughters who would sing as their mother sang. A home which would be his and the things most men regarded as important. A fair exchange, perhaps, for his endless quest for a lost world. For the empty travel and strange planets and the bleak life in ships which traversed the void.

He turned and faced her and saw the bronze of her hair, the smooth lines of her face, the eyes, jet with their smoldering flecks of ruby. He reached out and touched her and felt the life throbbing beneath her skin, the blood and bone and sinew which made her shape, the softness he remembered so well. Human and warm and vulnerable. He felt a sudden wave of protective tenderness and held her close as if to shield her from all harm.

"Earl?" She looked up at him and gently touched his cheek. "Darling, is something wrong?"

She had recognized the embrace for what it was. He forced himself to smile.

"No."

"Don't lie to me, Earl. I can feel it when you do."

"Nothing is wrong."

She was eager to be convinced and relaxed, smiling as she stepped back from his arms.

"I think it's time we were alone, darling. I have picked our room; it is a beautiful place. Let me show it to you."

"Later."

She did not argue, sensing with her woman's intuition his desire to be alone. Instead she said, "It is the third on the left past the room in which we ate. You will not be long?"

"No."

Daroca emerged as she entered the house. He looked after her for a moment, then walked to where Dumarest stood beneath the scented trees.

"A beautiful woman, Earl. You will never know how much I envy you." He paused and then, as Dumarest made no comment, said, "A stupid remark, but old habits die hard and much of my life has been spent in making banal conversation. Yet I was sincere. She loves you and will make you happy."

Dumarest said, "Perhaps."

"You doubt her? No. Something else, then?" He frowned as Chom's voice came booming through the open door. "Listen to that fool. He is trying to talk Karn into turning pirate or slaver, but he is wasting his time. Our captain is a man of honor. He will do his duty no matter what the personal cost."

"You are tired," said Dumarest. "You should eat and rest."

"Later, when my mind has quieted. Now, each time I close my eyes, I am back on that cliff riding your back to safety. And there is something else. Chom thinks that our ordeal is over. I am not so sure, and, I think, neither are you."

"No," said Dumarest bleakly. "I don't think that it is over."

He woke and knew immediately that something was wrong. He turned, reaching, but found only emptiness beside him. Mayenne was gone, the room in which they had slept, the window framing the scented trees. Instead he lay on a couch of some soft material in a room all of gold and crystal with cerise carpet on the floor and his clothes lying on a chair. Quickly he dressed and commenced to search. A door opened on a bathroom, another on a kitchen, a third on a long, low open space with a floor of polished wood and small tables bearing statues, ornaments, flowers caught in transparent blocks. A montage of things he had known before, assembled—where?

"Do you like it, darling?"

"Mayenne!"

He turned, quickly, staring at the figure at the end of the room. The light was subdued and he had been misled by the lilt in the voice. It was not Mayenne.

"You," he said. "Tormyle."

She smiled and came closer, dressed as he had seen her at the stream, the diaphanous gown parting to reveal soft and glowing flesh. There were alterations. The face was not quite as he remembered. Lolis had been beautiful, but young and with a certain vacuity. Now that touch of emptiness had gone. The hair too was different, glowing with the sheen of bronze, and the figure was more mature. The voice also. A blend, he thought, something of Mayenne added to Lolis. A composite.

"I asked if you like it, darling." Her hand gestured to the room, the apartment. "I made it just for you."

"As a cage?"

"As a place where we can talk. You would prefer that I whispered from a leaf? My shape to be something else? Earl, why do you fight against me? I want to be your friend."

He said bitterly, "You have an odd way of showing it."

"Because of the trials to which you were put? But, Earl, I had to make sure. I had to be positive. The experiment had to be carried to its logical conclusion. You would care for some wine?"

"No."

"Why not? You drink with the woman, why not with me?"

He caught the sharpness, the note of petulance, and frowned. Mayenne had been jealous and he had wondered why the alien should have adopted a female shape. The test, also, had contained elements of willfulness which would have been alien to a true machine. And yet what else could the thing be?

He said, "Can you drink?"

"But of course!" Her laughter was music. "Do you think

this shape is like those I sent against you in the valley? Earl, my darling, I build well. This body is totally functional. See?" She stretched and turned so as to display her curves. A decanter stood on a table and she poured two glasses of wine, swallowing hers without pause. "I can drink and eat and do everything a female of your species can do."

"Bleed?"

"That also." She came close and held out her arm. "Cut me if you wish. Use your knife against me. Kill me if it pleases you."

He could do it. He could slam his knife into her heart, but how long would she remain dead? Even if he managed to destroy the shape before him, how could it affect the planetary being?

"You don't want to hurt me," she said, and lowered her arm. "You are gentle, Earl, and kind, and you think of others. You have shown me what love really is."

He reached for his wine and sipped cautiously, wetting his lips while pretending to swallow. He felt the prickle of danger as if he stood at the edge of an invisible chasm in utter darkness. A thing not seen but sensed with the instinctive caution which had more than once saved his life.

"Love," she mused. "Such a complex emotion, as you once told me, Earl. And it comes in so many different forms. The love of a man for his brother, for his companions, an emotion strong enough for him to risk his life. The love of a man for a woman. A woman for a man. A passion strong enough to make him kill. Never before have I experienced such a thing. Once I would have thought it madness."

Dryly he said, "There are those who would agree with you."

"But not you, Earl."

"In some cases, yes."

"No. Such an emotion would not be love as you have taught me it should be. Greed, maybe, the desire to possess, a yearning to fulfill a personal need, but it would not be true love."

She had learned, he thought, and perhaps learned too well. He toyed with his wine, conscious of his inadequacy. He could have sensed a real woman's mood and played on it, appealing to her pride and intelligence, manipulating words and meanings to achieve a desired end. But a woman would have had obvious motives none of which could be applied to Tormyle. This thing beside him, no matter how she appeared, was not a woman but the manifestation of a planetary intelligence.

"You admit that we have answered your question," he said. "The thing you wanted to know."

"Yes, Earl."

"Then when can we leave?"

A couch stood against one wall. She moved toward it and gestured him to join her. As he seated himself, she said, "Why are you in so much of a hurry, Earl? I have provided for your friends. They have comfort and pleasant surroundings."

"It isn't enough. Men aren't animals to be satisfied with food and a comfortable prison."

"Other comforts, then? A larger house, a greater variety of food, entertainment which could amuse and please?"

Putting down his wine, Dumarest said, "You said the ship had been repaired and we made a bargain. We have kept our side of it. When are you going to keep yours?"

"Later, Earl."

"You will let us go?"

Her laughter was music. "Of course, my darling. You worry over nothing. But not yet. I have waited so long for novelty, do you begrudge me a little now that I have the chance to enjoy it?"

He said flatly, "More fights, Tormyle? More tests? More tricks to amuse you?"

"No." She moved against him, coming very close, her thigh touching his so that he could feel the softness of her flesh, the warmth of her body. A real woman would have felt like that, but she wasn't real. Always he must remember that. She wasn't real.

As if reading his thoughts, she said, "Touch me, Earl. Hold me. Close your eyes and be honest. Can you tell the difference between me and that other?"

He could, but he knew better than to say so.

"Can you imagine what my life has been?" she asked softly. "The long, so long, empty years. Always alone. I didn't realize how much alone until you came. Now things can never be the same as they were. I have seen what life can really be like, the interplay of emotion, the sense of companionship, the sharing. Can you understand, Earl? Can you even begin to guess what it means? The ability to talk to someone as I talk to you. The knowledge that there is something wonderful which I can share. To love and be loved. To belong to someone. To have another entity care for me so strongly that he would kill and die for my sake. You have it. To you it is a normal part of existence, but I have never known it until now. I want it, my darling. I want it and you can give it to me. You must!"

He said, very carefully, "Me?"

"You, Earl."

"I don't understand, Tormyle. What can I give you that you don't already have?"

She reached out to touch his shoulder and turned him so as to stare into his face. Her hair caught the light in metallic shimmers, bronze, beautiful, as were her face, her eyes.

"You are not a fool, Earl. You understand well enough. But if you want me to say it I will. I love you, darling. I love you—and I want you to love me in return."

Chapter
◆ FOURTEEN ◆

Vast caverns filled with crystalline growths, endless tunnels through which ran conductive fluids, the blazing heart of atomic fires; the brain, the veins, the heart of a planetary being. The control of tremendous forces were the hands which could reach across space, move worlds, tear apart the hearts of suns.

A world demanding to be loved.

Dumarest was thinking in mechanistic terms and that was wrong. Tormyle wasn't simply a gigantic artifact. There was more, a life-form in its own right, an intelligence which was too vast to comprehend. It was better to sit and look at the female shape and think of her as a woman with a woman's needs: to meet her on those terms and deal with her as he could.

He said casually, "You have learned more than I guessed, Tormyle. It seems now that you also have a sense of humor."

"Earl?"

"Surely you must be joking."

"You think that? No, darling, I'm serious. And would it be so hard for you to love me? If this shape doesn't please you, there are others I can wear. Shapes without number. And there is more I can offer. Think of what you desire and it will be yours. See?"

The apartment dissolved and became a great hall filled with bowing courtiers, creatures fashioned to obey his dictates. The hall opened to show fields of crops, houses, snaking roads filled with traffic. Mountains reared, golden, glittering with gems. They sank into an ocean filled with strange fish and on which armadas sailed. Ten thousand

140

women danced in the silver light of a sky filled with lambent moons.

All his for the price of love.

More power than any man had ever dreamed of. A world for his plaything in which he would rule as a king. A god.

A pet.

He lifted his wine as the apartment returned, his hand shaking a little as he drank, deeply this time, quenching more than a physical thirst. Every man had his need for heaven and she had shown him that and more. But at a price.

Unsteadily he said, "You offer much, perhaps too much, and I am overwhelmed. But you forget. I am mortal and will age. You will grow bored. What then?"

"I will never grow bored, Earl. Not with your love."

"And the rest?"

"Your age?" She laughed, triumphant. "Such a little thing. My darling, I can take your mind and the pattern which makes you unique and I can store it in a part of my being. You will never die. Your body, the shape you wear, may age, but then it can be replaced. We shall be together for an eternity, Earl. Always together. Always in love."

A girl in the grip of her first love affair making promises impossible to keep. For a year, ten perhaps, and then the novelty would fade. She would become impatient with his limitations and he would become, at the best, a tolerated pet; at the worst, a thing to be eliminated. Even if neither happened, what would happen to his pride?

He rose and moved restlessly about the room. It was warm, comfortable, but it had no door and no matter how pleasant a place it was still a prison. As the entire planet was a prison and one from which he had to escape.

He said, "You don't need me."

"That is nonsense, darling."

"You will forget," he said. "After we have gone, all this will diminish in importance. An interesting experiment which has yielded a new fact, no more. You feel this way because you have put too much of yourself in a female shape. You have built too well. Change and you will no longer feel the same. Love is not as you think. It can't be switched on. It is something founded in shared hardship, suffering and even pain. Unending joy would sicken and cloy by repetition. Surely you understand that."

She sat very still and when she spoke there was no laughter in her voice.

"You refuse me?"

Carefully he tried to soften the fact. "Not refuse. Not in the way you mean. But I am a man and you are a world. What could there be in common between us? You can give me everything I wish, true; but what can I give you? Protection? You don't need it. Comfort? How can that be possible? Companionship? I can't even begin to understand the complexity of your being. As I said, you don't need me."

"You are wrong, Earl. So very wrong. I need the one thing I cannot otherwise obtain. The thing which you alone can give."

An obsession, he thought, or perhaps the culmination of an experiment in which he was an integral part. Or it could be that he was observing the symptoms of a growing aberration. There was no way to be sure. He could be cunning and agree to do as she asked. With a normal woman who held him in her power that is what he would have done: given lip service and waited for an opportunity to escape. But how could he ever free himself from the tyranny of a planetary intelligence?

He said flatly, "What you ask is impossible. I can't love a world."

"You must stop thinking of me like that, Earl," she insisted. "I am a woman."

"If you were I would kill you. For what you did out there in the valley."

"The experiment?" She shrugged. "Certain things had to be determined. The girl, for example. You care for her. But why her and not me? How am I different from that entity for whom you risked your life?"

He said harshly, "Isn't that obvious? You have experienced none of the normal things which go to make a person. You are a beautiful pretense and nothing more. Damn it, you aren't even human."

"And if I were?"

He hesitated, sensing danger, conscious that he had already said too much. A woman scorned could be a vicious enemy and she was acting like a jealous woman, a woman determined to get her own way no matter what the cost. And he knew how ruthless she could be.

It was a time for lies.

"If you were it would be different. You are lovely, as you know, and any man would be proud to call you his own. But you are not human and we both know it." He added regretfully, "It is something I cannot forget."

"But if I were a real woman, Earl, as frail as you, as mortal?"

"Perhaps."

"And if I could bear you sons?"

He almost smiled at the impossibility, but this was no game, no pleasant bandying of words.

"Certainly. But that is beyond reason. Why don't you prove your love and let us go?"

"Perhaps I will, Earl," she said softly. "Perhaps I will go with you. You would like that. You and I together, sharing, enjoying all the things which lovers do. It can be done, Earl. You know that."

He tensed, sensing the closing jaws of a trap. Carefully he said, "I cannot begin to understand the full extent of your powers, Tormyle, but even you can't become wholly human."

"No?" Her laughter held a hint of mockery. "You know better than that, Earl. There is a way and you know it. You will give it to me, as a token of your love."

The apartment vanished. Abruptly he was in the open air, staggering a little from the sudden shock of transition, catching his balance as the ground seemed to move beneath his feet. Before him the house quivered, then dissolved into streamers of colored smoke. From within the mist he heard Chom's startled roar.

"The meat! The wine! What is happening?"

A gust of air blasted away the mist. Dumarest felt the pressure on his back and turned to see the great bulk of the ship standing at the end of the valley where the cages had hung suspended from their chains. It had been moved to this place by the power of Tormyle.

He heard Karn cry out and saw him running toward the ship. Daroca stared and headed toward him, Chom at his heels. Mayenne passed them both. She was shaking, her face wet with tears.

"Earl! I thought you were dead. When I woke and found you gone I didn't know what to do."

"We looked everywhere," said Daroca. "But I guessed what had happened. Tormyle?"

"Yes."

"A long, cozy chat?" said Chom. "A deal, maybe?"

"We talked, yes."

"About her letting us go?" Chom rubbed his hands. "I wish I could have joined the conversation. A woman like that, crazy for love, how often does a man get such a chance? You took advantage of it, of course. Used your attraction to get us free. A bonus too, perhaps? A cargo of precious metal to help us on our way? Food, at least; that meat was delicious."

Daroca said, "Chom, you disgust me. What happened, Earl? Has anything been decided?"

"I'm not sure."

"But you spoke?"

"Yes, and something was decided, but I am not sure exactly what."

He remembered the girl, the words she had used, the thin spite in her voice at the last, that and the expression of triumph in her eyes. Human emotions for an alien being, too human, and he wondered if it had all been part of an act. There had been something else too, a note of conviction that, in this game they were playing, she would surely win.

And he would help her do it.

Karn came back toward them from the ship. He looked distraught.

"It's still sealed," he said. "I don't understand it. Why should Tormyle have brought the ship here, if it didn't intend us to leave? Damn it, we did what it wanted; why can't it play fair?"

"You credit it with a sense of justice it doesn't possess," said Daroca, "and ethics it couldn't understand. Fair play is a uniquely human attribute. It is a voluntary sense of duty toward another which dictates that it is moral to keep a promise. It isn't even universal. On Krag, for example, there is a culture which has no time for such softness. They think it a mark of insanity. On that world it is normal to lie and cheat and steal."

"Philosophy," Chom sneered. "At a time like this we have to listen to your spouting. You said that I disgusted you, Daroca; well, you sicken me. It is all very well for the wealthy to prate of ethics, but when you've had to snatch a living from the dirt you have no time for such luxuries."

"I hardly call acting like a civilized human being a luxury."

The entrepreneur shrugged. "What does it mean to be civilized? To live in houses and obey laws and consider others? There are harsher jungles in cities than are to be found on primitive worlds. A code of ethics, then? If Tormyle said that all could leave but one and that one was you, Daroca, would you be willing to sacrifice yourself? If it chose another, Earl perhaps, would you insist that he stayed?"

"That is an academic question."

"Is it?" Chom's eyes were shrewd. "Perhaps it is, but there has to be some reason why we still cannot leave. Is that what happened, Earl? Was an offer made?"

"No."

"If it came to that, would you be willing to stay so that we could leave?"

"He wouldn't stay alone," said Mayenne. "I would never leave without him."

"Love," said Chom. "Madness. To hell with it. Karn, let's see if we can get into that ship somehow."

The ports were sealed as they had been before. Dumarest examined them, frowning. Chom and the officer slammed heavy stones against the locks. The metal resisted the impact. Chom swore as a stone split in his hands, and he flung aside the pieces.

"There has to be a way," he stormed. "We are intelligent beings with brains and imagination. A lock is nothing but a strip of metal—surely we can find a way to break it. Karn, can't we get in through the vents?"

"Without tools, no."

"Explosives?" Chom was clutching at straws. "A ram of some kind?"

A hammer was the best they could devise. Dumarest

swung the long shaft made from a sapling he had cut down with his knife. The head was a great stone lashed with strips of cloth. Three times he slammed the weight against the port, denting the metal before the lashings broke and the stone fell to one side. Panting, chest heaving from the effort of manipulating the heavy weight, he watched as Karn checked the lock.

"It's still fast," he said. "I don't think we can get in this way."

"We can try," snapped Chom. "Stop worrying about the damage to your precious vessel and help me repair the hammer."

At Dumarest's side Mayenne said quietly, "It isn't over yet; is it, Earl? If Tormyle was willing for us to leave, why should the ship still be sealed?"

"An oversight, perhaps." He was deliberately casual. "Or perhaps a final test. If we are intelligent we should be able to gain entry."

"We couldn't before."

"Our motives were different. Then we wanted weapons and shelter. Now we are all together and want to leave. Once we hammer in that port our troubles will be over."

He watched as Chom lifted the repaired hammer, thick shoulders heaving as he lifted the weight. He took two steps toward the port and halted, pressing at the air.

Karn said sharply, "What is wrong?"

"I don't know." Chom grunted as he pushed forward, the hammer falling from his hands. "Daroca?"

"It's a barrier," he said wonderingly. "Invisible, soft, but I can't pass. It seems to be all around the ship."

"Not the ship," said Karn. He had been investigating. "About us."

It circled them in a cylinder of confining energy through which they could see the trees, the cliffs and the ship now more remote than ever before. Dumarest looked at the others where they had spread to determine its perimeters. As he watched they fell toward each other, pushed by the relentless pressure he felt at his back, moving to halt in a circle ten feet in diameter. He lifted his hand. Two feet above his head he felt resistance. Stooping, he thrust his knife at the soil. It halted an inch below the surface.

"Earl?" Mayenne's eyes reflected her fear as she caught at his arm. "What is happening?"

"We're in a box."

"Another cage? But why, Earl? What does it hope to gain by tormenting us like this?"

In his ear a voice whispered.

"Earl, my darling, now you will give me the means to make us one. A gift to prove your love. Act quickly or it will be too late to save your friends." A pause and then, *"Your friends, darling—and yourself."*

The wall thickened and became opaque; only the low ceiling remained transparent and permitted the entry of light. Karn moved restlessly about the area.

"I don't like this," he complained. "I don't understand it."

"A test," Daroca mused. "Another device of Tormyle's, but to prove what? Earl, did it give you any clue as to what it intends?"

Dumarest made no answer as he probed at the walls, the ceiling, the soil beneath their feet. The barrier had solidified so that he felt what seemed to be marble, hard, cold to the touch.

Mayenne said, "Look! Something's happening!"

Four feet above the ground, hard against the curved wall, a panel had appeared, an oblong board with fifteen buttons in glowing scarlet each marked with a familiar symbol.

Chom said, "What is it? A combination lock of some kind? Are we supposed to solve the correct sequence in order to get out?"

"Those are the signs of molecular units," said Karn blankly. "I studied biochemistry once. But what are we supposed to do with them? Earl, do you know?"

He knew too well. They were to be arranged, set in the correct sequence for the production of the affinity-twin, the secret he had carried and guarded for so long. Dumarest looked at the bright roof and enclosing walls and recognized the trap for what it was. The enclosed space was small; the air could not last for very long. Sooner or later he would have to operate the lock and release them—and give Tormyle the secret.

To be used—how?

"These buttons are loose," said Daroca. He stood before the panel, touching them, the great ring on his finger glowing with reflected light. "They can be taken out and replaced and, obviously, they have to be rearranged in a certain order. But which?"

He began to move them, setting them in various combinations, his long fingers deft as he worked. Dumarest watched, his face impassive. The chance that Daroca could hit on the correct sequence was remote, but it existed and he could afford to wait.

"This is useless," said Daroca after a while. "There are too many possible combinations. Perhaps we have to set them in an order which has some relevance to biochemistry. Karn, you said you knew something about it. Is there an organism or a creature which would contain these elements in a peculiar order?"

"They are elemental building materials for organic life, but that is all I know." Karn scowled at them, bending close as if to study the markings in greater detail. He moved a few of the buttons at random, then shrugged. "There is nothing I can do to help. You might as well carry on."

"The air's getting thicker," said Chom. "Hurry."

It was imagination, thought Dumarest. The air could not be getting stale so soon. Then something caught at his throat and he heard Karn's incredulous shout.

"Gas! The place is filling with gas!"

Dumarest coughed, retching, his nose and lungs filled with the stench of chlorine. Mayenne doubled and fell, her eyes enormous as she fought to breathe. Daroca fell back from the panel, one of the buttons falling from his hand.

Dumarest scooped it up and faced the panel. He had no time for thought or for the testing of the possibility of a bluff. He was dying, they were all dying, and only his knowledge could save them. The last button clicked home.

The gas vanished. The opaque wall, the glowing ceiling. Only the panel remained, falling to lie face upward on the ground beneath the shimmering sky.

He dived for it, coughing. His eyes streamed as he reached for the buttons and tore them free, scattering them to either side.

Rising, he faced Tormyle.

Chapter

◆ FIFTEEN ◆

She was more beautiful than before, with subtle changes that likened her more than ever to Mayenne. But the Ghenka held a human warmth and slight imperfections while Tormyle was the personification of an ideal.

Chom sucked in his breath in naked admiration.

"My lady," he said. "This is indeed an honor. Never before have I seen a woman so rare."

She ignored the compliment, looking at Dumarest. "I must thank you for your gift, my darling. You see how easily I am pleased? Now, soon, I shall be wholly a woman, one able to bear you sons."

Her voice matched her face and her body, singing like music.

"What does it mean, Earl?" Mayenne came to his side, her hand resting possessively on his arm. She was jealous, hating her rival and afraid of her power. "How can a thing like that bear children?"

"She can't," said Daroca. "She is trying to upset you, Mayenne. Don't let her do it."

"But if she could," mused Chom, "what children they would be. Gods and goddesses to gladden the hearts of all who saw them. My lady, I am a humble person and do not look as fine as I once did, but I would love you forever if you would make me the same offer."

Smiling, she said, "You are not necessary. Soon you will leave. You will all leave, aside from Earl and the woman. I can use her."

As a receptacle for the affinity-twin. Dumarest glanced at the Ghenka, cursing himself for the danger he had put her in, the trap he had been unable to avoid: Tormyle's

149

mind in Mayenne's body, sensing her every emotion, experiencing what it was to be a real woman at last.

He said harshly, "You can't do it, Tormyle. It wouldn't work."

"It will, darling. I have assurance of that."

From whom? Chom? The entrepreneur was standing, puzzled, his face creased in a frown. Karn? He had eyes only for his ship. Daroca? He stood, bland, the hand bearing the ring stroking the side of his face. Himself? But if Tormyle could read his mind, why had it forced him to disclose his knowledge?

Had it been another whim? The desire to show him who was the master? A feminine willfulness induced by the shape it wore?

"No," he said. "I warn you, Tormyle. If you take over Mayenne's body I shall kill it. Do you understand?"

"More than you, I think, Earl," she said lightly. "You love Mayenne. I shall become Mayenne. When I do, you will love me. You will not kill the thing you love. You see, darling? It is all so beautifully simple."

The elementary logic of a child, but in the field of human relationships logic was of minor importance.

"I would kill her," he said flatly. "For her own sake, if nothing else. And you are wrong about me loving you. It wouldn't be like that. I would know that you were an intruder. If you've learned anything about love at all, you must realize that it is more than the desire for a body. There is a heart and mind and personality, a warmth and affinity which defies chemical analysis. She has it and you do not. As I told you before, you aren't a real woman. You are nothing more than a beautiful pretense."

She said coldly, "You could never love a pretense?"

"No."

"You fool!" Her voice was acid, devoid of all affection, the snap of a woman scorned. "Look! See your friends as they really are!"

It was an illusion, thought Dumarest; it could be nothing else. Karn was all metal and crystal, a hard, programmed mechanism with set paths and robotic ways. He gazed at the object of his worship, the world in which he lived and traveled between the stars. Chom was softness and oozing slime, decay and naked greed, feral hunger and a thousand grasping tentacles. The others?

He had the impression of webs, of spider-shapes crouching, scarlet, shaven, robed and bearing a hated seal. Then the moment had passed and all was as before.

Daroca lifted his hand and touched his cheek, his ring spilling fire. "You know. I can tell it by your eyes."

"You and Mayenne," said Dumarest thickly. "Agents of the Cyclan."

"There were agents on every ship in the area. Your probable paths were extrapolated and snares set before you. But you must admit that it was neatly done."

"Very neat," said Dumarest, looking at the girl.

"It was a trap which couldn't fail. I knew you would be suspicious and on your guard, but against a dilletante and a Ghenka?" Daroca shook his head. "Gorlyk was a fool who tried to live like a machine; it was simple to slip a drawing of the seal into his papers. I did not underestimate you, Earl, but with me to feed you scraps of information about Earth, the Ghenka to beguile you and Gorlyk to act as a decoy you didn't stand a chance. On Selegal you would have been taken. We had radioed ahead and men would have been waiting, a ship also to take you to a place from which you could never have escaped. A trap which couldn't fail," he repeated. "If it hadn't been for the beast, the damage, the one thing impossible to anticipate."

Luck, thought Dumarest. The thing which had saved him before, that and quick thinking and his own, natural suspicions. It was the one factor impossible to include in any calculated prediction, the unknown element which defied even the power of the Cyclan.

How much longer could it last?

Mayenne stirred and said, "Earl, you must believe me. It was a job at first; nothing more than that. Just something to be done for pay. But later, when we became close, I would have told you, warned you. You must believe that."

"It doesn't matter."

"It does," she insisted. "Surely you understand. I fell in love with you. Really in love. I was glad when the ship broke down. It meant that I didn't have to betray you and that, at least, we could die together."

"The logic of a woman," said Daroca. "But, then, all women are fools." He glanced to where Tormyle stood, watching, waiting, a peculiar expression in the shining eyes.

"You made a deal with Tormyle," said Dumarest. "Told it about the affinity-twin."

"Yes."

"What about Chom and Karn? Do you intend to kill them?"

"There is no need." Daroca smiled, at ease, in command of the situation. "They have been in stasis since your eyes were opened to the reality of what we are, and have heard nothing of our conversation. The planetary intelligence has been most cooperative since I showed it how to solve the problem of gaining your affection. When I noticed its penchant to adopt a female form I guessed the way things would go. Predicted, rather; even though I am not a cyber I have some skill. You know, Earl, too often we tend to become overawed by sheer size. A brain the size of a world can become just as confused as that of a man. However, that isn't important. What really matters is that I now have the correct sequence of the fifteen units of the affinity-twin. An eidetic memory," he explained. "A glance at the buttons was enough. When I give it to the Cyclan I shall receive my reward. Money, but far more than that. A new, young body in which to enjoy life. A fresh existence."

The bribe no old man could refuse, no matron resist. The bait which would tempt all those holding power into the net of the Cyclan.

Daroca lifted his hand with the flowing ring. "Don't try anything foolish," he warned. "I am armed and will kill if necessary. Now, Tormyle, with your permission, I will leave."

"Wait," said Dumarest.

"Why, Earl?" Her voice had regained its softness. "We don't need them. And you told me that I should always keep a bargain."

"The ship repaired and returned to where it was found," said Daroca, "in return for the secret which will give you everything you could ever want. A fair, exchange, I think." To Mayenne he said, "I must bid you farewell, my dear. Our association has been most profitable. I wish you a happy future."

He smiled and lifted his hand as if to wave.

Dumarest moved. He stooped and lifted the knife from his boot, the blade poised to throw. He saw Daroca's sudden look of fear, the realization that he held knowledge which Dumarest didn't intend he should keep. He had declared himself an enemy and would pay the price.

The ring on his finger spat a thread of fire and something shrilled through the air.

Then the knife was turning, glittering, reaching out to send its point crashing through an eye and into the scheming brain beneath.

"Mayenne!"

She was not hurt. The wild shot had missed and she stood, one hand to her hair, her face pale but very determined. As he watched, her hand plucked a gem from the bronze tresses. Before he could stop her, she had slipped it into her mouth.

"Good-bye, Earl," she whispered. "It is better this way. But I loved you. I loved you so very much, my darling. So very much."

The Ghenka poison carried in a jewel. Quick, clean and painless. At least she had proved the last.

Gently he lowered her to the ground, to the soft grass beneath the scented trees.

He walked through a parkland of emerald softness touched with scented airs, low trees and shrubs heavy with fruit and flowers, vagrant globes drifting in a kaleidoscope of form and brilliance. The playground of a child, the heaven of an artist, a haven of tranquillity and peace.

The ship had gone and with it Karn and Chom, to find themselves in familiar space. The bodies of the dead had vanished and Dumarest was alone with the woman-shape at his side. On the grass her feet were soundless and, when he closed his eyes, she did not exist. There was no warmth of human presence. She was there like the flowers, the trees, and like her they were fabrications of the moment, devices which could own nothing from the past.

She said, "Earl, I do not understand. Why did the woman choose to cease her function?"

The terminology of a machine. Harshly he said, "The girl was human. She killed herself. She died. She did not cease her function."

"But why? It was not the action of a reasoning, sentient creature. To destroy the prime function is totally illogical."

"Humans are not logical, as you should know by now. Mayenne killed herself because she knew what you intended and refused to be dominated."

Perhaps too because she was ashamed, and did not want to meet the accusation in his eyes, the doubts she imagined would be there. She killed herself to save him from an impossible situation, making the only restitution she could.

Bleakly he kicked at a rolling ball of purple and scarlet and smelled the scent of roses as it burst beneath his heel. Three others sprang from where it had broken, darting aside, teasing, offering distraction.

He added, "And because she had pride."

"Pride?"

"Something, perhaps, you wouldn't understand. In every man and woman there is a point beyond which they refuse to go. It can vary in degree and nature, but always it is there—an invisible line at which they call a halt. To pass it would, in their own estimation, make them less than human." He paused and then said, "What do you intend to do with me?"

"You know that, Earl. You have no need to ask."

"I'm not a pet, Tormyle."

"Call me Mayenne. I will be Mayenne and you will love me."

"No," he said flatly. "Can't you realize that your experiment is over? You have learned what you wanted to know and now it is finished. Be logical, Tormyle. There is no one else here now and nothing you can use against me. The girl is dead and, dying, she gave me freedom."

"Call me Mayenne."

"I'll call you what you are. A soulless, heartless machine which has somehow become contaminated with the essence of your discovery. Can't you realize how insane this situation really is? You, a planetary intelligence, demanding affection from me, a human being? Have you no logic? No pride?"

For a long moment she remained silent and then said, "Pride?"

"I'm a man; would it be sane of me to demand love from an ant? I could feed it, play with it, tease it, hurt and kill it, but nothing I could ever do would ever enable it to give me what I demanded. Not even if I fashioned a part of myself into a similar likeness. And there is more. No experimenter should ever allow himself to become involved with his experiment. To do so invalidates his findings."

A floating star tapped him on the cheek, singing with cadences of muted harmony. He knocked it away and it dissolved with a shower of trilling notes. Toys, he thought bitterly; compensation for what he had lost. These were fragile things to titillate the senses and provide a moment of amusement.

She said, "You spoke of sanity, Earl, not pride. Who are you to question my motivations? How can you begin to understand the needs of what I am?"

A prisoner, alone, crying for the touch of life, the common bond of protoplasm. He could understand that: the thing which made men feed scorpions and spiders, talk to them even, consider them as friends, as welcome pets. But never as lovers.

Madness, he thought. It was an aberration which had become an obsession, a blindness which had narrowed the universe down to a single point, a determination which could destroy him at a whim.

He said, "You have chosen to appear as a woman, so let us consider you in those terms. Mayenne is dead, therefore you have no reason to be jealous. The rest? You whine, plead, beg. The cheapest harlot in the lowest house would have more pride. Didn't you learn from Mari how we regard a woman who pays for love?"

He saw the tenseness of her face, the sudden hardness of her eyes and knew that he was hurting her, shocking her. To one side a clump of trees flew into the air, falling with a crash, a shower of dirt and stones.

"Stop it, Earl."

He laughed, deliberately feeding her rage, edging his voice with sneering contempt.

"Does the truth hurt, Tormyle? I thought that was what you valued: the cold, naked truth. Perhaps you can't stand it any longer. You've been alone too long, grown too conceited. Or perhaps you've become insane. Is that it?"

A chasm gaped, ran to within inches of his feet and then closed with a snap.

She said, "I could destroy you, Earl, and unless you stop talking this way I will."

"You could kill me," he admitted. "But what would that prove? That you are stronger than I am? We already know that. That you are more clever? I think not. If you destroy me, you will only have proved one thing—that you have failed. It would mean that you have become a petulant, stupid, illogical entity unable to either appreciate or understand a simple problem in human relationships; that your experiment has taught you nothing and that all the people you destroyed died for no real purpose." He felt his anger rising, his voice growing harsh. "Mari and the brothers. Lolis and that poor fool Gorlyk. Mayenne!"

"You hate me," she said wonderingly. "You really hate me."

He looked down at his hands; they were clenched, the knuckles white. Thickly he said, "I hate you for what you've done. If you were real, I would have killed you long ago."

"As you did the man?"

"And for the same reason. He deserved to die. But I don't have to kill you, Tormyle. You are destroying yourself. You have become infected with emotion and it will ruin your mind. Once that is gone, what is left? An endless quest for what you can never have. A search for contentment you can never know. I feel almost sorry for you. Pity you."

"Pity?"

"A human emotion which you have not yet displayed. Charity, consideration, concern for the weak and helpless. One day, perhaps, you will need it."

She stood very still, very beautiful in her resemblance to Mayenne, the light from the sky turning her hair into burnished flame. Then she changed a little, an inward thing, a hardness, a clinical detachment.

"Pity," she said. "An incredible concept—that *you* could pity *me*."

He tensed, waiting.

"Pity," she said again. "Pity!"

Then she was gone and with her went the trees, the grass, the drifting toys. Dumarest staggered as the ground became uneven beneath his feet, stones and boulders and pitfalls to every side. Above, the sky grew dark, the shimmer vanishing even as he watched. Air roared as it gushed into space, lifting a cloud of debris of which he was a part.

He was thrown high into the emptiness of space where only death could be waiting.

There was a sun smoldering low on the horizon, dullness mottled with flaring patches and edged with a spiked corona. Dumarest stared at it for a long time from where he lay, conscious only of the throb at his temple, the rawness of his chest and lungs.

He remembered the gusting roar of air as it streamed into space. The debris, the rocks and stones carried upward on the blast, the splintering impact as something had crashed against his skull. Tormyle must have saved him, flicking him casually to where he lay as a man might flick an ant with the tip of a finger. Pity? Concern? Charity? Who could tell? No matter what the reason, the planetary intelligence had saved his life.

He sat upright, fighting a wave of nausea. The side of his head was crusted with dried blood. More blood stained his lips and chin, marring the neck and front of his blouse, coming from the capillaries which had burst as the pressure had fallen and he'd tried to breathe in the void.

Rising, he stared at where he had landed. On all sides stretched desert, a sea of fine golden sand. He had no way of telling if the sun were rising or setting. If the first, he would be caught beneath its heat to die of thirst and exhaustion; if the latter, he could easily freeze. Nowhere could he see any sign of habitation.

The perversity of a woman, he thought. Tormyle could have set him down in the heart of a city or on a world

rich with water and growing things. At least he was alive
and he should not complain.

Wetting a finger, he held it high. There was no breeze.
One direction was as good as any, but only the right one
would offer hope of life. Shrugging, he began to walk
away from the sun.

An hour later he came to a road running like a thread
of silver over the desert. Now his choice of direction narrowed to a single alternative. Left or right? As he hesitated, he heard a thin sound from the left. A bee-hum
which slowly grew louder and resolved itself into a
wheeled vehicle powered by a noisy engine. A man sat in
the front. He wore rough clothing, a beard and a broad,
floppy hat made of woven straw. He slowed, halting as he
came level with Dumarest.

"You in trouble, mister?"

Dumarest nodded, finding it hard to talk. He gestured
toward his mouth. "Water?"

"Sure." The man handed over a canteen, watching as
Dumarest drank and rinsed his head and face. "Man, you
look like hell! You lost?"

"You could say that."

"Want a lift?"

The seat was hard, a board covered only by a thin blanket, but Dumarest relaxed on it as if he sat on cushions.
Leaning back, he examined the sky. It had grown darker,
pricked with scant stars.

"Can't imagine how you got out here," said the driver.
"There isn't a settlement for miles. If I hadn't come along,
you could have died. It's a bad place to be at night. Anyway, I can take you to town."

"Is it a big place?"

"Fair. Not big enough for ships, of course; they land on
the southern plain." He was curious. "What happened?
You been dumped, maybe?"

"Yes," said Dumarest.

"Nice going." The man was bitter. "The bucks think it
smart to take a man out, beat him up and leave him in
the middle of nowhere. You been playing around where
you shouldn't?"

"I upset someone," said Dumarest.

"A woman?"

More than a woman, but he could never explain. He sat back, feeling the ache, the strain of past activity, the reaction at his near-brush with final extinction. But there were compensations. He had escaped the Cyclan and not even its most skilled adepts could have predicted where Tormyle had placed him. The pattern had been broken. Now they had to search for one man in an entire galaxy, not an individual following probable paths.

"A woman, mister?" The driver was eager for conversation. "She had you dumped?"

Dumarest was cautious; the mores of this world were unknown to him. "Not exactly. I had an argument with someone. You get many ships landing here?"

"An argument, eh?" The driver sucked at his teeth. "Those damned bucks! Lording it over everyone they meet. You ought to be careful, mister. The next time you might not be so lucky."

"There won't be a next time," said Dumarest. "How about those ships? You get many?"

"A fair amount. You got money?"

"I can work. I'll get the money."

He would get the money and the passage on the ships which would take him where he wanted to go: to where Earth waited to be found.

For
Philip Harbottle

JONDELLE

CHAPTER

ONE

Akon Batik was an old man with a seamed face and slanting eyes flecked with motes of amber. His lobeless ears were set close to his rounded skull and his thin mouth curved downward as if he had tasted the universe and found it not to his liking. He wore an embroidered robe of black and yellow, the wide sleeves falling low over his hands. A round cap of matching color was adorned by a single jewel which caught the light and reflected it in splinters of lambent ruby. Casually he stirred the heap of crystals lying before him on the solid desk of inlaid woods. His finger was thin, hooked, the nail long and sharply pointed. At its touch the crystals made a dry rustling as they shifted over the sheet of paper on which they lay.

"From Estale?"

"Yes," said Dumarest. "From Estale."

"A hard world," mused the jeweler. "A bleak place with little to commend it aside from the workings which produce its wealth. A single vein of lerad in which are to be found the chorismite crystals." He touched them again, watching as they turned, his eyes remote. "I understood the company mining them was jealous of its monopoly."

"It is."

"And yet you have a score of them."

It was more of a question than a statement but one which Dumarest had no intention of answering. He leaned back in his chair looking again at the paneled walls, the painted ceiling, the rugs of price which lay scattered on the floor. Light shone in a yellow flood from recessed lanterns, soft, gentle, lulling with implied warmth and comfort. It was hard to remember that this room lay within a fortress of stone, harder still to bear in mind that not all the defenses were outside. There would be men, perhaps, watching, electronic devices certainly, means to protect and to kill if the need arose. Akon Batik had not grown old in his trade by neglecting elementary precautions.

5

He said, "Why did you bring them to me?"

"You have a reputation," said Dumarest. "You will buy what is offered. Of course, if you are not interested in the crystals I will waste no more of your time."

"Did I say that?" Again the long nail touched the little heap. "But it is in my nature to be curious. I wonder how a man could manage to elude the guards and the inspection at the field on Estale. A man working the vein could no doubt manage to retain a few crystals—but to leave with them?"

"They are genuine."

"I believe you, but my eyes are not as young as they were and it would be well to make certain." The jeweler switched on a lamp and bathed the surface of his desk with invisible ultraviolet. The crystals blazed with a shimmering kaleidoscope of color, rainbows painting the seamed cheeks, the slanted eyes, glowing from the dark wood of the paneled walls. For a long moment he stared at them, then switched off the lamp. "Chorismite," he said. "There can be no doubt."

Dumarest said, "You will buy them?"

The crux of the matter, but Akon Batik was not to be hurried. He leaned back, eyes thoughtful as he studied his visitor. A hard man, he decided, tall, lean, somber in his clothing. Pants tucked into high boots, the hilt of a knife riding above the right. A tunic with long sleeves caught at the wrists and high about the throat. Clothing of a neutral gray and all of it showing the marks of hard usage, the plastic scratched and scuffed with minor attritions. His eyes lifted to the face, studying the deep-set eyes, the determined set of the jaw, the firm mouth which could easily become cruel. The face of a man who had early learned to survive without the protection of House or Guild or Organization.

A traveler. A man who moved from world to world in search of something, or perhaps because he was unable to rest. A wanderer who had seen a hundred worlds and found none he could call his own.

Quietly he said, "Estale is a bad world and not one a traveler should visit. There would be little opportunity for such a man to work and collect the price of a passage. You agree?"

There were many such, dead-end planets, end-of-the-line worlds devoid of industry, poverty-stricken cultures in which a stranded traveler stood no chance of making an escape. Dumarest had seen too many of them. Bleakly he nodded.

"On Estale you work in the mine or you do not work," continued the jeweler. "And, once you sign the contract, escape is rare. The pay is low, prices high, a worker remains constantly in debt. Yet a shrewd man could beat the system. A man who saved every coin, who indulged in no pleasures, and who wasted no opportunity in order to build his stake. A man who would bide his time, work out his contract, and leave without suspicion." He paused and added, softly, "And who would suspect that a man riding Low would have a fortune hidden within his person."

And his visitor had ridden Low; the signs were plain. No body fat, a drawn appearance about the eyes, the hands thinner than nature intended. The result of riding doped, frozen, and ninety percent dead in caskets designed for the transportation of beasts. Risking the fifteen percent death rate for the sake of cheap travel.

"Will you buy the crystals?"

"I will give you one thousand stergals for them," said Akon Batik flatly, and translated the sum into more recognizable terms. "That is the cost of two High passages."

Dumarest frowned. "They are worth more."

"Far more," agreed the jeweler. "But commissions will have to be paid and you are selling, not buying. My profit will be little more than what I pay you—but you need have no fears once you leave my house. A thousand stergals. You agree?"

He smiled as Dumarest nodded, a quirk of the lips, more a grimace than an expression of amusement. Yet his voice held satisfaction as he said, "The money will be given to you as you leave. And now, a glass of wine to seal the bargain. You have no objection?"

It was tradition, Dumarest guessed, a ritual which politeness dictated he should share. And, perhaps, things could be learned over the wine.

It was dark, thick, and heavy with a cloying sweetness, pungent with the scent of spice which warmed throat and stomach. Cautiously he sipped and then said, casually, "You have lived long and are wise. Tell me: have you ever heard of a planet called Earth?"

"Earth?" Akon Batik stared thoughtfully at his wine.

"An odd name for a world, but no, I have not. A place you seek?"

"A world I intend to find."

"May good fortune attend you. Do you intend to remain long on Ourelle?"

"I don't know," said Dumarest cautiously. "It depends."

"On whether or not you find things to attract you?" The jeweler sipped at his wine. "I asked because it is barely possible that I may be able to find you suitable employment. Men who can acquire chorismite are rare. It could be that I will have a proposition to make you at some later time. Naturally, it will be of a profitable kind. You would not be averse?"

"I would be interested," said Dumarest flatly. He sipped again at his wine, wondering at the other's interest. A man like Akon Batik would not have a need for men to do his bidding; certainly he would not have to rely on strangers no matter how skillful they appeared to be. Setting down the goblet, he said, "I thank you for the wine and your courtesy. And now, the money?"

"It's waiting for you at the door." The jeweler pursed his thin mouth. "You are a stranger on Ourelle, am I correct?"

"Yes."

"It is a strange world and perhaps I could save you misfortune. If you are tempted to seek games of chance, do not play in the Stewpot, the Pavilion of Many Delights, or the Purple Flower. You may win, but you will not live to count your gains. The House of the Gong is as fair as any and you will be safe from violence."

Dumarest said, "You own it?"

"Naturally, and if you are eager to lose your money, I may as well regain what I have paid. Another thing: Ourelle is not as other worlds. If you remain in the city, that need not concern you; but if you wish to explore, take nothing for granted. You have plans?"

"To look around. To see that is to be seen. You have a museum? A scientific institute?"

The jeweler blinked his surprise. "We have a House of Knowledge. The Kladour. You will recognize it by the fluted spire. It is the pride of Sargone. And now, if you would care for more wine? No? Then our business is completed. If the need arises, I shall contact you. In the meantime, good fortune attend each step you take."

"And may your life be full of gladness," responded Dumarest, and knew by the sudden shift of light in the slanted eyes that he had enhanced his standing in the jeweler's estimation. A man who insisted on wine to complete a transaction would be sensitive to such courtesies.

A moving arrow of dull green guided him through a labyrinth of passages to the outer door where a squat man handed him a bag of coins, waiting phlegmatically as Dumarest counted them. The money safe in his pocket, he stepped into the street, blinking at the comparative brilliance of the late afternoon. An emerald sun hung low in the sky, painting the blank facades of the buildings with a dozen shades of green; dark in shuttered windows and enigmatic doors, bright and pale on parapets and trailing vines heavy with blossoms of blue, gold, and scarlet. Above the roofs, seemingly close, he could see a peculiar spire twisting as it rose to terminate in a delicate shaft topped by a gilded ball. The Kladour, he guessed, and made his way toward it.

In Sargone no street could be called straight. Every alley, avenue, road, and byway was curved, a crescent, the part of circle, the twist of a spiral, all wending in baffling contradiction as if designed by the undulations of a gigantic serpent. A guide had taken him to the jeweler's house, another would have taken him to the Kladour, but the street had been empty and the spire deceptively close. Dumarest had trusted to his own ability and soon found that he was completely lost.

He halted, trying to orient himself. The sun was where it should be, the spire too, but it was more distant now and the street in which he stood wended in the wrong direction. Traffic was light and pedestrians few. An alley gave onto a more populous street which irritatingly sent him away from his objective.

A man rubbed his chin, his eyes sharp as Dumarest asked directions.

"The Kladour? Hell, man, you won't find nothing there. You want the Narn. Everything to satisfy a man in the Narn. Girls, wine, gambling, sensitapes, analogues—you name it and it's to be had. Fights too. You like to watch a good fight? Ten-inch blades and to the death. Tell you what—you hire me and I'll take you to where you want to go."

A tout eager to make a commission. Dumarest said, "Forget it. I want the Kladour."

"First right, second right, first left, third left, straight ahead. If you change your mind and hit the Narn, ask for Jarge Venrush. If you want action, I can show you all you can use. Remember the name. You'll find me in the Disaphar."

Dumarest nodded and moved on. The second on the right was a narrow alley thick with emerald shadows, a gash cut between high buildings and prematurely dark. He trod softly, keeping to the center, ears strained with instinctive caution. Something rattled ahead and he tensed as a shape darted from behind a can. A small animal seeking its prey; lambent eyes glowed as he passed where it crouched, feeding. Beyond it, the the left-hand turn showed an opening little wider than the alley.

He slowed as he neared it, his skin prickling with primitive warning. It was too dark, too convenient for any who might choose to lie in wait, and the tout could have sent him into a trap. Sargone was a city no better than any other. It had its dark corners and own species of savage life. Men who lived on helpless prey. Robbers and those who would find it more convenient to kill from a distance.

Dumarest halted, then turned to retrace his steps, halting again as he heard the cry.

It was high, shrill, more of a scream than a shout, and it came from the opening behind. He spun, one hand dropping to the knife in his boot, the nine-inch blade glowing emerald as he lifted it from its sheath, faded sunlight bright on needle point and razor edge. Two steps and he had reached the opening, was racing down the alley as the cry came again. A woman, he thought, a girl, then corrected the impression as he saw the tableau ahead. Not a girl, a child, a small boy pressed tight against a wall.

He wasn't alone. Beside him stood a man, thickset, his hair a tangled darkness, his face drawn and reflecting his fear. His hands were clenched in baffled helplessness as he faced the three standing close. They were decked and masked, glittering tunics bright with a variety of symbols, the masks grotesque with beak and horn. Camouflage or protection—it was impossible to see what lay beneath the masks, but Dumarest had no doubt as to what they intended. Robbers, armed with knives, willing and perhaps eager to use them against defenseless victims. To cut and stab and slash in a fury of blood-lust. To kill the man and perhaps the boy. Degenerates out for a little fun. The scum inevitable in any civilization.

One turned as he approached. Dumarest saw the mask, the glitter of eyes, the sweep of the blade held like a sword in a gloved hand. It lanced forward in an upswinging thrust which would have disemboweled an uprotected belly. Dumarest jumped to one side, his own blade whining as it cut through the air, the edge hitting, biting, breaking free as it slashed through the hand just behind the fingers. Fingers and knife fell in a fountain of blood, the blade swinging up again in a return slash at the lower edge of the mask, the tip finding and severing the soft tissues of the throat.

Without pause, he sprang at the nearest of the other two, left arm blocking the defending blade, his own point lifting to aim at an eye, to thrust, twist, and emerge dripping with fresh blood.

"Hold it!" The third man had retreated, dropping his knife, his hand now heavy with the weight of a gun. "You fool," he said. "You interfered. No one asked you to do that. All we wanted was the kid. You could have walked past and forgotten what you'd seen. Instead you had to act the hero. Well, now you're going to pay for it." He poised the weapon. "In the belly," he said. "A hole burned right through your guts. You'll take a long time to die and scream every minute of it. Damn you! Here it comes!"

Dumarest moved, leaping to one side, his arm reaching back, than forward, the knife spinning from his hand. He saw the mask, the gun, the ruby guide-beam of the laser, and caught the stench of seared plastic and metal. Pain tore at his side and then the beam had gone, the gun swinging upward, the mask, the hilt of the knife protruding like an ugly growth from the flesh beneath.

Then pain became a consuming nightmare.

CHAPTER

TWO

He looked to be six pushing seven, a stocky lad with a mane of yellow hair and eyes deep-set and vividly blue. His back and shoulders were straight, his stomach still rotund from early fat, his hands dimpled, his mouth a soft rose. He stood beside the bed, very solemn, his words very precise.

"My name is Jondelle. I must thank you for having saved me when we were attacked in the city."

Big words for a small boy, thought Dumarest, but, equally solemn, he said, "It was my pleasure to be of service. Can you tell me what happened?"

"After you were shot?"

"Yes."

"Elray saved you. He helped you to our raft and brought you back home. I didn't forget to bring your knife. Do you want it now?"

"Please," said Dumarest.

"I've cleaned it," said the boy. "It was all sticky with blood but I washed it and polished it. Have you used it to kill many men?"

"No more than I had to."

"I saw how you threw it. Will you teach me how to throw a knife?"

"Perhaps." Dumarest sat upright on the cot. He was naked beneath the sheets, a transparent bandage tight against the left side of his body. Beneath the covering he could see the flesh almost totally healed. Hormones, he thought, or perhaps even slow-time, the magic chemical which speeded the metabolism so that a man lived a day in a few minutes. But he doubted it. The use of slow-time brought ravenous hunger and he did not feel that. And there were no marks on his arms to show the use of intravenous feeding.

"Makgar nursed you," said the boy. "She is very good at that, but I think Weemek helped."

12

"Weemek?"

"A friend who visits us sometimes. If you stay here, you will meet him. I call it a 'him,' but I can't be sure. He isn't human, you see."

Dumarest didn't, but he didn't correct the boy. He leaned back, faintly amused and more than a little puzzled. The lad spoke too precisely for his apparent age as if he'd had intensive schooling during his formative years. Or perhaps it was normal for childern of this culture to be so forward.

He said, "May I have my knife now?"

It was clean as the boy had said, the edge freshly honed, the steel polished.

"And my clothes?"

"Makgar has those. She has refurbished them. Is there anything else you want?"

Information, but that could wait. Dumarest shook his head, and as the boy left looked around. He was in a room made of slabbed stone, the ceiling low and heavily beamed, the floor of wood smoothed to a natural polish. Rugs softened the spartan simplicity, a few prints made bright patches of color against the walls, and a broad window was bright with a pale green light. The sun was high over rolling plains and fields thick with crops. Trees stood at the crest of a distant ridge and a narrow river wended down a slope to vanish in a curve which led beyond the house.

A farmhouse, he guessed. The center of an agricultural complex. Somewhere would be barns for livestock, silos for storage, sheds for machinery. Other houses also for the workers. He opened the window and breathed deeply of the air. It was warm, scented with unfamiliar odors, rich and invigorating. Suddenly he was hungry.

"You shouldn't be up," said a voice behind him. "Get back into bed now."

He turned and looked at the woman. She was tall, with a closely cut mane of dark hair, her dark eyes holding a hint of amusement and something of anticipation. Her figure was full and lush beneath a dress of some brown fabric belted at the waist. He feet were bare in leather sandals, her hands broad, the fingers long and tapered. The hands of a sculpter, he thought, or those of a surgeon. Unabashed by his nakedness, he stood and met her eyes.

"Bed," she repeated. "Immediately."

"You are Makgar?"

"Yes, but I am also your doctor, your nurse, and your hostess. Also I am very grateful and would hate to see you suffer a relapse. If it hadn't been for the protective mesh buried in your clothing, the beam of that laser would have killed you. As it was the heat was dissipated just enough to slow penetration. Now please get into bed."

He obeyed, conscious of a sudden weakness.

"How long have I been here?"

"Ten days. You lost a great deal of blood, but that I was able to replace. However, you were greatly debilitated, no fat and showing signs of long-standing malnutrition. I've had you under hypnotic sedation and used fast-acting hormones to promote rapid healing. I would have used slow-time, but, frankly, you were in no condition to take it." She paused, hesitating, and he guessed at her question.

"Six months working in a mine and skimping on food," he said dryly. "Then riding Low. It isn't the best way to stay in condition."

"I wondered," she said. "Thank you for confiding in me."

"You are the doctor—you need to know." He added, quietly, "You mentioned hypnotic sedation."

"A technique of my own. You felt no pain and were able to eat at regular intervals, but your privacy remained inviolate, Earl." She smiled at his expression. "Some things I had to know—your name for one. For therapeutic reasons, not official. We don't bother with such things here at Relad."

"The farm?"

"The area. At times you became a little delirious and the use of your name enabled me to strengthen your libido. Anyway, that is all over now. Good food and rest will make you as good as new."

"As my clothes?"

"You know?"

"The boy told me that you were refurbishing them. A big word for a small boy to use."

"He is a very unusual boy." She swallowed and added, "I am not good at displaying emotion, my training perhaps, but there it is. And some things are impossible to put into words. But know this. Anything I have, anything you want, is yours for what you did. Had Jondelle been taken—"

"He wasn't," said Dumarest.

"Elray was helpless. You mustn't blame him. He would die for the boy but—"

"He isn't a killer," said Dumarest flatly. "And against three men with knives what could he have done? Died, perhaps, and would that have saved the boy?"

"You saved him. Are you a killer?" She didn't wait for an answer. "No, you may have killed in your time but only in order to survive. And you are no stranger to violence; the scars on your body told me that. Knife scars, Earl—there can be no mistake. I've seen them before on men who fought in the ring."

Fought and killed to the roaring of a blood-hungry crowd. He smelled again the scent of blood, the taint of the air heavy with anticipation, saw the animal stare from civilized masks as cultured men and women screamed for violent death. The catharsis demanded by societies grown decadent, the chance for a traveler to make a stake, a young man a reputation.

"A man accustomed to violence," she said softly. "But more than that. Elgar told me of your speed, the incredible way in which you moved. To throw a knife as fast as a man can pull a trigger! To send it across twenty feet before the beam could reach you. Had it been less, you would not have been burned. You are no ordinary man, Earl Dumarest, but I thank all the gods that ever were that you were at that place at that time."

Her voice betrayed her. Impassive though her face remained, the tones carried a vibrant note of raw emotion. Another woman would have burst into tears, caught his hand, perhaps, even showed signs of hysteria. And it was more than simple gratitude. It was as if a terrible fear had been realized and the reaction remained, all the more strong because of thoughts of what might have been.

He knew that he could reach for her, touch her, and whatever he desired would be freely given. Instead he said, "Those men wanted to take the boy. Do you know why?"

She drew a deep, shuddering breath. "Ransom, perhaps?"

"Not unless you are rich," he said dryly. "Are you?"

"We have the farm and little else. You carry more money than we own."

"Assets, then? Is the farm of value?"

"Land is cheap on Ourelle. We have food and live well, but that is about all."

"Enemies?"

"No. None that I know of."

He said, flatly, "Someone for some reason wanted to kidnap your boy. He is your son, I take it?"

"The child of my body," she said. "Yes."

"Those men weren't there by accident," he said. "They knew what they wanted and where to find it. Does Elray often take the lad into the city?"

"No. Not often. He went to collect a part for one of the machines and thought Jondelle would be interested. They had walked for a while, at random, sight-seeing and visiting the Kladour. A normal day for any man to spend with a young boy. And then, as they were making toward the place where they had left the raft, those men attacked them. They must have intended robbery. When you appeared the one with the gun must have hoped you would believe him. A warning perhaps."

"Perhaps," he said.

"It had to be that. Why should anyone want to steal a boy? How would they know where to find him if they did? It was a coincidence—it had to be."

Dumarest doubted it, but one thing was obvious. It was a subject she had no wish to discuss with a stranger and it was none of his business. And he had no desire to become involved. The boy was not alone. He had his mother and a man who appeared to be his father, though the fact hadn't been clearly stated. He had a farm on which to live and there would be retainers of a kind, workers, those dependent on the owners, obligated to defend both life and property. The protection of a House, small though that House might be. And here, at least, he was isolated from the dangers of the city.

More protection than Dumarest had ever known. More comfort and security and certainly more love. He leaned back on the pillows, dreaming, remembering a time best forgotten when hunger had been a constant companion and rocks and stones his only playthings.

Makgar said, "You are tired. The boy woke you too soon and your wound is far from healed. I shall send you food and you will rest and soon will be well again. Need I say that you are welcome to stay as long as you wish?"

"You are kind."

"Not kind, selfish. You give this place strength and I—" She broke off, then resumed in a more casual tone. "I am a doctor and do not want to see my work wasted. You are ready to eat?"

There were steaks, thick and almost raw, seared on beds of charcoal, served with eggs and mounds of butter. He ate and slept and woke to eat again, a high-protein diet designed to restore lost energy and to replace the fat consumed during the past few months. In two days he was on his feet, taking long walks over the fields and working at laborious tasks in order to tone muscle and sinew. And with him, almost constantly, was the boy.

He was very solemn, dressed in dark brown pants and shirt, thick boots on his small feet, and a loop of beads hung around his neck. They were large, each the size of a small egg, brightly colored, and strung on a length of wire with the strong metal knotted between each bead. Seeds, thought Dumarest, the product of some exotic plant, attractive to the eye and amusing to a child. Yet at times it was hard to think of Jondelle as a child. His words were too precise, his manner too adult.

"How do you make sure the blade hits in the same place every time?" he asked as he watched Dumarest chop a log. "When I tried to do it, I hit all over the place."

"You aim with the haft of the ax," said Dumarest. "The point near your hands. The blade follows."

"Can you throw an ax as you can a knife?"

Dumarest glanced at a trunk lying several yards to one side. He hefted the ax, feeling its balance, then threw it with a sudden release of energy. The blade bit deeply into the wood.

"I wish I could do that," said the boy. "Will you teach me?"

"You can't be taught. You can be shown, then the rest is up to you. It's a matter of balance and judging distance. That and plenty of practice."

"The knife, then. Will you help me to learn how to throw a knife? To use one?"

"Your father should do that."

"Elray isn't my father. He married Makgar, but that is all."

It was confirmation of what Dumarest had suspected. Two dark-haired, brown-eyed people could not have a blond, blue-eyed son, yet even so Elray was in the position of a parent. It was his duty to teach the essentials to the boy in his charge.

Jondelle said, shrewdly, "We could be attacked again. It would help if I knew how to defend myself. Please teach me how to use a knife."

"You expect to be attacked again?"

"I don't know. But if it did happen, then I want to be able to do as you did. Elray won't teach me. He doesn't like violence. He says that civilized people don't need to use it."

"He is right," said Dumarest flatly.

"But if a civilized man met one who wasn't?"

A question too shrewd for any young boy to ask . . . yet what was age when it came to understanding? At six, Dumarest had been hunting game with a crude sling, with hunger the penalty should he miss. At seven— He drew a deep breath, reluctant to remember.

"You hold a knife so." He demonstrated. "Thumb to the blade, the point held upward. Don't try to stab. You could miss or hit a bone or wedge it in some way and so disarm yourself. You use the edge to cut, so." He swept the blade through the air, turning it so that the late afternoon sun shone on the point and edge. "And if you have to defend yourself, never hesitate. Go in fast and do what has to be done. Don't be afraid of getting hurt, accept the fact that you may have to take a minor wound, and try not to be afraid. Fear will slow you down and give your opponent a chance to get you before you can get him. Aim for the eyes and then—"

"That will be enough!" Elray had approached unseen, his boots silent on the soft dirt. He stood, his thickset body tense with rage, his face mottled with anger. "Jondelle, go into the house!"

Dumarest watched him go, looked at the watching eyes of a cluster of workers, small men with lank hair and a subdued manner, their women peering from the windows of the shacks clustered around the house.

"You are our guest," said Elray tightly. "But even if you were my brother, I would never allow what I have just seen. What kind of man are you to teach a boy how to maim and kill? To use weapons of destruction? Is this how you repay my hospitality?"

Dumarest looked at the knife in his hand, the whiteness

of the knuckles, and the trembling of the point. Quickly
he sheathed the blade.

"We owe you much," continued Elray. "I admit it.
But some things I will not permit. Jondelle is a child and
should be treated like one."

"He is a man," said Dumarest harshly. "A small one
and young, but a man just the same. He will grow and
meet others who did not have such squeamish guardians.
If they think him soft, they will push and he will have
no choice but to yield. He will lose his pride or, if he
has it, will make a stand. And, dying, he will not thank
you for the things you failed to teach."

He turned before the other could answer, striding
quickly past the watching figures, heading for the distant
ridge and the trees which laced the sky. Beyond lay more
open ground, undulating plains unmarked by road or trail,
the river a winding streak of pale emerald edged with
clustered rushes. To the north mountains loomed, their
summits capped with snow. A pastoral scene of peace and
beauty, an oasis of tranquillity in which a man could sit
and dream way his life. But beyond it, somewhere, lay the
city and the field and the ships which would take him back
into space and to other worlds. His world, perhaps . . .
already he had lingered too long.

It was late when he returned, the sky a glitter of stars,
of curtains of shimmering brilliance, of globes and clusters
and sheets of glowing luminescence. The normal night-
scene of any planet close to the heart of the galaxy, the
Center where suns were close and world teemed in profusion.

Lights shone in the house and clustered shacks and
the scent of cooking was heavy on the air. He heard voices
as he passed through the main door, and paused at the
sound of his name. Elray and the woman, he guessed,
talking about the stranger they had taken into their home.
He paused, listening.

"No!" Elray was firm. "I won't have it. Knives at
his age. It's indecent!"

"Earl is a man who has lived hard. He has different
values from your own." She paused and then added, softly,
"If he hadn't, would you be sitting here now?"

"Are you reminding me again of what you choose to
call my weakness?"

"It isn't weak to be gentle, Elray, but sometimes it can

be fatal. I want Jondelle to be strong. To stand on his own feet and to rely on nobody. Damn it, man! I want him to survive!"

Her cry came from the heart, the eternal cry of a mother afraid for her child. Dumarest felt its intensity, and so did Elray. When he next spoke, his voice was more subdued.

"I care for the boy, Makgar; you know that. It's as if he were my own. But what do we really know about Dumarest? A stranger. A traveler and perhaps more than that. The attack could have been planned, his intervention also. All of it designed to get him where he is at this very moment. And he is too close to Jondelle. The boy won't stay away from him, always he seems to be at his side, talking, listening, learning perhaps, or perhaps it is more than that. How can we be sure?"

"Three men dead, Elray. Dumarest badly wounded—that's how we can be sure. And—"

"Yes?"

"Their closeness worries you?"

"It does."

"And you can't guess the reason? Her voice held a tender note of understanding. "A traveler, you called him, a wanderer without a home or family to call his own. A man who, perhaps, yearns for a son. A boy to teach and train and make into an image of himself. I've watched them together and I know something of the loneliness he must feel. I had him under hypnotic sedation, don't forget, and in that condition there can be no deception. Dumarest is no enemy. He is a very lonely person who is looking for something. Searching for it. Perhaps, subconsciously, he may think that he has found it."

"The boy," said Elray thickly. "A surrogate son. And you? Are you eager to become his wife?"

Her amusement was genuine. "Elray? Are you jealous?"

"Can you deny it?"

"You're talking nonsense."

"You don't deny it," he said bleakly. "You can't, I've watched and I know."

Dumarest turned and moved softly through the door back into the star-shot night. He coughed, scuffed his boot, and slammed the panel hard against the wall as he reentered the house. Light shone through the open door of the room in which Elray and the woman sat at the table, bread, wine, the remains of a meal scattered before them.

Entering, he said, "It is time that I moved on. If you could give me a lift to the city, I would be grateful."

"You're leaving?" He caught the note of anguish in the woman's voice, saw the sudden look of relief in the man's eyes.

"Yes. There are things I have to do."

"But you aren't fit yet." Makgar rose to close fast the door and stood before him, the rise and fall of her breasts prominent beneath the fabric of her gown. "Your wound isn't wholly healed and you need more food and rest."

"I can get both in the city."

"I will be going there tomorrow," said Elray quickly. "You can ride with me."

"But—" With an effort she controlled herself. "I think you are being foolish," she continued flatly. "That is my opinion as a doctor. There is still the danger of complications from your wound. In five days I think you could walk to the city, but, at this time, to ride would be to take a foolish risk."

"There are doctors in the city," said Elray. "And the raft is stable. We will travel slow and in comfort." He added, "Stop fussing. Makgar. Earl is a grown man and knows what he wants to do."

"Yes," she said dully. "I supose that he does." Her eyes fell to the food on the table, lifted to meet Dumarest's level stare. "You haven't eaten," she accused. "We waited, but you didn't arrive and so—" Her hand made a little gesture. "At least you will eat before you go to your room?"

"Yes," he said. "I will eat."

CHAPTER

THREE

There were small sounds, the creak of timbers, the rustle of a leaf, the settling of boards and stairs. The starlight shone too brightly through the window and the air seemed to be filled with a restless urgency. Dumarest stirred, uneasy on the soft bed, instinct keeping him aware. He was leaving, a decision had been made, there was nothing more to do now but wait. Yet his uneasiness persisted and he could not sleep.

Rising, he crossed to the window and stared at the empty scene outside, the river a soft band of silver, the grass so dark as to be almost black. A few clouds drifted in the sky to the impact of a gentle wind. Softly he padded to the door and stood, listening. A murmur drifted to his ears as of voices wrapped and muffled and very distant. Dressing, he stepped outside the room and crept down the stairs. The murmur grew as he neared the door, strengthening as he opened it. A few lights shone in the clustered shacks and the sound grew louder. A chant, he realized, voices raised in muted harmony. A paean or an appeal—it was impossible to tell which. It rose and then died with shocking abruptness as a door opened to emit a flood of light. Framed in the opening Makgar stood, turned to face the interior from which came the thin, telltale cry of a newborn child.

"He will be well," she said to those within. "He will grow strong and tall and run like the wind. Your son will bring you joy."

The chant rose again as she closed the door and moved across the courtyard. She halted with a gasp as she saw Dumarest, one hand flying to her throat. She wore a robe loosely tied at the front, open at breast and thigh to reveal naked flesh. A thing quickly donned, he guessed, in order to answer an urgent summons.

"Earl! Is that you?"

"I heard the chant and came to see what caused it."

22

"A birth," she said. "There was some difficulty and they sent for me. A simple thing, but they are a simple people and cannot cope with the unexpected. Always they have to appeal to someone or something. Gods, spirits, even the wind and stars. Inbreeding has leeched all initiative out of their character, but they make good and docile workers."

"Where did you find them?"

"They've always been here, living in the woods and forests, primitive and riddled wih superstition. I suppose they must be the original people, though——" She broke off, staring at his face. "Is something wrong, Earl?"

"You called them the Original People."

"I meant those who were here first. Ourelle has been settled many times and there are all sorts of offshoot cultures. The planet is stable now, but there was a time when it was every man for himself and to hell with the consequences. You've seen Sargone? Of course you have . . . well, didn't you wonder why the streets are all curved? It was built by thieves and robbers who wanted a defense against line-of-sight weapons. At one time they levied tribute on every scrap of material entering or leaving the spacefield. Other fields were built, of course, and other patterns followed, but they have never really merged into a whole as they have done on other worlds. Sargone is the city-state, Relad the agricultural. To the west lies Frome and beyond it Ikinold. And then there is the sea-culture of Jelbtel." She made an impatient gesture. "This is no time or place for a history lesson, and I doubt if you are really interested."

"You would be wrong," he said. "I'm very interested. Particularly in the Original People."

"The Hegelt? That's what we call them. They are human but hopelessly superstitious and, as I said, inbred to the point of extinction. A cross would revitalize them, but they won't entertain the idea. No woman will give herself to a man not of her own people and no man will look for a foreign wife. My guess is that in a few more generations they will be either extinct or utterly degenerate. In the meantime they have their uses. Are you tired?"

"No."

"Then shall we walk a little? I won't be able to sleep now. Please?"

She took his hand and led him to a place beside the

river where the bank fell gently toward the rippling water. She first sat and then lay supine, one knee upraised so as to reveal the sweeping curve of her naked thigh. A posture of abandonment or of calculated seduction, or perhaps it was merely an attitude of total relaxation in the company of someone she could trust.

Dreamily she said, "Isn't it peaceful here? So very pleasant and calm. In time your life begins to adjust to the tempo of the elements and seasons. I think men make a mistake to cling to cities when they could live closer to nature."

"Nature isn't always kind," said Dumarest. He had sat beside her, facing the river, watching the ripple of the water. "What did you do before you married Elray?"

"I was a doctor."

"And?"

"A historian of sorts. I never really practiced medicine after I qualified. A chance was offered at the Kladour and I took it—biological investigation and gene structure of native life. That is why I know so much about the Hegelt. One of the professors had a theory, or had heard of a theory, that all men originated on the same world. Ridiculous, of course, but it was amusing to disprove it."

Dumarest said, "Did you?"

"Disprove it? Well, I didn't really have to. After all, the concept is fantastical nonsense. How could one planet provide all the people there are in the galaxy? And think of the different types." She stretched a little, careless of the way her robe fell from her shoulders. "Are you really interested in the Hegelt, Earl?"

"Not the Hegelt. The Original People."

"There is a difference?"

"The Original People are members of a religious cult whose basic tenet is that all mankind stemmed from a common source. They believe that source was a single planet which they call Terra. They are a secretive group who seek no converts and whose activities are shrouded in mystery. Have you ever heard of them? Is there any information about them in the Kladour?"

"To my knowledge, no."

"Can you be certain? In some old book, perhaps, a minor reference even. Anything."

She sensed the raw hunger in his voice, the hope, too

often thwarted, yet constantly alive. She lifted her shoulders from the sward, sitting with her hands clasped around her knees, looking at his profile, the hard line of the jaw stark in the glow from the sky.

Quietly she said, "There is nothing that I know of. But why are you so interested?"

"Terra is another name for Earth."

"Earth," she mused. "Once, in your delirium, you mentioned it. Earth. A place?"

"A world. My world."

"Could a planet have such a name?" Her voice was light, matching the tinkle of the water. "It's like calling a world sand or dirt or ground. This is earth." Her hand touched the soil. "But we call this place Ourelle."

"Earth is real," he insisted. "A world, old and scarred by ancient wars. The stars are few and there is a great, single moon which hangs like a pale sun in the night sky."

"A legend," she said. "I have heard of them. Worlds which have never existed. Jackpot and Bonanza, El Dorado, and Camelot. Eden too, though I think there is an actual planet called that."

"There are three," he said bleakly. "And there could be more. But there is only one Earth and I was born on its surface. One day I shall find it."

"But—" She broke off, frowning, and then said, carefully, as if talking to a child, "You were born on it, you say, and you must have left it. Then why can't you just go back to it?"

"Because no one knows where it is. It isn't listed in any almanac, the very name seems to have no meaning, the coordinates are missing. People think it is a legend and smile when I mention its name."

"A lost world," she said thoughtfully. "One on the edge of the galaxy; if the stars are few, it must be. There would be few ships and little trade. But you left it, you say?"

"As a boy. I stowed away on a ship and had more luck than I deserved. The captain was kind, an old man who regarded me as his son. He should have evicted me; instead he allowed me to work my passage. And then there were other journeys, other worlds."

Moving, always moving, and always toward the Center where planets were close and ships plentiful. Traveling for years until even the very name of Earth had been forgotten and it had become less than a dream. And the other years, the empty spaces, the constant search for someone, anyone, who would know the way back. The coordinates which would guide him home.

He felt the touch of her hand on his own and turned to face her, seeing her eyes, wide with sympathy, bright with emotion.

"I think I understand now," she said softly, "I knew you were searching for something and I thought—well, never mind. But I didn't guess—how could I have guessed? —that you were lost and searching for your home. Have you no clues? Nothing to guide you?"

Fragments. A sector of the galaxy, some notations, a name, other things. Enough to go on, if he could find the money to hire machines and experts, more to charter a vessel, still more to insure his survival. But, always, was the hope that he could find another way. A person who knew where Earth was to be found. Figures that would provide the answer.

"Earl!" Her fingers tightened on his hand and he sensed the heightening of her emotion. "Oh, Earl!"

Lightly he said, "There you have it, the story of my life. A runaway boy who thinks it's long past the time to go back home. Which is why I'm leaving tomorrow. Or is it today?"

She glanced at the stars and said, "Today. But must you go?"

"Yes."

"But why, Earl? You are welcome here. More than welcome."

"By Elray?"

"Of course! Surely you don't think that—" She broke off and then said, flatly, "You heard. You must have heard. You entered the house and then left to enter again. Well, what of it? What difference does it make?"

He made no answer, looking at the sky, at the silver thread of a metor reflected in the water of the river.

"We're married," she said dully. "On Ourelle such a contract is not all that important and can be broken any time either party wishes. But ours was never more than a marriage of convenience. My money paid for the farm and Elray was willing to work it. A mutual arrangement for mutual protection, because even on Ourelle a woman alone with a child finds life a little hard. And a boy needs a father,

a man to emulate, to follow, with whom to feel secure.
Earl!"

"No!"

"Jondelle likes you. He needs you. The farm is mine.
If—"

"No," he said again, harshly. "Forget it!"

She knew better than to argue, leaning back instead
to sprawl on the scented grass, the starlight warm on the
soft contours of thigh and shoulders, the rich swell of
her breasts. Tempting bait for a lonely man, more so when
coupled with the farm and the security it offered, harder
still to resist when there was a boy who had already won
more than his friendship. A child he could so easily
regard as his son. A good exchange for the bleak emptiness between the stars, the endless quest for a forgotten
world.

Quietly she said, "This is what could happen, Earl. We
could all go into the city, the divorce arranged, the
marrage performed, provision made for Elray. You would
rule here and you could watch Jondelle grow, teach him
the things he should know and guide him on the path he
must take. But you don't want that. So instead I'll make
you a proposition. Stay here for a while. Guard the boy.
Give him a year of your life."

A determined woman, he thought, and a clever one. In
a year he would be trapped, unwilling or unable to leave
the boy, ready to fall into a new arrangement. And it would
not take a year—not with her pushing and Elray aiding by
his own sullen aggression.

"Earl?"

"It's getting late. We had better get back to the house."

"Aren't you interested?"

"No."

"Not even for the boy's sake?"

"If you're afraid for the lad, then sell your farm and
move into the city. Hire guards and watchers. Better still,
take ship and hide on some other world."

"As you have done, Earl?"

He caught the inflection and remembered that she
had held him beneath her hypnotic influence, helpless to
resist any investigation she had cared to make. And a curious woman would not have stopped at merely discovering
his name.

"As I have done," he admitted. "But you know that."

"I guessed. I didn't pry, you have my word for that, but some things are obvious. A fear you try to hide, a thing you must keep secret and—" She broke off, looking at the sky. Earl!"

"What is it?"

"There! See?"

A patch of darkness against the splendor of the sky. An oblong which moved and grew even as they watched, to settle beyond the house and the cluster of shacks.

"A raft," he said. "Visitors, perhaps?"

A roar gave the answer. The crash of explosives followed by a pillar of flame, repeated as the workers screamed and ran into the sheltering darkness. More flame rising to paint the area red and orange, leaping tongues feeding on walls and roofs, filling the air with smoke and the stink of char.

Dumarest felt the woman leave his side and race toward the house. He followed her, caught an arm, flung her to the ground, one hand clamped over her mouth.

"Be silent," he hissed into her ear. "You promise?"

She nodded, gulping as he released her mouth, sobbing as she looked at the devastation.

"The boy, Earl! Dear God, the boy!"

He was in the house together with Elray and a handful of servants and, as yet, the house was untouched. Dumarest narrowed his eyes as he stared at the mounting glare. Against the burning shacks he could see bizarre shapes, men with protective armor pointed and fluted in spiked curves, heads masked and helmeted with plumes and ribbons. Madmen hell-bent on wanton destruction—or men who wanted to give that exact impression.

He watched as one lifted an arm and hurled an object into a barn. Thunder, smoke, and flame gushed from the open door. Others ran over the courtyard, lances thrusting at cringing shapes, keening laughter rising above the dying screams.

"Melevganians," said the woman. "From the lands beyond the deserts to the south. Madmen the lot of them. Earl! We must save the boy!"

He held her close to the dirt, one hand hard against her back, feeling the bunch and jerk of muscle as she tried to rise.

"We can do nothing," he snapped. "Not yet. And the boy is in no immediate danger." He stared at the house.

The windows showed no lights, the glass ruby with reflected firelight, and that was wrong. There were no internal lights —but it wasn't that—what was wrong was that no window had yet been opened. Elray must surely be awake, the servants too, and there would be arms, lasers perhaps, missile weapons which could kill an injured beast if nothing else. And a gun which could kill an animal could just as easily kill a man. Elray now should be behind an open window ready to defend his own.

He looked again at the attackers. A dozen, he guessed, at least ten, but it was hard to tell in the dancing firelight. They moved in sudden darts, stabbing, moving on, grotesque in their helmets and armor. A raiding party intent on easy destruction and wary of approaching the house and the danger it could contain—or a group eliminating opposition with calculated precision?

He said, "Are you sure of what they are?"

Again he felt her strain beneath his hand, then relax, sobbing.

Deliberately he slapped her cheek with his free hand. "Control yourself! Answer me: are you certain?"

"The way they're dressed," she said. "The way they are acting. Lunatics, insane, drugged and degenerate, and having fun. They will burn and destroy and kill everything alive. Everything, Earl! Everything!"

"Why isn't Elray shooting them down? Are there no weapons in the house?"

"A couple of rifles, but he won't use them. He hates violence." Her voice hardened. "The damn coward! If he lives through this, I'll tear out his throat! Earl, what can we do?"

A dozen men armed with grenades, lances, and probably missile weapons. Protected by helmets and armor and drunk on blood-lust. And against them he had only a knife.

He said, "Move toward the back of the house. Be careful; drop if you see anything and freeze until it's gone. Get inside if you can and get the boy. A rifle too, if you can manage. Then get back outside and head for the river. Follow it to the crest and hide among the trees. If anyone tries to stop you, shoot without hesitation. Shoot, then run."

"And you, Earl?"

"I'll attack from the other side and try to create a

diversion." He saw a gout of flame rimmed with flying sparks burst from a point close to the house. Against it armored figures began to move with grim purpose toward the untouched building. "Move!"

He rose as she slipped away, crouched, running in a wide circle so as to hug the edge of the firelight. A dark shape raced toward him, one of the workers breaking free, whimpering in terror, an armored figure close behind. As Dumarest watched, the lanced lifted, aimed, spat a tongue of fire. The worker exploded in a gout of flame.

Lasers would have been silent and more efficient but to madmen, reveling in the sound and fury of destruction, less satisfying. The lance was a double-duty weapon, a sharp point and a missile launcher of some kind built into the shaft. Dumarest sprang to one side as it leveled toward him, sprang again as fire jetted from the tip, a third time as flame and noise blasted from where he had stood. Then he was within the length of the weapon, left hand sweeping it aside, right foot lashing out in a savage kick to an armored knee.

He felt something yield and heard the figure scream with maniacal rage. A fist lifted, clenched, and swept down like a mace, firelight glinting from the spikes set on each knuckle. Wind brushed his cheek as he dodged and before the fist could strike again he was behind the armored figure, left hand clamped around the throat, the knife in his right scraping as he thrust it through the vision slit in the helmet. Twice he stabbed, blinding, killing, rending the brain, tearing free the steel as the figure collapsed.

Quickly Dumarest searched the body. A pouch held three round objects, grenades, simple things with a pin and safety catch. He thrust them into a pocket of his tunic. The lance was long, clumsy, a button set close to the end of the shaft. He looked toward the house. Three figures were close to the door, one almost touching the panel, the others a little toward the rear and to one side. Still more, apparently tired of ravaging the shacks, moved to join them.

The dead man made a convenient rest. Dumarest sprawled behind him, the lance resting on the armored chest, his eyes narrowed as he stared along the shaft. The weapon probably fired a rocket of some kind and he doubted if it would be too accurate. The light was bad, the shadows deceptive, and if he missed the figure close to the door he could well blow in the panel. He moved the tip a little, steadied his aim, and pressed the button.

Fire blossomed from the wall of the house high and to one side of the little group. Adjusting his aim, he fired again, twice more, then the weapon was empty. Before the house a man staggered, shrieking, beating at the fire which wreathed his helmet. Two others lay in twitching heaps, a third crawled like a broken insect over the dirt. As Dumarest watched, he rose, staggering, shaking his head: semi-stunned by concussion but otherwise unhurt.

Four down but there were others and the woman had to be given her chance. Dumarest stood upright, a grenade in his hand. He drew the pin and threw it toward the house, turning before it fell, running as it exploded, his figure clear against the light from the burning shacks. Somewhere beyond the fires would be their raft, probably unattended or, if guarded, watched by restless and impatient men. To those who had seen him it would be important—they would want to save it from damage, and they would follow.

Almost too late he saw the twin figures with raised lances, ribbons bright on crested helmets, firelight warm on points and flutes of armor. They stood at the end of the open ground, blocking his path, others running from the rear to trap him between. Without hesitation he lunged to one side, hit the burning wall of a shack, rolled through fire, holding his breath, eyes tight-closed, feeling the kiss of flame on his hands and face, hearing the crisp of his hair. The shack was small; momentum carried him to and through the opposite wall to roll in a shower of sparks on the ground beyond. Rising, he threw a second grenade, running before it exploded, hearing the roar, the screams, and shouts of command.

And another scream, high, shrill, coming from the back of the house.

CHAPTER

FOUR

Makgar had been taken. She stood, an armored figure holding each arm, very pale in the starlight. The house shielded the little group from the light of the fires, the shadow accentuating the darkness so that for a moment Dumarest couldn't see the third man. Then he moved and the light shone on yellow hair—the boy caught in his arms.

"Please," she begged. "Don't take the boy. Let him go. I'll give you anything you want, but let him go."

One of the men holding her tittered, his voice thin and high, crazed and ugly.

"What can you give, woman, that we do not already have?"

"Money. I'll sell the farm and give you what I get. More. I'll work and you can have that too. I'll be your slave if you want—but don't hurt the boy."

"A fine child," said the one who had spoken. "A strong child. A young one who can be—manipulated. Clamps and cramps and bindings to guide his growth. Racks and weights and implements to alter and stretch and turn him into a thing of joy. Have you seen our menagerie? Some of our specimens you would never take for men."

He laughed, the sound like the rasp of a nail on slate, a degraded keening devoid of amusement.

"No!" Sweat shone on her face and her eyes were wild. "Not that! Dear God, not that!"

"The prospect amuses you, woman? After all, why should he be as other men? An ordinary person when he could be fashioned to become a thing unique. The arms, for example, lengthened to twice what they would normally be. The legs too, the head shaped into a cone, the back guided into a serpentine curve. It amuses you to think of it?"

The man holding the boy said, "Enough."

"You object?"

"There will be no more such talk." His voice was deep, reverberating from the closed helmet. "We have the boy and now we can leave."

"So soon? When there is sport yet to be had? I think not." The thin voice held a menacing snarl. "The house still stands, the woman lives, and there is another. He too must be taken care of before the dawn."

"Do as you wish, but the boy must not be harmed. Attend me to the raft."

He stepped forward, confident of being obeyed, his figure huge as he stepped into the light from the burning shacks. Behind him the woman strained against the metal-clad hands which gripped her.

"Jondelle!"

The boy gave no answer. He seemed to be asleep in the big man's arms, his head lolling against the armored shoulder. Drugged, thought Dumarest, certainly not dead. They would have taken less trouble with a dead boy, and the lad was not that. He caught the movement of the lifting chest, the beads accentuating the slight inhalation, bright colors shifting beneath the light. On the pale cheeks the lashes looked like delicate lace.

The big man halted. "Come," he boomed. "Attend me. I shall not ask again."

The thin voice tittered, "You ask? Not order?"

"I ask."

"Then we shall accommodate you. We are reasonable men, most reasonable, but we do not take kindly to orders. And, as we walk, I shall think of how to amuse this woman. A fire at her feet, perhaps, not too hot or too large, but just enough to shorten her height. And then—well, such things must not be hurried. I shall dwell on it as we walk at your back."

As they passed, Dumarest rose like a ghost behind them. Helmets limited vision; they could see ahead but not to either side and certainly not where he followed. And there were no others at the rear of the house; he had made certain of that. But he would have to act fast before they met their companions.

Three men. The one holding the boy would be hampered, slow to turn, slower to act. The ones holding the woman were more dangerous, to beat them would need speed and accuracy, but if he could free her he would have an ally.

If she could forget her concern for the boy, resist her natural impulse to run toward him, and take advantage of her opportunity.

Stepping forward, he tripped up the man to her right. It was a thing quickly and easily done. One foot caught on his instep and lifted so as to catch behind the other. He toppled, dropping his lance, releasing his hold on the woman in order to save himself. As he fell, Dumarest lunged forward, gripped the other man's right shoulder, and jerked the trapped arm hard against his body. He felt the snap of bone as the elbow yielded beneath the armor and snapped at the woman as the hand fell from her arm.

"The other one. Take him!"

He snatched the knife from his boot as a spiked fist drove toward his face, feeling the rip as the cruel points tore at his scalp. The blade lifted and lanced at the helmet, seeking a slit and finding only perforations. Again the left fist came toward him like a club, catching his shoulder, ripping at the plastic to reveal the glint of metal beneath. Before it could lift again, Dumarest had swung up his left arm, lifting the visor and exposing the face beneath. It was painted, snarling, a vicious mask of animal ferocity. The mouth gaped to show filed teeth, closed to send them clashing against the steel of the blade. Dumarest jerked it free, thrust again at the glaring eyes, sending the point between the ball and the bony ridge of the eyebrow, driving it deep into the brain.

From behind came a frenzied screaming.

Makgar had taken her chance. The fallen man had tried to rise and she had jumped on his back, sending him to the dirt, her hands lifting his visor and busying themselves beneath. She raised them, red with blood, naked breasts heaving beneath the parted robe.

"He isn't dead," she panted. "But he can't see. I got his eyes. The boy?"

The big man had gone, the boy with him. Dumarest snatched up a lance and ran past the burning shacks. A dark figure came from one side, arms empty, a lance raised. Dumarest fired, thumbing the button, sending a stream of missiles toward him. One hit the ground at his feet, another slammed into the armored chest. The third was wasted.

"Jondelle," she said. "Quick!"

The fires fell behind, lapping at a wall of star-shot night. The contrast was too great; against the firelight all was darkness and illusive shadows. Dumarest halted, conscious of the danger, the fires at his back, and enemies waiting. The woman threw aside all caution.

"Quick!" she gasped. "Hurry!"

Somewhere was the raft and one man, more likely several. The big man with the boy and the others who must have been left on guard. Dumarest hit the woman, throwing the weight of his body against her flank, and sending her sprawling on the ground. He followed, holding her down as streaks of fire passed overhead to explode among the burning shacks.

"Earl!"

"Be silent!"

Sound could betray their position. He lifted his head cautiously, staring at the glittering sky. Against it something moved, dark, regular in shape, and slowly rising.

"The raft! Earl, they're getting away!"

She rolled from beneath his hand, rising before he could stop her, running over the grass toward the ascending vehicle. He reared upright, snatching out the last grenade, then throwing it aside as useless. He could throw it and maybe send it to explode in the body of the raft, but that would certainly kill the boy. But he could damage it perhaps, slow it in some way, maybe even bring it down. He lifted the lance, aimed, and touched the button.

Fire exploded against metal, a brilliant gush which showed the underside of the raft, the helmeted heads peering over the edge. Two of them. There would be another, the pilot, and maybe yet one more, that of the big man who held the boy. He fired again, the missile hitting the back edge, the light revealing the shafts pointing toward him. He fired twice more, guessing where the engine would be, the generator of the current which fed the anti-gravity units of the raft.

And then the lance was exhausted and he had thrown it aside, falling to hug the ground, covering his ears as the return fire blazed around him.

Miraculously he was unhit, rising as the missiles ceased, conscious of the ache caused by bruising fragments, a trickle of blood running over his face from a minor wound.

"Makgar!" He looked around, wiping blood from his eyes. "Makgar?"

She lay looking very small and fragile in the torn ruin of her robe, the bright fabric brighter than before with the ruby of her blood. Around her the soil was pitted with jagged craters, the dirt burned and tormented, wet where she lay. The distant firelight caught her eyes, enhancing their brightness, their pain.

"Earl?"

"They got away," he said flatly. "I think I damaged the raft so they couldn't move fast or far. And you?"

"My side. It was like being kicked. Earl—"

"Don't talk," he said. "Don't do anything. Just lie there until I return."

"You're going?"

"They left in a hurry," he said grimly. "Some of them may have been left behind. I want to make sure."

The area was lifeless, silent aside from the rustle of flame. Close to the house Dumarest heard the keening of the man Makgar had injured, but ignored him, moving to the back and an opened window, slipping inside with knife ready and eyes strained. The workers were dead, the servants huddled where they had run to Elray for protection. He lay beside a rifle, the side of his head a crushed mess, one hand outstretched as if in mute appeal. Perhaps he had tried to do that, talk instead of act, beg instead of using the rifle which could have saved his life. Dumarest picked it up, a good weapon, fully loaded, the missiles capable of penetrating any armor ever worn, Elray could have climbed to an upper room, picked off the invaders as they stood before the fires, shot them down as they tried to climb the stairs. Had he acted, the boy would be safe and the woman unharmed.

She looked at him as he stooped over her.

"Earl?"

"It's all right," he said. "I'm going to take you into the house."

"Elray?"

"Dead."

"I'm glad," she whispered. "He could have done something, used one of the guns, anything. He didn't have to let them take the boy."

"Maybe he didn't."

"They were waiting," she said. "In the house. They

grabbed me as I—well, never mind. That isn't important now. But he could have done something. He promised to look after the boy. He promised that."

She groaned as he lifted her, blood welling from the torn wound in her side, dark, turgid.

"It hurts," she whispered. "God, how it hurts!"

Her head lolled as he carried her into the house, her eyes blank, glazed with pain. He snapped on every light he could find, found her room, stripped off the bed covers and laid her on the sheet. Flinging the robe into a corner, he studied her naked body. The missile had hit her side, exploding, creating intense pressures, and causing havoc to the internal organs. He found warm water and washed the wound free of dirt and fiber, using clean sheets to bind it close, fretting out the material before applying it so as to promote coagulation. In a cabinet downstairs he found medical supplies and studied them, frowning. Quick-time would have helped, slowing the metabolism so as to make a day seem but a few minutes, but there was little need for it outside the ships which traversed space—the passengers who rode High using it to shorten the tedium of the journey.

He found antibiotics and a hypogun, loading the instrument and testing it against a sheet of paper, the air blast driving the drug through the material as it would skin and fat. Another vial contained a sedative, a third a means to kill pain. He carried them upstairs and injected them all.

"Earl." The drugs were quick-acting; incredibly she managed to smile. "You're efficient, Earl. I like that in a man. You know what to do and you do it without hesitation, but you shouldn't waste your time."

"It's my time."

"And my life—what there is of it."

"You're hurt," he said flatly. "Badly, but you're still alive. If you want to, you can stay that way. Give up and I might as well bury you now."

"I'm a doctor," she said. "You don't have to lie to me."

"Am I lying?"

"No, but—" She caught herself, forcing open her eyes. "I feel so sleepy and I mustn't sleep. There is something. The boy. Earl!"

"He'll be all right. The man who took him won't

let him come to harm. And we'll find him. I promise that."

She stirred, fighting the drugs he had blasted into her bloodstream.

Quickly he said, "Have you a radio? Some means of summoning aid?"

"No, no radio, we wanted to be isolated. Just—"

"Sleep now," he said.

"I mustn't." Again she dragged herself awake. "You shouldn't have given me that sedative. There are things I have to say."

"Later."

"Now, before it's too late. You've got to promise me . . . Earl . . . you must . . . "

She sighed and yielded to the drugs, relaxing and looking younger than he had ever seen her before. And yet she was far from being a girl, the lines of her body held a lush maturity, the muscles firm, the fat giving a soft roundness. He covered her, piling on soft quilts, arranging her pillow, and then, mouth cruel, he left the house and went into the courtyard.

The man she had blinded was still alive. He crawled in his armor like a stricken monster, keening, his spiked gloves scrabbling at the dirt. Dumarest watched him without pity, remembering the things he had said, the threats he had made. Catching a shoulder, he spun the man over onto his back, the ruined face ugly with its paint in the fading light of the fires.

"Listen to me," said Dumarest. "I want to tell you something amusing. You are blind and can't see, but I will describe it to you. A new formation of a man. A fire to char away his feet, a knife to remove his hands, his ears, his nose. The same knife to slit his tongue and to release the intestines from his stomach. Acid to burn a pattern on his flesh. You appreciate the image? A work of art suitable for inclusion in your menagerie. You will be that man, unless you talk."

The thin lips parted to show the filed teeth.

"My eyes! The pain—"

"Will get a damn sight worse if you don't tell me what I want to know! Who are you? Where are you from?"

"They lied!" The voice was a fretful whine. "They said there would be no opposition. Just a few Hegelt, a woman and a boy."

"Who lied?"

"Those who wanted to come with us. For amusement, they said. Money and a raft and we could do as we pleased. A raid, that was all. A night of fun. My eyes!"

"The man who took the boy. What is his name?"

"Why should I care?"

"Where did he come from?"

"What are strangers to us?"

"Damn you!" snarled Dumarest. "Talk!"

Incredibly the creature smiled. "I will talk. I am Tars Krandle, a noble of Melevgan, and if you will take me to where I can receive medical aid I will reward you well. Your own weight in silver, women of chosen attractiveness, a selection from my private—" He broke off, laughing, the thin sound echoing madness. "Or I will sing you the dirge of the Emphali. They sing when they are being slowly torn apart—did you know that? I have a most entertaining recording and will give you a copy, if you will only aid me. Or—" He tittered. "Or perhaps I won't talk at all. You can't make me. No one can force a member of my race to do anything they choose not to do. Not you, not anyone. We are the elect."

"You will talk." Dumarest rasped the knife from his boot and rested the flat of the blade against the flaccid cheek. "Feel that? It's a knife. I'm going to make it red-hot and then I'll touch you again. Need I tell you where?"

"You will not make me talk. No one can tell a noble of Melevgan what to do. We know how to live—and we know when to die."

"You will die," promised Dumarest savagely. "But you will take a long time and the waiting will not be pleasant. Feel the heat of the fires? They are close and could be closer. Now tell me who the man was and why he wanted the boy."

"I don't know. What are such things to me?"

"Where was he taking him?"

Dumarest jerked back as the man surged upward in a sudden explosion of energy, sensing rather than seeing the gloved hands rising, the spikes turned inward toward his head. Easily he avoided them, watching as they clashed together, to fall and beat at the armored chest, the protected groin. Screaming with maniacal rage, the Melevganian rose, his fists beating at the air, the open front of his helmet. Blood shone redly on the spikes as, still screaming, he staggered blindly into a glowing mound of ash, to fall, still shrieking, into the heart of the red-hot embers.

Bleakly Dumarest watched him burn. The man had created havoc, killed without compunction, and threatened horrors all for his own amusement. An insane monster who had chosen the manner of his own death—and who had died taking his knowledge with him.

He stretched, conscious of the ache in his body, the sting of the burns on hands and face, but there were things to be done before he could apply medications. The shacks had burned, the entire area a shambles, the dead lying with blank faces toward the sky. Dumarest let them lie. Beneath the helmets the faces of the armored men were the same as those he had already seen. The strangers, whoever they were, had all escaped in the raft. Two of them at least, he guessed. The big man would never have trusted the vehicle to the blood-crazed insanity of the Melevganians even if they had been willing to forego their amusement. But there had been another raft, Elray's, and he had to find it.

It was buried beneath a mound of splintered wood and stone, the metal bent, the engine damaged by fragments. He cleared it, working until the rising sun threw a pale green light over the area and his head swam with fatigue. And, with the dawn, came furtive shapes, the Hegelt returning to keen over their dead, their voices rising to blend with the morning breeze.

CHAPTER

FIVE

The room was as he remembered, warm, soft with golden light, the air scented with pungent aromas. At his desk Akon Batik wore the same robe of black and yellow, the jewel in his cap a living, ruby eye. He poured wine and said, after the first sip, "A sad story. A tragedy. But on Ourelle such things happen. On other worlds too, I have no doubt. But why have you come to me?"

"For help," said Dumarest. "For information."

"Which you think I can provide?"

"Which I think you may be able to obtain. A boy was stolen. A young lad who lived quietly on a farm. I want to know why."

Akon Batik shrugged, thin shoulders rising beneath his robe. "For ransom, perhaps? That is the obvious answer. For the whim of someone who had seen the boy and desired what they saw? For revenge against the mother? As a means to force others to obey their will? As a toy, a pet, or someone to train along a selected path? And what is it to you? A boy . . . there are millions of boys. One more or less—what does it matter?"

"It matters," said Dumarest. "To me."

"But not to me. You can appreciate that?"

A man of business who concerned himself only with profit and loss. On this and other worlds a man of sense and logic who took care of his own and remained clear of personal involvement. Dumarest sipped at his wine, not tasting the lambent fluid, knowing that he had to deal with the other on his own terms.

"You know the city," he said quietly. "You would be able to discover if men were hired to do a certain thing. You might even be able to find out who had hired them."

"Perhaps."

"I have money, as you know. I would be willing to pay for whatever help you could give."

41

The jeweler pursed his lips. "A business proposition? You present the matter in a more attractive light. But you said the raiders were Melevganians."

"There were others with them. Not Melevganians and maybe from the city. And certainly it was men from the city who tried to take the boy at first."

"Three men," said Akon Batik softly. "Yes, I heard of how they were found, but they were strangers." He paused, then added. "Perhaps it would have been best had you let them have their way."

A farm ruined, men and women slaughtered like beasts, and still the boy had been taken. Dumarest looked at his goblet, the tension of his hand.

"No," he said. "I couldn't do that."

"In any case, the thing is done and no man can reverse the passage of time. But I must warn you, those who took the boy are obviously strong. They will not be gentle should they find you an embarrassment. And, to be honest, I cannot understand your concern. He is not your son. You owe his family no allegiance. No one, as yet, has paid you to find him. Why are you willing to risk your life?"

"I gave my word."

"And, for you, that is enough." Akon Batik sipped thoughtfully at his wine. "I am not a sentimental man, but I can appreciate the strength of a promise given. Very well, I will do what I can. Be at the House of the Gong tonight and I will send a man to tell you what I have found. You will give him ten stergals."

"And for yourself?"

"You will give fifty to the man at the gate. You wish more wine?"

"Thank you, no."

"Then may good fortune attend you."

"And may happiness fill your days."

A cab took Dumarest to the Kladour and he stood looking up at the vast bulk of the building. The sun caught the fluted spire, the gilded ball on the summit, turning it into an eye-bright point of flame. Inside it was cool, wide halls sending soft echoes from the vaulted ceiling. A receptionist, a young girl, her face dusted with lavender, her eyes bright with inset flakes of reflective material, stared with frank admiration at his lean figure, curious as she noted his burned skin and singed hair.

"Could I help you, sir?"

"Yes. I have a problem. I am trying to find a man, a professor who works here or who used to work here. I don't know his name, but he once had a woman assistant. Makgar. He field was biological investigation and gene structure of native life. Can you help me?"

"No," she said reluctantly. "I'm sorry, I can't."

"But surely there would be records. It was a few years ago, I admit, but possibly someone would remember."

"Your interest?"

"I am making an investigation into the divergencies of various races from a common norm. I heard that the professor would have valuable information, and it is barely possible that I could help him in his own inquiries. If you could check with your personnel department?"

Professor Ashlen was well past middle age, with a balding scalp and muscles which had long since run to fat. He sat in an office musty with old files wearing a stained smock over a shirt of maroon and gray. He rose as Dumarest entered and held out his hand.

"You take it," he said. "You shake it and then let it go. It's an old custom."

"Yes," said Dumarest. "I know." The touch of the palm was moist, clammy.

"So few people do," said Ashlen. He sat and waved his visitor to a chair. "It's a little test of my own. If someone comes claiming to be an investigator of the human race, I assume that he has studied many cultures. If he has, then he would know why I put out my hand."

"You told me what to do," reminded Dumarest.

"So I did. That was careless of me. Now tell me: how did such a custom originate in the first place?"

"As a means of proving peaceful intention. I show you my bare hand and you touch it with your own. Naked hands can hold no weapons."

"And the other one? The left hand which is not extended?"

"Perhaps that held a knife behind the back," said Dumarest dryly. "Just in case. Do you remember a woman who used to work with you? Makgar. Tall, dark, well-built. A few years ago now."

"Makgar?" Ashlen frowned. "Is that what you came to talk about? I understood that you were interested in divergent races."

"I am, and the theory that all life originated on one world. But—"

"That is nonsense," said the professor firmly. "It is an attractive theory and one which rises from time to time, but, believe me, it has no foundation of truth. Men evolved on a variety of worlds much at the same time. There has been movement, of course, new worlds colonized and settlements founded, but to seriously consider that all men came from one small world is ludicrous. In fact, I proved it to be a complete fallacy."

"You and Makgar?"

"Makgar? Well, yes, she helped on the routine side, but I can fairly claim the credit for exposing the illogic of the contention. Of course, I can understand how such a notion could arise. Take Ourelle, for example. You are a stranger here?"

Dumarest nodded.

"A most peculiar world." Ashlen produced a map and unrolled it on his cluttered desk. "Here is the city of Sargone where we are now." His fingers rapped a patch of yellow. Here the plains of Relad where the majority of the Hegelt are to be found. Then here we have the Valley of Charne where there is a most peculiar race of yellow-skinned people. Note, the Hegelt are dark brown and the Charnians yellow. You see the implication?"

"Two races on one world," said Dumarest.

"Not so. The Hegelt are the original people and the Charnians the result of a later colonization. Then, to the north, we have the Shindara. And there are Frome and Ikinold and others. I won't bore you with their names. The point is they are all different in skin color, facial characteristics, and even physical peculiarities. It is natural to assume that if such variety could be found on one world, then they could have coexisted together in the past. On the mythical world from which legend has it they all originated."

"Earth?"

"You have heard the name?" Ashlen shrugged. "But then, as an investigator into the divergencies of race, you would. A part of the legend, of course. My own conclusion is that it is another name for Eden which, as you must know, was the name of the original paradise. Another legend born of the tribulations of the early settlers when times were hard. They consoled themselves with talk of fabulous places and a world on which no man had to work and everything was provided by some race of beneficent creatures called, I think, angels. However, as I was saying, the existence of many races on Ourelle does not prove that all the races in the galaxy could have at one time shared one planet. In fact, the reverse is true, because we know they came here in various waves of colonization. Small groups which remained apart and still do. Societies and cultures which have found a stability and a certain harmony."

Dumarest said, "Harmony? The Melevganians?"

"Perhaps I should have said stability, but the Melevganians—" Ashlen shook his head. "They are insane and I mean that in a literal sense. Their gene structure has been altered due to the mutation-inducing radiations of the area in which they live. Their sense of values has little if nothing to do with what we regard as the norm. They are willful, caring nothing for anything but their most immediate desire. Unpredictable, dangerous, and yet fascinating to any student of the human species."

"I saw one die once," said Dumarest. "He threw himself into a fire."

"Faced with an impossible situation they will seek self-destruction," said the professor. "A maniacal hate which turns against themselves at what they regard as a failure to master their immediate environment. And they have an infinite capacity for revenge. They reside here." His finger tapped the map. "A sunken area surrounded by high mountains. With rafts they could escape, but they have a limited technology and, fortunately for the rest of Ourelle, a disinclination to leave their own territorial area. They make raids at times, disgusting affairs, but mostly they are contained by the peoples in adjoining areas."

Dumarest said, thoughtfully, "But they have contact with the outside. They trade?"

"Yes. As I said, they have a limited technology and are unable to produce much of what they use. However, they do find gems and heavy metals in the mountains which surround them. There are rumors that they have slaves to work the mines, but no one knows for certain. My personal opinion is that they do. Their arrogance would not allow them to perform menial tasks."

Ashlen reached for a thick pile of graphs. "And now let me show you the result of my investigations. You will see that, based on a cross-section of a thousand samples, there is a distinct . . ."

Dumarest let him ramble on, sitting back in a wooden chair, his eyes thoughtful as he stared at the emerald patch of the window. A girl brought them cups of tisane and he drank the tangy liquid more from politeness than from any reason of thirst. Around him the Kladour hummed with quiet efficiency, the repository of knowledge on this world, the pride of the city. And yet it contained nothing he did not already know about the planet he sought, and he could tell the professor nothing he would be willing to accept. His mind was closed, his eyes blinded to the possibility that he could be wrong. He was science and science had spoken and the world on which Dumarest had been born to him simply did not and could not exist.

A familiar reaction and another hope frustrated, but he had come for more than information about Earth.

"The woman," he said as the professor paused. "Makgar. Tell me about her."

"A woman. A good assistant. What more can I say?"

"Did she have a child? A son?"

"I believe so." Ashlen frowned. "Yes, now that I come to think of it, she did."

"How did she get her position here?"

"How do I know? These things are done by personnel. I wanted an assistant and they found me one. She seemed to know her job."

Short answers of little value. Dumarest restrained his impatience. "Did she talk to you at all about her past? Was she born here? Do you know her home world?"

"She claimed to be a doctor. She could have been, it was unimportant and unessential to her duties. I don't think she was born on Ourelle. Something she said once about the light. She mentioned a place called Veido, it was in casual conversation, and she seemed to have made a slip of the tongue. That's why I remember it."

"Try to remember something else," urged Dumarest. "Has anyone, at any time, ever asked about her?"

"No."

"Why did she leave?"

"Really!" Ashlen blew out his cheeks, his eyes hard with anger. "I entertained you because I took you for a colleague, but you seem to be more interested in the woman than my work. She left, I think, to leave the city. I simply didn't take that much interest." He touched a button on his desk. "And now, if you will excuse me? The usher will show you out."

"A moment." Dumarest rose and stood, tall and somber at the edge of the desk. Looking down at the professor, he said, "One more question—and this time think about it. Did she, at any time, mention the father of her child?"

"I—"

"Think about it, man! Did she?"

Ashlen swallowed. "No, she didn't. Not once. I assumed that he was dead, if I bothered to think about it at all. But why ask me all these things? Why don't you ask her?"

"I can't," said Dumarest harshly. "She's dead."

CHAPTER

SIX

She had died in the afternoon when the sun was high and casting a delicate patina over her hair. She had lain in the body of the raft, cushioned by quilts and blankets, more covering her from feet to chin. She had been restless, febrile, with an ooze of blood seeping from between her lips. And Dumarest, haggard from days without sleep, had been unable to save her.

It had taken too long to repair the raft and the Hegelt had been useless. Numbed by their losses, they could only sit and mourn their dead. Even when repaired the craft was slow, drifting over the ground like a windblown feather, demanding constant attention to keep it aloft and on course. He had been forced to land many times to work on the engine, more to bathe her fevered cheeks and wipe the crusted blood from her mouth. She had tried to remain conscious, refusing more sedatives, knowing she rode with death at her side.

"I'm dying, Earl. Don't argue with me, I know."

"We are all dying, Makgar."

"Then I'm ahead of my time." Her hands moved, checking her body. "The spleen is ruined, the pancreas also. The intestines are in a mess and both stomach and lungs are perforated." She tried to smile. "I'm not in what you'd call very good condition."

"We'll make it."

"In this wreck? God knows how you ever got it going in the first place. You could almost walk as fast. And how much longer can you go without sleep?"

"As long as I have to. And you're going to keep going as long as you have to. Until we can get you to a hospital."

"To life-support mechanisms, regrafts and regrowths, slow-time and all the rest of it. It's already too late, Earl. I'd be dead now, if it wasn't for you. Earl!"

He caught her hand and felt the pressure of her fingers as she fought the pain.

Bitterly he said, "Where did you hide your medicines? The drugs we could have used. You had to have more than what I found."

"In the shack, Earl. The one in which the baby was born. I left my bag there, I didn't need it, and there was no need to take it. The baby," she said. "Dear God, how can things shaped like men be so vile? The baby—and my boy. Jondelle!"

He saw the agony on her face and tore his hand free, lifting the hypogun and blasting pain-killers into her blood.

"No!" She shook her head as he adjusted the instrument. "I don't want to sleep. I can't. The boy——"

"I'll find him, Makgar."

"You promise that? Earl, you promise?"

"I promise."

"He's so small, so young and helpless. I can't bear to think of him in the hands of those beasts. You've got to save him, Earl."

"I will. I give you my word."

A promise to ease the hurt of a dying woman, but one he would keep. She sighed and seemed to relax, her eyes closing.

"Earl," she murmured. "I love you. I've loved you from the first. Elray was right. I wanted you, not him. I told you that. You should have agreed."

It would have made no difference. Leaning close, he said, "Makgar, listen to me. Who knew that Elray was going into the city?"

"No one."

"You said he had to pick up a machine part. Was the time fixed?"

"I suppose so." She looked at him, startled. "Earl! Do you think that Elray—? No. He couldn't. He wouldn't."

There was no limit to what a hungry man would do, and the hunger for money could ruin a world. A date and time arranged, a route chosen, and who would think to blame him? And he had made no attempt to fight the invaders. He had died close to a rifle which could have saved them all. Had the big man paid him off with unexpected coin? A dead man could not talk.

"Earl." Her voice was fading. "Earl."

"Tell me about the boy," he said urgently. "Where should I take him? Who are his people?"

". . . love you," she whispered. "You and me and the boy . . . happiness . . . why did . . . Jondelle!"

"Makgar!"

But she hadn't heard. She had died in the afternoon sunlight with a thin breeze whispering a dirge and the scent of grass like delicate flowers. He had buried her beneath a flowering tree, leaving the useless raft as a marker.

A bad memory best forgotten.

He took a deep breath as he left the Kladour. The professor had been of no help, he had no idea where Elray had arranged to get his part, and the peace officers of the city were uninterested in anything which happened outside of their jurisdiction. There was nothing he could do but wait for the jeweler's messenger at the House of the Gong.

It was in the Narn, a sprawling, brawling place such as he had seen on a hundred worlds. An area filled with places of synthetic joy where men and women drank and gambled and tasted unwise delights. The voices of the touts were a droning susurration.

"See, be seen, watch, and be watched. The erotic fantasies of a thousand worlds assembled for your participation and watchful enjoyment. No limit, one fee, stay as long as you can stand the pace!"

"Honest tables and straight dealing. Free food and wine. Ten chips to leave with no matter what."

"Let the mystic crystals of Muhtua read the things which are to come. Good fortune, good health, and safe passage."

"Real knives! Real blood! Young buckos willing to take on all contenders! A hundred stergals if you stay unmarked for three minutes!" The tout caught Dumarest by the arm. "You, sir. I can tell you're no stranger with a blade. Easy money for a single bout."

With a fixed blade, lights adjusted to dazzle, a spray of numbing gas, perhaps, to slow him down. Dumarest shook off the arm.

"No?" The tout shrugged, sneering. "Afraid of a scratch or two?" He appealed to a group of onlookers. "You there, sir, you with that charming girl at your side. I'll bet ten stergals you have more courage. Ten coins in your hand if you enter the ring and a hundred more if you stay unmarked for three minutes."

He was young, little more than a boy, someone from the

edging farms, perhaps, after a little adult fun. The girl at his side gave him no opportunity to refuse the baited offer.

"Go on, Garfrul. Ten stergals! We could go to the Disaphar and try one of those analogues."

"The little lady has the right idea," shouted the tout. He tweaked the baited hook. "Ten in the hand before you start. A hundred, maybe, when you finish. Think of what you could buy . . . the best food in the Narn, the best wine. A place at the highest table. Who knows, with luck you could turn it into a fortune. It's been done before."

The boy hesitated. "I don't know," he said. "I'm not much use with a knife."

"You're fast," urged his companion. Her eyes were too bright, too eager, a she-cat lusting for excitement. "You can dodge around for a little while. Three minutes isn't long and think of what we could do with the money. A new suit, a new dress, a chance to better yourself. Oh, Garfrul! I'd be so proud of you! I'd tell all the girls— no I won't. If I did they'd be after you and I'm jealous."

Dumarest watched, knowing what was to come. Ten stergals for a slash which would sever tendons and leave the boy maimed for life. A double handful of coins for wounds which would leave permanent scars. An evening of innocent pleasure ruined before it had begun.

Abruptly he said, "Don't be a fool, boy. Don't be led to the slaughter."

The tout turned, snarling. "Why don't you mind your own business? He's old enough to make up his own mind. What's it to you what he does?"

Nothing, but he had blond hair and blue eyes and looked as Jondelle might look if he were lucky enough to stay alive.

To the boy he said, "You want to see what they were leading you into? Then follow me." To the tout he snapped, "I'll take your offer. A hundred stergals for three minutes, you say?"

"If you stay unmarked, yes."

"How much if I win?"

The tout blinked, his eyes wary, but the crowd was pressing close and he could visualize a full house. "Double."

"First blood, no breaks, an empty ring?"

"Sure."

"Then let's get inside."

Dumarest thrust his way into the booth, nose crinkling to familiar scents, blood and sweat and oil, the intangible odor of anticipation and the animal-stink of blood-lust. Behind him came the boy, the girl hugging his arm, her eyes unnaturally bright. After them came the crowd from the street, scenting violence to come, willing to pay the extra the tout demanded for the privilege of watching men cut and slash at each other with naked steel.

They filed into the booth, whispering as Dumarest examined the ring. It was a sanded area, twelve feet square, raised four feet above the floor. Overhead lights threw an eye-bright brilliance. He looked at them, squinting, seeing the other, unlit lights, aimed at each corner of the combat area. The lights which could be flashed to dazzle and bemuse a combatant who proved too dangerous.

"All set?" The tout came forward, smiling, knives in his hands, his champion at his side. He was tall, lithe, dressed only in pants and boots, his naked torso gleaming with oil and laced with the cicatrices of old scars. His hair was close-cropped to a rounded skull and his face, broad, flat-nosed, held the impassivity of an executioner.

"I'm ready," said Dumarest.

"Good. You'll have to strip, but I guess you know that." He watched as Dumarest removed his tunic and handed it to Garfrul. "You've been in a ring before?"

"I've watched a few times and we used to fight a little at a place I worked at once. Practice blades only, of course."

There was no need to lie when a part of the truth would serve as well.

"I thought so," said the tout. "I can tell when a man knows what he's doing. Get in the ring and I'll hand you the blade."

The naked edge was ten inches long, dull, heavy, and ill-balanced. Dumarest poised it, then held out his hand. "I'll take the other one."

"Something wrong?"

"You tell me. No?" Dumarest shrugged and threw aside the knife. "Then I'll use my own." He lifted it from his boot and turned it so the light flashed from the blade. "It's shorter by an inch," he said calmly. "I'm giving your boy an advantage. Now blow the whistle and let's get this over with."

The tout hesitated. "That all right with you, Krom?"

His champion shrugged, confident in his own prowess. "Sure."

Still the man hesitated, looking at Dumarest, his knife, his scars, uneasy at the fear that he had been led into a trap. Then a man yelled from the back of the crowd.

"Come on, there! Where's the action?"

Others took it up, a roar of sound, feral, demanding. Feet began pounding the floor, a rolling drumbeat of angry impatience. The tout sucked in his breath and stepped from the ring. His whistle killed the noise as if it had been cut by a knife.

Krom moved.

He was clever, skilled, moving more for the crowd than anything else, his knife held a little before him, waist-high, the point upward, the blade twisted a little so as to provide a thread of brilliance along the edge. He took a step forward, back, moved sideways, dancing on the balls of his feet, the point lifting, falling, rising again to eye-level. His stance was open, inviting, left hand held far from his body.

From the crowd a woman screamed, her voice brittle with hysteria. "Cut him, mister! Cut him good!"

Dumarest ignored her as he ignored everything but the man before him. Krom was good, a veteran of a thousand combats, his body trained to move by unthinking reflex action, the master of a dozen tricks. A professional who intended to win; but even if he had been a raw amateur, Dumarest would have been just as wary. Too many things could happen during a fight. Little things, a foot slipping, light reflecting from a blade to give temporary blindness, anything. And the luck which had stayed with him so long could even now be running out.

Krom attacked, blade lifted, the edge toward Dumarest's face, moving slower than it should. He caught it on his own knife, the steel clashing, clashing again as he returned the slash, the thin, harsh ringing echoing over the crowd.

Grandstand play to give the effect of savage violence. Korm was acting from habit, aiming at the knife, not at the man, stretching the bout so as to make it look good and to encourage others to test their skill. Dumarest could have cut him then, but he had his own motivations. A fight soon ended looked too easy. He wanted the boy to be sure of what was happening.

He backed, confident that there would be no real attack as yet, but alert just the same. He weaved, seeing the back of the blade turned toward him, allowing it to come closer than it might. He cut, clumsily, deliberately missing, Krom springing out of range with smooth efficiency, blades clashing as he blocked a second attack. Dumarest stooped, knocked up the knife arm, and sent the point of his weapon whining an inch from the glistening chest.

The crowd roared, screaming at the expected sight of blood, quieting as they saw the unmarked torso. A bell rang sharply.

"Minute one!"

They parted, standing at either side of the ring, crouched a little, light on the balls of their feet. Krom's left arm lifted, swept down in a sharp gesture. A signal, perhaps? Dumarest thought of the aimed lights, the other devices used in such a place to insure victory for the champion. Krom must know that his chest could have been cut in the last encounter, and a man of his experience would take no chances.

He came forward, knife held up and out, the blade flickering as it weaved a pattern. An amateur would have tried to follow it, to anticipate where it would be and when it would thrust or cut. Dumarest knew better. He backed, keeping clear, his own knife ready and waiting. He felt the ropes behind him, sprang to one side as Krom lunged forward, sprang again as the man turned and swept up the knife. He caught it on his own, lifted, and stared into the broad face.

Krom jerked up his knee.

Dumarest twisted, felt it slam against his thigh, and pushed hard against the trapped knife. Krom staggered back, off balance and temporarily helpless. Dumarest sprang after him, saw the uplifted blade, the tiny hole below the edge in the guard. He turned in midair, landing like a cat, leaping to the side of the ring as the invisible spray lashed toward him. Krom followed it, holding his breath, cutting upward so as to hit the wrist and slash the tendons. The knives jarred, held, broke free as Dumarest sprang to the center of the ring.

Above the sighing inhalation of the crowd he heard the harsh clang of the bell.

"Minute two!"

A lie, of course; the tout would be stretching the time. But lie or not, one thing was certain: the playacting was over. And more than playacting. Króm had used his spray, the puff of gas which would stun and slow, and while Dumarest remained in the center of the ring the lights could not be used. Now it was just one against the other with naked steel and skill, luck and speed deciding the winner.

Krom attacked, feinting, changing the direction of his cut, backing as the blades clashed to attack again. Dumarest moved in a tight circle, turned a little so as to present his knife-side to his opponent, mentally counting seconds. Twenty . . . Krom would be getting desperate. Thirty . . . now, if at all, he would put out his major effort. A trick he had learned, perhaps, a baffling move which had proven worthwhile.

From the crowd a woman shrieked.

It was a scream of utter agony, rising, demanding immediate attention. It shocked the crowd. It would have shocked any amateur fighter, causing him to turn, to expose himself for the necessary second to be cut.

Dumarest didn't turn. He knew the distraction to be what it was. Before him Krom's knife flashed, vanished, flashed again in his other hand. It came forward like a finger of light as his right hand lifted in an empty feint. Dumarest moved to his right, his left forearm slamming against Krom's left wrist, his own knife moving out to gently cut a shallow gash on the naked shoulder.

"Blood!" a man yelled at the sight. "He's cut him! He's won!"

The bout was over. Dumarest should have relaxed, lowered his knife, turned, perhaps, to the crowd in smiling victory. Turned—and taken Krom's knife in his kidneys.

He had won—but a dead man could collect no winnings and who would care about a stranger?

He saw the man turn, the knife back in his right hand, the point lifting to stab at his heart. Dumarest caught the wrist, fingers locking like iron around the flesh and sinew, halting the blade an inch from his skin. His own knife rose, the edge hard against the corded throat.

"Drop it!" he said and then, as Krom hesitated, "Don't be a fool, man! You've lost, but you can live to fight again!"

"Fast," muttered Krom. "Too damn fast. You could

have taken me in the first ten seconds. Althen was a fool to have picked you." The knife fell from his hand. "You're a pro. Anyone else would have killed me. Now what?"

"Nothing," said Dumarest. "I'm going to collect."

Jumping from the ring, he snatched his tunic from the boy's hands and headed to the box office. The tout was busy. He cringed as Dumarest caught his arm.

"Now wait a minute. There's no need to get rough. I was just checking the take."

"You owe me two hundred stergals. I want it."

"Sure, but—" Althen dabbed at his sweating face. "Look—you're a reasonable man. You know how we operate. Ten stergals, yes, but how can I pay more? I've expenses, the concession to pay for, other things. Profits are low and getting lower all the time. Tell you what, I'll settle for fifty."

Dumarest tightened his hand.

"You cheated me. You conned me into a trap. You had Krom beaten from the whistle." He looked at Dumarest's hard eyes, the cruel mouth. "I can pay," Althen admitted. "Just. But if you take it, you'll ruin me."

"Damn you," said Dumarest harshly. "What is that to me?"

CHAPTER

SEVEN

There were baths of steam and scented water, a masseuse with hands like petals with fingers of steel as she probed and eased the tension from skin and muscle. Her voice was a tempting whisper.

"You wish delights, master? A girl to beguile you, chemicals to maintain your interest, visual effects to increase your enjoyment. No? An analogue, perhaps? To experience what it is to wear another form, to mate in the shape of a beast, to hunt and kill, to feed—we have a wide variety. Still no? Then to sit and experience death in a dozen different ways. Sensitapes recorded with full stimuli from those who have burned, have fallen, have been slowly crushed. Or other things— No? As you please, master. You will sleep a little, then? An hour of blissful peace induced by the microcurrents at hand. No? Then rest, master, and let your thoughts wander. The bell will summon me in case of need."

The bell which commanded every joy invented by man—at a price.

Dumarest ignored it, lying supine, looking at the painted ceiling and the images it contained. Vague scenes summoned from the abstract design and fashioned by the power of his mind. Armored figures limned by flame, savage faces, another with a rim of blood around the mouth. Hair of jet, of gold, of brilliant flame. Women he had met and loved and lost. Worlds he had seen, the stars, a monstrous shape robed in scarlet engulfing them in a web. A boy with golden hair and vivid blue eyes.

Damn Garfrul. He had looked too much like Jondelle and he had been a fool. It had been stupid to interfere, more than stupid to fight. And he had shown the boy nothing except what seemed to be an easy way to make money. He would practice, think himself strong, and pay for it with vicious cuts.

His girl would see to that.

57

Dumarest remembered her face, the planes and contours framed by a wealth of midnight hair, the eyes which had betrayed her selfish nature. And yet was she so wrong to reach for what she desired? Lallia had been a little like that, strong and ruthless in her fashion, knowing what she wanted and honest enough to admit it. Lallia who had died on a world in the Web, killed by an agent of the Cyclan.

He thought again of the scarlet shape engulfing worlds. The symbol of the organization which sought complete domination of the galaxy. Its agents spreading to influence every sphere of importance. The cybers who were living robots devoid of all emotion, who could only know the pleasure of mental achievement. Men who had been taken as boys, to be trained, operated on, the thalamus divorced from the cortex, so they could never experience hate or love or fear. Creatures in human form who could take a handful of data and extrapolate from it in lines of logical sequence and so predict the outcome of any course of action.

The Cyclan which hunted him and would always hunt him as long as he held the secret of the affinity twin given to him by Kalin. Kalin of the flame-red hair. Red robes, red gems, red the color of blood which had stained his path for as long as he could remember.

But there were no cybers on Ourelle. The culture was too splintered, too divided, without strong government or rulers of influence. Ourelle, a backward world, almost ignored, an easy place in which to get lost.

Was that why Makgar had chosen it?

Dumarest turned again, restless, unable to wholly relax. The ceiling held too many images, inspired too many trains of thought . . . Jondelle and what might be happening to him . . . what could happen unless he was found. Why was he so concerned with the boy?

A promise given to dying woman. His word. It was enough.

To the air he said, "What is the time?"

"Three hours before midnight," a soft voice responded. "The night is dry but there is cloud."

Time to be moving. Outside the baths he paused and looked at the blaze of light which hung like a nimbus over the Narn. More light shone from where the field lay beyond the city, floodlights which showed every inch of ground with the perimeter fence. As he watched there was a crack of displaced air from high above and a ship, wreathed in the blue halo of its Erhaft drive, settled to the ground below.

A ship, small, probably engrossed in local trade, but a vessel he could take, the cash in his pocket buying him a High passage to where there would be other ships making longer journeys. But no ship he knew could take him where he wanted to go.

A woman said, "You look lonely, friend. That ship remind you of home? Why don't you come to my place and tell me all about it."

"Thank you, no."

"Not in the mood?" She shrugged. "Well, that's the way it goes."

She moved on and he walked to the House of the Gong.

It was large, bright, hung with a thousand lanterns in every shade and combination of color. Suspended gongs throbbed softly to the impact of an artificial wind and a larger gong, pierced, formed the entrance which was reached by a flight of low, broad steps. At their foot a cowled figure held a bowl of chipped plastic. Before him a plump man with his gemmed woman roared with sudden mirth.

"Charity? I don't believe in it. A man should stand on his own two feet and not depend on alms. Give me one good reason why I should put anything into your bowl."

The monk was of the Universal Church, drab in his homespun robe, feet bare in crude sandals. Within the cowl his face was lined, pinched by age and deprivation, but his eyes were young and bright with infinite compassion.

Quietly he said, "You are about to tempt good fortune, brother. May luck attend you. But think of those who have no luck and who lack for bread. It is summer now but winter will be with us soon. A bad time, brother, for those who have no money or friends."

"Not good enough." The plump man shook his head. "I'm still not convinced."

"You are a gambler, brother, and as such believe in symbols and omens. Who knows what brings good fortune? Your first stake thrown to the ground? Your first win tossed to the servants? A wise man would surely make a small sacrifice before he begins to play."

The woman said, "He could be right, Enex. Helga threw a beggar a coin once and won a thousand stergals."

A good psychologist, thought Dumarest as the plump man reached into his pocket. But the monks are past masters of the art. Throwing a coin into the bowl, he mounted the stairs.

Inside it was warm with gusts of scented air driving coils of colored smoke past lanterns hanging from the decorated ceilings. The place was as he expected, tables for cards, dice, spinning wheels. The games too were familiar: high-low-man-in-between, poker, spectrum, sevens, starburn, brenzo. A transparent, tube-like container held a mass of writhing spores, the voice of the houseman a steady drone.

"The battle commences. Bet now on your choice of red, blue, or green. The photometer will tell which color is ascendent at the expiration of sixty seconds. Bet now. No more bets. Play commences."

He pressed a lever. Nutrients flooded into the container, the spores eating, breeding, fighting, and dying.

"Yellow wins!" The container spun, emptied, grew bright with fresh spores. "The battle commences. Make your bets. The photometer . . ."

Dumarest passed on. A girl, dressed from throat to ankle in a clinging gown of embroidered silk, offered him a tray of food and drink. Hollow pastries and strong wine. Fuddled men made careless gamblers.

He waved her aside and headed for the restaurant. Akon Batik would be in no hurry to send his messenger. It would be good business to keep him waiting, gambling, perhaps, losing some of the money he had received for the chorismite. There would be time and to spare for a meal and Dumarest had early learned to eat while food was available. A traveler never could be sure when he would be able to eat again.

He ordered meat, light vegetables, cheese, and a weak wine. The meat was good and he ate it slowly. The cheese held a strange pungency and was speckled with seeds which dissolved to a tart liquid. The wine was dry, scented with roses, pink with streaks of red. He was emptying the bottle when a man slipped into the chair opposite.

"Dumarest? Earl Dumarest?"

Dumarest nodded.

"Akin Tambolt. You're expecting me."

"I am?"

"Sure. The jeweler sent me."

"Name him."

Tambolt laughed with a flash of strong, white teeth. "You're cautious; well, I can't blame you. In Sargone most things can happen and usually do. All right, let's use names. Akon Batik, good enough?"

He was young with a hard maturity about the eyes and mouth. A broad, thickset figure which would later run to fat unless he were careful. He was dressed in thick, serviceable clothing, pants and high boots, a shirt of ebon scratched to reveal flashes of the wire mesh beneath. A traveler's garb, or that worn by a man used to rough living. His hands were broad, strong, the nails blunt. One cheek bore a thin scar. His hair was thick, low over ears and neck, brown flecked with auburn. He wore a heavy signet ring on the little finger of each hand. Wide metal bands set with sharp stones. Serviceable weapons for a man who knew how to use them.

A bravo, thought Dumarest. An opportunist. A man who lived on the fringe and would do anything for gain.

Tambolt said, "There was talk of money. Twenty stergals."

"Ten."

"Ten it is, but you can't blame me for trying. Give."

"For what? Because you ask?"

"Do you want to learn what I know or not?"

"I'll find out," said Dumarest. "One way or another, I'll find out. You want to bet on it?"

For a moment their eyes locked, then Tambolt shrugged. "One day, perhaps," he said flatly. "But not now. How about some wine?"

Dumarest ordered a bottle and watched as the other poured himself a glass. "To your health, Earl. Have you eaten?"

"Yes."

"A pity, I'm starving." He called to the waitress and ordered. "You've no objection?"

"None," said Dumarest.

"That's generous of you, Earl. I like a generous man."

"I'm not generous," said Dumarest. "Just impatient. What have you to tell me?"

"Nothing. That is nothing which seems to be of use. The jeweler passed the word and asked in the right places. No one seems to have hired bravos to steal the boy. The lads you took care of in the city must have come from outside. That or no one admits to ever having seen them before. The others, those that hit you at the farm, not the Melevganians, the same."

The food came and he ate with a barely masked hunger.

"Of course the sources could be lying, but I don't think so. Akon is in well with everyone who matters and Sargone isn't all that large. People listen, they learn, and they talk if they can gain by it. Whoever wanted the boy must have played it close. They could have used their own men, in which case you're up a dead end."

"Perhaps not," said Dumarest. "The husband, Elray, could have told someone where and when he would be. The attack in the city doesn't make sense otherwise. No one would have known when to hit."

"The husband?" Tambolt swallowed the last of his meal. "You think he agreed to have his boy stolen?"

"Jondelle wasn't his child. He was dependent on his wife and maybe he wanted to make a break. If the opportunity was there, he could have taken it."

"Money for the child, some pretended grief, and then a quiet disappearance." Tambolt nodded. "It could have been done that way, but who would be willing to pay in order to get the boy? Usually it's the other way around. Steal the child and demand ransom."

"Yes."

"Which makes you think and gives rise to some interesting speculation. The boy must have a high value for someone. Perhaps whoever stole him knows the market and what the goods will bring. But you've thought of that, of course."

"Yes," said Dumarest again.

"Which maybe accounts for your interest? I'd wondered. You aren't related to the boy, so what's it to you if he gets stolen? But if you knew where the market was—"

"If I did I wouldn't be wasting time here," said Dumarest curtly.

"Maybe. Or maybe you know where it is and want to have the goods to hand." Tambolt sucked at his teeth. "Say, that meat was good. Mind if I have some more?"

"Eat as much as you like—you're paying for it."

"What?"

"From the money you hope to get from me. The ten stergals promised. It's down to seven now."

"Damn you!" Tambolt's hand clenched into a fist, light splintering on the sharp point of the gem in his ring. "You can't do that to me!"

"No?" Dumarest smiled without amusement. "Did you think I was so easy to con? Grow up, man. So far you haven't told me anything of value. You're a messenger, all right, so maybe it isn't your fault. But don't expect me to be grateful." Deliberately he reached for the bottle of wine and helped himself. "Your health. From the way you ate that meat things haven't been too good lately."

"You can say that again." Tambolt took a deep breath and unclenched his hand. "So I made a mistake," he admitted. "I tried to get more than was due and fell flat on my face. Well, it's a lesson."

He refilled his glass and sat back nursing the wine, looking older than he had, more haggard. A man who had dressed to a part, who had tried to live up to it and who now tasted the bitter fruit of failure.

"Akon gave me the job," he said. "I didn't know who or what you were—well, that doesn't matter now. How keen are you to find the boy?"

"Produce him and I'll give you the cost of a High passage."

"Traveler's talk. The way you assess values. Riding Low, High, Middle when you can get a berth on a vessel. You traveled much?"

"Yes."

"I've done a little. Not much, a couple of worlds, just enough to know that luck rides against me. I saw a man who had taken one chance too many on my last trip. When they opened the casket he was dead. Young too, younger than me. Ourelle seemed to hold promise, so I stayed. Now I haven't the price of a decent meal." He sipped at his wine. "Would you think that I've got a degree in geology?"

Dumarest was curt. "Does it matter?"

"What do you think? No, not really. Only I know rocks and formations and I've done a little prospecting. I've studied Ourelle, too, had a job in the Kladour for a while. They fired me because—well, never mind. Just say that we didn't see eye to eye on expenses. Field trips can come high. And I found a few things I didn't turn in." Tambolt looked at his rings. "Nice stones, aren't they? Fakes, of course, but they'd pass a casual inspection. Only the Kladour doesn't make casual inspections. I tried to build up the stake at the tables and lost the lot. One day I'll learn. When I'm dead maybe. When it's too late."

He emptied his glass and refilled it, gulping half of it in a single swallow as if making a defiant gesture to some private devil. Greed, perhaps, or inadequacy, or an intellectual blindness which made him underestimate all he met. Or, thought Dumarest grimly, he could be lying, presenting a facade he hoped would appeal.

Bluntly he said, "The boy?"

"You want to find him. Maybe I can help you."

"How?"

"You know, Earl. You must have thought of it. I guess you think of most things. Melevganians attacked the farm, but they weren't alone. The strangers took the boy. Where? We don't know. Who were they? We don't know that either. But maybe the Melevganians do. So reach them and make them talk. Right?"

He poured more wine as Dumarest made no answer.

"I'm beginning to understand why the jeweler picked me to carry his message. He's old and shrewd and can see the obvious. You want to go to Melevgan, there are gems there, things of value, and he knows we'd take him what we found. Fat profits and no risk. No wonder he's rich."

Dumarest said, flatly, "I'm after the boy, not a handful of stones."

"You could get both—or get neither. You think it easy? Going to Melevgan isn't like taking a stroll in the park. I've been there and I know. One wrong move and you'll wind up dead. You need me, Earl. Partners?"

Dumarest leaned back, sipping at his wine. From beyond the dining area came the susurration of gamblers at their play, the rattle of dice, the inhalations, cries of joy, and expressions of disgust. Devotees of the goddess of chance. Trying their luck as all men had to try it in order to stay alive. Yet not always were the odds so great. Most could pick their gambles, others could not. Jondelle for one.

He said, "What would we need?"

"A raft. Trade goods. Weapons and men. It won't come cheap."

"A thousand?"

"Not enough." Tambolt was emphatic. "A raft comes high—no one will rent one out so you'll have to buy. Trade goods will take half of it, weapons more, and then you'll have to find some men. They'll want high pay."

Dumarest thought of the farm and what he had left there. There and on the way to the city. He said, "We don't need a raft, only an engine. We can hire one with a driver to take us out to the farm. What do they need in the way of trade goods?"

"The Melevganians? Manufactured items; missiles for their lances, some electronic circuitry, drills, machine tools, stuff like that. The money will cover it, the engine too, but what about the men?"

Dumarest finished his wine. "I'll get the men."

CHAPTER

EIGHT

It was going to rain. Brother Elas could tell from the ache in his bones, the sure sign of inclement weather, and soon would come the winter, the snows from the north and the bitter, freezing winds. On Ourelle seasons were short and all too soon the sultry days of summer would be over, the sun hidden by cloud, the ground hard, and misery rampant. A bad time for monks as well as penitents. A bleak time for those who had nowhere to turn for aid but the church.

The thought of it made him shiver; imagination, of course, for the night was warm and the rain would do no more than bring wetness. But funds, as always, were low and he knew too well what was to come. Well, it was a thing that could not be helped and would have to be accepted along with the rest. With his duties, for one, and they were something which could not be shirked.

He walked slowly from the hut to where the church stood on a patch of waste ground. Small as such churches always were, a prefabricated structure built up with flimsy sheeting, the body containing his seat, the benediction light, the place for the suppliant. Brother Karl came to meet him, his young face showing signs of fatigue. Bowing, he said, "We are busy tonight, Brother."

"That is bad?"

"No, but—"

"You are tired."

"True, but even so—"

"You are tired," repeated the elder monk firmly. "A dull brain sees things not always as they are. You must eat and rest a little, and, Brother, remember what you are and why you are here."

A rebuke but a mild one, yet necessary just the same. The sin of impatience was close to that of pride and no monk of the Universal Church must ever forget for a moment that he was a servant and not a master. That

66

his duty was to help and never to demand. To learn that frustration was a part of life and his task seemingly endless.

Not an easy thing to accept, less so when the body was young and the soul restless. And yet Brother Karl would learn as they all had learned that the universe could not be altered in a day. That it was enough to take one penitent and give ease and comfort and to instill the creed which was the reason for their being. The one concept which alone could bring true happiness.

"There, but for the grace of God, go I."

Once all men accepted it, lived by it, the millennium would be at hand.

Brother Karl bowed, humiliated. "My apologies, Brother. I have still to learn."

"You have learned, but at times you forget to remember. Now go and eat a little and rest for a while. A fatigued body makes a bad servant and you have worked hard."

Too hard, he thought, as the young man moved away. Trying to do everything at once and yielding to irritation at the apparent slowness of progress. It was nothing new. All monks felt the same when they left the great seminary on the planet Hope, eager to take what they had learned and convert it into living fact. But he would learn as they all had learned that patience was the greatest weapon they possessed. Patience and dedication and, above all an infinite compassion.

He took his place in the church, bones creaking as he dropped into the still-warm seat. How long had it been since he had listened to his first suppliant? Forty years . . . it must be at least that, probably more. Almost a half century since he had gone to his first station to work with other, older monks, absorbing what they could teach, treading the path they had shown. He could have been the resident head now of an established church somewhere on a hospitable world, but always he had chosen to move on, to work at the beginnings, to go where he considered he was needed most.

Hard worlds. A hard life, but he would have chosen no other.

He blinked, conscious that his mind was wandering, and straightened, touching the bell to summon the first of the waiting suppliants. The man was thin, his skin febrile, his eyes unnaturally bright. He knelt before the benediction light, the waves of color laving his face with kaleidoscopic brilliance. His voice was a hurried murmur.

". . . and I took what wasn't mine. I stole a cloak and a pair of boots and sold them and kept the money. I was going to buy food but there was this place and I thought I could make it more so I gambled it and lost it and when I got back the baby had died. The money would have saved it, maybe. But I tried, Brother. I know I did wrong but I tried and now . . ."

Tormented by guilt he had turned to the only surcease he knew.

"Look into the light," said Brother Elas. "Let the light of forgiveness cleanse away your sin and bring ease to your heart. Look into the light."

The wash of color which induced a rapid hypnotic trance. The men would suffer subjective penance and rise to take the bread of forgiveness.

Others came, a stream of them with their petty crimes, most inventing their sins in order to receive the wafer of concentrates which helped them stay alive. Brother Elas did not mind; it was a small price to pay for the prohibition against killing instilled by the light. Smaller to embrace them in the body of Humanity, the great Brotherhood of Man where each should be the other's keeper and no man need live alone.

It was a long session, but finally it ended, no one answering the summons of the bell. Stiffly the old monk rose and left the church. It had begun to rain, a thin drizzle which made the ground slippery beneath his sandals, and increased the ache in his bones. Brother Karl, his face smoother now, his eyes less harassed, met him as he neared his hut.

"You have a visitor, Brother. I asked him to wait."

"Has he been here long?"

"Less than an hour. I would have called you, but he insisted that I should not. Shall I attend you?"

"No. Close the church; there will be no more penitents tonight. But if you could prepare me a little food . . . ?"

Dumarest rose as the monk entered the hut. He had been studying a fabrication of seeds and scraps of shining mineral, the whole worked into the likeness of a young man, robed, the cowl thrown back over his shoulders. Introducing himself, he said, "You, Brother?"

"Yes." Elas touched it, his thin hand gentle on the

ornate workmanship. "A memento from Kalgarsh. You know the world?"

"No."

"A hard place of poor soil and scanty crops. I was there very many years ago now. The women are deft and I tried to introduce a new art-form, souvenirs which they could sell to the tourists who came to watch the storms. The ground is arid, the winds strong and, at certain times of the year, vast clouds of colored dust hang like images in the sky. They gave me this when I left."

"A thoughtful tribute," said Dumarest politely.

"A small thing, but I value it. Vain, perhaps, but it is not always wise to forget the past and, at my age, memories hold undue tenderness. And now, brother, you have business with me?"

"I need your help."

"Mine, brother?"

"Yours and that of the Church." Dumarest told him of the boy and what had happened. "The mystery is why he should have been stolen at all. He belonged, as far as I know, to no rich House. Certainly his mother had little wealth. As a slave he would be of little worth and no slaver would have gone to so much trouble. He has been taken somewhere. I want to know where. If I knew why he was taken in the first place, it could help me to find him."

"I see." The old monk sat, brooding. "And your own interest?"

"A promise to his dying mother." Dumarest guessed what the other was thinking. "I can't keep the boy with me. If he has relatives, he must go to where he belongs. But I don't intend that those who stole him should keep him. They have too much to answer for. Perhaps, with luck, I shall make them pay for what they have done."

"With death," said Elas bitterly. "With maiming and violence and physical hurt. You are a hard man, Dumarest. Perhaps too hard. But how can I help you?"

"You and the Universal Church," corrected Dumarest. "You have monks on almost every world and I know the influence you have on those in high places. Friends who would be willing to help, if only to answer a question or two. And there could be others looking for the boy. You could ask, find out if such a boy is missing from his family, find his relatives, perhaps. Anything."

"And how could this be done?"

"You know, Brother. We both know."

By means of the hyper-radio incorporated into every benediction light, a network of communication which spread across the galaxy. To Hope itself where records were kept and the answer could, perhaps, be found.

"A boy," said Dumarest. "Young, lost, in peril of his life, perhaps. Someone who needs your help and the help you can give. I know that you cannot refuse."

Brother Elas sighed. The man was right, of course; he could not refuse, but there was so little to go on. A boy, young, blond, blue-eyed—the description would fit so many.

"Is there nothing else you can tell me? Was he born here on Ourelle?"

"I don't think so. His mother could have brought him from Veido—I don't know the planet."

"No solidiograph or list of physical peculiarities?" The monk spread his hands. "You can appreciate the difficulties. The more information I have, the better I will be able to help."

"I understand," said Dumarest. "And I think I can get you what you need. But I did not come here simply to ask. I have an offer as well. Make no mistake about what I am next going to say. I know that you cannot be bribed and need no payment for what I ask you to do. In fact, I'm going to ask even more."

"Yes?"

"The boy's mother owned a farm. She is dead now, her husband too. The title goes to the boy, but he is young and may never be found. I ask you to hold it in trust for him until it can be claimed. There is damage, but the house is intact and the crops ready for harvesting. There is water and plentiful timber. No one will argue if you choose to take it over and work it."

Elas said quietly, "You swear that what you have told me is the truth?"

"I am known on Hope. The High Monk Jerome will vouch for me."

"He is dead. Didn't you know?"

"The records, then."

The records which never died; the prospect was enticing. Elas sat back, thinking about it. A farm to provide food, warmth, and comfort against the bleakness to come. Shelter against the iron grip of winter. Brother Karl could handle it and find a vent for his energies in doing so. A place in which men could work and gain strength and recover their self-respect. A haven for the families who had no hope.

Dumarest rose. "You will need to think about it. I hope to leave within a few hours. A hired raft will take me to the farm. If you will send a monk, he can see the place and make his report. Also, I may be able to give more details about the boy. The raft, of course, will carry the monk back to you."

"Brother Karl will accompany you. And now?"

"Now," said Dumarest flatly, "I have to find some men."

They were where he expected them to be, crouched under scraps of plastic sheeting and hammered fragments of metal, discarded planks and strips of various materials. Poor protection against the rain, but all they had. The stranded, the travelers who lacked the price of a Low passage, those who had for some reason or other found themselves at the bottom of the heap. The desperate.

A man sat under an awning stirring a pot which stood over a smoldering fire. He looked up as Dumarest passed, his eyes suspicious, wary. Behind him a woman coughed and drew a moldy blanket tighter around her shoulders. Two others threw dice with blank interest, killing time with nothing to stake. A group huddled close for mutual comfort. A man pursed his lips as he mended a ragged tear in a boot. Another honed the blade of a knife.

Lowtowns were all the same.

Dumarest walked through it, catching the stench, the scent of dirt and bad health, of poor food and corrosive despair. And everywhere was the unmistakable stink of poverty.

He halted, lifting his voice.

"I want some men. An engineer able to repair a raft. Others with strong backs and shoulders. Who's interested?"

The man honing the knife rose and slipped the blade into a sheath at his waist.

"For what?"

"A journey. It's hard and rough and so I want men to match. You'll get food, clothing, and maybe the price of a passage when the job is done."

"High or Low?"

"Maybe High."

The man frowned. "Maybe?"

"That's what I said." Dumarest met his eyes, turned to look at the others who had clustered around. The man with the torn boot pressed close.

"I'm an engineer. You want a raft fixed, I can do it."

"You sure about that?"

"I'm sure." The man's eyes shifted a little. "You just give me the chance and I'll show you what I can do. You don't have to believe me, ask the monks, they'll tell you what I can do."

"You've been under the light?"

"Why, sure, how else could—"

"Forget it," snapped Dumarest. "Anyone else?"

A squat man thrust himself forward. He wore drab clothing, patched boots, and a mended shirt, but his cheeks were full and his shoulders square. He said, "I'm called Jasken. You want a good engineer, I'm your man. I can build a raft from scrap and if you want mining gear fixed, I can do that too. And I'm religious."

A man called, "What difference does it make?"

"He wents men who can fight and kill if they have to." Jasken didn't take his eyes off Dumarest. "All right, I'm willing to do anything to get a stake. What's your proposition?"

"I told you. Food, clothing, money if we find it, nothing if we don't."

"A journey. To where?" He whistled as Dumarest told him. "Hell, I've heard of that place. Mister, you don't know what you're asking!"

"Did I say it would be easy?" Dumarest shrugged. "I'm no monk and I'm not offering charity. I'm giving you a chance to get out of this stink and try your luck on some other world. You're an engineer, you say?"

"A good one."

"You'd better be. If you're lying, you'll regret it."

Jasken drew in his breath. "I don't lie, mister. I don't have to."

"Then why aren't you working? No rafts to be repaired on Ourelle? No mines with equipment to be kept operating? Tell me."

"They've got guilds. You belong to one or you don't work. Outside Sargone, maybe, but how do I get there? I landed three months ago after riding Low. I've worked maybe three weeks. Cut-rate jobs, but I was glad to get them. Then the guilds moved in and passed the word—employ me and ask for trouble. No one wants trouble." Jasken bared his teeth. "I've managed to stay alive, but it hasn't been easy, and I'd go to hell and back for a High passage."

"That's what I'm asking."

"Then that's what you'll get. Jasken looked at Dumarest, his eyes searching. "You're a traveler, I can tell. Haven't you ever been stranded? Don't you know what it's like?"

"I know," said Dumarest shortly.

"Yes, I guess you do. How many men do you need? I know them," he added as Dumarest made no answer. "I know who uses the Church and who doesn't The strong from the weak, those with the guts to take a chance and those who just want to sit and wait for a miracle. You'll let me pick them?"

His friends, those he could trust to back him if it came to trouble? Desperate men wouldn't be squeamish if offered a chance to make some easy money. It was a chance he was reluctant to take and yet Dumarest knew there was little choice. No matter whom he picked, they would have a common cause.

He said, "Pick about eight. I'll sort them out. Have them stand over by the church." As Jasken moved off, he returned to where the man sat before his pot of stew and stared down at him. "You. What's your name?"

"Preleret. Why?"

"Get on your feet!"

For a moment the man hesitated, than slowly rose, his eyes glinting.

"Listen, mister—I may not be much, but I don't get pushed around. Not by you. Not by anyone."

"Is that your woman?"

The man glanced to where she sat, shivering despite the warmth of the night.

"I'm looking after her."

"She's dying," said Dumarest bluntly. "In a week all you'll be able to do for her is to put her in the ground. I offered you a job, why didn't you take it?"

Deliberately the man spat. "I've been conned before, mister. Work hard, keep loyal, and collect the pot at the end of the rainbow. To hell with it. On Frendis I worked for six weeks gathering the harvest and found I owed more at the end of it than I'd earned. On Carsburg three months on a construction gang with the promise of a fat bonus, overtime, and double pay on holidays. There was no bonus, no overtime, and no damn holidays. You know what I got out of it? A new pair of boots. To hell with promises!"

"And her?" Dumarest jerked his head at the woman. "To hell with her too?"

"Damn you! Don't you think I know how bad she is? What are you trying to do?"

Dumarest dug coins from his pocket, let them clink in his palm. "This will save her," he said quietly. "Money to buy her the drugs and attention she needs. A place in the infirmary, food to build her up, put flesh on her bones. Are you too proud to take it?"

"Mister, where she's concerned I'd eat dirt. No, I've got no pride."

"I want you to come with me," said Dumarest. "All I can offer you is a chance—but what have you got now? Nothing. She'll die and you'll follow." He handed over the money. "I'm not bribing you; the money's yours whether you come or not. But think about it. If you want to come, I'll be back here at noon."

"I—" The man swallowed, staring at the money. "Mister, I—"

"Noon." said Dumarest. "At the church."

He walked away to where Jasken waited with the men he had selected. Preleret would be at the rendezvous, despite what he'd said, he had pride and would be grateful. The touch of the money would work its magic, what it could do and what more could bring. Health, escape and, perhaps, happiness. He would be there and would provide a little insurance against the rest. The others to be picked from those Jasken had chosen.

CHAPTER

NINE

The farm looked as he remembered, the house with closed windows looking like blind eyes, the door still closed by the planks he had nailed across the panel. Before it lay the ash from the fires, spread now, evened out by the wind so as to give the appearance of dingy snow. The invaders lay where they had fallen, bizarre armor dusted with gray, blown ash heaped in little drifts to blend them with the ground.

Dumarest studied the area. A mound of dirt showed where the Hegelt had buried their dead, a smaller one beside it where he had buried Elray. All was covered with ash. There were no footprints. The small, dark people had mourned their dead and then departed, driven away by fear of ghosts or later vengeance. They had been leaving when he had nursed the raft toward the city.

Brother Karl said, "An ugly scene, brother. It does not belong in such a gentle place."

"No."

"Shall we land?"

"A moment." Dumarest called to Tambolt where he rode with the others in the repaired raft. "Make a swing about the area. A large one, out to those trees on the ridge. I want to make sure no one is lurking about."

"You expect trouble?" The driver of the hired raft pulled uneasily at the collar of his shirt. "Now look, mister. I was hired to carry you out and then lift the monk back to the city. Nobody said anything about heading into a war."

Dumarest said, "Land close to the house. A few feet before the front door."

"Shall I start to unload?"

"Yes." Dumarest glanced at the bales in the body of the vehicle, the trade goods Tambolt had purchased. "But be careful. Drop one and we could all go sky-high."

"Explosives? But—"

75

"Just be careful."

The planks yielded with a squeal. Dumarest threw them aside and walked into the familiar area. It was dim, light streaming past him through the open door throwing vague shadows in the passage and foot of the stairs. They vanished as he opened more doors, filling the house with an emerald luminescence.

"A fine house," said the monk. His eyes were bright, eager. Already he was mentally allocating quarters and evaluating what needed to be done. That room for the administration, that for the benediction light, another to dispense medicines. Trees could be cut to provide timber for shacks. Clay could be dug, molded, and fired for drainage pipes and an extension of the water supply. Baths could hug the river, the silos repaired, the sheds, the workshops. Stone and mud to provide extensions to the house. The materials were at hand and they would not be short of labor. "A fine dwelling," he said again. "A haven for those in need during the winter."

"To be held in trust," Dumarest reminded. "For the boy."

"Of course, that is understood." Brother Karl looked at the ugly stains on the floor of the room in which they stood. "The owner died here?"

"The owner's husband. She died on the way to the city. You saw her grave."

"Of course, I should have remembered. Well, where shall we begin?"

The room was a study, the desk filled with scraps of paper, old bills, records, lists of plantings and stores. Dumarest looked at a folded document, the title to the farm, and learned from it nothing he did not already know. He handed it to the monk and stood, frowning.

"The boy was close to her," he said. "Upstairs, perhaps, in her room?"

It held memories he did his best to ignore. Hours spent in bandaging, cooling fevered skin, of replacing covers thrown aside. A wardrobe held an assortment of clothing, serviceable gowns, mostly, thick coats with hoods, strong boots for use in mud. A shimmer of color revealed a low-cut, narrow-waisted dress of diaphanous material. A party dress or one worn by a woman attending a high function. The fabric of the neck and waist was frayed as if adornments had been torn from their foundation.

Gems, perhaps? The jewels which had provided the money to buy the farm?

Dumarest delved into a small chest and found a litter of cosmetics, paint, brushes, vials of perfume.

"The boy's room, perhaps?" suggested the monk.

It was small, snug under the eaves, warm and bright with gay color. Animals of a dozen varieties traced in glowing pigments on the walls, soft covers on the rumpled bed, a shelf which held an assortment of toys, things carved from wood, made of stuffed fabrics, combinations of stones and seeds.

His clothes looked very small.

Dumarest checked everything, his jaw hard, muscles prominent along the line of bone. Jondelle had been asleep, lost, maybe, in childish dreams when the attack had come. He would have woken, frightened, perhaps calling for help. And then the brutal shape of the armored man, grotesque, terrifying, bursting through the door. An arm to clamp him hard against the unyielding chest, a gloved hand rammed over his mouth. And then the sting of the drug which had made him lax, unconscious, easy to handle.

He felt a hand touch his arm. The monk was anxious.

"Is anything wrong? You look—"

"Nothing." Dumarest drew a deep breath into his lungs. "Nothing is wrong."

"Your face—" Brother Karl shook his head. "Your expression. I have seen such before, brother . . . on the face of a man intent on murder." He paused, then added, "There is nothing here. The dispensary, perhaps?"

It was white, clean, a table which could serve as an emergency operating theater, a sterilizing unit to one side, ultraviolet lamps to cleanse the air of harmful bacteria. A cabinet holding drugs, disarranged from Dumarest's earlier searching. Records of treatments given.

He found his own and tore it into tiny fragments as the monk examined the rest.

"Nothing." The monk looked baffled. "And yet she must have treated him, examined him at least. Small children are subject to minor injuries and, as a doctor, she would have been interested in the progress of her child. And why no solidiographs? There isn't a likeness of the boy in the house."

"She was a woman," said Dumarest thoughtfully. "A doctor too, but first a woman."

He went back upstairs and found the chest with its litter of cosmetics. He tilted it, strewing its contents on the floor, fingers stiff as he probed the bottom. With sudden impatience he lifted his clenched hand and slammed it down hard against the base. Wood cracked, splintered as he tore it free. The monk edged close as he lifted what lay beneath the false bottom.

Medical records. A solidiograph of a smiling baby, another, taken later, of a blond-haired, blue-eyed child standing before a clump of trees.

The monk said, "The boy?"

"Yes. Jondelle. The medical records will give you his physical characteristics." Dumarest studied the remaining item. A card of flexible plastic bearing a photograph, a name, a series of fingerprints, a list of coded symbols. A means of identification carried by anyone who worked in a high-security area—or a record of one which should have remained in a file.

He looked at the face, younger than he remembered, but no less determined.

"The woman?" The monk was curious. "The boy's mother?"

Dumarest nodded, reading the name. "Kamar Ragnack. She made an anagram of the first three letters of each of the names. I don't know why, but it's obvious she was trying to hide." He handed the papers and card to the monk, retaining the solidiographs, turning them so as to look at the boy from every angle. "You can copy these," he said. "They should help."

The monk took them, tucked them into his robe. "And now?"

"You go back to the city and we'll be getting on with what has to be done."

The hired raft was empty, the driver impatient to be gone. Dumarest watched as the craft lifted, the monk raising an arm in farewell as it carried him away. Tambolt had landed close to stacked bales. He said, "I scanned the area. Nothing."

"No signs of fires, ashes, torn dirt?"

"Nothing, Earl. I flew low and checked everything. No one's been here and certainly no one is watching." He looked at the ashes of the fires, the armored dead. "It looks as if you had quite a time here. Did you learn anything about the boy?"

"No."

"You wouldn't tell me if you had—but we're partners, remember?"

Dumarest looked past him to where the others sat in the body of the raft. Jasken, Preleret, four others. One, older than the rest, said, "You promised food and clothing, Earl. I'm not complaining, but it's been a long drag. When do we eat?"

His name was Sekness, a quiet man who had remained neat and clean despite his privations. He carried a short club and had lost the little finger of his right hand.

"As soon as you prepare some food." Dumarest jerked his head toward the house. "Get into the kitchen. There's food in the store and meat in the freezer." To one of the others he said, "Help him. Jasken, how's the raft?"

"Not too good." The squat man scowled and rubbed his hand along the edge of his jaw. "The engine's no problem, but the conducting strips aren't what they should be. We're low on lift. I'd guess that we're operating at about sixty percent efficiency. We can carry the men or the load, but not both."

"That's fine," snapped Tambolt. "We're beaten before we start. A hell of an engineer you turned out to be!"

"I fitted the engine," said Jasken stolidly. "Find me new conducting strips and I'll have it as good as new, but even then you'd be in trouble. The raft isn't big enough for what you want. Those bales are heavy and we're talking about eight men. Add it all up and you've got too big a load."

"We'll manage," said Dumarest.

"How?" Tambolt was savage. "I told you the money wasn't enough. "Damn it, man, have you any idea of what lies ahead? Rough ground most of the way, chasms, mountains, patches of forest. And don't think it's like what we've already covered. Past the Relad the terrain alters. I warned you it wouldn't be easy."

"If it was, I wouldn't need you," said Dumarest evenly. "Or a raft, the goods, the men. I'd have gone alone. Now stop complaining and get the bales loaded. Preleret, come with me."

In the house he jerked open a wardrobe and gestured to the clothes inside. Elray's clothes.

"Help yourself. Take what you need and share the rest among the others. Can you use a rifle?"

"If I have to, yes."

"Carry this." Dumarest handed him one of the two weapons the house contained. "There's cartridges in the drawer; make sure they are all loaded on the raft. Touch nothing and make sure that no one takes what isn't theirs. You understand?"

Preleret nodded.

"How's your woman?"

"Fine. The medics said that I got her to the infirmary just in time. She's going to be all right. They even said they might find her a job, nothing much, just doing the dirty work, but it'll provide food and shelter until I get back."

"You'll get back."

"I intend to." The man hesitated. "Earl, I'm not good at saying things. You know? But—"

"Get your clothes," said Dumarest. "And keep that gun handy. I might need you to use it sometime. You follow me?"

"Sure, Earl." Preleret drew a deep breath. "You don't want thanks and I'm not good at giving them. But I'll pay you back in some way. Don't worry—you can rely on me."

Dumarest nodded and left the house. Outside Tambolt was supervising the loading, Jasken adjusting the bales so as to trim the raft. He glanced up as Dumarest passed, seemed about to say something, then changed his mind. The sprawled shape of an armored figure rested to one side; Dumarest passed it, halted where small craters pocked the ground, ash filling their bottoms and rounding the jagged rims. He stooped and picked up the lance he had used. A missile had struck the shaft and he looked at the ripped metal, the savage blade with its crusted point. His eyes lifted to where Makgar had lain, rose again to stare in the direction the raft had taken.

It meant nothing. They could have turned, circled, taken any direction once out of sight. The air held no traces and, even if it had, the wind would have blown them away. As it had blown the ash, the scars of the battle.

From behind Tambolt said, "Dreaming, Earl?"

"Thinking."

"About the raft? It won't carry the load and us too. We could drop some of the stuff and leave some of the men behind. Or we could take it all and leave them all.

I don't like either solution. We need the goods and we're going to need the men."

"And food," said Dumarest.

"More weight, but you're right. Men have to eat. Damn it, Earl. What can we do?"

"Use ropes. Twenty-foot lengths tied to the raft and hanging over the edge. Tie loops at the ends and we'll settle them under our arms. The raft will lift and we'll follow it. With the lift and the forward movement, we should be able to cover ten or twenty feet at a bound. Simple."

"Simple," agreed Tambolt. "On flat, soft ground and with a steady hand at the controls. But what about when the ground gets rough and there are crosswinds? The men won't like it."

"They'll like it," said Dumarest grimly. "Or they can lump it. But one thing is certain; they aren't going to quit. Once we start, we keep going until the end."

"Until we reach Melevgan."

"Until we find the boy," Dumarest corrected. He looked at the broken lance in his hand and flung it so that it stuck in the dirt. "Until we find those who took him. Now let's go and eat."

CHAPTER

TEN

The first day they covered a hundred miles, running behind and under the raft, loops tight under their armpits, slack in their hands, a hopping, bounding journey which left everyone but Dumarest and Jasken exhausted. At night they camped, eating the first big meal of the day, high-protein food, low in bulk but high in energy.

Tambolt stared at the lance Dumarest held out to him. "What's this for?"

"We're standing guard." The lance was one of four salvaged from the farm, reloaded from the goods they carried. "You, me, and Jasken. We'll overlap the shifts, two on and one off."

"I can't. I'm beat."

"You can," said Dumarest grimly. "And you will."

"The others—"

"Haven't the strength." Dumarest thrust the lance into Tambolt's hands. "All you have to do it to keep your eyes open. You see anything, you yell. If it comes at you, give it the point. If we're attacked, fire the missiles. There's nothing to it."

At dawn one of the men complained of his ankle. It was swollen, tender to the touch. Dumarest ripped up a shirt and bound it tightly, then fashioned splints with a crossbar to take the strain. Wincing, the man rose, testing it.

"I can't do it. I'll have to ride."

"You'll travel like the rest. Nurse the ankle and use the other foot—and this time be more damn careful."

The man was stubborn. "I ride or I quit. Leave me some food and one of the lances and I'll make my own way back."

"You don't ride and you don't quit," said Dumarest. "You're coming, if we have to drag you. Now get in that rope and remember what I told you. Hurt the other ankle and I'll leave you behind to rot. Now move!"

They made less progress that day, more the day after. The ground became rough, great boulders and swaths of jagged stone slowing them down almost to a crawl. A patch of forest had to be circumnavigated and hills climbed. By the time they reached the mountains the men were fit, hard and as agile as cats. But they had reached the end of the line.

"We're low on food," reported Sekness. "Enough for a couple of big meals or a half dozen small ones." He looked at the mountains soaring before them. "There could be game up there, but I doubt it. There'd be nothing for it to live on."

"There's no game." Tambolt was emphatic. "But Melevgan lies over the other side. If this damn raft was as it should be, we could get there in a day."

Jasken said, "There's nothing wrong with the raft. I'm getting tired of you whining about it."

"You're riding all the time," snapped Tambolt. "Try swinging on one of those damn ropes for a change and see how you like it."

The engineer shrugged. "Each to their own skill, mister. You think it easy handling this thing, then you try it. I've got to guard against crosswinds, updrafts, dips, and crests. To go fast when I can and to slow as I drop. If I misjudge, you'd fall, get dragged, and maybe break a few bones."

Dumarest said, "Sekness, prepare a meal, a big one. Tambolt, Preleret, get the others and unload the raft."

"Here?" Tambolt frowned. "What's the point, Earl? We've got to get the stuff over the mountains, not leave it here."

"I'm going to scout the ground," said Dumarest patiently. "We might need all the lift we can get. Now let's not waste any more time arguing about it. I want to get it done before dark."

Unloaded, the raft lifted easily beneath Jasken's hands. He sent it upward and toward the soaring barrier with Dumarest at his side studying the ground below. A defile wound, climbing and relatively smooth. It ended in a blind canyon beyond which lay a mass of jagged stone slashed with deep crevasses. Higher lay sheer falls, ledges which led nowhere, overhanging cliffs, and slopes of loose debris. The stone, harsh, blue-tinted in the emerald light, was dotted with sparse shrubs, spined and thorny growths and hooked vines covered with savage burrs.

Jasken said, "No one could climb up that. Nor down either. I'll try farther along."

It was the same. To either side the mountains presented an impassable barrier to men on foot. Jasken swore as the raft jerked beneath them, falling to rise again with a scrape of metal against stone.

"Thermals," he said. "We're too close. There are updrafts and pockets, side winds too. You seen enough, Earl?"

"Go back to the camp and try again. Head straight for the summit."

There was a place a third of the way up, a pocket in the side of the mountain, edged by stone and invisible from below. The interior was fairly smooth, dotted with minor boulders but with enough room to land. Higher there was another and the summit was bare. Jasken grunted as the raft veered to the impact of wind.

"You want me to go over?"

"No, turn back. If anyone's down there, I don't want them to see us."

"Not sure of the reception?"

"That's right. Have you marked those areas we found or do you want to take another look?"

"I know where they are. You thinking of shifting the load a piece at a time?"

Dumarest nodded; it was the only way.

"We won't be able to carry much at a time. A third of the load with a single man. Four trips each time." Jasken sent the raft flying clear of the mountain as he headed back to the camp. "Why don't you head straight for the top and be done with it?"

Dumarest said dryly, "Have you met the Melevganians?"

"No."

"But you've heard about them?"

"Sure, but—"

"Would you like to be sitting on top of that mountain with goods of price and the nearest help way down at the bottom?"

"No," said Jasken thoughtfully. "I guess not. The time element's important. I hadn't thought of that. Is that why you didn't want to be spotted? But how could they climb the other side of the mountain?"

"I don't know. Maybe they couldn't, but Tambolt said they mine it. And, maybe, they could have a raft. When we meet, I want all the advantage I can get." Dumarest stared down and ahead. The sun was setting, thick shadows hiding the lower regions, the campfire a speck of brightness against the night. Too bright, an attraction for unwanted eyes. If the food was cooked, it would have to be extinguished. To Jasken he said, "No guard for you tonight. Eat and get all the sleep you can. Tomorrow, check the raft. As soon as the sun has warmed the air, we'll begin."

"That'll be close to noon," said Jasken. "I can't work in the dark and it'll take time for the sun to warm those rocks. Uneven temperature means uneasy air and we'll have to get in close. I'd say about two hours to noon. With luck we can get all the men and goods up to the top by late afternoon."

Dumarest went with the first load, riding with a third of the bundles, frowning as the raft jerked and responded sluggishly to the controls. Twice Jasken attempted to land, veering away at the last moment as rising air made the craft unstable. The third time he set it down with a gasp of relief. He looked at his hands, trembling from overstrain, then wiped the sweat from his face and neck.

"That was tough," he said. "It'll get easier from now on. Maybe I should lighten the load a little, make five trips instead of four."

"Try it," said Dumarest. "Bring a man with you on the next trip, another on the third. Then the rest of the goods and finally the rest of the men." He added, "Make sure the man is armed."

A caution born of long experience with strange places. The mountains looked barren, but the Melevganians were close and it would be stupid to take appearances for granted. Dumarest checked the area, the rifle he carried held in readiness, but found nothing alarming in the small pocket in which he and the bales stood: some openings like tiny caves about the size of a fist, a straggle of thorned vegetation, and a patch of spined scrub. He climbed the outer wall and stared down at the bleak expanse below. If the raft should crash, he would be trapped. It would be barely possible to fashion a rope and to cut footholds, blast them, even with the missiles in the bales, but he had no food and only a little water. One slip and he would fall to lie with broken legs or punctured lungs. A damaged ankle, even, would mean his death.

He turned and stared up at the soaring expanse of the mountain. One of the chain, Tambolt had said, which ringed Melevgan. There could be a pass, somewhere, but there was no time to find it. Only a raft could surmount it and traders did not leave their rafts. If there were any inside, they would not be used for raids.

He sat on one of the bales, thinking, taking small sips of water to combat the moisture-sucking heat. The pocket was like an oven reflecting the rays of the rising sun, accentuating the heat with every passing moment. At midday it would be like a furnace.

Jasken returned with a second load, smaller, more easily handled. This time he landed at the first approach, snapping at the man he carried.

"Get this stuff off, fast. Move!"

The man was the one who had injured his ankle. He carried a lance which he let fall as he grappled with a bale. Dumarest took another, Jasken a third. Within minutes the raft was empty and rising for another journey. As it fell, Altrane yelled, "The next time bring some food. Water too. Understand?"

Dumarest said, "Get these bales stacked in a neat pile. And pick up that lance."

"Why?" Altrane was sullen. "There's plenty of room here; what's the use of double-handling?"

"Do it. Jasken needs all the room he can get. And don't forget what we're carrying. If he should drop, slam against one of these bales, you won't have a thing to worry about. You'll be dead."

He was exaggerating, but the threat brought action. Altrane placed the last of the bales and stood, sweating, his tongue moistening his lower lip.

"Have you got any water? I'm parched." He took the container Dumarest offered and drank greedily, water falling past his chin to splash on the ground. "Thanks."

"Now the lance."

"You think I'll need this thing?" He picked it up and reasted it against the bales so that the point stood upward, wicked in the light. "What's going to attack us up here? The vegetation? The rocks? You know, Earl, at times I think you're a little too cautious for your own good. A little too careful. There's a name for it."

Dumarest said, flatly, "Tell me."

Altrane scowled, remembering the way he had been treated when he had hurt his ankle. It had healed, true, but it could have grown worse and no thanks to Dumarest that it hadn't. Tambolt would have been more understanding. He could get along with Tambolt. They would have been in and out by now, taking half the goods and men, a quick trade and a big profit. And he wouldn't have used his position to push a man around.

"Tell me," said Dumarest again. "What do they call a man who's too careful?"

"Nothing." It was easy to think of what he'd say and do if the chance arose. but, now that it had come, he wasn't too eager. To change the subject, Altrane said, "How much do you think we'll make?"

"I told you what you'll get. A High passage if we find enough, less if we don't."

"Yes, but suppose we make a lot more than a High passage all around? Tambolt was saying that there are fortunes in these mountains. Jewels to be had for the taking. We could really hit the jackpot. What then, Earl?"

"Nothing. We made a deal."

"You mean that no matter how much we find, all you're going to give us is the cost of a High passage? Hell, man, you call that fair? Tambolt was saying—"

"Tambolt talks too much," snapped Dumarest curtly. "And so do you. What's the point of arguing about something we haven't even found yet? Now keep quiet. Sound travels in mountains like these."

"So what? So who's to hear us?" Altrane was livid. "Listen. Let's get this straight. Are we going to share equally or not? I—"

"Shut up!"

"What? Now you see—"

"Shut your damned mouth!"

Dumarest tensed, listening. From somewhere above and to one side came a scrape, the bounce of a falling stone. More followed the first, a little rush of loosened debris, the rocks clattering as they jounced over the slope. He climbed the wall and looked over the edge in the direction from which the sound had come. He saw nothing aside from the blue-tinged rock, the scabrous green of the straggling vegetation. A fragment yielding beneath the impact of temperature change, perhaps? A root, slowly growing, slowly pushing until eroded stone showered in a tiny avalanche?

He looked higher up the mountain, the sun-glare catching his eyes and filling them with water. He blinked, caught the hint of movement, and heard Altrane's incredulous shout.

"Dear God! What is it?"

An armored thing, ten feet long, plated, clawed, a tail raised to show a sting. Thin legs scrabbled as it raced forward, blue-tinted to match the rocks among which it lurked, the legs hooked with barbs, sending stones rolling down the mountain. A mutated, scorpion-like creature which scented water and food.

Dumarest sprang back as it reared above the edge of the pocket. falling as his foot turned, rolling to rise as the thing lunged toward him. He sprang high, a claw snapping beneath his boot, landed on a rounded back to spring again as the tail stabbed where he had stood. It brushed his side and he felt the bruising impact through his tunic. The plastic tore and a green venom stained the mesh beneath.

"The lance, man!" he shouted. "Use the lance!"

Altrane crouched behind the bales, shaking, paralyzed with fear. He screamed as the thing touched the obstruction and rose above it, the scream rising to a shriek as a claw snapped and tore flesh from his arm: He ran, hitting Dumarest in his wild flight, trailing blood as he raced to the wall at the edge of the pocket. The thing turned, the lance falling, the shaft bending beneath the grip of a claw. Dumarest dodged, jumped to one side, and ran to where the bales lay scattered. The rifle lay beneath them. If he tried to get it, he would be dead before he could drag it free. He sprang to the top of the bales, leaped over the plated back and ran to the opposite side of the pocket to where Altrane stood, whimpering, clutching at his wounded arm.

The thing froze. It stood, almost indistinguishable from the stone, stalked eyes questing, tail raised to strike. It could scent prey and was temporarily undecided in which direction to go. Dumarest tensed, watching. If the thing moved away from the bales, he could get the rifle or the lance. The lance, he decided. It was in the open and closer to hand. The shaft was bent and the missile launcher useless, but the blade and point were still serviceable. With it, he could slash at the legs, the eyes, crippling and blinding the creature and gaining time to recover the rifle and the death it could give.

He said, "Move, Altrane. Run along the edge of the wall."

"No! I can't! It'll get me!"

"Not if you go fast enough. Make a feint, then dive the other way. I've got to get hold of that lance. Bare-handed we haven't a chance."

"I can't, Earl! I can't!"

Dumarest stopped, snatched out his knife, threw it in one smooth gesture. It spun, reached the armored back just behind the eyes, and fell to ring against the stone. The plating was too hard to penetrate, as Dumarest had known it would be, but the impact stirred the creature. It spun, claws and tail uplifted, racing forward as Dumarest flung himself behind the bales. He heard the impact, the rip of tearing fabric, and felt a numbing impact against his boot. The sting had caught the heel. He jerked it away before it could strike again, rolling around the end of the scattered bales to snatch up the lance. The blade made an arc of brightness as it whined through the air, the sound of an ax hitting wood as it struck the joint of a segmented claw.

A yellow ichor welled about the blade, gushing as Dumarest tore it free to spatter on the ground. A fetid odor rose from where it lay.

"The rifle," snapped Dumarest. "Get it. Use it. Move!"

There was no time to see if Altrane obeyed. The thing had lunged forward again, legs rasping on the ground, moving at incredible speed. Dumarest backed, the lance held before him stabbing at the eyes, ducking under a sweeping claw to slash at the legs, to spring over the back as the tail slammed toward him, moving by unthinking reflex action, only his speed enabling him to survive.

It was a contest which couldn't last. Already he was tiring, the heart pounding in his chest, sweat dewing face and hands. A slip and the thing would have him, the massive claws crushing his body, driving splintered ribs into his lungs or pulping his intestines. A moment of inattention and the tail would descend like a mace on skull or shoulder, snapping the bone in arm or leg, the sting tearing at naked flesh or penetrating his clothing. And it was too well armored to be seriously hurt by the lance. Too agile to be crippled to the point where it would be helpless.

He risked a glance to where Altrane stood, numbed by his terror, useless to help.

The eyes, he thought. It had to be the eyes. Blinded, the creature might freeze long enough for him to reach the rifle.

He lifted the lance, the shaft bent now at the point where it had been crushed. Gripping the butt, he swung it in a circle, light catching the smeared blade, air whining as he backed. There was no time for careful aim. As the thing darted toward him, he threw the lance, spinning, toward the stalked eyes. Almost he missed. The blade struck one of the thick protrusions, the shaft the other, but too low for what he had intended. Hurt, the creature halted, backed a little, claws questing.

Dumarest moved.

He felt the rasp of chiton on his back as he raced, stooped, beneath a claw. The thing had been stunned a little, slow to respond, but he heard the scrape of hooked feet on the ground as it turned, the wind from the stabbing tail. Then the bales were before him and he dived over the nearest, hitting the ground, rolling to throw his weight against the one on the rifle. He rose, the muzzle spurting flame as the creature reared above him.

He saw the bullets hit, blasting the eyes, the head, the open jaw. Yellow ichor gushed from the holed carapace, sickening with its odor, and a claw fell, slamming against his side, throwing him hard against the bales.

He fired again, aiming by instinct, seeing the joint of the great pincher shatter beneath the impact of the missiles. Other thunder joined his own. Preleret, standing on the raft, white-faced, the rifle he carried tight against his shoulder.

"Earl!" he called. "Earl!"

The creature turned, gusting air in a thin, high parody of a scream. Dying, it threshed about the pocket of stone, bales flying, air thrumming to the lash of its sting. Dumarest heard a shriek, the blast of Preleret's rifle and then, after what seemed a long time, silence.

Stiffly he rose. His side felt numb and blood ran from his nose, the corner of his mouth. He looked at the

twitching shape, the raft, the figure of Altrane lying limp
to one side. His chest was torn, his skin puffed and swollen from the poison of the sting which had taken his life.

"God!" Jasken drew in a shuddering breath. "Look at
the size of that thing! Are you all right, Earl?"

He was bruised, his shoulder and ribs aching, but nothing
was broken and he would survive. As Altrane would
have survived, if he'd had the courage to act. Dumarest
looked at the dead man, then at the dead creature.

"Get ropes on it," he ordered. "Lift and drag it clear.
Dump it lower down the mountain, but leave it where it
can be seen."

Preleret was shrewd. "As a warning?"

"As bait for any others that might be lurking around.
I want no more surprises. If they come looking for easy
meat, they'll find it in one of their own kind. We can
watch, shoot if we have to, hold our fire if we don't."

Jasken said, "And the man? What about him?"

"The same."

"Well, now," said Jasken slowly. "Altrane wasn't much
good, I'll admit. I guessed wrong with him. A troublemaker
and greedy to boot. But to dump him, just like that? As
food for things like the one that attacked you? Somehow it
doesn't seem right."

"You want to take him back and show him to the
others?" Dumarest shrugged as the man made no answer.
"He's dead. He doesn't care what happens to him now. But
if the others see him, they'll get scared. Split the load.
Bring up two more on your next trip. They can see him
when they get here and not before. Now move! I want
to get to the summit before dark!"

CHAPTER

ELEVEN

They spent the night on a windswept plateau, the men nervous, staying awake and ready to shout the alarm at every sound. The bales and raft made a protective ring over which they stared into the star-shot night, seeing a danger in every shadow. At dawn they dropped into the valley, half the men at the first load, the goods, Dumarest staying until the last. The sun was bright as they left the foothills and began to cross cultivated ground. Fields of crops, orchards, bushes bearing a variety of fruit. Men and women worked the fields, small and dark, looking up as they passed, then returning to their duties.

"The Hegelt," said Tambolt. "Some of them must have been here when the Melevganians came and others have probably been brought in. They breed fast and make docile workers."

Dumarest looked ahead. They were pulling the raft now, the engine providing barely enough energy to lift the vehicle a few feet above the ground. It was slow progress, but safe and he wanted to give the impression that the craft was damaged. A precaution against theft or confiscation. A workable raft to the Melevganians would be a temptation they might choose not to ignore. A damaged one would be of little value.

"There!" Tambolt, at his side, lifted an arm, pointing. "You can see the city."

It was low, long, a rambling collection of buildings constructed in a dozen varieties of style. Grim blocks shouldered fabrications of sweeping curves and fluted roofs, tiered pagodas and convoluted spirals of no apparent purpose. Most had broad, external stairs, wide balconies and walks supported by stalked columns. The windows were paneled in fretted iron-work, panes of many shapes and colors, wide sheets of reflecting crystal, rounded bull's-eyes, curves and abstract shapes which followed no apparent symmetry. From peaked, flat, and rounded roofs fluttered pennons and gaudy ribbons, figures of weird beasts and inflated constructions striped and mottled in a variety of hues.

An amusement park, though Dumarest. A collection of individual designs interspersed with fountains which threw a rain of sparkling water into the air, of flower beds and patches of sward and mobiles which turned and chimed with soft tintinnabulations. A child's playground—or a city built by those with childlke whims.

A raft rose as they approached and swept toward them, settling a few yards ahead. It held men dressed in hatefully familiar armor, armed with lances which they kept leveled as the little party came to a halt. Another man, not armored, stepped from the raft and waited.

The reception committee. Tambolt dropped his rope and caught Dumarest by the arm as he stepped forward to where the man stood.

"Let me handle this, Earl. Don't forget they're crazy. A word and they'll be at your throat. The same word, spoken in a different tone at a different time, and they will give you everything they own. Logic doesn't work here. Not your sort of logic, at any rate."

Dumarest made no answer, looking instead at the unarmored Melevganian. He was tall, thin, his face painted in tiny flecks of color. His hair was dark, clubbed at the rear with a gemmed band. He wore soft shoes and pants, a wide belt above which showed the jeweled hilt of a knife, a short jacket, open in the front to reveal a painted chest. His lips were full, sensuous, his teeth cruelly pointed.

He said, "This is the land of the Melevganians. You are strangers."

"Traders," said Tambolt smoothly. "Men who have come to bring you things of interest. To offer our services and to bask in the sun of Melevgan."

"Which will never fade."

"Which will never fade," repeated Tambolt. "Have we your permission to remain?"

"And if it is refused?"

"We shall leave."

Dumarest saw the painted face convulse, the lips tighten, and one of the thin hands lift toward the knife.

He said quickly, "My lord, if we have offended, we crave your forgiveness. The sun of the elect is bright in our eyes and dulls our mind. Of course we cannot leave without your august permission. In all things we are your servants."

"You are gracious." The man relaxed, his hand falling from his waist, his thin, strident voice softening a little. "You please me. You carry goods, you say?"

"A few things of little worth—yet you may find them amusing."

"That could be so."

"If it is your wish to see them, the bales will be unpacked at your command."

"Later. The Guardians of Melevgan do not concern themselves with such things. But, later, if it is my whim, I shall inspect them."

"As you wish, my lord."

"You speak well," mused the man. "And you please me, as I have said. The elect are generous to those who do them service. Go now, to the house bearing the image of a hanging man. Food will be provided."

"My lord." Dumarest bowed. "May I have the honor of knowing to whom I speak?"

"Tars Boras. Commander of the Guardians and a noble of Melevgan. We shall meet again."

Tambolt released his breath as the man returned to his raft and was lifted away.

"You took a chance there, Earl. Asking his name like that. He could have turned against us."

"He didn't."

"But he could have. I told you to leave everything to me. I know how to handle them."

"Maybe." Jasken had overheard. "But it looked to me as if he were about to blow his top before Earl took over." He scowled after the vanishing shape of the raft. "The arrogant swine! I've met characters like him before. They think they own the galaxy because they've got wealth and power and consider everyone else to be less than dirt. Well, maybe we can teach him a lesson."

"No," said Dumarest.

"How come, Earl?"

"I don't want you thinking that way. We want something from these people. If we have to eat dirt to get it, then that's just what we'll do. Now let's find the house of the hanging man."

It was deep in the city, a squat cone with a staircase

spiraling outside to a pointed summit on which stood a
gallows and the figure of a suspended man. A wide door
admitted the raft and internal stairs led upward to a
semicircular chamber bright with rainbows from a dozen
windows glazed with tinted crystal. Other chambers opened
from the first containing baths and soft couches, a room
with a table containing smoking meats. Hegelt women
served them, silent on naked feet, shapeless beneath robes
of nondescript gray.

Tambolt said, "For these who don't know better, let
me give a warning. Don't touch the women or interfere
with them in any way. They keep to themselves and the
Melevganians won't have anything to do with them. Men
don't mate with animals and to them that's just what the
Hegelt are. If you touch them, you'll demean yourselves
and the rest of us with you. I want to get out of here
alive and rich, but at least alive. You understand?"

Preleret said, "I'm not interested in these girls. I've got
a woman back in Sargone. All I'm interested in is money."

"And there's plenty of it around," said one of the
others. "Did you see those jewels that character was
wearing? How much do you think the stuff we brought is
worth, Tambolt? Can we screw up the price, maybe?"

Greed, thought Dumarest, but it was an emotion to be
used. Had been used. He pushed aside his plate and left
the table. In the large, semicircular room he stepped to
one of the windows and tried to look outside. The tinted
panes distorted his view, imperfections in the crystal blur-
ring clear vision either by accident or design. Were all
traders arriving in Melevgan put in this house to wait the
pleasure of the elect? Was it a means to keep them from
learning too much?

To one of the Hegelt women he said, "Are we permitted
to leave?"

"Master?"

"Can we go outside?"

"There are Guardians below, master. It would not be
wise to attempt to pass them."

Prisoners, then, or guests who had to remain where
put. Dumarest tested one of the windows, remembering
the spiral staircase outside. The guards would be inside the
building watching both raft and door. Or perhaps they
stood outside the wide panels. If he could reach the external stair and drop from it, he could leave unseen.

The window seemed jammed. He moved to another, the girl padding behind him.

"Master, why do you wish to leave and go outside?"

To learn. To ask about the things he wanted to know. To discover, somehow, if the boy was in the city. Perhaps Tars Boras would tell him, but he doubted it. The man had been too ready to reach for his knife, too quick to take offense. Questions about Jondelle would only serve to drive him into a rage. A rage all the more intense if he'd had anything to do with the raid.

A third window resisted his pressure. The woman said, "Upstairs, master. If you want to see outside. There is a window which opens."

It was in a small room musty with the scent of neglect. A rumpled heap of clothing stood in a corner, plastic ripped and torn, in one place stained with something which could have been blood. Dumarest thought of the shape of the man hanging above. A real man, perhaps? One killed in a sudden rage and left to hang? Coated, maybe, with a preserving agent to provide a macabre decoration?

The window opened with a creak, a gust of cool air blowing away the odors of the room. A narrow ledge opened on an empty space. Dumarest leaned over and saw the upper limit of the spiral staircase below. It was seven feet from the window, a narrow band three feet wide winding around the outside of the building. Like a helter-skelter, he thought. If it had been smooth, he could have ridden down it on a mat.

Overhead the gallows creaked a little beneath the impact of the wind. He stared up toward it, seeing the hanging shape, the distorted grimace on the face beneath its transparent plastic film. The face was unpainted, the teeth unfiled, the skin a golden copper, the hair streaked with blond. A stranger who had said the wrong thing at the wrong time and who had paid the price.

The gallows creaked again as Dumarest eased his body through the window, to hang a second before falling to drop on the stairs.

They were greased and had no rail.

He felt his boots slip and flung out his arms as he fell. His hands hit the slimed surface, slipped as his body rolled over the edge, caught as they hit the patch wiped clean by his legs. The wind gusted between his body and the building, forcing him outward from the wall. He glanced down. The next turn of the spiral was twelve feet below and to his rear, carried outward by the expanding base of the building. He could fall and hit it, but if it were greased, his body would be thrown to one side as his boots hit the uneven surface. A second spiral lay below the first, yet more beyond that. If he fell, he would bounce from one to the other to the ground a hundred feet below.

He felt his hands begin to slip, the grease on his fingers making it impossible to hold his weight against the wind. Gritting his teeth, he clamped his fingers on the stone, pulling, the muscles in arms, back, and shoulders cracking beneath the strain. The edge drew close to his eyes, his chin. He thrust his head forward and felt stone beneath his jaw. A surge and he had his elbow on the edge of a step. Another, a knee. He paused, gasping, spreading his weight over the treacherous surface. Slowly he eased his body back onto the stairs, rolling tight against the wall. He slipped a little and halted the movement with the heel of a boot. Cautiously he rose and, as if stepping on eggs, moved slowly down the stair.

He jumped while ten feet above the ground, landing in a flower bed, rising to brush dirt from his clothing before venturing into the city.

It reminded him of Sargone, the streets all in curves and random windings. But where the city of Sargone had been built by thieves for protection, this had been constructed by random directives and distorted imagination. The curves were interspersed by zigzagging lanes of varying width, streets which looped in circles for no apparent reason, roads which ended against the blank walls of buildings. And everywhere the Hegelt with brooms to sweep and dusters to polish, crouching back as arrogant Melevganians strode past, in pairs, singly, riding on litters, or dreaming as they glided on tiny rafts suitable only to lift and carry a man at little more than a walking pace a foot above the ground.

The clothes they wore matched the buldings in the variety of their style and color. Some had painted faces and hair laced with gemmed ribbons; others wore drab smocks and tangled manes, their faces pale, introspective. Some grinned at secret amusement; others scowled with inner rage. A kaleidoscope of dress and expression, but all had the height, the fish-pallor whiteness, the hauteur which stamped them for what they were.

Dumarest felt a touch and turned to see a man standing before him. He was smeared with red and black, a rag about his loins, an elaborate headdress of feathers, gems, and trailing ribbons on his shaven skull. His hands groped before him, but he was not blind.

"There is something before me," he keened. "A solidification of the air, for my theories cannot be mistaken. Nothing can exist unless I give it permission to have being. Therefore what I touch must be an illusion. I will summon my mental powers and dissolve it, send it back to the chaos from whence it came. The purity of my mind must not be contaminated by unreal phenomena. Begone!"

Dumarest stepped aside and the man walked past, mouth wreathed in triumph.

"Thus I have yet more proof of the ascendancy of my mind. The universe exists because of my wish. Darkness and chaos comes with the closing of my eyes. All things are made by the concentration of my thoughts. Truly, I am a veritable god!"

A madman, but others were not so deluded. Dumarest felt the impact of eyes and saw a pair of Melevganians looking toward him. They were young, painted of face, aspiring Guardians, perhaps, or those similar to the ones who had raided the farm. Warrior-types enamored of the lure of combat. Dangerous.

To run would be to betray himself. Instead he strode forward to meet them, making his voice thin, keening.

"You will direct me toward the House of Control. Immediately!"

He had white skin, dark hair, the arrogant manner of a man born to command. He had the height and had adopted the hauteur. His clothing was what any of them might have chosen to wear. And he had attacked in the meaning of their culture.

"Quickly!" His hand dropped toward his knife, lifted, weighted with glistening steel. "Direct me!"

One of the men drew in his breath. "There is no such place as that you seek."

"There is. There must be. I say that it exists and so it must. Quickly, now. Direct me or pay for your disrespect!" He lifted the knife and slashed suddenly at the nearer of the two men. The point caught fabric, ripped, showed naked flesh beneath. "You!" The point lanced at the other man. "You smile! I saw you smile!"

"No! You are mistaken! I—"

The man sprang back as Dumarest sent the blade of his knife whistling through the air. The cut was deliberately short, but he couldn't know that. Couldn't know either that the grating voice was a facade.

"You dare to defy me? You offer a challenge? So be it. To the death, then. To the death!"

They ran, madmen giving respect to madness, or perhaps they were saner than he had given them credit for being. They had seen his eyes, the determination they held. Men who killed and burned and treated violence to others as a game could deserve no mercy. Had they stood, he would have marked them. Had they fought, they would have died.

A voice said, "That was pretty cool, mister. Do you hope to get away with it?"

Dumarest spun, the knife falling as he saw who had spoken. She reclined in a litter supported by four male Hegelt, kilted in scarlet with a broad sash of the same color running from left shoulder to hip. Their feet were sandaled and they stood, staring ahead as if utterly indifferent to what was going on around them.

The woman said, "Put away that knife, Earl. You won't be needing it."

"You know me?"

"I know about you," she corrected. "I know that you shouldn't have left the house and I know that those two freaks you scared won't remain that way for long. They'll be back spoiling for trouble. You could probably take care of them, but they'll have friends. If you don't want to wind up gutted and hanging from a pole, you'd better get in here."

The litter was roofed with tapestry supported on thin columns at each corner, curtains drawn back and held by scarlet cords. It dipped a little as Dumarest spread his length on the cushions, rising with a soft hum as the anti-grav generator compensated for the extra weight. The Hegelt didn't have to carry the burden, only pull it and steady its progress.

"Home," ordered the woman and, as they began to trot forward, released the scarlet cords and allowed the curtains to fall. Leaning back she said, "Earl Dumarest. A nice name. I like it. Welcome to Melevgan, Earl—but what the hell took you so long?"

CHAPTER

TWELVE

She was long and slim with a ripe maturity which had fleshed her bones so that the sweep of thigh and calf matched the swell of hips and breasts. She wore a wide belt of crimson leather studded with gems, pantaloons of some diaphanous material, softly yellow, caught at the ankles and slit so as to reveal the flesh beneath. Her torso was bare aside from a short jacket, open at the front and cut high above the waist. Beneath it her breasts, high, proud, showed their soft rotundity. Her skin was a golden copper traced with curvilinear lines of vivid blue. Her eyes were painted, crusted with sparkling fragments on the upper lids, the brows thin and arched like a drawn bow. The hair, loose around her shoulders, was copper touched with blonde, dusted with sparkle to match her eyes.

Dumarest watched as she smiled, the full lips parting to show broad, white teeth. He thought of the hanging man he had seen. Was she a member of the same race? She was certainly not a Melevganian.

He said, cautiously, "You were expecting me?"

"You or someone like you. Didn't—" She broke off, her eyes cautious. "My name is Neema. Doesn't it mean anything to you?"

"No."

"Then—" She broke off again, shrugging, her breasts lifting beneath the jacket. "A coincidence; well, they happen. Let's just say that I was expecting someone. I thought you were him. Apparently you're not. So what brought you to Melevgan?"

"You know that," he said. "If you know my name, you must know why I'm here."

"To trade—or so your partner told me. I've been to the house. When you couldn't be found, I came looking for you. It's lucky that I did. How long did you think you could last wandering around the city on your own?"

They were lying very close, side by side in the soft crimson light within the litter, his head a little above her own so that as she looked up at him he could see the sharp triangulation of her jaw. Her smile reminded him of a cat. Her perfume of a field of flowers on a sultry summer's day.

"You're a strong man, Earl, and in any other city you'd have no trouble getting by. But this isn't a normal city. The Melevganians are insane; didn't you know that? They don't like strangers. You may have got away with it with the pair you faced down, but there would be others, and one of them could have recognized you for what you are. A hunt would have started with you as the quarry. Have you ever been chased by a mob? It isn't pleasant. I've seen it happen and I never want to see it again. The noise—like slavering dogs. The end—they like to hear a man scream."

And then they'd take him, thought Dumarest grimly, and hang him on a building for use as an ornament. Yet the woman was a stranger. He said so and she shrugged.

"I'm tolerated. Accepted even. I came here five years ago and was lucky enough to be able to treat one of the nobles. He'd gone into psychic shock and was running amok. It was either kill him or calm him down. I had some drugs and managed to get close enough to blast them into his hide. When he recovered he gave me a house, servants, the freedom of the city. I've been tolerated ever since." She drew in her breath. "The man I was with wasn't so lucky."

"Are you a doctor?"

"I've trained in psychiatry. I knew what things were like here and made preparations. Two years in a mental ward learning how to handle the insane, studying at night, saving every penny in order to get the equipment—" She broke off and then said, flatly, "We should have stayed in Urmile."

"Your home?"

"Yes. A small, restricted town with established families and a stagnant culture. I'd moved around . . . Frome, Ikinold, Sargone . . . and I guess I got restless. With money you can travel the galaxy; without it you spend your life in a trap. So I went back home and worked to hit the jackpot. Melevgan is rich. If you can survive here, you've got it made."

Greed, the most potent force in the universe, the drive which made men risk their very lives. Dumarest looked at the woman, seeing the thin lines which traced a path beneath the paint on her face, the shadows which ran from nose to mouth. She had seemed young but mature; now he knew that she was older than he had first guessed.

He said, "And do you like it here?"

"Living among a load of nuts? What do you think?" Her laughter was brittle, devoid of humor. "Can you even begin to imagine what it's like? I'm tolerated, sure, but at any moment one of these painted freaks might decide to find out what I look like inside. Every moment of every day I live balanced on the edge of a volcano. I have to pander to them, guide them, eat dirt, and talk smooth. If it wasn't for some of the more stable members of the nobility, I wouldn't be able to do it. They're crazy by our standards, but sane when compared to the rest. And I have my defenses."

She lifted her left hand and Dumarest saw the heavy bracelet, the thin tube extending from a web of filigree which extended over the back of her hand.

"A dart gun. I wear a pair of them. If any of the Melevganians gets too way out I put him to sleep. One day I'll miss or the guns won't work or there'll be just too many of them. It's only a matter of time."

She rose as the litter slowed, drawing aside the curtains as it came to a halt. Ahead the street was blocked by a mass of people. From the crowd rose a thin keening and Dumarest felt his nerves twitch as to the scratching of a nail on slate.

"Langed! What is wrong?"

The Hegelt on the front right-hand side of the litter spoke without turning his head.

"The way is blocked, my lady."

"Then turn around. Go back and find another route. Quickly!"

She dropped the curtains as the litter began to turn. Her face was strained, anxious.

"The fools!" she stormed. "The dumb, ignorant, stupid fools!"

"The Hegelt?"

"Yes." She caught his hand as Dumarest made to draw back the curtain. "Don't look. Don't let them see you. A crowd like that means trouble. Mass hysteria building to break out in a wave of violence—and those damn fools headed straight toward it."

He looked at her hand where it gripped his own. It was trembling. Gently Dumarest disengaged her fingers.

"Why?" he said. "Why should they do that?"

"The Hegelt? Who knows? They could be the ones to get it, but they never seem to care. Or perhaps they wanted to put me in danger." She scowled, suddenly ugly. "They don't like me. No one in the entire city likes me. They're jealous of what I've got and what I am. Everytime I go out I can feel them watching me. Earl! I—"

Abruptly she broke into a storm of weeping, her hands clinging to his shoulders, the nails digging into the plastic of his tunic. He held her close, soothing, his face bleak as he looked past the shimmering glory of her hair. A woman with more greed than sense or perhaps one whose greed had led her into a trap. Contaminated by the insanity among which she lived, the twisted logic of those around her warping her own mental processes, eroding the emotional restraints common to a normal mind, giving her a paranoid complex.

Or perhaps she was a woman in an extremity of fear who had reason to be terrified and who had succumbed to emotion when it could no longer be contained.

Raising his voice Dumarest said, "Langed! Take the shortest route to your mistress' home. If you see a crowd, avoid it."

"Yes, master."

"And hurry."

Neema had regained her self-control by the time they arrived at a domed structure striped with swirls of red and yellow and vivid blue. Dumarest followed her inside to a small chamber softly feminine with subdued light nacreous through windows of shimmering pearl. A Melevganian stood waiting, tall, his face a psychedelic nightmare. His robe was of a dull orange and fell from shoulders to floor in an unbroken line.

He said, curtly, "I am told that the goods the traders brought have been purchased by you."

Neema bowed, her voice soft. "That is so, my lord."

"I want them."

"Then they are yours, my lord."

"And if I do not choose to pay?"

"They are yours, my lord," she repeated. "Mine will be the honor of serving the elect."

The nightmare face opened to show filed teeth.

"You speak well, Neema. It pleases me to take them. The Guardians need the missiles the bales contain for the protection of the city and thus the protection of yourself. And there are other things of value. Our equipment at the mines lacks efficiency, but that can now be remedied. You have done well."

"Your words are a kindness, my lord," said Neema. "May I be so bold as to ask after your son?"

"He does well."

"And his sleep?"

"No longer does he wake the house with screaming. Your potions have worked their magic. You will send more to my house before it is dark." The tall figure threw a bag to the floor. It fell on the carpet with a rattle of stones. "For the potions."

"You are most generous, my lord."

"It pleases me to be so. Farewell!"

Dumarest stooped and picked up the bag as the man left. Not once had the eyes in the painted face looked at him; to the Melevganian he had simply not existed. Opening the pouch, he looked at the mass of gems. His expenses, back; a High passage for each of the men who had accompanied him; more.

But the bag was empty of the one thing he wanted.

To Neema he said, quietly, "You jumped the gun. Those goods weren't yours to sell."

"No?" She met his eyes. "Think again, Earl. Your partner sold them to me for half of what you hold."

Tambolt eager for a quick profit and a safe skin. It was like the man to act without thinking and yet surely he could not have been so naïve as to have taken the first offer. Dumarest held back the gems as she reached for them.

"You have that in writing?"

"Don't be a fool. Of course not." She sighed at his expression. "I was working on commission. Fifty percent of what I could get. I know the market, you don't. I know how to get the money, you don't. You heard Tars Qualelle. He just took the goods and would have taken your life too had you protested. I had to con him. That money is for the drugs I supply to keep his idiot son quiet at night. It's the only way to do business here in Melevgan.

I've had five years' practice. Don't you think I deserve a commission?"

"Fifty percent?"

"Twenty-five then. Damn it, Earl, what's the matter? Isn't the money enough for you?"

"I wanted more than money. I wanted information."

She listened as he told her about the boy and why he had come to Melevgan. Crossing to a cabinet, she produced wine and filled two glasses. As she sipped, her eyes met his, very direct, calculating even.

"This boy—Jondelle—is he worth anything to you?"

"In money? No."

"Then why are you concerned about him? No," she added before he could answer. "Don't bother to tell me. If you don't want to cash in on him, then there's only one reason. You like him. You made a promise and you're going to keep it. Fair enough. But he isn't in Melevgan."

"Are you sure about that?"

"I'm sure." She sipped again at her wine. "What's it worth to me if I help you?"

Dumarest hefted the bag of gems, the stones emitting a harsh rattle.

"Not that. Not money. I need help. If I help you, will you help me in return?"

"If I can, yes."

"You're cautious," she said. "I like that. You don't promise what you can't give, but once you give your word that's it. I'll tell you what I want. I want to get the hell away from here. From Melevgan and all the nuts around me. I want to be able to see a man without wondering if he's going to shove a knife in my side as I pass. To be able to entertain friends for dinner, to walk unarmed, to look a man in the eye and tell him what I think instead of having to crawl and eat dirt. I want to escape."

She paused, breathing deeply, her breasts prominent beneath the jacket. She looked at the goblet in her hand and abruptly swallowed what it contained, glass rattling as she refilled it from the bottle.

"I want to escape," she said again. "Dear God, Earl! You can't guess how much I want to escape."

"Take a raft and go," said Dumarest flatly. "It's as simple as that."

"You think so?" Her shrug was eloquent. "The only rafts with enough lift to pass the mountains are held by the Guardians. The rest are toys, powerful only enough to drift. They can't be adapted. The only free raft in the place is the one you came with. The only way I can get out as if you take me. You, your raft, your men to give protection."

"The raft is damaged," lied Dumarest. "It burned out on the way down."

"Then you're in trouble." Again she emptied her glass. "The mountains can't be climbed and the Guardians won't help to lift you over. Get it repaired or you'll stay here for life. It won't be a long life," she added. "And it won't be an easy one. Traders are tolerated to a certain extent because the Melevganians need the things they bring. But they've got no patience. Start moving soon or you won't be able to move at all. You'll be too damn busy to do more than sweat and breathe. Can the raft be repaired?"

Dumarest was noncommittal. "Perhaps."

"I'm rich," said Neema. "I've been here five years and I haven't wasted my time. Get me to Sargone, Earl, and I'll double what you hold in your hand. Is it a deal?"

"If I can get you out, I will."

"Your word?" She smiled as he nodded, relaxing as she helped herself to yet more wine. "Now, maybe, I can sleep tonight." She glanced at him, her eyes suggestive. "Earl?"

"The boy," he said. "Tell me what you know about him."

"About the boy, nothing. About the men who took him, not much more. Four of them arrived here a short while ago, about two days before you said the boy was taken. They had a raft and some goods and traded at a profit. One was a very big man, Euluch. Heeg Euluch. I heard one of the others call him that. He collected a few wild aspirants to Guardianship and left. That's all I know."

Dumarest looked at the bag in his hands. He dropped it and crossed the space between himself and the woman in three long strides. Gripping her shoulders he said, harshly, "That isn't enough, woman! Tell me more!"

She winced, pulling at his wrists.

"Earl! You're hurting me!"

"Talk, damn you!"

For a moment their eyes met and then his hands moved, knocking aside the tubes aimed at his face. Tightly he said, "Use those things on me and I'll break both your arms. You want to leave here, Neema? All right. I'll take you. But first you've got to tell me what I want to know. Where is Jondelle?"

"The boy? I don't know."

"But the men who took him. You know more than what you've told me. Where did they come from? What did they look like?"

"Like men," she said, sullenly. "Euluch was a giant, the others normal. They had yellow skins."

"Charnians?"

"They could have been. They grow them like that in the Valley, but people get around, Earl. They could have come from anywhere on Ourelle."

Or off of it, he thought grimly. But to start thinking that was to compound the difficulties of the situation. He had to work on the assumption that the boy was still on this world and those who took him a part of it.

"Those who went with Euluch," he said. "The Melevganians. One was named Tars Krandle. Could he have been a relative of Tars Boras or that other one, Tars Qualelle? Is Tars a family name?"

"Yes," she said. "But it's also a title. Something like 'champion,' or 'defender.' Every Guardian is called Tars something or other, but the relationship is so weak as to be almost meaningless. Inbreeding," she explained. "The son takes the title of his mother, the husband his wife. About a quarter of the population is of the Tars family and all of them are Guardians. Then we have the Yelm; they concentrate on agriculture and the food supply. Then there is the Aruk; they—"

"Never mind," snapped Dumarest. He was in no mood to learn about the Melevganian culture. "Would anyone be worrying about him or the others who died?"

"No," said Neema. "Not now. Short memories," she explained. "And no Melevganian gives a damn about another once he's grown."

"So a stranger arrived here on a raft and traded some goods," said Dumarest slowly. "Then he asked for a few volunteers to help him to steal a boy. Offered money and a night of fun if they would agree. But how could they have trusted him? He could have been a slaver or someone after a few specimens for a zoo. How did they know he would bring them back when the job was done? A man willing to kill in order to steal a boy wouldn't have stopped at cutting them down to rid himself of an inconvenience. The Melevganians may be crazy, but they aren't complete fools. They would have safeguarded themselves in some way. How, Neema? How did they do it?"

Slowly she poured herself more wine, drank, and looked thoughtfully at the goblet.

"Neema?"

"You're hard, Earl," she said. "Hard and shrewd. I wasn't going to tell you this because—well, never mind. You won't stop until you get the answer. Four men arrived on that raft. I made Euluch the same proposition I made you, but he didn't want to know. He was busy, he said, and had no time to rescue a stupid woman. Now I know what he had in mind."

Dumarest said, quietly, "And?"

"Four men arrived on the raft, but only two left with the Melevganians. The others were kept behind as hostages." Neema lifted her glass and drank it empty. When she lowered it her, full lips glistened with moisture. "They're still here. Chained and working in the mines. Sweating themselves to death as you will be—unless you can mend your raft."

THIRTEEN

Jasken said, "I don't like it, Earl. I don't like it one little bit."

He turned and looked back the way they had come, at the raft which had brought them, floating now a hundred feet from the opening where they stood, armored men casual as they lounged in the body of the vehicle. He stepped to the edge and looked down at the side of the mountain. Stone fell sheer from where he stood, rose above in an unbroken wall. He turned again, scowling, shaking his head as he rejoined Dumarest.

"A hell of a place for a mine," he grumbled. "What happens if there's a fall? How do we get out if they decide to leave us here?"

"They won't," said Dumarest. "You're an expert on mining equipment. You've agreed to check some of the machines and to see what can be done about repairs. Before you can fix them, you'll have to return to the city and I must go with you. They value the machines more than a couple of potential slaves."

Jasken grunted, unconvinced. A plume of dust fell from overhead followed almost immediately after by a dull concussion.

"The crazy fools are blasting!" Jasken glared at the Melevganian who stood with another to one side. All wore thick coveralls of dusty scarlet. Their faces bore whorls of granular paint. The Geth, those who were in hereditary charge of the mines.

One of them came forward and said, "We are ready for you to begin."

A command loaded with the arrogance which was natural to Melevgan, but tempered by hard experience and brutal fact. Rocks did not leap to obey and stone cared nothing for titles and self-delusion. Of all the Melevganians the Geth were the most sane.

Dumarest said, "My companion will study your machin-

ery to see what needs to be done. I will examine the mine
to evaluate matters of priority." He added, "With your
permission, naturally, my lord."

Geth Iema frowned. "I do not understand."

"It is not enough to increase the efficiency of, say, a
drill," explained Dumarest. "Of what use to fill the air
with dust when there is no means of ventilation to carry it
away? The workers will choke and die and production
slowed to a point lower than it was before. No, before we
can make the best of the machinery available a survey will
have to be made."

The overseer blinked, struggling with unfamiliar logic.
Slaves were slaves. If they died, they could be replaced.

"It will not take long, my lord," said Dumarest quickly.
"And there is no need to concern yourself. I can manage
alone."

From somewhere down the tunnel a high-pitched scream
rose to break with a screech of metal. A unit, overloaded,
burned out and perhaps damaged beyond repair. Geth Iema
made up his mind.

"You will do what needs to be done," he ordered. "I
shall wait for you here. You will touch nothing but the
machinery, talk to no one but the overseers. Go!"

The tunnel was long, winding, thick with dust which
hung like a pale mist in the air. Galleries opened from
it and lights showed yellow in the gloom. Jasken halted,
wet a finger, and held it high above his head.

"No ventilation to speak of," he said. "These tunnels
must branch for miles to either side. How the hell do they
manage to breathe without pumps and fans?" He reached
out and touched a support. Dust showered as he shook it.
"Rotten. The timber's just a shell over leached wood. It
needs replacing. Every damned support in the place needs
replacing. If we had any sense, Earl, we'd get out of here."

"Later," said Dumarest. "After I've found out what I
came for."

"You think you can find those men?" Jasken shrugged.
"Two men among all the rest? Well, I agreed to play along
and that's just what I'll do. I'm only hoping that Tambolt doesn't take it into his head to leave us behind."

"He can't."

"What's to stop him? The woman won't care who she
pays as long as she gets away and Tambolt won't care

who he leaves behind as long as he makes his profit. Maybe you're trusting him too much, Earl."

"He can't leave," said Dumarest patiently. "I've got a part of the engine. He can't use the raft until he gets it."

Insurance, he though. A precaution as leaving Preleret in charge had been a precaution. A man could be overpowered, killed even, and a part found if given time enough, but both should give all the protection needed. And if anyone was curious about the raft, its failure to operate would back his lie.

He said, "Let's get deeper into the mine. I want to find where the men are working. You can check any machinery in sight and provide a distraction if one is needed. Now let's get on with it."

Grumbling, Jasken obeyed. The mine twitched at his nerves, filling him with foreboding. The tunnels were too narrow, the dust too thick, and the supports worried him. Falls, in such a place, would be common. There was little danger of damp in a mine so high, and the rock would not burn and thus offer the danger of explosion, but every mine had its dangers and he could scent them like a dog.

Ahead, the tunnel widened, branched, lights showing the way to a gallery and a narrow face. The crack of whips echoed thinly through the air, followed by a rumble and a thin scream. Dust billowed, catching at throat and lungs. From somewhere a machine hummed with a strident irregularity.

It crouched like a monster against a wall, steel claws ripping at the stone, sending it showering back to where men crouched sorting through the debris. Other men humped the discarded rubble to where a fissure gaped in the floor. From it rose a stream of air, dry, acrid. A vent to a lower cavern, Dumarest guessed. An underground chamber which must open somewhere to the outer air.

He looked at the workers . . . slaves, collared and chained with flexible links to a stake driven into the wall. Over them stood Melevganians similar to the ones he had seen when entering the mine. They stood, arrogant, whips in their hands, sending the lash at random intervals at the naked bodies of the crouching men. From time to time one of the workers would rise, bowing, handing a stone to one of the overseers.

For reward he was given a cup of water and a thin slice of concentrates.

A nice system, thought Dumarest savagely. The men worked or they were whipped. They found gems or they starved. He caught Jasken's arm as the man stepped forward, his face ugly.

"Hold it!"

"But, Earl! Those men! Look at the swine lash at their backs."

"We can't alter it, so we must accept it," snapped Dumarest. "And we didn't come here to get ourselves killed. Try anything and you'll wind up with a chain around your neck." He pointed over to the other side of the gallery where a machine stood unattended and silent. "See what's wrong with that. Make some noise. I'm going to look around."

He stepped forward, bowing to the overseers who stared at him with incurious eyes. He was unchained and so could not be a slave. He was here so must have been accepted and passed by the outer guards. Therefore he could be ignored.

In a patch of shadow he dropped and said to a sweating man, "I'm looking for someone. He hasn't been here long and would have a friend. A man with a yellow skin. Have you seen him?"

Pale eyes glared at him from a haggard face. "Don't stop me working, mister. I can't take much more of the whip and I haven't eaten all day. Don't stop me working!"

Dumarest passed on. Men were busy slamming heavy bars against the stone, others dragging at lumps of rock loosened by hammered wedges. Noise and dust were everywhere. Men gasped, dived for a stone, fought over it as dogs over a bone, the winner going to collect his reward.

Food, water, a chance to live.

A whistle shrilled and work ceased, slaves passing down the gallery with buckets of water, handing a cup to each man. Dumarest watched as Jasken busied himself with the machine, metallic bangings coming from where he worked. There were no Hegelt; the small, dark men probably died as soon as impressed. There were tall men with slanted eyes, others with ebon skins powdered with sandy dust, some with white and olive. None he could see with yellow. The Charnians must be elsewhere.

He found one at the end of a low gallery, bent double

as he drove a short pick into the stone. The smooth skin was blemished with scars and welts, ugly bruises and scrapes which oozed blood under the dust. He jumped as Dumarest touched him, cringing, one arm lifted as if to ward off a blow.

"What's your name?" Dumarest asked.

The Charnian looked up suspiciously, but the hard eyes meeting his forced an answer. "Sheem. Why do you want to know?"

"I've been looking for you, Sheem. . . . Heeg Euluch," said Dumarest. "Tell me about him."

"Are you his friend?" Hope shone in the bloodshot eyes. "Has he returned? I knew that he wouldn't let me down. When did he arive? How soon can I get out of here?"

"He's no friend," said Dumarest harshly. "He hasn't come back. He's living it high somewhere while you rot in this stinking mine. Think of it," he urged. "A nice place with a woman, maybe. Some wine, cool, in goblets wet with condensation. Soft food of a dozen different flavors. Decent air to breathe and maybe a gentle wind to carry the scent of flowers. Why should he worry about you?"

The man looked at the pick in his hand, the knuckles taut beneath the skin.

"The pig," he said thickly. "The stinking pig."

"He used you," said Dumarest. "He got you to help him do a job and then he dumped you. A nice man. Your friend? With a friend like that, who needs enemies?"

The man shook his head, unbelieving. "He wouldn't. He couldn't."

"He did. Do you think all this is a dream?" Dumarest gestured around the shaft, the heaps of debris. "He left you as a hostage and he knew damn well what would happen to you if he didn't come back. Where did you meet him?"

"In the Valley. Me and Famur grew up together and wanted to spread our wings. We met up with Euluch and did a few things together. Then this job came along."

Dumarest said, "What was the name of the other man, the one who went with Euluch?"

"Urlat, Chen Urlat."

"From?"

"I don't know. He was with Euluch when we joined up with him." The man blinked and swallowed. "Listen, mister. Can you buy me out of here? I'll do anything if you'll get me free. Please, mister. Please!"

"There were two of you. Where's the other one?"

"Famur? He's dead. A rock fall caught him the second day they threw us in here. You'll get me out, mister? Please!"

A whip cracked sharply and the man screamed as the lash curled about his shoulders. An overseer stood, stooped in the gallery, the whip lifted for a second blow. Dumarest rose, turning so the lash missed him, bowing to hide the hate in his eyes.

"My lord?"

"You must not talk to the slaves. When they talk, they do not work. If you stop them working, then you will join them."

"I hear and obey, my lord." Dumarest fought the inclination to grab the whip, to send the lash across the arrogant face, to smash the painted visage with the heavy butt. "But I was examining the rock. The tool the man is using is not the best for the work at hand. If the haft was longer and the head less wide, a greater efficiency would be obtained. With your gracious permission, my lord, I will continue my studies."

"You will not talk?"

"How could I disobey the instructions of the elect, my lord? As you command, so it will be."

The Melevganian nodded, arrogance blinding him to the ambiguity of the reply, but making no effort to move away from where he stood. From where Jasken stood by the machine came a sudden whine of energy, the shrill of an unloaded drive. His yell of triumph rose above the sound.

"Got it! Now if someone could get me a drill?"

The overseer turned, his attention caught by the distraction, and Dumarest stooped, his voice low.

"Quickly, now. Where did Euluch intend taking the boy?"

"I don't know. He didn't say."

"But you knew what he was after?"

The man shrugged. "Sure. A kidnap job for a fat payoff. A pity it was a bust."

"It was no bust," said Dumarest harshly. "And Euluch knew exactly what he was doing. Some Melevganians to do the dirty work and a couple of fools to use as hostages. You and Famur. Your friend is dead and you could follow.

If you got out of here, where would you look for Euluch?"

"You going to get me out?"

"Maybe . . . now talk."

From somewhere along the gallery came the crack of a whip followed by a scream of pain. The sound killed the Charnian's hesitation. "In the Valley. There's a tavern, the Sumba. I'd look for him there." His hand reached out and caught Dumarest by the arm. "And now, mister, for God's sake! Get me out of here!"

Dumarest shook off the hand and rose, his eyes bleak. No man should be chained like an animal and forced to work as a slave. But he had no pity for anyone who had agreed to steal a child.

"You're a man," he snapped. "Get yourself out. You've got tools which could be used as weapons. There's a fissure in the mine which must lead to the outside. Talk to a few others, kill the overseers, and make a break for it."

"I can't! They'd kill me!"

"Yes," said Dumarest flatly. "If you don't make it, they'll kill you. But they're going to do that anyway, so what can you lose?"

FOURTEEN

It was late when they left the mine, the emerald sun low over the mountains, casting broad swaths of shadow from the jagged summits over the foothills and cultivated ground. Jasken sat next to Dumarest in the body of the raft, uneasy because of the armored figures which sat like statues at front and rear. His voice was low, anxious.

"I didn't think they'd let us out, Earl. That overseer, Geth Iema, was pretty definite."

"He liked the way you fixed that machine," said Dumarest. "You impressed him. Maybe you should think about taking his offer. A house, servants, jewels, and soft living. All you have to do is to keep the mine equipment functioning."

"And if one day I can't?" Jasken shuddered. "Did you see those poor devils? Chained and beaten and breathing that stinking dust? One slip and they'll have me among them. One wrong word to an overseer even would do it." He glowered at the armored figures ahead. "They like their own way, these people. Geth Iema didn't want to let us go."

It had taken smooth talk, lies, and extravagant promises, but Dumarest knew they were not yet in the clear. Out of the mine, perhaps, but Melevgan was a prison in itself. And the longer they waited, the more dangerous it became. Jasken was of value to the Melevganians, himself and the others easily available labor for the mines.

Loudly he said, "I think you should take the offer. With the things we brought with us you could do quite a few of the needed repairs. And I can bring in anything you need. Tambolt and a couple of the others can stay as hostages and maybe we could build up a real service between here and Sargone." He added, for the benefit of listening ears, "And it would be an honor to serve the elect. Even to be close to them gives a man a sense of pride."

Jasken turned, his eyes incredulous. "Earl! What the

hell's got in—" He broke off as an elbow jabbed his ribs.

"You agree it's a good idea, Jasken?" Dumarest kept his voice loud. "Think of it, man. A fine house and all you could ever hope to gain. You know the work, for you it would be easy, and we can arrange to have tools and parts lifted in at regular intervals if the Melevganians agree. How fast do you think you could increase production?"

"I reckon to double it within two months," said Jasken, catching on. "Those hand tools are hopelessly inefficient. Once I get the drills working, the men can concentrate on searching the debris instead of wasting time hammering at rock. Of course, that's assuming you can bring me in those parts I need. How long do you think it will take?"

"Not long. Do another check tomorrow and let me know what you want. With the Melevganians' permission I could leave the day after and return in about a week. Would you need Tambolt to help?"

"Him and a couple of the others," said Jasken, and continued as the raft drew near to the city. "I like the idea. We should celebrate it tonight. Some wine, maybe, and anything else that's going. How about the raft?"

"Forget it." Dumarest touched the engine part in his pocket. "It's useless. I'll have to ask the elect to let us use one of theirs. I can bring in a replacement when I return."

Childish banter, but to warped minds eager to hear the things they wanted it might help to ease suspicion. And it did no harm to remind the Guardians that their raft was little better than a heap of scrap metal. A lie, but one which could help to spring the trap they were in. Dumarest was uncomfortably aware of the snare which had closed around them.

Neema was aware of it too. As they entered the House of the Hanging Man she nodded to Jasken and caught Dumarest by the arm.

"Where the hell have you been? I've been waiting for you; we've all been waiting. Damn it, Earl, what kept you so long?"

"We had trouble getting away. Are you ready to leave?"

"I've been ready for over a year now, but I know what you mean." She touched the thick belt around her waist. "Yes, I'm ready."

Tambolt came toward them, his face savage. "The raft, Earl. It won't lift. The engine won't even start. I tried it and—" He broke off, looking at Dumarest's face. "Something wrong?"

"I don't know," said Dumarest coldly. "You tell me. Why did you try to start the raft?"

"I—" Tambolt swallowed. "I was testing it, that's all. Me and Haakon." He gestured toward one of the men standing in a little group beside the vehicle. "He checked and said that a part was missing. Earl! How the hell are we going to get away from here?"

Dumarest ignored him, walking over to the raft and looking inside. The interior held boxes of food, containers of water, bales and bundles together with items of clothing, vases, statues, things of price.

At his side Preleret said, softly, "I tried to stop them, Earl, but they wouldn't listen. They wouldn't have left without you, though; I'd have seen to that."

"The goods," said Dumarest. "The woman's?"

"Some. Those bales. The rest is from the house."

"Who took it? Arion? Haakon? Sekness? Tambolt?"

"Not Sekness."

Dumarest turned to face the other three. "Take these things and put them back where you found them. Tambolt, you should have known better." He thinned his lips as they made no move to obey. "You damned fools! The Hegelt know everything you do and they will talk about it. Report it, even. They have no reason to love us and can get a reward from the Melevganians for keeping watch. Try stealing and you'll wind up in the mines. If you want to know what that means, ask Jasken. He's been there."

"It's rough," said Jasken. "Do as Earl says."

"Now wait a minute!" Arion edged forward. "Tambolt said it would be all right and why shouldn't we take all that's going while we've the chance? I—"

Sekness rapped his club on the edge of the raft. It made a hard, metallic sound. "I'm with Earl," he said. "I don't like stealing, but I'm not the boss and you wouldn't have listened to me. Now the boss says it goes back. Do it!"

His club fell again, the sound menacing.

As the men began unloading the raft Dumarest said, "I

suppose you authorized this, Tambolt, before you knew you couldn't leave?"

"I just wanted to get everything ready, Earl." Tambolt tried to smile, then shrugged instead. "All right, I was wrong, but it seemed a good idea at the time. Maybe I just can't leave nice things alone, but they were sitting there just waiting to be taken. And it wasn't exactly stealing. I mean, if other traders use this house, they could have taken them. We couldn't really have been blamed. And the Melevganians have so much they wouldn't have troubled themselves about a little."

The eternal self-justification of a thief. Dumarest turned away, not bothering to argue, and found Neema again at his side.

"The raft, Earl?"

"It's working." He handed Jasken the part he had removed. "We'll be leaving in the early hours."

"Not before?"

"No. I've tried to persuade our hosts that we have no intention of leaving until the day after tomorrow. They may not believe what they heard, but we've got to keep up the pretense."

She said, shrewdly, "Is that why you made the men take back the things?"

"The fools!" His face darkened with anger. "It may be too late. If the Hegelt noticed what had happened the Melevganians could be warned by now. But if they're put back, we stand a chance. Someone might drop in for a look around. If they do, they could punish the Hegelt for lying. Or they could think it was a mistake. If the stuff isn't to be seen and is found in the raft, then we wouldn't have a hope of getting away."

"We haven't much even now," she said bleakly. "I was treating one and he talked. A manic-depressive on the slope of his cycle who wanted a boost. I gave him a little more than he bargained for. A hypnotic which I daren't use too often but carry for emergencies. They don't intend to let us go. At the moment they're playing with us, with you, that is. A cat and mouse game. Maybe you can talk them out of it, but I doubt it. The young Guardians think you killed their companions. The ones who went off with the big man."

Dumarest said, "Why would they think that?"

"The lances. You've got three of them. I saw them

and so the Hegelt must have too. You're right about them reporting to their masters. Only the Guardians carry lances and it doesn't take genius to guess where you got them from. Earl! I'm scared!"

She came into his arms and he held her, oblivious of the others, feeling the trembling of her soft body against his own. An emotional breakdown, he thought. Over-strained nerves giving way before imagined dangers. Perils all the more terrifying because, as yet, they were not real.

He said, "Can you get us some weapons, Neema? More lances, perhaps?"

"No." She stepped back, breathing deeply, her face calming as she met his eyes. "The Guardians hold them close. I had a laser when I arrived here, but it vanished. The Hegelt, I think. I could get some, I suppose, but it would be dangerous."

Too dangerous. Suspicion once aroused needed only a touch to turn into action. And, if what she had learned from her patient was true, the Guardians were watching and ready to spring. His playacting with Jasken may have lulled them. It would be greater sport to wait, to let their victims think they had an open road before snapping shut the trap. An amusement the Melevganians would appreciate. He hoped so. In their sadism lay Dumarest's only chance of escape.

From where he stood beside the raft Jasken called, "It's fixed, Earl. What happens now?"

"We wait." Dumarest studied the open area in which the raft lay. The wide doors gave to the street, stairs led upward to the living quarters. There could be traps in the floor or secret panels in the walls, but he doubted it. Such things were the product of timidity and the people of Melevgan were far from that. Insane, perhaps, but certain of their superiority. "Try to block the doors, Jasken, then stay here with Preleret on guard. Check the load and make sure we can carry everything we need to take. Dump out what's in the raft if you have to." He caught Neema's expression. "You can take what you carry, but the rest of the stuff might have to go. Do you mind?"

"No," she said. "And?"

"We're going to have a party."

It was a masquerade of shouting men and gushing wine, of food nibbled and thrown aside, of hands reaching for the soft-footed Hegelt women. Of big talk and songs and apparent drunkenness. A macabre performance for the benefit of the Hegelt and the Guardians to whom they might report. A thing promised, expected, and so provided to allay suspicion.

But not all the food was barely nibbled and cast aside. Experienced travelers knew the value of a full stomach and they had heard Dumarest's orders and knew better than the woman that nothing but a little water would remain in the raft. Life was more important than goods, and weight too precious to be wasted on baubles.

At a window Dumarest watched the sky. Night had fallen, the stars blazing in a fiery arc, and he cursed the sheets and curtains of brilliance which haloed the firmament. He wanted cloud, thick, shielding, a pall to dim the vision of any who might be watching. Later, perhaps, it might come. Later. For now they could only wait until the city quieted, until any watchers might grow drowsy at their posts.

Neema came to him. She had been a little careless with the wine as had Haakon and Arion despite the repeated warnings. Too much had been swallowed instead of being slopped and now their boisterous laughter had a genuine ring of abandon. Dumarest caught Sekness' eye and the man nodded. They would keep silent when the time came or he would take action with his club. Without weapons they were passengers; for now they could accentuate the pretense that all were getting helplessly drunk.

Neema wasn't wholly pretending. She blew out her breath and leaned against his arm as Dumarest turned from the window.

"Five years," she said. "Five lousy years. I can't believe that it's almost over. You know what I'm going to do when we reach Sargone, Earl? I'm going to have the best that money can buy. Baths, clothes, foods, wines, you name it and that's what it will be."

"You've got that already," he said.

"No. The things, maybe, but not the background. I'm sick of being served by slaves. I want people I can talk to and laugh with and know that they're doing things for me because they want to, not because they'll be whipped and maybe killed if they don't. And there are other things." She leaned a little closer. "One thing in particular. Five years in Melevgan, Earl. Can you guess what that means?"

"You told me."

"Not all of it. Not the worst part. I'm a woman, Earl. I need to be loved. What's the good of money and clothes and all the rest of this junk if it doesn't fill a real need? Five years wasted, Earl. You understand?"

A woman, older than she appeared, a little drunk and more than a little sentimental. A refuge, perhaps, from imagined fears. A release from tension. Her own, private safety valve from the emotional pressures within. Dumarest remembered the environment in which she had lived, the contamination of those around her. An insidious thing which could warp without suspicion, altering viewpoints, and changing logic so that the unthinkable became the commonplace, the unusual the norm.

Quietly he said, "In Sargone, Neema, you'll find all that you need."

"I've got it here, Earl. Almost. Have you ever thought about it? Everything you could ever hope for aside from one thing. And then that thing arrives and your world could be complete. And it could be, Earl, for the both of us. I can manage the Melevganians. They're insane, sure, but I can manage them. And then we could really begin to live. You and me, Earl, here, in a fine house with all the servants we could use and all the things money can buy. A dream come true, Earl. Here, in the hollow of your hand. Close it and it's yours."

From terror to overconfidence, from despair to high-flying euphoria, and all in a few hours, accentuated, perhaps, by the wine. An emotional change common to manic-depressives and coupled with her betrayed paranoia. A combination which was more explosive than a bomb.

Dumarest felt his skin crawl as he looked into her eyes. They were wide, flecked with motes of shifting color, windows on a mind which drifted in unknown regions. A word and she would be at his eyes or in his arms. A rejection might cause her to turn to suicide or to run screaming in the street to condemn them all.

"A dream, Neema?" He forced himself to smile, to be casual. "But didn't you have it once?"

"I thought I had, Earl, but it didn't last. We came here knowing exactly what we had to do. For a while things were fine and then—" She shrugged. "He was weak, Earl. Stupid. He wouldn't listen to what I said. A trained fool who knew too much to take advice."

And who hung now, swinging from a gallows as an

ornament to the house in which she offered herself to another man.

"You wouldn't be weak, Earl. You're strong and know what has to be done and when to do it. A woman would be safe with you. You would take care of her, look after her, protect her. And you would do more than that, my darling. So very much more." She caught his arm. "Come with me, Earl. Come with me. Now!"

Tambolt grinned as they walked past the table, his mouth wet with wine, his eyes envious. Dumarest, conscious of the watching Hegelt, lifted a bottle and tilted it to his lips, his throat working, but swallowing nothing. He dropped the bottle with a gusting sigh, reached for another and repeated the performance, letting it fall to smash and lie in a puddle of wine.

"A song," he ordered. "Give us a song." Sound to add to the illusion of gaiety. "And how about these girls, here? Can't they dance? Music, girls, and dancing. This is a party!"

The sound rose behind him as he followed Neema from the room, dulled as he closed the door, became muted as he trod at her heels into an upstairs chamber. A couple of hours, he thought. Three at the most. He could manage her that long.

"Wine, Earl?"

The Hegelt had rearranged the room according to her instructions, given while he was at the mine. A bottle and glasses stood on a low table, the wide bed was bright with an embroidered cover, a censer stood beneath a thin spiral of rising smoke, the scent of incense hanging heavy in the air.

He took the wine, lifting it to his lips, but making no effort to swallow. Over the rim of the goblet he could see her eyes, still wide, still filled with vaguely shifting emotion.

"You love me, Earl," she said. "Say it!"

He stood, watching, silent.

"Say it!" Her voice rose a little. "I want you to love me, Earl. I love you and it isn't fair that you don't love me. You must love me. You do love me. Say it. Say, 'I love you, Neema.' Say it!"

He threw the wine into her face.

It hit, bathing her with ruby, wine running from her eyebrows, the tip of her nose and the point of her chin, dripping to the upthrust breasts beneath the low-cut gown, wet, shocking in its unexpectedness. She swayed back, blinking, hands lifting, light gleaming from the bracelets, the filigree on the backs. His left arm rose, knocking them higher as his right hand swept around to slap her sharply on the cheek.

"I told you before," he said harshly. "Use those darts on me and I'll break both of your arms."

"Earl! You—"

For a moment her sanity hung in the balance. Rage climbing, mounting, tearing at her mind with destructive fury. Rage too great to be contained. He had seen it before, in a man who had driven spikes into his blinded face and had thrown himself into a fire because of the frustration it had caused.

And then she collapsed, shuddering into his arms.

He carried her to the bed and laid her on the cover, holding her until the storm subsided, until she rose, her face wet with tears, streaked and stained by the wine.

With water he washed it clean, the golden skin now devoid of cosmetics looking haggard and a little pathetic.

"Earl!" Her hand lifted, touched her forehead. "I've got to get away from here. At times I go crazy. It's something inside, like a bursting in the mind. I can't think straight and logic has gone all to hell. I could have killed you then. I would have done it, given the chance. Nothing seemed to matter, but that. To kill you. To see you dead."

"I know," he said. "I know."

"You can't." She looked at him, her eyes clear now, a little red from her weeping. "Or perhaps you can. But you'd have reason for wanting to kill. I didn't. The Melevganians haven't, not really; they just yield to a whim. Or is it a whim?" she whispered. "Everything seems so logical and reasonable at the time. It's only afterward that it can be seen for what it is. Crazy talk and crazy behavior. And it's getting worse, Earl. I used to be able to fight against it, take drugs to control it; recently I just haven't cared."

"You'll be all right, Neema. Once we get away from here, you'll be among normal people. You could have treatment to even you out. It's nothing to worry about."

She smiled and reached out to touch his face. "You're kind, Earl. Hard, but kind. Gentle, too."

"Gentle?" His own hand touched the place where he had slapped her. The skin showed red, but there would be no bruise. "You'd better get a little rest. A few hours at least. I'll call you when it's time to go."

"No! I—" She wanted to trust him and could not call him a liar to his face. Could not put into words the doubt he knew must exist. That he would go and leave her behind. Instead she said, "My face! I must look a mess!"

Smiling, he said, "No. You look what you are. A very attractive woman."

"You think so? Earl, you really think that?" And then her arms were around him, the scent of her hair in his nostrils, the warmth of her breath against his cheek. "Don't leave me, Earl. For God's sake, don't leave me. I'm afraid. I want something to hang onto. Earl! Stay with me until it's time to go!"

CHAPTER

FIFTEEN

In the darkness the stairs were a death-trap, but if there were watchers, it was the last route they would expect him to follow. Shoulder hard against the sloping wall, Dumarest crept down the external spiral, eyes straining as he looked at the sky, the streets below. He could see no guards and the air was clear of rafts. He reached the bottom and rapped on the door. Twice, a pause, then twice more. It opened with a faint creak of timbers and in the dimness he could see the bulk of the raft, the others waiting in the vehicle, starlight catching their eyes.

Jasken had opened the door. He said, "All clear, Earl?"

"As much as it will ever be. You know what to do?"

"Lift high once we're clear and then head due west. But, Earl, Sargone lies to the south."

"We go west."

"To avoid pursuit." Jasken nodded. "A good idea. I should have thought of it."

To avoid pursuit and to head toward the Valley of Charne, but Dumarest didn't mention that. He glanced at the raft, checking that each was in his place. Jasken at the controls, Preleret with the other rifle to the left side, himself to the right. Tambolt and Sekness each with a lance at front and rear. Haakon and Arion lay in the body of the craft, breathing deeply, useless. Neema squatted beside them.

Dumarest handed her the remaining lance. "Can you use it?"

"I think so."

"Aim it like a stick. There's a button in the butt. Press it and release a missile. They've got explosive heads, so make sure they don't hit too close." He added, for the benefit of them all, "Don't start firing until I give the word. If we're stopped, I want to try bluffing our way out. Say nothing, do nothing, but keep alert. Right, Jasken, let's go!"

The engine hummed, rose to a noisy pulsing, settled

126

to a whining drone as the raft lifted from the floor. Carefully Jasken guided it from the building, then fed more power to the anti-gravity units. The ground fell away, shadows passing over them from adjacent structures, dropping to expose them to the burning light from the stars.

The heavens were too bright. Dumarest had hoped for cloud, but none had come and he dared wait no longer. Dawn must find them safely over the mountains.

Tambolt sucked in his breath.

"We're going to make it, Earl. By God, we're going to make it!"

His words were thick, slurred a little, despite the cold showers and drenchings he had suffered. Dumarest looked down at the house with its grisly adornment. The Hegelt had left an hour earlier to report, he hoped, that the party had ended in a drunken stupor. The Guardians could have been deluded. If so, their only real danger lay in running into a random patrol.

They rose still higher, the city falling beneath until it looked a garish toy, lights showing the shape of buildings, the tiny figures of Hegelt at their never-ending task of keeping the place clean. Dumarest leaned over the side, his eyes narrowed.

"Neema!"

She joined him immediately, her hair brushing his cheek. "What is it, Earl?"

"That crowd down there. Normal?"

"Nothing's normal in Melevgan. It could be the start of a hunt—sometimes one of them is crazy enough to volunteer for quarry, or sometimes, for no apparent reason, they gang up on one of their own kind. Usually someone they reckon may have lived too long. Or it could be a group-session. They gather, start keening, and whip themselves into a frenzy." She drew in her breath, an inward sigh of annoyance. "I can't be sure. It's too far away. It worries you, Earl?"

At a time like this everything was a cause for worry. They had lifted high when leaving the city to escape observation; a raft heading upward was invisible to anyone not looking at the sky. But other rafts, lower, might spot them occluding the stars as they headed west. To drop lower might be safer, but they would lose maneuverability close to the ground. And, if seen, could arouse suspicion.

All they could do was to remain alert and trust to luck. It ran out halfway to the mountains.

Preleret saw it first. He said, "Something coming, Earl. From the left and below."

A dark shape touched with starlight. A large raft filled with armored men.

Tambolt said, "We could blast it, Earl. Spray it with missiles from the lances. Hit them before they know it."

"No."

"But—"

"Shut up! Don't talk and keep those weapons out of sight."

Two rifles with fifteen-shot capacity. Three lances with ten missiles each. Thirty shots aimed by inexperienced hands. Two-thirds of them would never reach the target. The rest might kill, maim, and, perhaps, smash the engine. Then would come the return fire from those who had managed to survive. The alarm would have been given and they would be defenseless before another attack.

And, as yet, the raft hadn't seen them. It was riding level and several hundred feet below. With luck it would pass.

In the body of the raft Haakon turned, rose on all fours and shouted, "Wine! Bring more wine! I want more wine!"

Sekness moved, his club lifting to fall with a dull crack, but the damage had been done. An armored head tilted, starlight showing the slits, the dark patches beneath which were eyes. A gloved hand raised, pointing; a lance aimed itself; another, a dozen.

Dumarest said quickly, "Sing. Tambolt, Jasken, pretend you're drunk. The rest of you drop—and hide those weapons."

He lowered his own rifle as the raft below swung up to ride level, leaning over the edge, grinning, waving his hand in cheerful greeting.

"Hi, there! A nice night for a ride. You should have been at the party. We had quite a time. Wine, women, song." He jerked his hand to where the others stood, bawling. "Want to join in?"

"You will halt immediately!"

"Sure." Dumarest waved at Jasken. "You heard the man. He wants to join us. He can't do it while we keep moving."

"And be silent."

"The singing? Anything you say, my lord. We're going to work for you, did you know that? Me, these two, the others we left behind in the house." He shook his head, appearing to regain control of himself. "My lords! If we have offended, we apologize. Have I the honor of talking to Tars Boras?"

"You know him?"

"I have had the honor of his company. It was he who gave us permission to test our raft tonight. He was most gracious."

For a moment the armored figure standing upright in the raft stared blankly at Dumarest, the closed visor giving him the appearance of a bizarre robot. Then he said, "You will turn and follow me back to the city. If you deviate from our flight path, you will immediately be destroyed."

"As you command, my lord," said Dumarest. "As you wish, so shall it be."

Jasken said, "Earl?"

"Do as he says, but as you turn win us a little height."

Dumarest crouched as the raft swung in a tight circle, moving across the interior to touch Preleret on the shoulder. He kept his voice low.

"They've got us covered. If we start anything and don't get them first, they'll blast us all to hell. Sekness, how are you with a rifle?"

"I can use one."

"Take mine. It's ready to shoot. Semiautomatic—just aim and pull the trigger. Move over to the right. Preleret, you take the left. Rise when I gave the word and take care of anyone aiming anything at us. I'll see to their raft." Dumarest picked up the lance Sekness had discarded.

Neema said, "Can I help?"

"No. You stay out of this. Tambolt, you cover Jasken. If anyone tries to get him, you get them first. But don't use the lance unless you have to. Ready?" He peered over the edge of the raft. "Now!"

He rose, the lance in his hands, the point steadying as he aimed the shaft. Ahead armored figures held leveled lances, but he gambled that they would be slow to open fire. Slow enough for the two marksmen to take care of them with the rifles. He heard the sharp explosions, saw the Melevganians fall backward as bullets tore through their decorative armor, others turning to fall under the merciless fire.

As they fell, he was touching the button beneath his thumb, missiles spouting from the tip of the lance. Four shots, all concentrated on the driver and the controls of the vehicle. As they exploded, he yelled to Jasken.

"Turn! Lift! Take evasive action!"

Missiles streaked toward them as the man obeyed, lines of fire cutting the air beneath and to one side. One struck the rear edge of the raft, flame gushing over the side as it exploded against the bottom. Tambolt shouted, lifted his lance, swore as Dumarest tore it from his hands.

"What the hell are you doing?"

"Saving our fire-power." Dumarest looked back at the other raft. It was tilted, slowly falling, men clinging to the sides. His missiles had wrecked the controls. "We've had our share of luck. The next time they come, we'll need every bullet and missile we have."

"If they come."

"They'll come," said Dumarest grimly. "Keep watch while I check the damage."

The stray missile had hit a few feet from the extreme rear of the raft, the explosives tearing a jagged patch. Arion's head had been lying where it had hit. The raft rose a little as Dumarest threw his body over the side.

"Can't you get us higher, Jasken?"

"I'm trying. That missile didn't do us any good. We've lost some lift."

"Do the best you can." Dumarest stooped over Haakon. His legs were singed, but otherwise he seemed unhurt aside from the lump on his head where Sekness had clubbed him. He groaned as Dumarest slapped his cheeks.

"What—"

"Up! Hang over the side. Be sick if you want to, but get active. Up, damn you! Up!"

"My head!" The man struggled upright, his eyes bloodshot, creased with pain. "Where's Arion?"

"Dead and over the side. You were lucky. Try to stay that way." Dumarest looked at the woman. "Give him some water, drugs too if you have any. I want every eye we've got open and on the lookout. When the Melevganians come, I want to see them before they see us."

They arrived as the raft neared the summit of the mountains, a black oblong against the stars, flying high and fast and intent on the kill. Plumed helmets showed over the sides and the starlight glinted from the points of bristling lances.

Tambolt said, "We could drop, Earl. Get below the mountains and use them as a shield."

"No."

"It would give us a chance." His voice was firm, his semidrunkenness evaporated by tension. "We might even be able to land."

A possibility Dumarest had considered and rejected. They could land and hide and wait out the day and hope that they wouldn't be spotted. But to land in starlight on the side of a jagged mountain without lights to guide them and no assurance they would find a suitable place was to tempt luck too far.

"No," he said again. "And we can't drop. If we do and they spot us, we'll be pinned against the wall of the mountain."

"Then all we can do is to hope they don't see us," said Tambolt. "Hope—and pray." He stared upward, his hands clenched as the other raft drew near and passed overhead. "They've missed us. Earl, they—" He broke off, cursing as light blazed around them. "What the hell's that?"

A flare, dropped from the other raft, drifting down on its parachute and bathing them in the eye-bright glow of burning magnesium.

They had seconds before the heavens would rain fire.

"Move!" Dumarest yelled at Jasken as he snatched the rifle from Sekness' hands. "Preleret, get that light!"

He dropped to one knee, aiming at the raft and the helmeted heads behind the bristling lances, squinting against the glare which dazed his vision. The rifle kicked against his shoulder as he sent a stream of bullets to smash into slotted visors. Missiles flared up beside him as Tambolt joined in, trying to destroy the armored men before they could open fire.

Preleret grunted, aimed, fired, and fired again. The flare exploded into a shower of burning fragments which fell, dying, to the ground below.

"Quick, Jasken! Get under them!" Dumarest threw aside the empty rifle and snatched up a lance. Haakon rose, wavering.

"A gun," he said. "Give me a gun."

His head dissolved. His chest puffed out in a mess of blood, ribs and internal organs, spattering fragments and scraps of lung as the missile exploded. Others followed, a rain of streaking fire which passed to one side as Jasken turned the raft. Sekness cried out, looked at the ripped hole in his side, and then, without a sound, toppled over the edge. A missile, lucky or more carefully aimed, had exploded against the rear where he had stood.

Two more flares illuminated the night. Dumarest ignored them, concentrating on his aim. Fire blossomed against the base of the raft above, ripping metal just behind where he estimated the controls to be. More gushed a little to one side, then he held down the stud and emptied the weapon, sending the missiles through the widened hole.

Two passed right through; the others met opposition. He heard screams, the roar of explosions, and the sound of grating metal. A Melevganian toppled over the edge, wailing as he fell. Another leaned over, grotesquely misshapen, showering a sticky rain. The raft lurched to one side, fell a little, veered sluggishly as it turned.

"Under them!" snapped Dumarest. "Stay under them!"

Their altitude was to his advantage—as long as it was not too great. They could not fire without leaning over the edge and exposing themselves and, if their target was too close, couldn't bring their lances to bear. But there was a danger and he recognized it.

"Preleret! Watch that hole I made. If anyone tries to use it, get them."

"I'm low on shots, Earl."

"Then make them all count. Use a lance if you have to." He threw aside the one he had used. There were two others: the one Tambolt had used probably almost empty, the other full. Ten missiles. It should be more than enough.

Jasken said, "Earl!"

The other raft had twisted again, jerking sidewise and rising a little so that it was a little to one side. Abruptly it fell.

Dumarest fired as he saw the raised lances, aiming not at the helmets, but at the side of the raft below them. The missiles would explode on impact, and the armor they wore would protect the Guardians from flying fragments, but the concussion would daze and, perhaps, stun.

The lance was inaccurate and he had no missiles to waste on elusive targets.

The thing was to stun, confuse, to kill if he could, but, above all, to prevent an accurate return fire. A rain of missiles which would reach the raft and blast its occupants into smoking shreds.

Speed alone was the only real defense. Six lances were leveled toward him, their tips circling a little as the Melevganians aimed the shafts. Dumarest fired at once, sending as many missiles to roar in a continuous explosion against the side of the raft, hearing the crack of Preleret's rifle, Tambolt's hysterical shout.

"Dodge, man! For God's sake, get out of the way!"

Dumarest felt the raft drop beneath him as Jasken cut the lift. It fell as an armored figure rose, his lance streaming flame. A streak of fire cut past Dumarest's head; another ended in a gout of flame at his rear. Two more reached for Jasken, a third slamming into the metal at his side.

Then the armored shape dissolved into bursting metal and flesh as Dumarest fired. He had three missiles left. He sent them all into the raft at where he guessed the engine to be. The explosions grew, turned into flame, licking, roaring high as the raft spun away hopelessly out of control . . . to tilt and shower bizarre figures from the interior, screaming as they fell to spatter on the rocks below.

"Earl!" Jasken was dying, his voice a raw thread of agony. He crouched against the side of the raft, a pool of blood around his feet from the gaping wounds left by the fragments which had ripped open his stomach. "The controls, Earl. I can't handle the controls!"

"Take them," said Dumarest to Tambolt. "Neema?"

She had been hurt, blood on her shoulder, the front of her dress, her left arm hanging limply at her side. She knelt, examining the engineer, rising with a helpless shake of her head.

"I can't help him, Earl. A missile got my bag. Me too. We have no drugs, nothing to ease his pain. He's suffering. My God, he's suffering, but there's nothing we can give him."

Nothing but the pressure of a hand, the fingers hard against the carotids to bring swift unconsciousness and merciful oblivion. Dumarest eased the man to the floor of the raft, laying him down where Haakon lay in an untidy heap.

"We'll bury them in soft ground somewhere," he said. "Somewhere under a tree with a stone as a marker."

Tambolt said, "On the way to Sargone?"

"On the way to the Valley of Charne," said Dumarest flatly. "I've still got to find Jondelle."

CHAPTER

SIXTEEN

Konba Tach rose as usual a little before dawn, ate the food his wife had prepared, and then went out to his farm which clung to the side of the mountain. It was, he felt, going to be a good day. Already the mist which filled the valley with the setting of each sun was thinning, lowering to show other farms to the sides and below . . . a collection of small patches of ground, painstakingly leveled, walled, and planted with neatly arranged crops. Unga beans, mostly, with some klwem, artash, and a few shrubs of prenchet which provided a useful narcotic. There were herbs also and bushes which bore leaves for the making of tisanes, tall grasses which could be beaten and dyed and woven into delicate fabrics. And flowers. Everywhere, in the valley, there were flowers.

He stooped over a swollen bloom and inhaled the sweet perfume. Rising, he looked at the raft which had arrived with the sun.

It was not a local vehicle. The sides were scarred, torn, the metal showing the marks of violence. Those within looked in little better shape . . . a woman, pale, her left arm bandaged and in a sling . . . the man beside her, tall in his gray clothing, his eyes watchful . . . two others who drooped as if from exhaustion. Travelers from a far place, Konba Tach guessed. Strangers to the valley. Perhaps they had been caught in the storms common to the Wendelt Plain; but no matter who they were or why they looked as they did, custom demanded they be offered food and refreshment, the hospitality of his home.

Bowing, he said, "Strangers, you are welcome."

"Is this the Valley of Charne?"

"It is. My name is Konba Tach. My wife and children are not yet at work, but greet you in my name. If you will alight, it will give me honor to attend to your needs."

"You are more than kind," said Dumarest. The neatly arranged plants betrayed the poverty which must exist

135

here, forcing the use of every inch of ground. "We gladly accept your offer of refreshment. Have you hot water? Bandages?" He gestured to where Neema stood. "The woman has been hurt."

"All shall be provided." Konba Tach lifted his voice as he gave orders to the woman peering from the open door of the house set into the flank of the mountain. "Now, if you will follow me?"

They washed in a tub half-filled with water which stung like ice, the bath both refreshing and stimulating appetites. The food was hot, consisting of beans flavored with herbs and mixed with succulent fragments of pulpy vegetable. It filled but did not satisfy, a low-protein diet which gave little energy and was mental poison to a growing intelligence. The reason, perhaps, why Konba Tach remained on the farm, why his son would follow him, his daughters continuing the same life. A family trapped in the ways of their forebears, struggling constantly to exist on a patch of ground leveled from the side of a mountain instead of striking out to the more fertile plains beyond.

And yet they seemed happy enough, the house clean, the children neat, the woman deft as she cleared the table and provided cups of fragrant tisane.

"That was good," said Tambolt. "The first hot meal we've had in how long, Earl? Ten days?"

"Twelve," said Preleret. His hands shook a little as he lifted his cup. "Ten days since we buried the others."

A long time to travel without supplies. They had drunk when they had found water, eaten a few roots and juiceless berries, remaining constantly on the alert for questing Melevganian rafts.

Tambolt refilled his cup from the pot of tisane.

"Well, we made it. We're safe now. We can get the raft fixed or buy another one and head to Sargone. Right, Preleret?"

"When Earl says."

"The boy." Tambolt frowned. "The Valley of Charne is three hundred miles long. There is one major and two minor cities and God knows how many farms and settlements. How the hell are you going to find one small boy in a place like this?"

"If he's here, I'll find him," said Dumarest. To Neema he said, "Let's take a look at that arm."

It was bad. Beneath the crusted bandages the flesh was torn, imbedded with minute fragments from the bursting missile, the tissue tender and inflamed. Dumarest lowered his head, sniffing, catching the sickly odor of putrefaction. He reached for water and bandages, his face impassive.

"It's bad," said Tambolt. "If she isn't careful, she could lose the arm, her life as well. At the hospital in Sargone she could have the best of attention."

"She'll get it," said Preleret. "They must have doctors in the Valley."

"Sure, but—" Tambolt broke off, his eyes thoughtful. As Dumarest finished the bandaging he said, "Earl? Could I have a word with you? In private?"

Outside he walked to where the raft stood in a patch of crushed grass. The mist was lower now, showing the floor of the valley, vapor pluming to hide the shapes of buildings which stood like toys dwarfed by the immensity of the mountains.

He looked at them for a moment, then said, "Earl, just where does Preleret stand? As regards our deal, I mean."

"Deal?"

"The money you hope to get for the boy. I know why you're after him and I'm with you all the way. We've done well, but we could double it easily. Maybe more. That kid must be worth a fortune to whoever wants him. Once we find the goods we—"

"Jondelle isn't 'goods,'" said Dumarest harshly. "He's a boy. He isn't something to be found and offered to the highest bidder. He was stolen, his mother shot, his stepfather killed. He isn't a bag of jewels or a bundle of loot. He is a human being. Remember that."

"Sure," said Tambolt hastily. "It was just a manner of speaking. I feel for the kid as much as you do. But where does Preleret fit in?"

"He's willing to help."

"For free?" Tambolt shrugged. "Well, I'll leave it up to you, Earl. Maybe we could give him something for his trouble. A share, a tenth, say; I'll go to that. But if he gets greedy, we'll have to cut him down. You agree?"

Dumarest looked down at his hand. He was gripping the side of the raft and the knuckles were white. He removed it, walking to the wall, looking at the slabs of stone, the tiny lichens growing in the windblown dirt accumulated between the cracks.

He said, "First we have to find the boy. What we do with what I get for him can wait, but I promise you this. Half of what I get for him is yours. I'll take care of Preleret."

"Fair enough, Earl. And the rest? What we got for the goods?"

"After expenses we cut it three ways."

"Three?" Tambolt frowned. "That seems high, Earl. Too high for a man straight out of Lowtown. Why not give him the High passage you promised?"

"He gets a third," snapped Dumarest. "After expenses. If it hadn't been for him, Tambolt, we'd be dead now. His rifle gave us the edge when we needed it most. A third and I'm not going to argue about it."

Tambolt shrugged. "All right, Earl. You're the boss."

"Yes," said Dumarest. "Remember that."

Preleret was asleep when they returned to the house. He lay spread across the table, his head cradled in his arms, his breathing stentorian. He woke, blinking as Dumarest touched his shoulder.

"Earl?"

"Go and dip your head in the tub outside. We're leaving. You can sleep later in a soft bed with clean sheets." Dumarest turned to Neema. "How do you feel?"

"Dopey." She held a saffron pod in her hand and chewed on another. "Our hostess gave me something to ease the pain. It does, too, but I'm feeling all detached as if I'm floating."

"Prenchet," explained Konba Tach. "It can be a great comfort in times of distress." His eyes widened as he looked at the gem Dumarest dropped into his palm. "My lord?"

"A gift. For you, your wife, your children." Dumarest knew better than to pay for the hospitality they had received. Poor as he was their host had his pride. "Clothes, tools, and seeds. Money to take you to a new farm," he hinted. "Fertile ground and animals to supply meat for your table. If you accept it, I shall gain honor."

Konba Tach bowed, hiding the glow in his eyes.

"Sell it to an honest man," said Dumarest. "Better still, deposit it as collateral in a bank. . . . Where is a tavern known as the Sumba?"

"I do not know, my lord." Konba Tach was apologetic. "Rarely do I leave the farm and we have no money for the things to be found in taverns."

"A doctor, then?"

"Gar Cheng is a good man. Descend to the floor of the valley, head to the west; he lives at the house with a triple pagoda. On foot the journey takes a day. With a raft less than an hour." He bowed again. "My lord, may good fortune attend each step you take."

"And may happiness fill your days."

Gar Cheng was a small, wizened, snapping turtle of a man with a straggle of thinning hair and a mouth which looked as if it had tasted a rotten fruit. He hissed as he examined Neema's arm, his dark eyes accusing as he stared at Dumarest.

"This woman should have received immediate medical attention. To have neglected the injury was inexcusable. Why have you waited so long?"

"We had no choice, Doc." The narcotic she had chewed had slurred the woman's voice. "And we had no drugs or prophylactics. Don't blame Earl, blame circumstance." She began to giggle.

"Prenchet," said Dumarest. "She'd chewed a pod before I could stop her." He held out the other. "Bad?"

"Undesirable. In its raw state prenchet is a strongly addictive narcotic. At times I wonder how the hill farmers manage to resist its lure." The doctor shrugged. "Well, no matter. "The damage has been done and, at least, she will have interesting dreams." He probed at the mangled flesh. "Have you money?"

"Yes."

"That is well. If you hadn't, I would still treat the woman, but in that case all I could do would be to amputate. Later you could buy a prosthetic or a regraft, but that, of course, would be up to you. As it is, I can perform extensive surgery which, coupled with the use of hormones and slow-time, will repair the damage. Such treatment is expensive. Aside from the use of my skill there are others to pay and the things I need do not come cheap."

"Get them," said Dumarest. "Do whatever is needed. She can pay."

"In advance?" Gar Cheng frowned at the gems Dumarest

placed in his hand. "I'm not a jeweler. These stones mean nothing to me. Have you no cash?"

Neema giggled again. "What's he want, Earl? Money?" She tugged at the belt around her waist. It revealed the flash of jewels, the glint of metal. "Here's money. How much do you want? Five hundred stergals? A thousand? Help yourself."

Dumarest helped himself to a handful of coins. "Two hundred," he said, counting. "I need it. All right, Neema?"

"Sure." She swayed, eyes closing. "Anything you want, Earl. Anything you want. Me, the loot, anything. Just ask and it's yours."

Gar Cheng took the belt from her hands. She was lax, breathing deeply, already lost in narcotic dreams. "I will take care of this. Later, when she has recovered, she can settle my bill. And now, if you will excuse me, there is much to do and no more time should be wasted."

Outside the others waited in the raft. Preleret was asleep; Tambolt nodded as he sat at the controls. Reaction had caught them, the effect of the food, the relief of having arrived safe at the Valley of Charne. Dumarest felt the grit in his eyes, the sapping ache of strength used and almost exhausted. He wanted to find the tavern, the big man, the boy, but caution dictated delay.

The big man had killed and could kill again. He would be fresh and alert and perhaps suspicious of strangers. Against him an exhausted man would stand little chance and a dead man was useless to Jondelle.

Tambolt said, "What now, Earl?"

"Sleep," said Dumarest, deciding. "A few hours at least."

"And then?"

"We find the Sumba."

CHAPTER

SEVENTEEN

It was not what he had expected. The Charnian in the mine had called it a tavern, but it was far more than that. A vastly sprawling place of bars, and baths, and discrete rooms . . . of open spaces and amusements, fountains and tinkling lanterns. In the mist it looked ghostly, unreal, patches of light swelling to vanish in blurs of fading color, others blooming to take their place. By day it was an intricate complex of rooms and halls and covered ways, by night a fairylike palace of music, perfume, and mysterious enigma.

"One man," said Tambolt. "In a place like this."

"We'll find him," said Dumarest. "If he's here. You're good at that kind of thing, Tambolt. And you've got eyes and ears, Preleret. Move around, watch, ask a few questions. You're looking for a big man, almost a giant. Heeg Euluch. If you spot him, don't talk to him and try not to arouse suspicion."

Preleret said, "And if we find him?"

"There's a bar, the Paradisa Room. If I'm not there, wait for me. I'll drop in as often as I can. Move now. We've wasted enough time."

Too much, thought Dumarest as they moved away, vanishing almost at once in the swirling mist. A whole day . . . and yet it couldn't be helped. They had needed the rest and a place like the Sumba wouldn't come really alive until the night. If Euluch followed the usual pattern of his kind, now was the best time to find him.

He stepped ahead, cautiously, hearing water gurgle to his right, a gusting sigh from his left. Fountains and wind-operated bubble-throwers, both devoid of their visual magic in the clinging mist which filled the valley. The path grated underfoot, the sound changing from the rasp of gravel to the crunch of shell, to the ting of metal, to the splash of rain. An attendant, his eyes masked by fog-penetrating goggles, loomed from one side. He carried a club.

"You are bemused, sir?"

"A little."

"Then you are new to the Sumba. The paths tell a discerning ear which direction they take. Music toward the palace of joy, light, enchanting, a little more somber on the return. To the gaming rooms? Then we have the unmistakable clink of coin, the familiar rattle of dice. To the baths? What else but the tinkle of water. To the bars? The gush of wine and the susurration of murmuring voices. A most cunning introduction, as I think you will agree. But then, the Sumba is no ordinary place."

"No," said Dumarest.

"Of course for those who do not care to wander the night the inner complex yields on to each and every room and chamber of intriguing delight. If I may guide you, sir, I will show you the way."

"I'd like to look around," said Dumarest. "Is that possible?"

"At any time during the day, most certainly. At night?" The figure shrugged. "The mist holds a magic which must not be dissipated. A pleasant companion gains an added mystery when wreathed with the vapors of Charne. To stroll along the paths is an adventure for foot and ear with each step filled with potential romance. There are ladies here, sir, of high quality who would not care to be exposed to eyes which stare too hard and look too long. Discretion, sir, is all, and in the Sumba we are most discreet. Wander as you will, but wander as you are. The rule, sir, and rules must not be broken. Those locked in the passion of love must rest assured that none can see better than they. And love, sir, on soft couches all around which only a questing foot can find, is easy to find for one who stands and waits."

Harpies haunting the mist eager to sell fleshy delights, and perhaps more than harpies. Or, no, the guards would take care of that with their goggles and clubs. Here the rich and depraved would be safe from those eager to rob without finesse.

"A large place," said Dumarest. He had been taken for a stranger seeking casual amusement. A ready-made excuse and a natural protection.

"Very large," agreed the guard. "If you wish, I could

find you pleasant company. A girl from Ikinold, perhaps?"

"Or a boy from Relad?"

For a moment the man hesitated, then said, regretfully, "A boy, sir, yes, but not from Relad. Shall I—"

"Later," said Dumarest quickly. "First I shall look inside. If you will guide me?"

Triple doors kept out the mist, polarized so as to keep in the light. Inside it was warm and dry with only a hint of vapor marring the clarity of the air. The Paradisa Room was a transposed portion of jungle with false vegetation covering walls and ceiling, a dozen varieties of fruit hanging low, mechanical simulacra moving, peering from behind leaves and boles to vanish as soon as seen. The air was heavy with tropical odors, stirring with the sub-audible beat of drums, of rain, of distant thunder.

The bar was in the shape of split trees, the drinks served in plastic fashioned into the likeness of fruit shells. Dumarest ordered and sat nursing his drink. He did not have to wait long. A girl, wearing only a string of beads and a dress of synthetic skin which left one shoulder and breast bare, sat beside him. The dress was cut to the hip and showed the silken sheen of her thigh. Her feet were painted blue, the nails red, the soles a dusty green. The motif was continued over her body and gave her face a mask-like appearance.

"You are alone," she said. "In the Sumba no one should be alone. For a stergal I will talk to you for thirty minutes. For ten I am yours for an hour to do with as you please."

"I am looking for a friend of mine," said Dumarest. "Perhaps you know him. A big man. Heeg Euluch."

"You may call me Odenda. For a stergal I will talk to you for thirty minutes."

"Go to hell," said Dumarest. He caught the bartender's eye and waved him over. The man stared blankly as he repeated his question.

"Euluch? Never heard of him. You want another drink?"

Dumarest dropped a coin on the bar. "No drink. Just answers. If you know the big man, tell him a friend wants to see him. I'll be moving around."

He had told the others to be cautious, but he made no attempt at caution himself. He passed through the rooms, buying unwanted drinks, asking always the same question, always receiving the same answer. No one knew the big

man. No one knew anyone named Heeg Euluch. But someone would carry the word and, maybe, the man would be
curious enough to show himself.

If he was here. If the man in the mine had told
the truth. If he just wasn't wasting his time.

Back in the Paradisa Room Preleret was waiting. He
caught Dumarest's eye, saw the faint signal, and shook his
head. Tambolt came in a moment later. He grinned at
Odenda, then looked at Dumarest with amazement.

"Earl! What the hell are you doing here? I thought you
were busy with—well, you know. How did you make
out?"

"Fine. I was lucky, Famur wasn't. The big one and
Urlat got away. You want a drink?"

Tambolt had a drink. Odenda came to Dumarest and
slipped her arm through his. Softly she said, "One stergal
and we talk. Ten and you play, if that is your desire.
Twenty and I will tell you what you want to know."

"I told you once—"

"—to go to hell. Yes, I heard you. Are we in business,
mister, or not?" In the painted face the eyes were
hard, the lips parted to show teeth too white and too
sharp. In the dim light of the bar she reminded Dumarest
of a Melevganian.

He said, "Twenty stergals for an introduction to a
man I want to do business with? You must be crazy."

"Ten then."

"Five—payable after we've met."

"Mister, when that happens I won't be around. Give
me the money." She tucked it somewhere within her
dress. "Heeg Euluch is a big man in more ways than one.
He owns part of the Sumba. Are you really his friend?"

"Money is. I can help him to get it."

"If you can't, then start running." She shrugged as
Dumarest made no effort to move. "Well, it's your neck.
Go to the gaming room. Play a little spectrum. Wait."

The game was a seven-card deal, two draws, the object
being to make a complete spectrum, red low, violet high.
A game with too many variables for Dumarest's liking, but
he played as ordered. After thirty minutes in which he
won a hundred stergals a voice whispered in his ear.

"All right, mister. You want to meet Heeg Euluch.
Come with us."

Two of them, young, lithe with the arrogance of those accustomed to power. They led him from the gaming room down long passages, through doors, and into an empty chamber. Another door and he faced a man behind a desk. A big man with hair tight against his skull. Eyes almost lost in folds of fat, the material of his shirt tight across his shoulders.

As the men who had escorted Dumarest left the room he said, "You wanted to see me? I'm Heeg Euluch."

Dumarest frowned. The voice was too high, even allowing for the distortion of a helmet. And there was a softness about the shoulders, a weakness about the chin.

He said, "Stand up."

"What? Now—"

"Up," snapped Dumarest. "Get on your feet!"

The man grunted, rising to stand behind the desk. He was big, his paunch round, sagging, thighs like the boles of trees.

"All right," said Dumarest. "It's polite to stand when greeting a visitor. Now let's end this charade. You're not Heeg. Where is he?"

The man shrugged. "Don't take it hard. We had to be sure you knew him. Heeg! Come out now!"

A door at the rear opened and a giant stepped into the room.

He was huge with muscle where the other was bloated with fat. His head towered, the features hard, his mouth a slash of savagery against the thrust of his jaw. A man who would think nothing of killing, cheating, abandoning those who worked with him, of stealing a child—if by doing so, he could gain personal advantage.

"I'm Heeg." His voice was deep, resonant. "You seem to know me, but I don't know you. Who told you where to find me?"

"Sheem. He wasn't happy at the way you left him."

"That's his grief. And?"

"I was wondering what happened to Chen Urlat. We had a deal going."

"Forget it. Urlat's dead."

Urlat and the two others who had been in the raft. The Melevganians who had probably been lasered down together with Urlat and dumped over the side so as to leave the big man in undisputed possession of Jondelle.

Dumarest said, "I've come to buy something—you know what. Are you able to sell?"

"Maybe." The hard eyes grew thoughtful. To the fat man Heeg said, "You've got something to do. Do it."

"But, Heeg—"

"Go and get us some wine. Move!"

"Good," said Dumarest as the man left. "We don't need witnesses. You have the boy?"

"And if I have?"

"I'll buy him. Ten thousand stergals. The cash in your hand by noon tomorrow. A deal?"

"There's a door behind you," said Heeg. "Get on the other side of it."

"All right," said Dumarest. "I was keeping it low. You can't blame me for that. Deliver the boy and I'll put twenty thousand in your hand."

He had hit the right level. The man frowned, greed bright in his eyes, then he shook his head.

"I want thirty."

A bargaining price and inwardly Dumarest relaxed. The man could be lying, the boy could have been passed on if that had been the original intention, but he doubted it. A man like Heeg would hold to out the last, upping the price as high as the traffic would bear. Or he could be trying a bluff; the boy could be dead. He felt the tension return at the thought of it. With an effort he remained calm.

"You ask too much. The market won't stand it and I've got to get my profit. Of course, if you want to pass him on and get robbed on the deal, that's your business. How much were you offered? Ten? Twelve?" He caught the betraying tension, the tiny, revealing signs learned from endless hours facing others across countless gambling tables. "I'm offering a fat profit and no risk. Just hand over the boy and I'll take care of the other end." He paused and added, casually, "Do I know who arranged this?"

"You're smart," grated Heeg. "Maybe too damned smart. Make it twenty-five."

"Twenty." It would be a mistake to agree too quickly. "I can get that with no grief. It's just a matter of waiting. And why should I deal with you anyway? I don't know you. Why should I take your word?"

"About what?" Dumarest shrugged. "The money? You don't hand over the boy until you get it. You don't know me? What the hell does that matter? I know you and what you did. You jumped the gun, is all. You beat me to it. Well, it happens. You spend time arranging a deal and then someone gets in first. But you're being sold short. So why not cut out the middle man? I'm willing to buy what you hold. Twenty thousand. A deal?"

Heeg scowled. A big man who relied on brute strength rather than mental agility, a greedy man and therefore weak.

"Add five and the boy's yours. It's my last word. Take it or leave it."

"I'll take it, but I've got to see him." Dumarest met the other man's eyes. "I want to know he's still alive," he said coldly. "Dead he's useless to you and me both. I don't intend buying something I can't sell. Where is he?"

"Here," said the big man. "In the Sumba. In the Mirage."

CHAPTER
EIGHTEEN

He looked very small and very pathetic as he sat in a small room containing only a bed, a rug, a single chair. He wore a jumper suit of dull green, pointed shoes on his feet, the beads around his neck the only touch of cheerful color. Instinctively Dumarest took a step toward him, grunting as he collided with a smooth, unyielding surface.

Heeg laughed. "Neat, isn't it? You see the kid, but he can't see you. You can watch him, but you can't touch him or talk to him. Well, there he is. Twenty-five thousand and he's yours. Satisfied?"

"No." Dumarest reached out and touched the surface depicting the boy. A mirror, he guessed, portraying a scene relayed by other mirrors and lenses. He looked upward and saw a disk of light. "This could be a projection. The boy could be dead and this a taped recording."

"It isn't."

"I've got to be sure. I want to touch the boy, talk to him."

"You want too damn much," snapped Heeg. "You've seen the mechandise. You can talk to him when I see the money. Have it here at noon tomorrow and we'll make the swap. Now get the hell out of here. That door will take you outside."

The mist was thick, clammy now that the night was old and the air chill. Dumarest heard the path beneath his boots, the thin shattering of crystal, too reminiscent of a child's tears. Had Jondelle cried? Sitting like an animal in his cage of a room, had he known the bleakness of despair? Or was he numbed by events beyond his experience, withdrawing into his own world of private fantasy, finding comfort in the familiar touch of a bedcover, the beads placed by his mother around his neck.

A guard loomed from the darkness. "Sir?"

"The Paradisa Room. Direct me."

It was busier now, men and women filling the air with

148

strained gaiety. Preleret nursed a drink in a corner. He caught Dumarest's eye, finished his drink, and went outside. Five minutes later Dumarest followed.

In the mist he said, "Get Tambolt. The boy's here. I've seen him. I'm going to get him out."

From a locked building, probably guarded, in an area shielded by mist. But Heeg would not have trusted too many with his secret. And he could be overconfident, planning, no doubt, to take the money and keep the boy.

Waiting for the others to return Dumarest prowled the area. From somewhere a woman laughed, the sound sensual in the mist. There was a creak and the echo of hard breathing. Running feet filled the air with a medley of sounds and a mechanism nearby filled the mist with a gush of cloying perfume.

He halted, looking helpless, swearing as he turned, apparently hopelessly lost.

"Is anyone here? I need help."

A shadow thickened, revealed itself as a guard. "Sir, I am at your ser—"

The smooth voice broke as Dumarest slammed his fist into the stomach. As the man doubled he struck again, the edge of his stiffened hand impacting the nerves in the side of the neck. The man was not dead, but would remain unconscious for an hour. Dumarest tore off the goggles, donned them, rose gripping the club. Around him the grounds of the Sumba sprang to life.

It was a pale, eerily green scene, people showing as warm figures against the trees, the buildings. Other guards stood or strolled at the side of the echoing paths. Dumarest followed one, lifting an arm in casual greeting as the man turned. Goggled, dressed in neutral gray, the club at his side, he looked enough like a companion to lull the man's suspicions. By the time the guard realized his mistake it was too late. Then another, and Dumarest walked with spare goggles and clubs to where Preleret and Tambolt stood blinking in the mist.

"Take these." He handed over the equipment. "Stay off the paths and follow me. If anyone tries to stop us, get them before they can give the alarm."

The building where he had seen the boy lay a short distance from the main complex, joined to it by a covered passage. It was a low place with a roof almost flat, a hexagonal structure with blank walls and two doors.

Dumarest passed the one by which he had left and halted at the other. It was on the far side, away from the main buildings, faced by a pool of water set in a sloping lawn. Beyond it rose the high wall of the enclosure.

From the other side of the building came the sound of tinkling glass.

"Quick!" whispered Dumarest. "On the roof!"

Two guards came around the building as they settled on the edge of the eaves. Their voices were low, slurred by the mist.

"Seems pointless to me. No one ever comes this way at night. Nothing to see or do."

His companion shrugged. "Heeg said to keep watch, so that's what we do. Maybe he's afraid someone will fall into the pool."

"We'd hear them if they did. I've got some prenchet here, want a chew?"

"Well—" The guard hesitated. "Just a little, then. A third of a pod."

They passed and Dumarest relaxed a little. To Tambolt he whispered, "Stay here and keep watch. I'm taking Preleret over the roof."

It was tiled with wide slabs of thin pottery and had no trap or other means of entry. Dumarest sprawled over it, his ear hard to the chill surface. He moved, listened, moved again. A thin hum came from below, machinery of some kind, a device to eliminate the mist from the air inside. Lifting the knife from his boot, he thrust the point between two of the tiles, levered upward, thrust his fingers beneath the edge.

Preleret joined him and together they lifted the slab and set it soundlessly to one side. Warm air gusted from the opening. Beneath lay a blank surface, the softly humming bulk of a machine. Beside it lay the rim of an access trap. It opened to a room bright with reflections. Dumarest dropped through, Preleret following, images flashing all around as they lifted the goggles from their eyes.

"A maze," whispered Preleret. "Mirrors everywhere. What the hell is this, Earl?"

An amusement for those so inclined. Aritficial mirages supplied by electronic means so that those entering would be surrounded by a constantly changing variety of scenes. They would wander, turning, baffled by reflective surfaces, bemused and deceived by visual images.

There were no scenes now, the electronic devices inoperative, but the mirrors remained showing their figures in a dozen different positions. There would be small rooms leading one into the other, twists, turns, angled passages and still more compartments. In one of them must be the boy.

Dumarest lowered the goggles. The reflections vanished to be replaced by the eerie greenness of transmuted infrared light. A point glowed brighter than the rest, a concentrated blob of unrecognizable shape surrounded by a nimbus of light. A living thing radiated heat. The blob could be the boy, the nimbus the room in which he sat.

"There," he said to Preleret. "Lower your goggles and you can see it. Maybe twenty yards ahead."

"Twenty?" Preleret sounded dubious. "Three more like."

Dumarest turned, lifting his goggles. Preleret was looking in the wrong direction. He dived, hitting the man low, knocking him to one side as something burned a hole in the mirror before which he had stood.

"Earl! What—"

The mirror shattered, falling in a rain of glinting crystal. Framed hugely in the opening Heeg Euluch said, "I expected something like this. Well, it seems it was a good idea to check my investment." He lifted his right hand, the laser it contained. "Too bad you couldn't play it straight."

"Thirty thousand," said Dumarest quickly. "Pull that trigger and that's what you lose."

"Begging?"

"Talking sense." Dumarest rose, turning so as to hide the club at his side. "Talking money. You like money, Heeg. That's why you killed to get the boy, why you don't want your partners to know what you have. They'd want a cut and you don't want to give it to them. Thirty thousand and it could be all yours. Yes?"

"No." The laser wavered a little, moving from Dumarest to Preleret and back again. The arc widened as Dumarest edged from the other man. "This is the end of the road for you both. You get it first." The laser jerked at Preleret. "And you get it after you tell me a few things." The gun moved toward Dumarest. "And you'll tell me. That I promise."

Dumarest threw the club.

It flashed, spinning as he jumped aside, slamming

against the laser and knocking it from the big man's hand. Before it had fallen Dumarest was on him, the knife in his hand a glittering arc as it flashed upward at the stomach. It hit, slashed the yellow fabric of the tunic, halted as it struck the mesh beneath. Body armor—he should have expected it.

He sprang backward as the giant hands reached for his eyes, felt the impact of something solid, then fell in a rain of shattered glass. He rose as Heeg reached for the laser, drawing back his arm, sending the knife like an extension of his hand to bury itself deep in the corded throat.

Bleakly he watched the big man die.

"Fast," said Preleret. He had scooped up the laser and held it as he stared wonderingly at Dumarest. "I knew you were quick, but not that quick." He looked at Heeg. "You tried to gut him. You could have got him in the throat to begin with, but you tried to gut him. Why, Earl?"

A farm ruined, a woman killed, a boy stolen, workers slain by imported devils. Jasken gone, others, blood spilled for the sake of gain.

"He asked for it," said Dumarest coldly. "Now let's find the boy."

A solid cube lay in a nest of supporting stanchions approached through a maze of carefully aligned planes of mirrored glass. A bolt fastened the door. Dumarest tore it free and heaved at the portal. It opened to reveal a tiny room, a bed, a single chair, the small figure of a boy who looked up, his eyes wide in the rounded pallor of his face.

"Earl! Is that you?"

"Jondelle!" He came running as Dumarest dropped to one knee, throwing himself into the extended arms, his small weight hard against his chest. "Are you all right?"

"Yes, Earl." The voice was muffled. "I've been very lonely and scared, but I knew you would come to save me. I just knew it." The supreme faith of children which gave to their heroes the attributes of a god. "Are we going home now?"

Up to the roof where Tambolt waited. Down to the ground and over the wall with the laser to cut down all opposition and the raft to waft them to safety.

"Yes," said Dumarest. "We're going home."

CHAPTER

NINETEEN

The wine was as he remembered, red, sweet, cloying to the tongue, but now it seemed to have an added flavor which made it impossible to drink. Dumarest set down the goblet as Akon Batik spoke.

"A successful termination to a dangerous enterprise, Earl. You have reason to be gratified. More, perhaps, than you realize. Now, if you will let me handle the transaction, much profit may be gained by all."

"No," said Dumarest. "The boy is not for sale."

"But—" The jeweler broke off, then shrugged. "A matter of terminology. You, naturally, can claim to be rewarded for what you have done. There have been high expenses and much risk. Those who care for the lad will not be ungrateful. I think five thousand stergals would not be too much to expect. I will give it to you—on taking charge of the boy, of course, and will reclaim it later."

"No." Dumarest looked at his wine. "You mentioned a proposition the first time we met. A job of work to be done. Is it still available?"

"Unfortunately, no."

"The need no longer exists?" Dumarest shrugged. "Of course not. Neema is safe now. She no longer wants someone to go to Melevgan and rescue her. That was the proposition, wasn't it? That I should go and collect her so that you could collect fat profits at no risk. The fee, her jewels—you are a shrewd man, Akon Batik."

"One who takes advantage of an opportunity, Earl. If that is to be shrewd, then I must confess to the fault. But you must admit that, as far as you were concerned, I proved of service."

"Tambolt," agreed Dumarest. "A man sent to me because he was a man I could use. But I think he was a little more than that. Your agent to keep an eye on things, to work on your behalf. Unfortunately you didn't know him all

153

that well. Tambolt would sell his own mother for gain."
He added, "I think he believes I tricked him. I promised
him half of what I would get for the boy—which was a
half of exactly nothing. He had to be content with his third
of the agreed profit."

"The reward—"

"I didn't go after Jondelle for reward! I went because
—well, never mind."

"A promise," said the jeweler softly. "Your word. Sometimes I am amazed at the stupidity of men. What was
the boy to you? Why did you have to risk your life to
get him? To kill and have men killed. And never was
the boy in any real danger. Time would have cured all.
An exchange, as you have said, the passing of money and
he would have been returned. It was simply a matter of
negotiation."

"As you say—a matter of negotiation."

"Exactly. So why should you deny yourself the chance
of gain? Five thousand, ten High passages, a small fortune.
Shall we drink to it?"

Dumarest said, "No. I do not care for your wine. It
has a taste I can't stomach."

"A taste?" The jeweler frowned. "You suspect poison?"

Dumarest rose and moved from the chair where lasers,
if any, would be aimed. He said, coldly, "Not poison—
vileness. A man cannot be blamed for his nature, but some
men go too far. Money becomes their god, their only
reason for being, and, when it does, they stop being human.
They become like the things found under an over-
turned stone. Spiders sitting in a web of intrigue, manipulating men and women, arranging, hinting, offering, doing
nothing but creating desolation. I should kill you. I should
bury a knife in your throat as I did Heeg Euluch. You
arranged with him to steal the boy. You contacted Neema
by radio and there are radios in Charne. Maybe Elray was
first approached, or he could even have contacted you—it
doesn't matter now. When you failed to get him in the city,
you obtained other help. Fast rafts, willing men, agents to
do your bidding. Or perhaps you had everything arranged
in case of initial failure.

"You are shrewd and clever—and you deserve to die.
But I won't kill you. I don't have to. Time will do that
soon enough. You're old, Akon Batik. Too old to be
given the mercy of a quick end. So sit and wait for your

bones to stiffen and your faculties to weaken. Until, maybe, someone treats you exactly as you treat others."

Outside the air was clean, invigorating after the nest in which the jeweler sat. Dumarest hailed a cab and was driven to the hotel. It was a big place, the best in Sargone. Neema met him as he entered the suite. She was radiant, her arm healed, neatly and quietly dressed in a gown which covered her from neck to ankles.

"Preleret's gone, Earl. He's taken his cask and his woman and gone riding High. To Rodyne, I think. He said that you didn't need thanks, but he left them just the same."

"A good man," said Dumarest. "He'll be happy."

"As I will be."

"In Urmile?"

"On some other world. I've had enough of Ourelle, Earl. Now that you don't need me to look after the boy—" She paused and said, softly, "Earl?"

Gently he shook his head. "No, Neema."

"Well, I asked." She managed to smile. "You're not a man to be held by any woman, Earl. I know that, but I had to try. Did you see the jeweler?"

"Yes, but I learned nothing new. I guess I lost my temper. It was a mistake, perhaps, but I couldn't help it."

"Did you kill him?"

"No."

"Then you didn't lose your temper. You simply told him a few things he should have known. And, perhaps, verified things you had suspected." She came very close, resting her hand on his arm. "I'll be off now. The boy is in the other room with the monk and his people. I don't suppose I'll ever see you again, but I'm going to think of you often. So good-bye, my dear, and may good fortune attend each step you take."

"And may your life be full of gladness."

She kissed him once and then was gone, leaving the room strangely empty, a hint of her perfume hanging in the air as if she had become a disembodied ghost haunting him with vague regrets of what might have been.

A woman, a home, a son, perhaps, like Jondelle. Drawing a deep breath Dumarest went into the room where the boy waited with Brother Elas and two others.

He sat on the edge of the bed, very busy with his

beads, running them through his fingers, lifting them to his ear as if to listen to forgotten voices. Toys lay beside him, a fluffy, round-eared, bright-eyed creature with a snub nose and cheerful smile almost as large as himself. A spaceship which could be dismantled and reassembled. A colorscope which showed endless patterns at the touch of a button, the shapes rearranging themselves beneath directed compulsion. Some books, blocks of transparent plastic containing variable images, a knife.

Jondelle lifted it and threw it clumsily at the pillow. The plastic blade bent and left the material unharmed.

"One day, Earl, I'm going to learn to throw it just like you."

"One day," he said.

"And then no one will be able to take me away again. They won't be able to hurt anyone like they did Elray and Makgar." The full bottom lip trembled a little. "I shall kill them if they try. Oh, Earl! Why did they do it? Why?"

Dumarest held him, feeling the small body shake, the wetness of sudden tears. The adult words had gone, the calm behavior, now there was only a very small and bewildered child.

He said, "It's all right, Jondelle. Everything's going to be all right from now. A bad thing has happened, but it will pass. You have had bad dreams, haven't you? Well, sometimes life is like a bad dream. But you forget dreams and you can forget unhappiness. So you must try to do that. You promise?"

"I promise."

"Good. Go with Brother Elas now and wash your face."

"You'll be here when I come back?"

"Yes," said Dumarest. "I'll be here."

He rose as the monk ushered the boy from the room, looking at the others for the first time. A man and woman, neither young, both blond, blue-eyed, looking as if they were brother and sister.

"Tharg Hamsen," said the man, extending his hand. "And my wife, Wilma."

Dumarest took the extended hand and pressed it.

"You know the old customs; good." The man smiled, then became grave. "To talk of thanks at a time like this is to use empty words. You have found our grandson— what can I say?"

"Nothing." Dumarest looked from one to the other,

seeing the similarities, the telltale marks of blood-relation-
ship. Selective inbreeding, he guessed, common on many
worlds among races which aimed at a desired goal. But
neither would have chosen Makgar for their son's wife.
She had been totally different from what they would have
accepted as a desirable mate. Carefully he said, "Your
son must have presented you with quite a problem."

"Jak?" The man frowned. "No, he was a good boy. I
cannot understand what you mean."

"You are obtuse, Tharg." His wife with her woman's
intuition had grasped Dumarest's meaning. "Earl is being
delicate. But you are mistaken, my friend. The woman
you knew as Makgar was not Jondelle's mother. She bore
him, true, but while Jak provided the seed she did not
provide the egg. You understand?"

"A plant?"

"Yes. The fertilized egg taken from the womb of one
woman and planted in the womb of another. Tharg?"

"Jak and May were on Veido, a working honeymoon.
She was newly pregnant and they were as happy as a couple
can be. There was an accident, a ground car—the details
don't matter. Jak was killed instantly, May was injured,
dying, and with her would die the child. The child and
the precious genes it carried!" He paused, breathing deeply,
continuing in a calmer tone. "Perhaps you don't understand. We are inbred as you can see and that tends to lead
to a degree of sterility. Jak was our only child, the last
of his line. If his genes were lost, it would set back a
program for unknown years. The work of a hundred generations lost because of a trick of fate. I—"

"They were connected with a scientific establishment on
Veido," said Wilma as he broke off. "Kamar Ragnack—
Makgar—was a technician attached to the medical side.
She and May were friends and she volunteered to have
the fertilized egg transplanted into her womb. It was done.
May died. Time passed and the baby, Jondelle, was born.
It is essential to the well-being of a newly born child to
stay with its mother and so we arranged for them to occupy
a small house close to the city. And then, one day, the
woman vanished taking the child with her."

Dumarest said, "Was there duress?"

"None." The woman looked down at her hands. They
were clenched. Slowly she unfolded them. "I can understand," she said. "As a mother I can understand. And

Jondelle was not a normal child. He was bred to develop a high sympathy-reaction, a survival trait which we consider to be important. It was just that Kamar couldn't bear to part with him. She wanted him beside her, to keep for always. The normal reaction of any woman toward the child of her body. I can understand—but I don't find it easy to forgive."

"Six years," said Tharg heavily. "Asking, searching, offering rewards. A long time."

Long enough for men like Akon Batik to have scented the bait. For Elray to have realized the value of what he had. For a home to be disrupted and the boy used as a pawn.

Dumarest said, "Was there another reason why Makgar could have taken the child? To protect him, perhaps?"

"From whom? Us?"

A suspicion, but one which was always with him. "Are there cybers on Veido?"

"Yes," said Tharg. "There are."

"And on your own world?"

"Kreem? No."

"Perhaps you had better make sure there never are," said Dumarest. "The Cyclan are always interested in potential advantage. A boy, bred to hold the qualities you say, would be most useful. Well, you have him . . . take care of him."

"Need you say that?" The man sighed. "I understand. The galaxy is full of enemies and who is Jondelle not to have his share? But he will be protected; have no fear of that. We know how to take care of our own. And we know how to reward those who wish us well."

"Money," said the woman. "But more than that. Something you value more than the cost of a few High passages. Brother Elas told us of your search. He learned of it from the records on Hope. Perhaps we can help you to find your home."

"Earth?"

"The legendary world," said Tharg quietly. "Some believe in it, most do not. There are those who are convinced it was the home of the human race. A place from which they fled in terror." His voice deepened, contained echoes which rolled like drums. "From terror they fled to find new places on which to expiate their sins. Only when cleansed will the race of Man be again united."

The creed of the Original People. Dumarest turned from where he stood beside the window, staring, mind burning with a sudden suspicion. The Original People. These? Were they members of the cult? It so, they would never admit it and he would lose anything he hoped to gain by pressing too hard. Already they had said too much if they followed the ancient ways.

"I have investigated old legends," said Tharg blandly. "From what I can discover, Earth must lie somewhere in the seventh decan. It is a planet circling a yellow, G-type star. It should not be too difficult to hire a computer to determine the exact position of each such star in that area."

Another clue to add to the rest. The final one, perhaps, to solve the problem of where the planet of his birth was to be found.

The door to the bathroom opened and Brother Elas ushered Jondelle into the room. It was time to say good-bye.

"I wondered if you'd be here, Earl. But you promised and I knew that you would. Earl, can't you come with us?"

"No." Dumarest dropped to one knee as he had done once before, feeling again the small body in his arms, the weight against his chest. "I've other things to do, Jondelle, and so have you."

"Shall I see you again?"

"Perhaps. Who can tell what the future will bring? But I shall always remember you."

"And I you, Earl." He stepped back, very small but very upright, his square shoulders framed against the bed and the toys his grandparents had brought. The people who would give him all the love and security he would need. The things every child should have by right. He held out his hand, an odd gesture recently learned.

"Good-bye, Earl."

Dumarest took the little hand, squeezed it. "Good-bye, son."

Beyond the window lay the city, the spacefield, the ships which would carry him on his way. They seemed blurred and he guessed it must be raining.

Outstanding science fiction and fantasy

☐	**NECTAR OF HEAVEN** by E. C. Tubb.	(#UJ1613—$1.95)
☐	**WORLD OF PROMISE** by E. C. Tubb.	(#UE1579—$1.75)
☐	**THE TERRA DATA** by E. C. Tubb.	(#UE1533—$1.75)
☐	**THE BOOK OF DREAMS** by Jack Vance.	(#UE1587—$2.25)
☐	**DOWNBELOW STATION** by C. J. Cherryh.	(#UE1595—$2.50)
☐	**COSMIC CRUSADERS** by Pierre Barbet.	(#UE1583—$2.25)
☐	**LORE OF THE WITCH WORLD** by Andre Norton.	
		(#UJ1560—$1.95)
☐	**KILL THE DEAD** by Tanith Lee.	(#UE1562—$1.75)
☐	**THE GREEN GODS** by N. C. Henneberg.	(#UE1538—$1.75)
☐	**PURSUIT OF THE SCREAMER** by Ansen Dibell.	
		(#UE1580—$2.25)
☐	**SABELLA OR THE BLOOD STONE** by Tanith Lee.	
		(#UE1529—$1.75)
☐	**THE LUCIFER COMET** by Ian Wallace.	(#UE1581—$2.25)
☐	**SERPENT'S REACH** by C. J. Cherryh.	(#UE1554—$2.25)
☐	**IRONCASTLE** by Philip Jose Farmer & J. Rosny.	
		(#UJ1545—$1.95)
☐	**ROGUE SHIP** by A. E. van Vogt.	(#UJ1536—$1.95)
☐	**THE GARMENTS OF CAEAN** by Barrington Bayley.	
		(#UJ1519—$1.95)
☐	**THE BRIGHT COMPANION** by Edward Llewellyn.	
		(#UE1511—$1.75)
☐	**LOST WORLDS** by Lin Carter.	(#UJ1556—$1.95)
☐	**STARMASTERS' GAMBIT** by Gerard Klein.	(#UE1464—$1.75)
☐	**SAGA OF LOST EARTHS** by Emil Petaja.	(#UJ1462—$1.95)
☐	**LOST: FIFTY SUNS** by A. E. van Vogt.	(#UE1491—$1.75)
☐	**THE MAN WITH A THOUSAND NAMES** by A. E. van Vogt.	
		(#UE1502—$1.75)

THE NEW AMERICAN LIBRARY, INC.,
P.O. Box 999, Bergenfield, New Jersey 07621

Please send me the DAW BOOKS I have checked above. I am enclosing
$_____ (check or money order—no currency or C.O.D.'s).
Please include the list price plus 50¢ per order to cover handling costs.

Name _____

Address _____

City _____ State _____ Zip Code _____
Please allow at least 4 weeks for delivery